Ruins of the Galaxy Book 8: Quantum Assault

This novel is a work of fiction. Names, characters, places, and incidents are either products of the author's imagination or used fictitiously. Any resemblance to actual events, locales, or persons, living, dead, or undead, is entirely coincidental.

Version 3.0

1st Edition

QUANTUM ASSAULT

BOOK EIGHT IN THE RUINS OF THE GALAXY SERIES

J.N. CHANEY
CHRISTOPHER HOPPER

JOIN THE RUINS TRIBE

Visit **ruinsofthegalaxy.com** today and join the tribe. Once there, you can sign up for our reader group, join our Facebook community, and find us on Twitter and Instagram.

If you'd like to email us with comments or questions, we respond to all emails sent to ruinsofthegalaxy@gmail.com, and love to hear from our readers.

See you in the Ruins!

STAY UP TO DATE

J.N. Chaney posts updates, official art, previews, and other awesome stuff on his website. You can also follow him on **Instagram**, **Facebook**, and **Twitter**.

He also created a special **Facebook group** called "JN Chaney's Renegade Readers" specifically for readers to come together and share their lives and interests, discuss the series, and speak directly to me. Please check it out and join whenever you get the chance!

For updates about new releases, as well as exclusive promotions, visit his website, jnchaney.com and sign up for the VIP mailing list. Head there now to receive a free copy of *The Other Side of Nowhere.*

https://www.jnchaney.com/ruins-of-the-galaxy-subscribe

Enjoying the series? Help others discover the Ruins of the Galaxy series by leaving a review on **Amazon.**

CONTENTS

PREVIOUSLY

Last time in Ruins of the Galaxy Book 7: Terminal Fallout...

DISTRAUGHT by the overwhelming loss of Capriana Prime, the Gladio Umbra sought refuge on the Sekmit home world of Aluross in an attempt to heal and rest. Still, a few among their number left to attend to matters on their home worlds.

Rohoar, mwadim of the Jujari, departed for Oorajee to rally his people following their defeat against the Paragon fleets. Meanwhile, Sootriman left for Ki Nar Four, reacting to racism she encountered while aiding survivors on Capriana Prime's far side.

On Aluross, however, Magnus and Awen's shore leave was cut short when Freya, pride mother of tribe Linux, leveraged them into liberating the Sekmit from the Republic's planetary governor.

But plans unraveled quickly for all the gladias. Rohoar encountered Moldark's essence during a death match for the throne, while Sootriman uncovered a plot to destabilize her planet. And back on Aluross, Magnus discovered that So-Elku had been collaborating with the Republic Governor and Senator Robert Malcom Blackman.

In the end, Rohoar evaded Moldark, managed to win the fight, and maintained his throne. Sootriman successfully rooted out the spies sent to undermine her rule. And Magnus killed Senator Blackman in the governor's mansion. But as the Gladio Umbra reunited, they found an emboldened enemy pulling planets into the newly formed Luma Alliance of Worlds.

That, and as Rohoar experienced firsthand, Moldark was very much alive…

And he is coming with a vengeance.

PROLOGUE

"HAVE you had a chance to think over our offer, Governor? Or does the prospect of bleeding out alone in the Falcion quadrant still interest you?"

Governor Morandu drummed his fingers on his desk with all the subtlety of an adolescent Mammothian bear. Ever since Master So-Elku had announced the formation of his new alliance to rival the Galactic Republic's failing infrastructure, the Luma leader hadn't left Morandu alone.

"It's a very enticing offer," the governor replied. "Though it's painfully obvious to everyone in the quadrant what you're trying to do."

"And that is?" So-Elku said from the holo window floating above Morandu's ebony desk.

"Take advantage of the Republic's demise—"

"I am bringing new stability to the galaxy."

"New stability?" Morandu stopped drumming his fingers. "You didn't think things were stable before?"

"And you did?" So-Elku cocked his head to the side, eyes narrowing.

"Protected trade routes, insured markets, access to education—"

"And a seat at the senate table." So-Elku waved his hand. "You're practically a spokesperson for the old Republic, Morandu. They would be proud if they were still around to care."

I swear, Morandu thought to himself. *If he interrupts me one more time*. "Be that as it may, there are still some of us who believe the Republic's days aren't over. There are plenty of worlds still loyal to the cause."

"The cause? And who do you think is going to patrol your trade routes now that their fleets have been decimated? Who is going to ensure the galactic markets will maintain integrity? And whose senate tower are you expecting to meet in?"

"Those things will be worked out in time."

"They might." So-Elku leaned in toward the camera. "But will they be worked out before pirates sabotage your lancite shipments? Before someone else determines who you can and can't trade with? Before your precious senate gathers enough votes from people who don't even know you to determine Undoria's future?" The Luma Master scoffed and then leaned back in his seat.

Morandu picked up the data pad and looked at it as if reviewing the entire proposal his staff had spent the last five days pouring over. "Frankly, So-Elku, I'm not sure how the Luma Alliance of Worlds is any better. At least with the Republic, we have history, and we know what we're getting—what we're fighting for."

"History?" So-Elku steepled his fingers and put them to his lips but did not speak right away. He let the one-word question hang in the air so long that Morandu almost broke the silence.

So-Elku spread his hands as if giving an offering to the mystics.

"Three hundred years, the Galactic Republic has ruled the quadrant. And before that? The Sentient Species Alliance—one hundred fifty years. And then the Star Faring Council for four hundred years. And before that?"

Morandu hesitated. He wasn't sure whether this was a rhetorical question or not. But when the silence stretched on, he replied, "Chaos."

"Chaos. Yes." So-Elku nodded, placing his fingertips back on his lips. "But not for everyone."

"Oh?"

"Us, Governor Morandu. There was no chaos for the Order of the Luma. Because we were here long before the Galactic Republic, and we will remain long after its carcass has stained the ground with its blood. So, if you want to know what you are getting, you are welcome to avail yourself of our vast library. Should you wish further evidence as to how we are already working with those worlds under our care, you are welcome to contact them at your discretion. That said, I would ask you one thing, dear Governor."

"And what's that?"

"Don't wait too long to reply. I fear we cannot guarantee your safety indefinitely."

"Indefinitely? As in, you've already begun?"

"Of course." So-Elku rested his hands on his chair's arms. "You boast the largest deposit of lancite in the quadrant, rivaled only by the mines of Limbia Centrella in Omodon. Did you really think the pirates and their hordes wouldn't come running the moment they knew the Republic fleets were eviscerated?"

"But we've not detected any pirates—"

"And nor will you, so long as our patrols remain in orbit."

Now it was Morandu's turn to lean forward. "You have ships in orbit over us? But we haven't detected—"

"No. You haven't. And you won't. That, my good governor, is what makes us more powerful than the Republic ever hoped to be." So-Elku stroked his neatly trimmed beard. "Tell me, have you heard of Governor Wade's recent abduction?"

"From Deltaurus Three." Morandu gave a small nod. "Though I'm not sure where this is going."

"He was arrested by the Galactic Republic on Minrok Santari on charges of conspiracy and high treason."

"I had not heard."

"No." The Luma continued to stroke his beard. "No, you wouldn't have, I suppose. He was among the first to pledge their allegiance to the LAW. And when the Republic heard?"

"He should have been more careful."

"Perhaps. But it doesn't matter now, anyway."

"Why's that?"

"Because the Governor has been safely reunited with his people and is enjoying the protection and assurances of the LAW."

"But I thought you said he was arrested on charges of—"

Morandu was interrupted this time by a series of images showing devastating damage to some building's interior. The images cycled through, one after another, filled with scenes of broken blastcrete walls. And bodies—*Repub Marines*, Morandu noticed. "What am I looking at?"

"The brig beneath Admiral's Hall at the Naval Academy of Tellstall."

Morandu swiped the images aside and pointed at So-Elku. "Did *you* do this?"

So-Elku nodded once.

"Do you realize what you've done?" Morandu slid to the edge of his seat. "You've—you've just declared open war on the Galactic Republic!"

So-Elku lifted one eyebrow as if Morandu had just read him an inconvenient weather forecast. "You seem rather exasperated. Is there something you feel I should be concerned with?"

Morandu felt beside himself at this man's brazen disregard for the consequences of his actions. "Are you mad, man? Have you completely lost your mind?"

"As a matter of fact, I am mad, Governor. I'm mad that the Republic thinks they have the power to do whatever they want to whomever they want, whenever it suits them."

"But you, you killed Republic Marines in order to—"

"To liberate a prisoner of their war and an illegally detained citizen of the Luma Alliance of Worlds. We protect our own, Governor. And we don't merely safeguard those systems whose economies or natural resources happen to suit our needs one moment and not the next. Nor do we leave your commodities to be determined by the whims of a senate who has no more vested interest in your world's wellbeing than you do in theirs. Oh, no. We protect equally, represent equally, and trade equally."

"And yet you would attack a naval academy? This is not the Luma we've known."

"But it is the Luma the people need to rescue them from an empire."

"Empire?"

If So-Elku was supposed to look ashamed at Morandu's disgust of the word's use, he didn't. "And what would you call the Republic then? Hmm, Governor?"

Morandu huffed. "Well, certainly not an empire."

"Really? Then how would you categorize the centuries of disproportionate agreements, broken promises, and backroom deals, all at the expense of innocent lives? How do you reconcile heavy-handed treaties that strip worlds of their customs and dignity, all in the name of the greater good? And what about the capital world being annihilated by their own ships? Does that not sound like an empire to you, Morandu? Because if it doesn't, then I don't think you and I will ever see eye to eye on how the galaxy really works."

"And how does the galaxy really work?"

So-Elku leaned into the camera. "Sign the covenant agreement, and you'll never have to wonder again. We'll show you."

Morandu sat back in his chair, facing the snow-capped mountains of the Westernlands that loomed outside his window. They stood like a row of impassable sentries, keeping solemn watch over the broad planes that stretched to the opposite horizon.

"I'm no fool," Morandu said to himself, eyes searching the sky for some silent confirmation.

He knew the enemy assaults would come. Every rogue scavenger this side of Kandameer would be aiming for Undoria's lancite mines now that the Republic orbital blockade was gone—their ships departing more than two weeks ago. In truth, Morandu was surprised the enemy hadn't come already, which is why So-Elku's claim of having hidden LAW ships in orbit was that much more believable.

And he resented So-Elku for it.

Not because Morandu didn't want the security for his planet. He did. And, secretly, he mourned the fact that Undoria had become so reliant on the Repub navy that they stopped building their own ships decades ago.

Nor did he despise what the Order of the Luma stood for. All those things So-Elku said about the Luma's history were true. They really *had* been around for millennia, and they would most likely be around for many more.

"So what's bothering you, Elias?" He drummed his fingers across his belly. "Why the apprehension?"

There were so many reasons. He feared being caught, yes. If the Republic found out that he and his cabinet had been reviewing a proposal from a rival organization, he'd—*what?* "You'd be imprisoned in the brig on Minrok Santari, just like Wade."

But it was more than that.

This was about So-Elku having envisioned, formed, and launched an entirely new alliance in less than four weeks since Capriana Prime's demise. To Morandu, it felt like a widower was out dating women at the nearest cantina a month after the wife's passing. "More like the next day."

So it was the principle of the thing then—*is that it, Elias? You're upset that So-Elku doesn't have the same allegiances, doesn't bleed Repub red?*

But, then again, why would he? The Luma had never been allies of the Republic—not really. Wherever there was a planet to protect and a species to preserve, the Luma were there, battling the Republic's every attempt to pull that world into the fold. But all of that was gone now.

The galaxy as Morandu knew it was fading away faster than he could have imagined. How such a mighty and majestic entity had come crashing down so quickly was, well, it was astonishing. And here was So-Elku and the Luma ready to offer a solution.

"Like it was planned all along," Morandu whispered. But then he shook the thought away. *No. There's no way the Luma could have orchestrated the events over Prime*, he told himself. This was simply So-Elku seizing an opportunity.

But if Morandu were honest, the galaxy would need something to align with. There were plenty of rogue star systems that could threaten Undoria if he didn't do something quick. And Morandu guessed his wasn't the only post-Republic world that would need protecting.

"What other option do you have?" He looked to the mountains again and offered a prayer to the mystics. Then he chuckled. "Aren't the mystics offering you the alliance?" Maybe there was some hope to be found in this new agreement after all.

Morandu's chamber door trilled.

"Come," he said. As soon as the metal panels separated, he heard the sound of blaster fire coming from somewhere in the distance.

"Governor Morandu," said Ingrid Sellner, his Chief of Staff.

Morandu stood up. "Ingrid. What's going on?"

"The building is under attack."

"Mystics." *It was happening already*. "Who?"

"We—" She hesitated and pinched the bridge of her nose. "We don't know yet, sir. But right now, we've got to get you to safety."

"Yes. Yes, of course." He moved around the desk and headed toward Sellner. Two security staffers stepped into the room; one offered Morandu an armored vest, and the other carried a riot helmet.

"Please put these on, sir," Sellner said.

He nodded and then donned the vest and helmet. The sounds of blaster fire were getting closer, coming from somewhere down the marble hall outside his office. "How many?"

Both security guards looked at one another and then to Sellner. "That's hard to say, sir."

"So many?"

"Not exactly." Sellner nodded at the two guards who then stepped into the hall, raising their blasters. "I'll explain as we move. But we've got to go right now."

Morandu nodded and followed her out to where five more guards waited, their weapons pointing down the hall. These were not the Republic Marines who usually stood guard throughout the building—those had left with the warships. Instead, these secondary security forces were responsible for the property's general safety. Morandu had much less confidence in them than the Repub security detail that always accompanied him everywhere he went, but in the event of an attack, he'd take anyone who knew how to point and shoot a gun at the bad guys.

"Back stairwell, sir," Sellner said, tugging on the governor's elbow.

"Right. Yes."

The security guards formed a diamond shape around him, moving as one toward the marble stairwell on the building's east side. Light from large windows flooded each switch-back landing, giving another beautiful view of the mountains. Meanwhile, the sounds of footfalls mixed with Morandu's heartbeat as he struggled to keep from tripping over his own feet. Three decades behind a desk had not done wonders for his college physique.

"So what is it you were going to explain?" Morandu asked Sellner.

"The attack seems to be an internal power grab."

"Internal? As in among the staff?"

"Yes, sir."

"Who's involved?"

Blaster rounds struck the stairs just below Morandu's feet. He skidded to a stop and nearly tumbled down the steps as one of the security guards cried out and fell face-forward into the hallway below.

The other security guards returned fire, suppressing the enemy just long enough to get the governor around the next turn. More blaster rounds struck the walls and broke through the tall windows, showering Morandu in crystal shards. He covered his head and ducked as the guards let loose another volley of return fire.

"Who's doing this?" Morandu cried over the now-constant sound of blaster fire mixed with troopers' boots crushing glass into the red carpet.

"We can't say, Governor." Sellner turned on the landing and took a step down when more bolts exploded around her feet. Three security guards collapsed, and Sellner was struck in the knee. She pitched forward, hands aloft, and screamed as a second and third round hit her chest and shoulder. She was dead before she hit the red carpet on the fourth floor.

Morandu swore and tried reaching for her, but someone pulled him back into the protection of the turn-around. Blaster fire was coming from the floors above and below him. Only three guards remained—one returning fire to slow the pursuit of enemies above, the other trying to clear a path through those below.

When the guard nearest Morandu slumped forward, the governor picked up the blaster and started firing under the ceiling and into the hallway below. He couldn't see anything just yet; there was too much smoke. The smells of burning flesh and singed carpet fibers stung his nostrils. Morandu fought the urge to vomit. If this was the end for him, he didn't want to be found in a pool of his own bile. He wanted to go down fighting.

The guard above him cried out then tumbled backward and landed in a heap beside Morandu's feet.

"Maybe we can go out the window," Morandu yelled. It was a desperate move, he knew, but they were pinned down.

"No good," the remaining guard said. "Four stories, straight down. You won't survive."

"And we won't here either."

Then, without any warning, the incoming blaster fire stopped. Morandu looked at the guard and then peered around the pillar toward the lower hallway.

"Governor," the guard said, placing a hand on his shoulder. "Please be careful."

Morandu nodded and then took a step down. He half expected his foot to get blown off. But it didn't. So he took another step, and another, all the while trying to peer through the smoke. Behind him, Morandu heard the guard following, one step at a time. An eerie silence befell the ornate marble corridor, the architecture and decorations of which went back four centuries to Undoria's Neo Revival period. A figure stepped through the smoke, hands open and raised.

"Who's there?"

"Katie," a quivering voice said. "Katie Tomanova. I work in finance. Please don't let him shoot me."

A second figure emerged behind her, this one holding a blaster muzzle against the back of Katie's head. Morandu didn't know her, but she was dressed in the business attire of any one of hundreds of people in the capitol building.

Morandu squinted, trying to make out the face of the assailant, and then he raised his gun like he'd seen all the holo stars do. "Put your weapon down and let her go!"

"Only if it suits our purposes, Governor Morandu," said a soft and even-toned voice. While the hostage-taker looked male and was dressed in casual business attire, his voice wasn't gender-specific. If anything, it seemed to Morandu like several other voices spoke behind the assailant's in a sort of dissonant harmony.

"And what are your purposes?" Morandu asked, taking another step down. The security guard cautioned him against going further, but Morandu waved him off.

"It is not among our purposes to inform you," the man replied. There was something about his eyes that seemed very strange to Morandu. It was almost as if dark clouds had settled over each eye socket. They hadn't, of course; the idea was purely metaphorical. But the man's countenance disturbed him.

"If I can't know your purposes, then how can I assist you in achieving them?" Morandu made a show of looking around and then took another step down. "You are clearly here for me. So why don't we start with who you work for. The Verv? Simbilant?"

"We work only for ourselves, Governor. And we have no need of your assistance. All paths inevitably lead to the one we desire."

Morandu stepped onto the hallway's landing and took his time moving toward the hostage, his sights still trained on the assailant behind her.

"Please, Governor Morandu," Katie said. Her eyes pleaded with him to do something.

"I'm going to take care of you, Katie Tomanova who works in finance. Just hold on."

She yelped as the gun pressed her to take another step forward. "I don't want to die."

"Just let her go," Morandu said, lowering his weapon. "Take me instead."

"But, governor," the man said, cocking his head sideways. "We don't want to take you."

"You—you don't?"

"You have entertained the Luma. We want to kill you."

The guard behind Morandu fired a single round that punched a hole in the assailant's forehead. Katie screamed and then ran into Morandu's arms just as the body hit the floor with a sickening crack.

"I've got you," Morandu said, one hand over the woman's head, the other still wrapped around the blaster's handle.

Then something flickered through the air like the fin of a Nethermink salmon streaking upriver. Morandu didn't actually see what it was, but the smoke seemed to ripple overhead.

"You cannot escape the shadows, Governor Morandu," said the guard in a strange voice—

The assailant's voice, Morandu realized. He spun around with Katie in his arms, raised his gun, and fired three shots into the guard's chest. The man's body convulsed, and the darkness left his eyes.

There was another flutter in the smoke, and then Katie's head rolled up to look him in the face. "Goodbye, Governor Morandu." And with that, the Obscura used Moldark's power to devour the man's soul.

1

"And then what did you do to him?" Piper asked.

She clutched one of Rohoar's thick paw-nubs as they walked along with one of Fînta's long bridges spanning two massive trees. The treetop village bustled with activity in preparation for the night's meal, which was made even more exciting because the tribe-mother Freya was scheduled to arrive.

"Rohoar?" Piper shook his paw a little. "Are you listening?"

"Rohoar punched him twice more," Rohoar replied.

But Piper could tell he wasn't fully listening to her. His thoughts were somewhere else. "And then what?"

"And then he swung at Rohoar and missed, hitting a column instead."

"And then what?"

Rohoar let out a hot breath that parted the air on her face.

Piper winced. "Did you brush your teeth today?"

"Which question do you wish Rohoar to answer first?"

Piper considered this. "The first one, because I think I already know the answer to the second one."

"And then Mahkmaim struck Rohoar here"—the Jujari pointed to the small of his back. "It was very painful."

"Ouch. I'm so sorry." Piper paused. "And then what?"

Rohoar sighed again. "This is a very tiring game for Rohoar's head. May we continue later?"

Piper felt disappointed, but she understood that the big doggy had traveled a long way. "I guess. But, but, will you still tell me how you killed Mahkmaim at the end? Maybe later, for a bedtime story?"

Rohoar's ears perked up. "You would wish this for a bedtime story?"

"So, that's a yes?"

Rohoar looked behind them.

"What's wrong?" Piper glanced over her shoulder too. But all she could see were Gladio Umbra and Sekmit working along the platforms and bridges.

"Awen must be watching," Rohoar said softly.

"Awen?" Piper wrinkled her nose. "Why?"

"She told Rohoar not to tell you these bedtime stories—ones she called *very violent*. They are not good for human children, she said."

Piper waved a dismissive hand through the air. "Oh that's just shydoh speaking." Then she grabbed Rohoar's paw with both hands and tugged on it. "Please? I love these kinds of bedtime stories so much."

Rohoar slowed and glared down at her with a furry eyebrow raised. "Are you certain you do not have Jujari blood, small one?"

"Me?" Piper's eyes went wide, and she looked down at her chest and arms. "I don't think so. Why?"

"Because Jujari pups also love such stories. Rohoar thinks you are part Jujari somewhere."

"Yeah. Probably. It's why we get along so well."

Rohoar let out a low *woof*. "Rohoar agrees."

"Anyway, I'm really super happy that you and the other Jujari are back now. And I know you have an important meeting to go to. Plus, I imagine it's hard for you too, you know." Piper looked around and raised her chin at the sprawling village.

"What does Rohoar know that Piper assumes Rohoar should know?"

"The things." She nodded toward the nearest Sekmit and then said in a hushed tone, "The kitty cats." When Rohoar *still* didn't seem to understand what she was trying to say, she yanked on his arm, forcing him to stoop over so she could talk in his ear. "Don't you want to attack all these cat people?"

"They are not cat people, tiny human."

"Yeah, but, they look a lot like them, and you're a big doggy—"

"Not a doggy."

"—who probably wants to eat them. Am I right?"

Rohoar tried working his paw out of Piper's grip like working his arm out of a coat sleeve, but she wasn't going to let go until he answered the question. "Fine," he huffed. "Yes. It's very tempting to eat them."

"See? I knew it."

"But Rohoar will refrain. There is too much to be done."

"I bet they want to scratch your nose."

Rohoar placed his other paw atop his snout. "Why would you say that?"

"'Cause. That's what cats on Capriana Prime do. Did." Suddenly, Piper felt very sad. Thinking of how many people died on the planet still hurt her heart. But now, there were no more people there, no more dogs or cats or corgachirps—real ones and fake ones.

"You are sad thinking of Rohoar fighting with the Sekmit? Because Rohoar can assure you, he will refrain from disemboweling them or making necklaces from their entrails."

"No." Piper let go of Rohoar's paw. "I'm just sad at how many people have died in all of, well, since I left Capriana. It almost feels, feels…"

"Feels like what?"

"Like it's my fault."

Rohoar stopped walking and knelt in front of her.

The bridge swayed a little as Piper looked up at his large fuzzy face. "What?"

"Listen to the air of Rohoar's speech. You have not caused this, tiny human. All of what we see now is the result of those set on destruction. If we perish in the middle of stopping them, or we kill others to complete our tasks, then this is only evidence of how deadly our enemies are. But we? Rohoar"—he touched his chest—"and most especially Piper"—he touched hers—"we are those who seek to preserve life. Take it if we must, but always preserve wherever we can. Yes? Understanding?"

"Understanding," Piper said. She wiped tears from her eyes and snot from her nose with the back of her hand.

"Good. We must always be appriprensive, facing fears together, as one."

She thought about correcting him but felt too grateful for his words to her to ruin the moment. "Yeah. Appriprensive. Thanks, Rohoar. I needed that."

"And Rohoar also needed what you said to him."

"What I said?"

"Yes. You taught me bahdish bahdang. About appriprensive. Rohoar used this to think of his pack, and it was his tribe who rescued him from Moldark and Mahkmaim."

"It was?"

Rohoar nodded. "Without them, Rohoar would not be here to encourage you." The Jujari's eyes got glossy, reflecting the torch-fires as they lit up across the Fînta. "We need one another. And this"—he made her form a fist and then punched his hand with it—"this is how we win."

Piper threw her arms around his thick neck and squeezed. "This is how we win," she echoed, whispering her thanks into his ear. Then she kissed him on his soft cheek and watched him walk to his important meeting.

It felt good to have the whole team back together again. While not everyone in the room was a company commander or team leader, Magnus had told Caldwell that he still wanted them present as they embodied the heart of the Gladio Umbra. And right now, the team needed every ounce of heart they had left. Magnus felt—no, he knew—that whatever came next would take everything they had to give.

The gladias gathered in Minx's command hall—a timbered room with wooden benches and tables, a central stone fire pit, and small alcoves along the walls. TO-96, Azelon, Colonel Caldwell, and Willowood stood at the room's front and talked casually while some of Minx's inner guard passed out glasses of water to those seated. Rohoar and his Jujari sat atop two tables, and Sootriman and Ezo lazed near the fireside, their arms around each other—well, more like Sootriman holding Ezo.

Ricio, Captain Forbes, and Lieutenant Nelson each had called in various leaders under their commands. Willowood asked Scion, Incipio, and Tora to represent Paladia Company, Azelon pulled in Cyril, Berouth, and Gilder. Moreover, all of Granther Company's members were present as Magnus sensed he was going to need to restructure the outfit based on whatever came from this meeting. The Gladio Umbra's losses on Prime, combined with the ever-changing tactics of the enemy, required that the outfit remain lean and versatile.

"All right," Caldwell said, quieting the room by holding up his cigar. "Let's settle in and get started. If my mustache is right, and it's rarely wrong, we've got a splickton of work in front of us. TO-96's bolts aren't getting any shinier, and my ball carrier ain't losing any wrinkles."

This produced a smattering of laughter around the room.

"The most important news, as you've probably all heard by now, is that we have reason to believe that Moldark is still alive."

Whatever lightheartedness floated through the air from his earlier statement hit the deck in a hurry from this one. Heads nodded, and faces grew stern—Magnus's especially. Having already talked with Rohoar while the Jujari were en route from Oorajee, Magnus could hardly believe the story was true. And he wouldn't have, were it not for the Jujari who told it. Not only was Rohoar a Unity user, but he was one of the most honest people Magnus had ever met, if not *the* most honest. The Jujari's complete incomprehension of hyperbole made him extremely forthcoming, if not annoyingly so.

Caldwell gestured toward Rohoar. "You have the floor, mwadim."

Rohoar stood, addressed his fellow gladias, and then told the story of his encounter with Moldark's essence while in Oosafar, beginning with the strange appearance of Paragon ships in Oorajee's orbit. Later he recounted the fight with Mahkmaim, taking special care to point out the other contender's noble attributes. Magnus found this particularly moving, given the fact that the Selskrit had tried to kill Rohoar for the throne.

Then the mwadim told of the sudden shift in Mahkmaim's demeanor and the conversation with whatever new spirit possessed the Selskrit leader. As Rohoar described his soul being sucked from his body, Magnus noticed several people in the crowd move in their seats. At last, Rohoar outlined Mahkmaim's mercy killing in a final effort to dispatch Moldark. He spoke with such reverence that Magnus thought maybe the two warriors had been estranged brothers and not rivals to a throne.

"Thank you, Rohoar," Caldwell said as the Jujari sat down. "I don't think I need to tell you all that the pucker factor on that one is just north of hearing a LIMKIT 4 landmine click when you sit down in a latrine."

A hand went up. It was Zoll. "Colonel. Do we know how Moldark was able to possess this other Jujari? Was he killed over Prime, and his spirit got loose or something?"

Heads nodded throughout the room.

"Colonel," TO-96 said. "If I may."

"Go ahead, Ballsy."

TO-96 turned to face the room. "As you may recall, after we analyzed the data of the *Black Labyrinth's* final moments, we had determined that the probability of Moldark escaping the ship's destruction was less than 3%."

"I remember that," Zoll said. "Sounds pretty low."

"It does," the bot replied. "Which we all took comfort in. However, we decided to employ additional data captured from Azelon's sizable and robust sensor array that probed the surrounding space—"

Magnus shot Awen a look and then mouthed the words "sizable and robust?"

She shot back with "probed?"

"—we discovered several anomalies consistent with biological transport infrastructure." TO-96 projected a large holo display of data, laid out in mind-numbing three-dimensional grids.

"What are we looking at here?" Bliss asked. "This makes no sense to me."

"Show them the rendering," Ezo said to TO-96.

The bot nodded. The data vanished, and the image of a single starship appeared.

"The *Peregrine*," Forbes said, sitting forward on his bench.

"Precisely, Captain Forbes," TO-96 replied.

"So, he did escape," Zoll said.

"We believe so, yes," TO-96 said. "This news, combined with Rohoar's generals' eyewitness accounts of Paragon warships firing on Oorajee, leads us to conclude that Moldark is still alive."

"But I thought you said those ships were destroyed," Abimbola said to Rohoar.

"Most were," the mwadim replied. "But we estimate that some may have survived."

"Estimate?" Abimbola asked.

Rohoar grunted. "Something blocked our pack's sensors. We felt as if something survived though. I will try to explain this. It was as if something blotted out space, hiding it from the sight of our eyes. As if blood stained a piece of leather. As if a sandstorm covered the sky across the horizon. As if—"

"Got it, mwadim," Abimbola said.

"I concur with the Jujari's findings," Azelon said. "After reviewing everything the Tawnhack sent us, I was able to determine that there was, in fact, some form of dark matter around the last known coordinates of the Paragon ships in orbit over Oorajee."

"Dark matter?" Awen asked, seemingly intrigued but this new bit of information. Willowood's body language suggested she, too, was keen on whatever Azelon had to say. The two women shared a look.

"Does this mean something to you?" Magnus asked.

Awen deferred to Willowood with a nod.

"It could," the older woman said. "Dark energy makes up more than half of the universe, and dark matter almost a third. While most dark matter is naturally occurring, it exists passively, like a substrate beneath the rest of what we see and experience."

"Anyone else lost?" Robillard asked. His question produced a series of verbal consents and head nods.

Caldwell raised his cigar for silence and then pointed it at Willowood. "Please, continue."

She gave a quick half-smile. "Think of it like bedrock. We all know it's there, but no one thinks about it."

"Except geologists," Magnus said.

"Correct. And, I guess you could say we're"—Willowood glanced at Awen and the other mystics—"the geologists."

"So you know what was blotting out Rohoar's sensors like a moon over the sun?" the Jujari asked.

"Not exactly," Willowood replied. "But I think it's important we find out what it was."

Magnus couldn't put his finger on it, but there was definitely a change in the elder woman's mood. Even if it was imperceptible to everyone else, he chalked the insight up to being an old Marine hunch. "And why's that? Begging your pardon."

Willowood pursed her lips in thought before replying. "Dark matter doesn't just pop up and interfere with normal matter. If anything, it stays behind the scenes, giving everything else that's known something to stand on, as it were."

"So the fact that it messed with Jujari sensors concerns you," Magnus said.

"That's correct. It might be nothing."

"But it might also be something. And if so, I assume you have a working theory?"

Willowood sighed. "No. No theories yet. Which is all the more reason we need to discover what caused it. Until then, I think Moldark is in the wind. If we try to follow him now, we'd just be wasting time. Better to focus on the things we can change until…"

"Until what?" Magnus asked.

"Until Moldark comes to us."

Well that was definitely not awesome. Even though he hated the uncertainty of Willowood's statement, he trusted her. She'd come to Caldwell with answers when she had them.

"What do you need for your investigation?" Caldwell asked.

"The data from TO-96 and the Jujari sensors for a start. The gladias of Paladia Company will handle the rest."

Caldwell nodded. "Which leads us to our next topic of discussion while we wait for our esteemed hostess, Freya, to arrive: that of the golden bath babies that Magnus and Alpha Team encountered at the Governor's mansion. Magnus?"

Magnus tapped on the data pad and then pushed it into the middle of the table closest to him. It projected a large holo display of video captured from his helmet cam during the battle with the Luma warriors. The footage showed Magnus firing on the robed assailants and retreating through the mansion.

"As most of you know, I made the call to personally pursue Senator Blackman after Awen made the surprise discovery that he had not only survived the assault on Prime but was involved with Governor Littleton's activities here on Aluross. While Blackman"—Magnus glanced at Caldwell—"succumbed to injuries sustained during the ensuing conflict, the more important revelation is his connection to So-Elku's new Luma Alliance of Worlds."

Magnus froze the video on a panoramic shot of the Luma flooding the building's rear entrance just before the BATRIGs opened fire.

"Golden bath babies," Zoll said, nodding slowly. "Now I get what you meant, Colonel."

Caldwell smiled through his cigar smoke but kept his eyes focused on Magnus. "Describe your encounter, Lieutenant."

"They had powerful Unity shielding, that's for damn sure," Magnus said. "And not like the kind we encountered when we lost Simone on Worru. It was stronger—as if my blaster fire was absorbed, and then used against me, much like I've seen some of our gladia do." He gestured toward the mystics. "In the end, it was only the mech's overwhelming fire rate that punched holes in their shields and put down the enemy." He pushed play and allowed the video to show the counterattack. The BATRIGs' withering firepower decimated the enemy and tore the building's backside to shreds.

Several people whistled at the action, and more than one gladia let out an enthusiastic "La-raah!" When the footage ended, Magnus turned off the holo and removed the data pad from the table.

"I'm gonna turn this over to Willowood," Magnus said, and then stepped aside.

"Thank you, Magnus." Willowood laid her own data pad on the table and brought up a holo presentation she'd prepared. The first segment of video, care of TO-96, was lifted from So-Elku's planet-wide broadcast. "As we learned from So-Elku's national address on Worru, the warriors Magnus encountered are what So-Elku is calling the Li-Dain." The video slowed as the broadcast camera swept along a row of Luma dressed in their distinctive and already infamous gold-colored martial apparel. "Based on the name, Magnus's description, and the footage from the encounter in the governor's mansion, it appears that So-Elku has taken the traditional Li-Loré arts well past their non-lethal genesis."

"The lie-lilly past their say what'asis?" Bliss asked, looking around. "Anyone else lost."

"She'll explain, Bliss," Caldwell said as he pumped his hand in the air. "Slow your sweet gourde."

"Copy."

"As I was saying," Willowood said. "Li-Loré is an ancient martial art form developed by the Luma Elders specifically to guard the Luma Master. On a few rare occasions, it was also used during covert negotiations."

"So, so, are you talking spy splick?" Cyril asked. "'Cause that 100% reminds me of a level in *Nova Ops Two* where—"

"The nature of those operations varied, Mr. Cyril," Willowood replied, doing an exemplary job of acting professionally toward Cyril's playfully obtuse question. "Most of them surrounded the protection of high-level government officials, especially during sensitive negotiations with the Galactic Republic."

Cyril sat back, folded his arms, then leaned over to Abimbola. "Spy splick. Called it."

"Can you tell us a little bit more about Li-Loré?" Abimbola asked. "I think we have seen some of it from our own mystic-gladia, yes?"

"Certainly." Willowood advanced her presentation footage to content taken aboard the *Spire* in one of the training hangars for Paladia Company. Several dozen gladias in Novian power suits moved in unison, sweeping, pushing, and punching their arms and legs in coordinated patterns. "Abimbola is right. When you've seen us use our powers in the Unity, in either hand-to-hand combat or against enemy attacks, you're seeing a version of Li-Loré. What you see here is a *tyka* of Awen's and my own design. We've developed it specifically for use in the Gladio Umbra. While there are certainly offensive capabilities, as some of you have no doubt witnessed, it is primarily a defensive tool used to deflect an enemy's aggressive energy."

"Those bath babies were doing a whole lot more than deflecting," Rix said. "The way they were shooting at Magnus made me wanna piss my mech."

"And I don't blame you," Willowood replied. "Those 'bath babies,' as you called them, were extremely powerful, using abilities well beyond anything they would have learned in the Li-Loré. Awen?"

Awen nodded and stepped forward. Then she advanced Willowood's data pad presentation to show an animated image of what looked to be a cross-section of three ground layers. But rather than show topsoil, gravel, and bedrock, this animation showed a surface level of moving yellow light, a second level of churning green, and a bottom layer of sparkling magenta. Various metrics and thin pointer indicators moved with each liquid layer, showing amplitudes, volumes, energy waves, and several other lines of data most likely lost on the majority of the audience. Even still, it looked impressive.

"What you see here, with no small thanks to Azelon, is the closest we can come to a graphic representation of the Unity."

"Where you all spend most of your time," Forbes offered.

"That's correct, Captain. This"—she pointed to the yellow top layer—"up until I went to metaspace for the first time, is what we have always called the Unity. It is the realm in which all Luma have learned to operate since the beginning of our order—*their* order. It enables us to see and move within the second sight.

"But when I encountered the Novia Minoosh and the codex, we learned that the Unity encompasses more layers and is much deeper than we ever knew." She touched the green section. "The Foundation layer presents a whole new creative realm within the Unity. From it, we understand the formative nature of the unseen and find the basis for all manner of matter manipulation. But this layer"—Awen touched the glimmering magenta region—"this is what we know as the Nexus. Think of it as a massive root system that exists in the lowest plain. Its energy interconnects everything else, both seen and unseen, known and unknown. It is the most powerful of all three Unity layers, and the level we know the least about."

"Is Awen then suggesting that these Lily-Danishes have access to the other realms?" Rohoar asked.

Awen smiled at the mispronunciation. "Yes, mwadim. Just as we gladia do. But where we have tried to harness its power for defensive means—being the *umbra* of our Gladio Umbra—these warriors with the Luma Alliance of Worlds have used it to conjure highly aggressive results."

"As we saw in the attack against Magnus," Sootriman said.

"Correct. They are powerful, and if we know So-Elku, they will be pressed to grow in their giftedness and understanding of this new power."

"If there is one thing So-Elku was known for," Willowood said, coming to stand beside Awen. "It was his relentless desire for perfection. When used for noble ends, sought through good ways, it had amazing results. So-Elku had ways of pulling the best out of everyone, as Awen can attest. But when a powerful person makes compromises to attain good things, well, I think we can all see the results today."

Abimbola raised his hand.

"Bimby," Caldwell said.

"So, if this is the spearhead of the LAW, then what were they doing here on Aluross?"

"Trying to take over our trinium deposits," said a female voice at the back of the hall.

Magnus looked across to the dimly lit entrance and saw Freya stride into the room accompanied by Wobix and eight other green-robed narskill warriors. The soldiers moved without making a sound and carried wooden staves and Thørzin bows.

"Your highness," Caldwell said. He raised his hands, reminding the gladias to stand.

Minx rushed to Freya's side and brushed her head along the tribe mother's neck. Minx's other servants lifted their chins in respect but stayed where they were around the room. Then Minx turned to address the Gladio Umbra. "I present ní Freya ap Linux."

"Thank you for honoring us with your presence," Caldwell said, motioning to give her the floor.

"Feared Aggressor Caldwell," she replied as she crossed the room to stand beside him. "It is good to see you again. And you, manservant of Awen."

Magnus coughed once and then raised his chin as Awen had taught him. "Ní Freya."

She gave him a dismissive glance. But half-hidden in her countenance, Magnus could have sworn he saw a look of approval.

"First," Freya said as she lazily looked around the room. "I'd like to congratulate you all on a job well done. While your methods were unorthodox, the coverage surrounding the explosion at the Governor's mansion seems to support the Republic's desire to cover up his —how shall I put it—unfortunate fetish for Elonian and Sekmit companions alike." Freya gave Awen a knowing smile.

"Needless to say, I don't think we'll be hearing from the GR anytime soon, except to attempt making reparations, which everyone knows they can't afford." She sniffed the air as if picking up the scent of something rancid. "Now, however, it seems we have a new pest in the garbage heap, one who had already gotten to the Governor."

Magnus suddenly wondered just how much Freya had heard before she made her appearance. Then again, this was her world, and it was highly likely that she'd already received intelligence from any number of sources—including from people who had listened in on the conversation via the Unity. Not that it mattered. The Gladio Umbra were guests; still, he didn't like having his brain tapped.

"This LAW you speak of," Freya continued. "If they are seeking to fill the void that the Republic once filled, then they will need the one thing that all advanced civilizations require for their drive cores."

"So, so, you really have, like, trinium here?" Cyril said. "On Aluross?"

"Yes, my nervous chattering human."

"But, uh, there aren't records about that. Like, none. And believe me, if there was, I would have seen them. Because, well, because I study that sort of thing and—"

Cyril froze when Freya whipped her hand up with a *swoosh* sound.

"Part of our agreement with the Galactic Republic was a mutually beneficial condition of absolute secrecy. In effect, it meant there would be no rivals to the Republic's claim, and we would be safe from unwelcome interest in our mines. Thus, the reason you are not aware of our trinium deposits is that we did not wish for you to know."

"Yeah, yeah, but it's more than that, I think." Cyril swallowed. Magnus had to give the kid credit—he sure did have some stones going up against Freya. That, or he was just completely ignorant of how lethal this species was, which didn't seem likely given the kid's level of study. "Every world with trinium deposits worth making alliances over is easy to spot because of the radiation. It's an unstable isotope. Obviously. If Aluross had trinium in any substantial proportions, we would have known. Everyone would have known. Like, the whole 'a long time ago' kind of knowing."

"That's because our trinium is hidden, chatterbox."

"But that's impossible."

"Cyril," Caldwell said with the warning tone of an impatient parent.

"No, no, I don't mean to say Miss Freya is lying or anything. Unless she *wants* to deceive us because then she'd be lying. And that's bad. But I don't mean to imply that she's stupid either, because, wow, that would be really disrespectful of me."

"Cyril," Caldwell barked. "Stand down."

"Yes, sir. Bravo roger niner, right away, Charlie."

"So what you're saying is that Blackman was here on behalf of the LAW," Awen said to Freya. "You think he was working to turn the Repub's planetary governor, and all in the hope of acquiring your trinium mines."

"That is my hypothesis, yes."

"Interesting." Awen looked at Magnus. "Makes sense."

"Which is the real reason why you wanted us to help you give Littleton the boot," Magnus said in a sudden epiphany.

The tribe mother eyed Magnus like she was ready to eat him for a snack. "As I said, this has been a closely guarded secret."

"So why tell us now?" Magnus asked.

"Because while the Republic may not return for the trinium, the LAW will. The Republic has other mines on other worlds, ones not currently embroiled in a scandal. But the LAW? They have no other sources for trinium, and ours is the largest and most accessible to them. If their plans really are to expand control over the quadrant and beyond, they won't be going anywhere unless they take Aluross first."

"So you used us," Magnus said. "And I'm guessing Lani DiAntora wasn't working alone either. You prompted her to send us here."

Freya cocked her head sideways at Magnus. "You know, for a manservant, you are both perceptive and irreverently outspoken."

"What can I say?" Magnus shrugged, then he winked at Awen. "My overlord lets me have a long leash."

Caldwell turned to Freya. "Ní Freya, I think you can understand how we feel at the moment."

"Comfortable, safe, and grateful for the protection the Sekmit have provided for your people?"

The colonel grunted with a half-smile. "We are, yes. But—"

"Tell me, Feared Aggressor of the Hundred Worlds War, would you have come to help us without the offer of protection for your people, as suggested by Captain DiAntora? And would you have risked your lives at the Governor's mansion if our objections were simply over mineral rights and natural resources?" She waited for Caldwell to reply. But when he didn't, she moved on. "Or would you have stayed clear and told us to take up our issues with the governor, ambassadors, and the senate?"

"Well, you did threaten us if we opted not to help you. And you mentioned the economic sanctions if the Repub caught wind of what was going on."

"And yet, in the end, why did you decide to come, and further, to help us, Feared Aggressor? What was it that so moved you on all points?"

The Colonel seemed to mull this over for a moment as he chewed on the end of his cigar. "I realized you wanted the same peace and security for your people that I wanted for mine."

"And, for the Sekmit, this includes our natural resources." Freya relaxed her stance then assumed a more wistful tone. "In hindsight, we were unwise to give up so much to the Galactic Republic when we first joined. But we feared that we were not strong enough to defend ourselves from them once the mines were discovered. Nor did we trust them to keep the trinium a secret if we refused their offer."

"And you're still not strong enough?" Caldwell said.

"Against a weakened Republic with the wisp of a navy? They would not be so foolish to try, as we have grown more powerful over the years. But the LAW?" Freya purred and twitched her nose. "They are more cunning and will no doubt be provoked by the loss of Senator Blackman and some of these golden cherubs, as you call them. That, and the Elder Queens seem uncertain of our people's fate. Which is why we wish you to stay and help us defend our planet once more."

Many of the gladias moaned at this prospect. But in the blink of an eye, Wobix and his narskill warriors had their Thørzin bows drawn and energy bolts ready to fly. Several gladias stood, some prepared to raise weapons, others holding out their hands to try and calm the situation.

"Stand down," Colonel Caldwell ordered with a commanding voice that cut through the air. Likewise, Freya hissed some command in the Sekmit tongue that seemed to take Wobix a few seconds to pass on to his warriors. Eventually, the tension subsided, and people retook their positions.

"Well, as you can see, ní Freya, this isn't exactly sitting well with everyone," Caldwell said.

"But is the LAW not our common foe?" Freya asked.

Caldwell blew out a puff of smoke. Magnus guessed the Colonel's conundrum. The fact was, the Gladio Umbra hadn't gotten to this part of the dialogue yet. "I don't know, gladias. Is the LAW our enemy?"

Magnus was caught off guard by Caldwell's candor. It wasn't standard procedure to open up such a question in front of so many players, including a possible foe. Maybe the Colonel was slipping. Or perhaps he was just trying to get everyone on the same page.

"Let's face it," Caldwell said. "We might as well talk this out together and all get on the same page. Hell knows our hosts aren't gonna wait forever. Anyone?"

"They're enemies," Zoll said. "Their precious golden-wrapped diaper babies tried to kill Magnus."

Several people laughed at this.

"But does the LAW offer a sense of needed stability in light of the Republic's fall?" Magnus offered, much to everyone's surprise. He didn't mean it, of course. But he was trying to do a little of what Awen had told him to. "I'm just trying to make sure we're looking at all sides of this conversation." That, and he wanted to make sure everyone saw what was at stake if they indeed decided that the LAW needed to be taken down.

Awen raised her eyebrows at him. "They tried to kill you, Adonis."

"Because I went after Blackman."

"And Blackman was responsible for Capriana Prime," Forbes added.

"In part, yes." Magnus nodded. "But if we decide that the LAW is a real enemy, then it means we're all in. It means that we believe So-Elku will do anything he can to acquire power, and we're basing that off one encounter."

"No, we're not," Awen said, arms folded.

Magnus gave her a look as if he wanted her to repeat the statement. This was a new direction for her. The last time the GU had met like this, she'd contended that it was too soon to know what the Luma Master's motives were.

"We're not basing this off one encounter," Awen continued. "It's

So-Elku's pattern. He tried to manipulate me into giving him the stardrive. He conspired against Willowood and the others, and he kidnapped Piper. Then, through Blackman, we learn that he worked behind the scenes in ways we're not even fully aware of to attack Capriana Prime and then create his own alliance network. And now his forces show up here? To take political control of Aluross?" She shook her head, more to herself than anyone else it seemed. "No. I think it's clear that So-Elku's sense of peace and justice is based only on what he deems it to be. He's not willing to talk it through. He's not willing to see all sides. That man"—she pointed to one side as if to make a point—"has abandoned the Luma way in favor of something else, and he must be stopped."

A heavy silence fell over the hall. People looked to one another as if in search of silent confirmation. Magnus knew that it was one thing for a warrior to offer reasons to charge into battle, but it was another thing altogether when Awen did.

"If we're saying this, then we're going back to war," Caldwell said.

"Yeah, but we all knew that was coming anyway," Bliss said. "Colonel, sir."

"I'm with Bliss," Robillard said. "If we sit around here too long, we're bound to grow tails."

The Sekmit snapped their heads to him.

Robillard pumped his hands in the air. "Not that there's anything wrong with that. I'm just saying."

"Company commanders?" Caldwell said. "I want a vote. We're doing this together or not at all."

Magnus was the first to put his hand up. "I haven't come all this way just so some crazy-ass Luma totalitarian can spoil everything.

And while I'm not about to rejoin the ranks of the Corps, the GR was still better than the LAW any day."

Heads nodded, and a few gladias let out quiet *la-raahs* as each company commander's hand went up in a unanimous vote.

Caldwell held out his cigar. "Motion carried." Then he let the weight of the vote settle on everyone and took the opportunity to take a long draw on his tobacco; mystics knew Magnus would have done the same. "But that still doesn't answer our question about helping the Sekmit. So we need to decide whether it's better to take the fight to Worru or stay here and defend against another possible power grab."

"We assaulted Worru once," Bliss said.

"Yeah, and barely made it out alive," Robillard replied. "I'm not sure we're up for that yet."

"It certainly was a challenging raid," Abimbola said as he flipped a poker chip and caught it. "But one worth taking, as it was a mission to both rescue"—he nodded at Willowood and her mystics—"and recruit"—he looked to Forbes and Nelson. Then he slapped the poker chip on the back of his hand. "This time, however, we would be going to destroy that which the Master Luma has constructed." Abimbola looked down at the chip. "And the gods tell me it is not the time."

"Reliance on deities is irrelevant to my logic systems," Azelon said. "However, in light of the Miblimbian's logic, I too calculate a minimal degree of success were our forces to attempt any sort of outright assault against Worru at this time."

"And remaining here on Aluross?" Caldwell asked.

"Depending on the numerous enemy attack scenarios, ranging from covert to overt, as well as the type of trinium deposits the Sekmit are guarding, I calculate a much higher degree of success if we remain here and aid Aluross against a possible invasion. Statistically speaking, an offensive endeavor must have five times the fighting force to successfully overpower any given defense. Our combined energies place us in the eightieth percentile of success given all the variables currently at my disposal."

"Ezo likes those odds," Ezo said.

"As does Rohoar," said the Jujari.

Freya turned to Caldwell. "Should I be concerned that you have some among your number who speak of themselves distantly?"

Caldwell titled his head. "Normally, I'd tell you to be concerned. But these ones are okay."

"As you say."

"Additionally," Azelon said. "If So-Elku acquires the Sekmit's trinium supply, assuming it is as abundant as proposed, then Freya has a very valid point. The LAW would have an ample supply of fuel, enabling them to extend their reach into other systems. As it stands now, with Republic supply lines dwindling by the day, Worru will be limited to whatever it has on hand."

"So you can bet they'll be coming back," Sootriman said. "Ain't nothing like an old fashioned chokehold to get someone kicking and punching for air."

Caldwell spread his arms apart. "So, what will it be, gladias?"

"Stay," said Abimbola.

"We stay and fight," Zoll said. "Dominate."

"Liberate," several more cried out.

Once the enthusiasm died down, Magnus looked at Freya. "Seeing as how you're getting yourself a battalion of mercenaries, mind showing us what we're defending and exactly why Cyril says there's no record of it?"

"It would be my pleasure, manservant."

2

David Seaman and his commanders watched the security camera footage of Governor Littleton's mansion inside the war room in Admiral's Hall. And none of them dared move.

The briefing required the highest security clearance. This, of course, was not a problem, as the leaders and commanders of the newly titled Neo Republic unanimously voted to elevate Seaman from commodore to acting chancellor until such time as new bylaws could be drafted to account for the Republic's unprecedented fragmentation. Likewise, Seaman made eight appointments to fill the seats of Central Command. These people would be responsible for seeing to the safety and security of the Neo Republic's sovereign citizens and military assets—what little remained. The CENTCOM assignments included Admiral Lani DiAntora, now Chief of Naval Operations, and General A. H. Lovell, now Commandant of the Marine Corps.

With lights low and blinds drawn, Seaman and his advisers watched the holos as men and women in formal attire ran from

Littleton's bedroom, shrieking in terror. People stumbled over one another as security guards pushed them down the hall. Several guests fell to the ground, preoccupied with tapping on their data pads.

Several smaller holo windows appeared at the end of the conference room with feeds that looked as though they'd been taken from the data pads.

"What you see here are the posts from the guests' devices," said General Kalene Williams, Commander of Naval Intelligence.

"Freeze," Seaman said. "Play window three."

The computer did as he instructed.

"Maximize," Seaman added.

The graphic scene of the governor's bedroom caused a few CENTCOM members to gasp, some placing hands over their mouths. In the holo, Littleton swore his innocence despite several scantily clad women lying across his bed and a floor covered in blood.

The chancellor looked across at DiAntora, checking to see if she was alright. Most of the females seemed to be Sekmit, though it was hard to be sure with the shaky video and the low light. DiAntora, however, remained the stoic picture of a proud Sekmit and professional Republic military commander.

"Resume primary screen and maximize," Seaman ordered the AI.

The security camera view returned, showing the guests running down stairs and filling the main reception hall.

"Advance to marker twenty-one twenty-nine," General Williams said. The program responded and showed security forces firing at the reception hall's second-story balcony.

Seaman searched for a target but saw nothing. "What are they firing at?" But Williams didn't reply, choosing instead to let the video continue to play. Some strange invisible presence moved along the balcony and then came down the stairs, firing round after round into the security guards.

At first, Seaman assumed it was the work of an entire platoon—there was no way that anything less could put so much firepower downrange. But then, as the chancellor started to notice that all the blaster rounds were emanating from a single source, he realized it was a very small group. Perhaps even one person. "But that's impossible," he said to himself.

Within moments, the unknown assailant had killed everyone in the entire reception hall.

"Did it stop?" Seaman asked Williams. "What's happening?"

"Just wait," she replied nodding toward the holo.

Just then, a uniformed man slid across the floor as if dragged at the ankle by the wind. Then a chair flipped up, all by itself, and the man was hoisted into it.

"Holy mystics," Seaman said, leaning forward. "Is that Senator Blackman?"

Williams nodded. "We have a 98% match, sir."

"Vesper's crag, I can't believe I'm seeing this."

"Neither could we, sir."

"And what's that uniform he's wearing?"

"Just wait, sir." Williams waved a finger in the air to raise the audio volume.

"Why'd you betray the people of Capriana Prime, you son of a bitch?" said a rough voice. The sound seemed strangely familiar to Seaman, but he couldn't quite place the speaker.

Blackman coughed and then seemed to try and make a deal

with his unseen adversary. Suddenly, his head snapped sideways, and the voice told the senator to answer the question.

"I didn't mean to," Blackman said. "It was an accident."

Then Blackman's right knee exploded in a blast of light, severing his lower leg. The senator screamed and begged for someone to rescue him. The two spoke some more, and then Blackman's other knee exploded as blood and bone splattered across the floor.

"Mystics, he's going to murder him," Seaman muttered.

As the senator and the unseen vigilante spoke, names like Moldark and So-Elku came up, as did themes of loyalty, betrayal, and vision. Something even depressed the logo on the senator's breast pocket. The patch was an encircled flame filled with a field of stars, bordered by some text too small to read. Finally, Blackman said one word. "Magnus."

"Magnus?" Seaman looked at DiAntora. "Does he mean the former Marine Lieutenant?"

But Lani barely looked at him.

The holo screen went white, and the speakers clipped from an audio spike. The mansion's front doors exploded, and then a dozen unusual-looking figures walked in. They were dressed in some sort of billowing golden pants and matching robed tunics, tied at the waist.

"What in the hell is going on here?" Seaman said, hardly able to believe anything he was seeing. He swore it was a holo movie, not real-life security footage. "Is this some sort of joke?"

Williams shook her head. "Keep watching."

Another dozen joined the twelve figures as they spread out and headed toward the senator. Then two blaster bolts punched through

Blackman's body, and he slumped forward and spilled out of the chair onto the floor.

The next few moments were a flurry of bright flashes and strange explosions. The golden warriors seemed to channel energy from the ether and send it careening toward the ghostly figure, who Seaman could only assume was Adonis Magnus. At twenty-four to one, Magnus seemed to retreat toward a rear hallway, followed by the golden robed assailants.

The pursuit finally ended when what looked to be four mechanized armor platforms unloaded on the mansion, cutting the gold attackers to ribbons. The sheer amount of withering firepower was astounding, blowing apart columns, ripping up tile, and tearing through walls. Then the four mechs turned and leaped off the back veranda. Just when Seaman guessed there could not be any more carnage, the camera feed froze on a bright white light illuminating the four mechs in midair.

"And that is the last frame we have," Williams said. Everyone sat, staring at the image for a few moments before General Lovell called for the lights.

Seaman glared at the wall. After a few seconds, he turned back to look at those around the table, including Lani. "Did you know?" he asked her.

"Know what, Chancellor?"

"Oh, cut the splick, Lani." He thrust a finger at where the holo screen had been. "That was the Lieutenant that *you* offered asylum to. And those mech's looked an awful lot like the ones the Marines encountered at Elusian Base and again on the beach outside the Forum Republica. You're telling me the Sekmit had nothing to do with, with"—he couldn't find the words—"with whatever mess that was?"

"The decisions of the leaders of Aluross are their own, regardless of—"

"Spare me the deflection, Admiral. Did you know?"

"It's complicated."

"Mystics!" Seaman threw himself back in his chair. "What the hell is going on around here? It's like the galaxy is falling out from underneath us, and I don't even know if I can trust the people at this table."

"You're tired," DiAntora said. "You haven't slept, and—"

"I don't need it right now, DiAntora. I need answers."

"Well, sir," Williams said. "It's not over yet."

The chancellor eyed her. "Excuse me?"

"We have more. And it explains the situation behind Governor Wade's defection to So-Elku's organization."

"You mean the Order of the Luma," Seaman replied.

"No, sir. I don't." Williams turned and activated the holo screen again. "We received the following footage through some of our shadow ops channels in the pre-dawn hours today."

An image appeared of Master So-Elku standing behind a podium in front of the Luma's Grand Arielina. Wiliams hit play.

"Citizens of Plumeria," So-Elku said. "Distinguished guests, and all those watching across Worru, it is my duty and my great honor to address you today."

Over the next several minutes, Chancellor Seaman and the other CENTCOM members watched and listened as So-Elku discussed the fall of the Galactic Republic—*an entirely premature assertion*, Seaman thought, *since we're still sitting right here*—the absence of clear leadership, and the need for a new alliance to pick up where the Republic had left off.

The Luma Master then proceeded to outline what he called the Luma Alliance of Worlds. All at once, Seaman connected the organization's logo to the patch on Blackman's chest. How the senator survived Capriana's destruction, Seaman had no idea, but he guessed it was with So-Elku's help. *You bastards*, Seaman thought while clenching his teeth. The new alliance also went a long way in explaining Wade's actions, just as Williams surmised. Seaman was starting to see a pattern.

Finally, So-Elku raised his hands and presented an army of golden-robed warriors. "I give you the Li-Dain Protectorate. Sworn Guardians of the LAW, and Mystics of the Nexus!"

"Turn it off," Seaman said. "Lights."

The room filled with heavy sighs and the squeaks of bodies shifting in leather seats as everyone prepared themselves for whatever came next. Several commanders took sips of water while others made notes in their data pads.

Seaman collected himself and placed his hands down at the head of the table. "Anyone else have any bad news they'd like to share before we move on?"

"Actually, yes," said Trade Commissioner Jere Davis. He swiped up on his data pad, sending a file to all those seated at the table. "This report outlines the activity of several emergent anomalies in shipping routes."

"Anomalies?" Seaman said, eyes narrowing. "You're talking pirates?"

"Among other things, yes, Chancellor. We've seen upticks along the Kandameer belt, Khimere, the Meridian Outskirts, and Pellu to name a few."

"Mystics."

"But it's more than that, sir." David used his data pad to project a holo screen that identified ten or so specific planets located throughout the four quadrants. "Notice anything?"

It was DiAntora who responded first. "The pirates are targeting the systems with the most trinium and lancite deposits."

"Correct," Davis replied. "Which leads me to believe that they're not pirates, at least not all of them."

"Explain," Seaman said.

"Most scavengers don't have the resources to go up against these worlds. Even without Republic protection, the planets we're talking about still have sizable defense networks."

"So you're saying it's someone else?" said Henry Sherwood, the newly appointed Finance Commissioner.

"I'm saying I think someone is using the pirates to create a screen while they work inside channels." David nodded to General Lovell.

"Nineteen hours ago, security forces reported that our planetary governor on Undoria was assassinated." Lovell sent several images and a video montage floating over the table. "The operation appears to have been conducted among Governor Morandu's own staff." Lovell expanded a video showing the governor's people turning against him during a firefight. The whole end scene seemed staged, but cryptically so, as if it was some elaborate double-cross scheme.

"An inside job?" Seaman squinted at the images. "But that doesn't make sense."

"It does if you consider who Morandu was speaking to moments before his assassination." Lovell pushed a Repub transmission record into the holo display, one that listed all incoming and outgoing communications for the last twenty-four hours. The final entry showed a blank space for the caller's name, but it did show a planet of origin.

"Worru." Seaman shook his head. "This was So-Elku."

"That's what the evidence suggests, sir."

"Which would also explain why he was going after Aluross," Seaman added. "He wants the trinium."

"But how would he know about it?" Sherwood asked. "That supply line is one of our most closely guarded secrets."

"Blackman," Seaman said. He rotated his glass of water on the table, staring at the contents. "He sold out Prime, and he's giving up our secrets. All for a seat at the table of whoever's dice are luckiest."

"The bastard's dead now," Lovell said.

"But how deep will his betrayal cut us?" Seaman looked up at Lovell. "How much more does So-Elku know? We're not in a place to protect those worlds, and he knows that."

"But if he gets his hands on enough resources to fuel ships, he'll—"

"He'll what, General? Provide energy to every planet with a warship and build himself a fleet of LAW loyalists? Take over the quadrant? Sounds like a workable plan to me."

Lovell worked his jaw. "Yes, chancellor. It does."

Seaman looked around the table. "The reality is that while we're reeling from losses no one ever imagined, So-Elku is building momentum around his new endeavor faster than we're going to be able to respond. And he's clearly willing to use any method necessary to manipulate or coerce leaders into going along with him. This means if we have any hope of keeping the Neo Republic together and stopping him, we can't rely on brute strength like we used to. We've got to be more cunning." He tapped the tip of his index finger on the table. "We've got to outsmart the fox at his own game."

"And you have a plan on how to do that?" Williams asked.

Seaman sighed. "No, General. But that's why I appointed the smartest leaders I know to help me come up with one. If not"—Seaman pointed to the frozen images from Undoria and Morandu's dead body—"you can sure as hell bet we'll be next."

A long pause circled the table as each official seemed to consider the task that Seaman proposed.

"Who else has the footage from inside Littleton's mansion?" DiAntora asked the table.

"Those were our proprietary security feeds," Williams said. "Unless someone's figured out our quantum encryption algo, no one."

"So all the public has is the footage from the social feeds and maybe some shots of the exterior?"

"That's a safe guess, yes," Williams replied.

"Then I'm willing to bet that's all So-Elku has too."

Seaman eyed DiAnora. "You have an idea?"

"I think so," DiAntora said. "It's a long shot. But it just may work."

Seaman gave her a crooked smile. "Right now, I think long shots are the only things we're gonna get, Admiral. Let's hear it."

3

Psykon stood over Moldark's slumbering form and studied the decaying admiral's body. The Elemental had done well in keeping the host's life force suppressed but not as well in maintaining the flesh. Pockmarked scars riddled the scalp and face, and the teeth had become pointed and gnarled. Dried blood stained the corners of Moldark's mouth, and Psykon guessed the man had recently lost a tooth.

"Are we ready to begin again?" he asked his ten *sedgewicks*, practitioners of hidden ways. They stood around the table, hands pressed together in front of their chests, and bowed.

"We have found the vessel of your choosing," Vingroth said. "He is on Fiad Six, as expected."

Psykon nodded. "And he is alone?"

"No. He holds council."

"A fitting test."

"And if we are forced to abandon?" Vingoth asked. "Will we not be lost to the ether?"

Psykon looked down at Moldark. "It is not we who are at risk, second son."

"I understand."

Psykon looked around the room. "Into the darkness."

"Into the darkness," the sedgewicks replied in unison and then filled the chamber with a low hum. Psykon placed his fingertips on Moldark's temples and then closed his eyes.

MOLDARK'S EYES SNAPPED OPEN, and he rose off the stone table as a corpse coming back to life. Then he glared at Psykon's hooded face. "What did you do to me?"

"We did nothing to you, Mithriel," the Obscura leader replied. "That would break the terms of our agreement."

"But you made me lose consciousness." Even as Moldark said the words, he recognized the severity of the situation. He had never been asleep before, as the biologics called it, since his was a perpetual existence, so long as his ethereal presence remained intact. The lack of sleep was one of the many reason's Kane's body was deteriorating more quickly than he had expected. This was, after all, his first human host. But all this was beside the point. "You have done something to me. Lie to me, and I will devour you." Moldark looked at ten other Obscura members standing around the table. "I will devour you all."

"In order to fully examine your being, we discovered that we must ease your awareness of reality." Psykon explained this as if it was nothing more than a temporary inconvenience. "The examination was less than ten common minutes and completely harmless."

Harmless? It was the first time in Moldark's entire existence that he could not remember the space between two points of time. How could something so disruptive be written off as *harmless*? It was time to end these impudent worms.

"Our agreement was that you would allow us to study you," Psykon continued. "We have. And so this concludes your end of the obligation. Now it is time for us to fulfill ours."

Moldark cocked his head at Psykon. "Is it now." Perhaps he was being too hasty, as this certainly seemed a favorable shift. He slid off the table and stretched himself. The domed, black-stone room was bare of any decorations or furniture and lit by only five torches fixed against the curved wall. "And here I thought you said this would take days."

"Has it not been two?"

Moldark peered at Psykon. "But I only arrived yesterday, and we've only attacked one victim."

"The Jujari, yes. Alas, we have learned all we can from you."

"And your findings?"

Psykon's shoulders seemed to lower ever so slightly. "It was just as you said. Your innate abilities are beyond our grasp."

It was just as Moldark suspected; these fools lacked the means to sift through the vastness of his being. "Pity. And yet you never did tell me what enemies we had in common."

"Would it change anything now?"

Moldark considered the question. These strange people were worthy of eradication, as many of them seemed to be human—*the takers*. Still, if they had a common enemy, perhaps using the Obscura for a period could achieve mutual goals—at least until Moldark decided the black beings had served his purposes. "That all depends on who has wronged you, doesn't it."

"Would you wish to help if it suited you?"

"You're playing me, Psykon. And it wears on me." Moldark thought of ending this now, but, strangely, he was not hungry. Consuming Mahkmaim's soul during the battle against Rohoar had sated him longer than he expected.

"We seek vengeance against the Order of the Luma," Psykon said. "And against the leader who perseveres them, one Teerbrin Vanik So-Elku, Master of the Luma and the Luma Alliance of Worlds."

MOLDARK LEANED against the sanctuary tower's railing and looked down. The main square, a hundred meters below, was emptied of people as all of Psykon's followers had gone home for the evening. Meanwhile, the Obscura's First of Many was one pace away, hidden in the roof's shadow.

The city was unusual. No lights dotted the dwellings, no cook fires filled the dark grey sky, and no birds darted from one overhang to the next. Instead, the buildings pushed toward the horizon until they blended with the grey sands and black rocks of the desert. Even the faded star provided little warmth to the barren landscape.

This is no way to live life, Moldark thought. What was more, these people, this world—all of it—seemed dead. Of course, Moldark knew the Obscura were very much alive. He could smell them if nothing else. But how they maintained their biological existence was a mystery.

"So you wish to kill So-Elku and the Luma," Moldark said as he withdrew from the railing and turned toward Psykon. "Why? And why bring me up here?"

"Tell me," Psykon said, raising a pale hand toward the barren cityscape. "What do you see?"

"I tire of your questions to my questions, Master Obscura."

"Then entreat me once more as I endeavor to explain."

Moldark kept his eyes locked on Psykon's hooded head.

The Obscura leader lowered his hand. "As you wish. Then I will tell you what I see. People shunned because of their oaths, forced from their homes, and hunted in the streets like dogs. A people forced to take refuge as far as their ships would carry them, and settle under a foreign sun in an inhospitable world where nothing would give them away, drawing the eye of the hunter."

"The Luma?"

Psykon nodded and then turned his head toward the city. "We were once like them—content. Free. We explored the unknown realms of the galaxy, wayfarers on the winds of the Unity."

"So you are Unity users."

Again, Psykon nodded. "Back then, the Order was in its infancy, a fledgling spark in the cosmos. But as users became more adept at navigating the Unity's waters, many felt that some sort of structure was needed. Boundaries. Limits of what was right and what wasn't."

"Let me guess," Moldark said, still trying to peer under the man's hood. "You didn't like where things were headed and then got kicked out."

Psykon turned to Moldark. "They decided how the Unity could be used as if it was something they could control, and then formalized their decisions. But it did not include our kind, our ways."

"Standing up to the majority can be very expensive."

"But we didn't stand up," Psykon said. "Not at first. Our ancestors bowed to the will of the council in the hope of preserving the peace, even though they knew the Order's statutes were far too limiting. So, we abided. We endeavored to do things their way while still making ourselves heard."

"A noble attempt," Moldark replied. "Though still weak." He found it curious that such timid ancestry could birth such resilient and resourceful progeny. The dark city's black-stone buildings reached toward the grey sky like a thousand steel fingernails scraping across slate. This place was truly a wonder, forged from the planet's crust with brute power. And yet, for all its ominous strength, there was a wildness to the city that felt unpredictable and feral.

Psykon took a breath to continue. "As time went on, our ancestors became convinced that the Luma were nearsighted."

"Inevitable," Moldark said.

"The council claimed that they wanted peace, but with so much of the Unity's power relegated to the shadows, we knew that was impossible. Where they were trying to constrain the cosmos, we wanted to let it out."

Moldark looked at Psykon. "Let it out?"

Psykon nodded as he looked out over the city. "Some people build dams to constrain water to their wills. Others break dams to see where the rivers flow. What the Luma saw as destruction, we saw as"—Psykon paused to study Moldark's face—"tranquility."

"You rebelled against the institution."

"In a manner of speaking." Psykon took another deep breath. "Our ancestors were forced to practice in the secret places, searching to make the unknown known, to release that which was locked. The more they discovered, the more they became convinced that the Order needed to embrace what they'd discovered. But their ideas were rejected." Psykon stepped toward the railing. "They called us devils, demons, and dark users. They branded us with irons." Psykon pulled up his sleeve to reveal the soft part of his wrist, and Moldark saw a scar made of two pairs of parallel lines intersecting one another. "And then banished us into the hill country of the Kindu Sharee on Worru."

"You were there?" Moldark said, looking up from the scars. "You survived for so long a period?"

But Psykon shook his head. "We bear the marks of our ancestors by choice. Their plight will not be forgotten."

"How quaint."

"Surely, as one who has been driven from his homeland, you can relate, Mithriel."

It still bothered Moldark that the Obscura knew something about him—how much remained to be seen. "Do not think to compare my people to yours, Psykon. That would be a mistake you will not recover from."

"My apologies." Psykon leaned against the railing and took a deep breath. "When our ancestors would not cease their practices, the Luma came to the Kindu Sharee to hunt our people. They slaughtered us in the streets, burned our homes, wiped out our villages, and razed our temples." The Obscura gestured to the tower's keep. "This stands to memorialize those who died on Worru as much as it does to gather the willing in pursuit of the sacred constant."

"The sacred constant?" Moldark asked.

Psykon turned and titled his head. "Chaos, Mithriel. The only surety that the cosmos can offer."

"So you seek chaos? I thought you said tranquility was your aim."

"To unhinge artificial constraints that would keep the Untiy's wild power bound, yes."

Moldark sneered. "Charming people."

If Psykon was offended, he did not show it. Instead, the man surveyed the city as the dim sun set on the horizon. Then he reached to the ground, picked up a stone, and held it in his palm for Moldark to see. "What would happen to this stone if I allowed it to escape the bonds that constrict it?"

"I'm beginning to see why they called your ancestors crazy," Moldark said.

Psykon dismissed the comment and then invited Moldark to study the object. All at once, the stone turned to powder. Moldark did his best to hide his surprise. But then the powder reconstructed itself into four different shapes of lesser size, each with their own unique characteristics. The smaller objects dissolved back into powder again and then reformed to one stone. Only this new rock was a pyramid in shape. Then Psykon lowered his head and blew the stone away, sending a plume of black dust to the wind. "Now it is free to become whatever it will be next."

"So the Luma banished you for playing with rocks. That's understandable."

"They taught us to break apart, reform, and then watch what will come." Psykon gazed over the city again. "The survivors escaped Worru knowing the Luma would not rest until everyone was dead. So our ancestors boarded the only starships they had access to and set off to find a new world as far from Worru as possible."

"And here you are, thousands of years later, and you want revenge on the Luma for killing your ancestors."

"There is more to the story, Mithriel."

Moldark placed his hand on Psykon's shoulder. "And I'm sure there is someone who cares. Though, tell me this: how do you biologics survive on a planet where there is so little to sustain you?"

Psykon pulled away from Moldark's hand. "Of the Obscura's many chaos practices, one of them involves liberating the flesh of its finite constraints. Without it, X would have been uninhabitable for us."

Moldark winced. For a people so powerful, they clearly lacked imagination. "You named your planet X?"

"An ode to keeping things unnamed and, therefore, unknown. Here, without organic matter to nourish us beneath a star whose light cannot nourish us, we have found a way to both survive and remain hidden in the darkness until such time that we can avenge our ancestors and crush those who keep the universe from tranquility."

"The Luma," Moldark said.

"Yes."

Moldark stared at the Obscura leader for a moment and then turned toward the city again.

"Something concerns you?" Psykon asked.

"Your ships," Moldark replied.

"What about them?"

"You outmatched mine over Oorajee. Naturally, I assume you can outmatch whatever opposition the Luma could muster. Why not simply destroy So-Elku and his followers yourselves?"

"Alas, our ships are held together and powered by the one thing the Luma have a hand in controlling."

Moldark bit his lip in thought and then said, "You use the Unity for your ships?"

Psykon nodded. "Forged from the magma of this planet and bound together by the Unity, our ships are nigh impervious to conventional weapons. Additionally, they do not require a drive core, at least in the way that you think of trinium-powered cores.

But were they to near Worru, the Luma might easily thwart an assault and render our vessels no more than rubble if given enough time."

While impressed with their resourcefulness, Moldark was impatient. "Then use your bianima abilities to take over some other civilization's fleets and assault them."

"And yet, as I explained, we lacked the capability," Psykon said. "That is until you arrived. Furthermore, with your powers, we no longer need ships to exact our revenge. Only your presence."

"And let me guess. You're offering me your ships."

"We are."

"The ones made of rocks."

"Do not be deceived, Mithriel. The power that sustains them far exceeds anything in this universe, as you yourself have borne witness to."

"Except for the Luma."

"Which you will never have to worry about again, should you choose to assist us."

Moldark ran his tongue over the front of his teeth. He nicked the flesh and then tasted blood. "How many ships?"

"As many as you like," Psykon said, raising both hands toward the horizon. "This planet composes them. We can begin at once."

"And then you create my quantum tunnel."

"Now, if you wish."

Moldark raised his eyebrows. "And my army?"

"As I mentioned, we will introduce you."

"And I risk nothing but my time?"

"Nothing but your time," Psykon echoed in reply.

Moldark didn't wish to remain on X any longer than he needed to, let alone stay in this universe. But the prospect of devouring So-

Elku and the rest of his robed hirelings was far too intriguing a possibility to pass up. Moldark eyed Psykon and spit a mouthful of blood on the keep's floor. "I can afford a little more time."

"Very well," Psykon replied. "Let us return to the sanctuary. We will need all the power of the Obscura."

4

Magnus sat with Awen in the rear of a hovertrain pod, listening to the hum of the repulsors push the hull along the track. The gladias and Sekmit from the leaders meeting filled out the other twenty seats and took up a second and third pod further back. Everyone spoke in hushed tones and seemed to be enjoying the ride across Aluross, especially Piper. She was glued to the windowplex canopy in the pod's nose, speaking with her grandmother, Colonel Caldwell, and Rohoar.

Outside Magnus's viewport, the countryside raced by in a blur of greens and blues. Rolling hills undulated like the swells of a jungle ocean. Far in the distance, Magnus noted a line of snow-capped mountains and felt the train start to bend toward them.

"You're awfully quiet," Awen said, touching his elbow with her hand. "Something on your mind?"

Magnus cleared his throat. "Sorry, just daydreaming, I guess."

"About?"

"Stuff."

Awen scratched the side of her forehead, seemingly unimpressed with his reply. "Stuff."

"Yeah. Why?"

She chuckled. "Stuff's pretty vague, Adonis. Care to elaborate?"

"Nah."

"Oh my gosh." She punched him in the arm. "You're ridiculous, you know that?"

He made a show of rubbing imaginary pain in his bicep. "I'm not the one who's going around punching innocent people."

"Whatever." She gave him an adorable half-smile and then looked away.

"Honestly? I was just thinking…"

Awen turned back and gave him an exasperated "I'm waiting" kind of look.

"…About…"

"You're killing me right now, you know that?"

Magnus smiled and then looked back out the window.

After a moment, Awen said, "So, are you going to tell me or not?"

"Hovertrains," Magnus said, still facing the window.

"Hovertrains?"

"Yeah. I was thinking about whether or not I could survive a jump from a hovertrain better in Mark I or Mark II armor." Magnus didn't need to see Awen to know she was about to punch him again. Sure enough, her fist hit home, harder this time, and Magnus flinched because it actually hurt.

"Why don't we open the window and you can find out," she said.

"But I'm not wearing any armor."

"Exactly."

"I'm not following."

"It's for the sake of science." Awen waved a hand through the air like she was addressing a lecture hall filled with students. "Every sound scientific experiment must have a control."

"Cute." Magnus rubbed his bicep again but for real this time. "You've got really boney fingers, you know that?"

She shrugged and then looked down the aisle toward the front window. Piper was pointing things out as fast as she could see them and saying "Look at that!" and "What's over there?" and "Did you see it?" so fast no one had time to respond before she moved on to the next item of interest.

"You really wanna know what I was thinking about?" Magnus asked Awen.

"Eh, not really. Heard it's overrated."

"Sure."

She faced him and gave one raised eyebrow. "If you insist."

Magnus raised his chin toward Piper. "Her."

Awen looked to the front of the train and then back at Magnus. "Piper?"

"Uh-huh. Been thinking about what happens to her when all this is over." Awen's eyes took in Magnus's face for a few moments before he finally said, "What is it?"

"You know, for an overly muscled dispenser of death, I have reformed you quite well."

"That's a little harsh."

"But true nonetheless." Awen put her hands in her lap and faced forward like a prim and proper Luma who was all too proud of her accomplishments. But she hadn't assumed the posture for two seconds before Magnus leaned in and kissed her. She tried pushing him away, but the effort was halfhearted. Eventually, she relaxed and returned the kiss.

"Oooo," Piper said from up front. "Shydoh and Mr. Lieutenant Magnus are kissing. Look!"

"We've been found out," Awen said, pulling away a few centimeters.

"Spies everywhere," Magnus replied. He kissed her again and then sat upright.

Piper waved at him and gave a big grin before resuming her incessant analysis of the oncoming terrain. "Look, the mountains are getting closer!"

"So, what happens to her when all of this is done?" Awen asked Magnus.

"Not sure." He shrugged. "Willowood will probably find a place for them to settle down away from anyone who might want to hurt her."

"Plenty of neutral planets out there."

Magnus nodded. "I just can't imagine what the rest of her life will look like in light of everything she's seen, you know?"

"I think about it every day," Awen said. "I can't imagine growing up without a mother."

"It sucks."

Awen furrowed her brow. "You?"

He gave a small nod and swallowed the lump in his throat; it hadn't been there a second ago.

"I—I didn't know that."

"Because I never said anything."

"What happened?" she asked.

But Magnus didn't want to talk about it. "Story for another time." He pointed at Piper. "But she's gonna need a whole lot of love to make up for Valerie's absence, I can tell you that much."

"Well, she'll have her grandmother, so that's something."

Magnus sighed and then looked out the window. "Yup. That's something."

A moment passed between them before Awen said, "But you don't think it's enough, do you."

"It is what it is." He watched tree limbs and birds zip by.

"No, it's not. You haven't been sitting here in total silence for the last twenty minutes just to conclude that things are what they are. You have something else in mind." Awen paused. "Mystics, you—you want to adopt her?"

Magnus looked over at Awen. "Keep your voice down. And I never said that."

"But that's what you—"

He nudged her.

More quietly, she said, "But that's what you were thinking, wasn't it."

"No." He looked back out the window.

A few seconds later, Awen leaned against his arm. "You really want to adopt her, Adonis?"

"It crossed my mind. I mean, if Willowood didn't feel up for, you know—"

"Raising her?"

"Right. But she's gonna want to. The lady kicks ass and doesn't look like she's gonna retire anytime soon."

"Yeah, but you never know." Awen scooched herself in tighter. "Kids can be a lot of work."

"A lotta work." Her warmth felt good against his side.

"You need a lot of patience."

"Lotta patience."

"And you're gonna need a partner to raise her right."

"Partner, yup." Just then, Magnus pulled back. "Whoa, what?"

"Whoa what, what?"

"Are you talking about—"

"Who, me?" Awen touched her chest. "No."

"Okay, because, I thought you were gonna say—"

"Say what?"

Magnus spread his palms. "You know."

"Marriage? No. Are you crazy?"

"Yeah. I mean, no. I'm not crazy. You're crazy. I mean, you *would* be crazy, but you didn't mean that, right?"

"Yeah. Totally not." Awen sat back and crossed her arms. "Because, at a time like this, that would be just—"

"Crazy."

"Absurd."

The two of them sat in silence for a minute, listening to Piper go on and on about one thing after another.

"But if I was gonna ask someone to be her mom," Magnus said.

"Uh-huh?" Awen said, leaning back into his arm.

"Hypothetically speaking."

She waved her hand to the side. "Completely hypothetical."

"You would, ya know."

"Yes?"

"You'd make a great mom, is all."

Awen smiled at him for a second and then sat back in her chair.

Magnus was expecting more somehow. A shout of glee, perhaps. Or maybe a few words spoken in anger, expressing how she was still too young to settle down. Instead, what he got was an Awen who seemed utterly content with the idea of being an adopted mother to

Piper and, by extension of Magnus's daydream, a partner of one kind or another to him. And she looked even more attractive than ever.

You're getting old, Adonis, he thought to himself. *Going soft and losing your edge.*

But, somehow, he wasn't sure that going soft was a bad thing.

As the train darted into the tunnel at the base of the mountains, Wobix stood up beside Freya's seat, opened a comms channel to the other pods, and turned to address the riders. His voice carried through the vehicle via the overhead speakers. "Ní Freya wishes to inform the gladias of the Gladio Umbra that from this point forward, communications with the rest of your team in Fînta are not permitted. Please remain seated." Wobix closed the channel and returned to his seat.

Long white lights strobed past the windowplex as the hovertrain shot through the mountains. Subtle air currents buffeted the pods from side to side, gently rocking everyone inside.

"So the trinium is under the mountains?" Awen asked Magnus in a hushed tone.

"That's my guess." He pulled his data pad from the seatback and brought up a topo map of the region. Since the device lost its unisatlink connection moments ago, he couldn't track their real-time location on the hovertrain. But it didn't concern him as he was going for a more traditional analysis anyway. "Looks like this mountain range runs north-south for a few hundred clicks." Magnus pointed to the white and grey spires that stood in stark contrast to the lush green jungle to the east.

"That doesn't seem right," Awen said.

"What do you mean?"

"Well, for one thing"—she tapped on the mountain range—"while there could be a large trinium deposit under here, we're not talking the size that would merit the kind of secrecy Freya talked about. Plus, sensors would pick up the radiation. These mountains would be glowing on even the most cursory scans."

"So now you're a geology expert too?" Magnus replied.

She waved a dismissive hand in the air. "All cultural majors include geology courses. Natural resources can drive economies, right?"

"Yeah, but nobody pays attention in those classes."

Awen shrugged and gave him an innocent grin.

He chuckled. "You never cease to surprise me."

"And I'll never stop."

"Is that a fact?"

Awen ignored the call to verbal sparring and looked at the data pad again. "Anyway, for another thing, if our destination were under the mountains, you'd think we'd have started slowing or turning by now. You feel anything?"

"We're not slowing, and I haven't felt us turn."

"Exactly."

She had some excellent points, and the hovertrain had approached the mountains at a perpendicular angle. "So, if we're not slowing and we're not turning"—Magnus slid the map view to the west—"that means we're headed straight out to the Leonï Ocean." The body of water looked to cover most of the western hemisphere. Magnus froze. "You think the deposit—"

"Is under the ocean?" Awen glanced up at Magnus as she finished his question. "That much water would act as a natural radiation shield. And, depending on what kind of scope we're talking, it could definitely be on the larger side. I mean, if it's even a quarter the size of this ocean, it would easily be—"

"One of the largest trinium deposits in the quadrant." It was his turn to finish her sentence.

"Right," she said, head nodding as the economic potential dawned on them both.

"No wonder So-Elku sent Blackman," Magnus thought aloud. "This wasn't about allegiances just to garner political support."

"This was about securing resources." Awen reached over and started tapping through menus on Magnus's data pad. She pulled up a list of the confirmed and suspected LAW worlds that TO-96 had compiled so far. "Darture and Timidithia in the Lepeedu system, along with Deltaurus Three. Know what they have in common?"

"No, but I bet you're gonna use that smarty pants education of yours to wow me."

"Precious and noble metals, including rhodium, palladium, iridium, and—you guessed it—"

"Trinium."

Awen nodded. "Then you've got Rithcosia, Fiad Six, and Vega."

"Let me guess. They've all got insane deals on vacation properties right now."

She shook her head. "Lancite."

"As in drive core catalyst lancite?"

"Exactly. And I can bet you that Undoria is next if So-Elku hasn't gotten to them already."

"More lancite?"

"Largest mines in the Falcion quadrant," Awen said. "The only planet that has more is Limbia Centrella, but not even So-Elku is getting in there."

"You mean a planet full of Abimbolas poses a threat?"

At hearing his name, Abimbola looked back at Magnus from the next row. "What threat do I pose?"

"A big one, Bimby," Magnus replied, reaching up and patting his shoulder. "Don't you worry." Then Magnus sat back and switched off his data pad. "If you control the flow of energy, you control the quadrants."

"Basic economics," Awen said.

"Well, hell. Here I thought So-Elku was just trying to make friends."

"Because he's so good at that."

Magnus pulled away from Awen and gave her a startled look. "Why, Miss Awen. Do I detect sarcasm there? That's hardly becoming of a Luma emissary."

"You and I both know she died a while ago."

"Oh yeah? When was that?"

"When some lancite-hoarding Miblimbian"—she stressed the word in Abimbola's direction—"drugged me and stuck me in a jail cell with a naked monkey butt."

"Attractive naked monkey butt," Magnus said, crossing his arms. "Don't want people thinking I've got an ugly ass."

"I have seen it," Abimbola said. "And it's ugly."

"Shut up, Bimby."

"You first, buckethead."

The moment that the hovertrain emerged from under the mountains and plunged into the ocean, the pod filled with sounds of delight—most notably from Piper. She squealed and clapped her hands, pointing at brightly colored fish and massive coral cliffs. Floodlights mounted along the hovertrain's translucent tube and on the support columns illuminated the fathom's deep underwater world. Sea creatures that Magnus had never seen before swished, sucked, sponged, and twirled themselves along under the gleam of the lights.

Magnus looked over and saw Awen staring straight up. The pod's formerly opaque roof had either retracted or changed composition, allowing for a panoramic view of the underwater environment. A giant whale-like beast with eyes the size of a human lumbered lazily over the tube, while a school of fish whose tails seemed to be on fire zipped beneath. Apparently, the Sekmit weren't the only unique species on Aluross.

"You're staring at me," Awen said without looking at Magnus.

"And?"

"Shouldn't you be admiring the wildlife?"

"Who says I'm not?"

She punched him again without even looking. He liked how much she was enjoying this ride and wondered if this was how she was as a kid—curious and amazed at the world around her. Amid so much war and violence, Magnus liked being reminded of the simpler things in life. Like joy and wonder. He needed more of that. So he studied Awen for a moment more and then took in the sights for himself.

Over the next several minutes, the hovertrain descended deeper and deeper. Magnus cleared his ears several times and noticed that the lights illuminated less of the water as darkness crept in around them. The tube itself was getting thicker too to compensate for the increasing pressure.

After a while, the lights along the tube's support structure vanished, and the occupants sped along in total darkness, save for the glow of soft floor lighting.

"Where'd everything go?" Piper asked from up front.

She conversed with her grandmother for a few minutes before Willowood pointed out the front window. "Look, Piper."

Far below, Magnus noticed the faint green glow of massive spheres connected by long glowing lines. As the hovertrain continued to descend, the circles not only became clearer, but they seemed to multiply across the seafloor. More glowing lines stretched out and connected an ever-increasing field of green orbs.

"They're domes," Awen said. "And those are tunnels."

"Ho-ly-splick," Magnus whispered. "It's an entire mining network."

The hovertrain began to decelerate as it approached the nearest dome—and that's when Magnus realized just how massive the domes were. He kept thinking that the pod was about to slip inside the base when the tube just kept going, and the dome kept rising. Higher and higher it loomed until finally he noticed the entry port half a klick ahead. "It's gotta be at least 100 meters high," Magnus said.

"This one is 133 meters, to be exact, manservant," Freya said from the pod's front.

Magnus raised his eyebrows. "Noted."

"Some are larger," she added. "But this one serves as one of our main reception centers." Then Freya stood and spread her paws. "Welcome to the trinium mines of Neptali."

The hovertrain entered the neon-green geodesic dome along the base, and Magnus's eyes went wide. Inside, the structure loomed overhead, constructed of a glowing latticework that cast white light on the floor below. Meanwhile, a hexagonal-patterned green shell covered the trussing, shimmering with a smooth iridescent finish.

The pod's doors opened, and everyone filed onto a landing platform made of dense coral. As Magnus looked down and studied the chamber floor, he noticed that everything—from the giant office-style building in the hall's center to the various cafe storefronts, umbrellaed seating areas that gave some cover from the dome's bright glow, and storage-style outbuildings—was made of the ocean's natural resources.

"They've built this right out of the seafloor," Awen said in an awe-filled whisper as if her words might spoil the mystery and bring the whole thing down. "It's…"

"Incredible," Magnus said, taking her arm as they moved down a ramp. Smooth black stone lined lushly landscaped walkways while red and blue coral composed the buildings. Alurossian dapple-palm fronds swayed in some sort of artificial breeze, and seaweed-thatched roofs rustled in the wind. There were even several species of birds that flitted about from tree to roof to column. Meanwhile, the smells of exotic fruits and something else that Magnus couldn't place filled his head. "You smell that?" He rubbed his thumb and index finger together. "Kinda spicy, kinda minty."

"Catnip," Awen replied.

Magnus chuckled. "Everybody's got their fix."

"What's yours?"

Magnus shrugged. "Whatever perfume Elonians wear."

"Nice try, Adonis. That only means you're attracted to a few million women on my home planet."

"Like I said."

She threw an elbow just above his hip.

He winced and rubbed his side. "You've got boney elbows too."

FREYA LED the party onto a moving walkway that sped them away from the main hall and into one of the smaller tunnels. Magnus guessed this was one of the connection lines between domes. Its structure was like that of the reception hall, complete with white-glowing trussing and the green exterior shell. But unlike the hover-train tube, the bright interior lights made it almost impossible to see into the ocean.

After a minutes-long ride, Freya stepped off the walkway and into a second geodesic dome. While just as large as the first, this chamber was less ornate and boasted an imposing command structure in the middle. The circular red-coral building had blackened glass windows on all nine levels and was topped with an array of electronic equipment that spiraled the rest of the way to the dome's ceiling. But despite its imposing presence, the structure still managed to maintain much of the ornate architecture and lush landscaping of the first dome's buildings. It said, "I'm here to do business, but I'm gonna look good in the process."

"Welcome to our mining command complex," Freya said as she turned to address the gladias. "From here, we can monitor our entire trinium mining operation."

A hand shot up from among the Gladio Umbra. Freya eyed it suspiciously. Then Wobix leaned in and whispered something in her ear. Freya raised one eyebrow and then pointed at the person raising the hand.

"Should have guessed," Magnus said in Awen's ear. "It's Cyril."

"Madame Freya queen, ma'am," Cyril said. "How many mining nodes does your operation contain? Subsequently, what is the average collection rate of raw substrate? Subsequently—haha, I said that already—what's the mine's overall output of refined trinium? How do you protect your workers? And do you—"

"Wobix will do his best to answer whatever questions we feel are pertinent to your aid in protecting our mine," Freya said.

Wobix's ears lowered—he was clearly not enthused about being the "chattering human's" point person.

The group followed Freya into the command complex and rode elevators to the third floor—at least according to Magnus's best guess. All script was written in the Sekmit language, which resembled small patches of claw marks rather than any legible Repub-alliance text.

Everyone stepped onto a wide landing and looked through a curved glass wall. Below, a sloped theatre that boasted dozens of work stations ended at a ten-meter high holo screen filled with camera feeds, flow charts, and data lists. Magnus expected something thorough, but this place brought new meaning to the term anal-retentive. Every worker, every surface, every screen looked immaculate. Even the air smelled clean.

Inside the command center, Magnus spotted dozens of machines on the holo feeds, each boring through tunnels or grinding away at rock walls. Other screens displayed the inside of extensive facilities that seemed dedicated to refining operations—not that he had any particular knowledge on how to refine trinium—it was just a guess. But the multi-level magnetic containment fields, glowing vats, and conveyor system gave him a pretty good idea of what he was looking at.

"Whoa, you're running proprietary index algorithms," Cyril exclaimed just before running smack-dab into the glass partition. The gong-like impact made the glass wobble as Cyril fell back into Rohoar's arms.

"Please mind the windowplex," Wobix said with a stern tone. Then he hissed at one of his narskill warriors who sped away. Less than ten seconds later, another Sekmit arrived and began wiping Cyril's collision marks from the glass with a spray bottle and a rag.

"These kitties sure do keep a clean litter box," Magnus said to Awen.

She giggled softly and gave him a look that was somewhere between "Stop making me laugh," and "You're going to get us in trouble."

"So sorry about that, ma'am Freya lady, sir," Cyril said, rubbing his forehead. "I got excited about your base operating system because it seriously looks like you paid a lot of money to—"

"To keep as much of this a secret as possible, chattering human," Freya said. She eyed Cyril until the young man took a step back in line, and then she scanned the rest of the crowd. "As you can see, from here we can monitor every mining node within the network. While I will not betray exact specifications to you, I think you can rightly assume that our operation is vast, extending a considerable distance across the ocean floor."

Magnus leaned over to Awen. "Is it just me, or does anyone else think it's ironic that a bunch of cats have to build biodomes over their mines to stay clear of the water?"

"Magnus, quiet," Awen said, hitting him again.

"Was there a question?" Freya asked, eyes locked on Magnus.

"Uh, no, tribe mother," he replied. "Just admiring your operation, is all." But then Magnus did have a few questions. "On second thought, the water."

"What about it?"

"It masks the trinium signature on the planet."

Freya nodded once. "It does, manservant. You are perceptive."

"But its gotta probably also totally trap the radiation, amplifying its intensity," Cyril said, eyes locked on some monitors in the control room. "How do you, ya know, keep your engineers from suffering high rad exposure?"

"Our security measures are the state's art, as you say."

"State of the art," Cyril said. He must have felt everyone glare at him because he threw his hands up. "What? She, she, she said it wrong."

Freya continued. "As are the armored suits that all workers are required to wear once they enter the node network."

Magnus studied one of the engineers in a control room monitor. The suit looked like something Azelon might dream up, more battle armor than scientific outfit. It boasted plate armor across all vital systems, curved leg and arm guards, gauntlets, and a feline-like battle helmet. Magnus leaned over to Awen. "Only thing they're missing are blasters."

"Something else to say, manservant of Awen?"

"Just saying your armor is very interesting. That's all."

She nodded and then turned to keep speaking.

Magnus thrust his hand up. "I do have one more question, your highness."

"Easy, Adonis," Awen said through a tight smile.

"Speak," Freya said.

"The Repub ever come down here?"

The pride mother rotated her head but kept her eyes locked on Magnus. "Only once, during our initial alliance negotiations. But that was years ago."

"So, are there plans on record outside of your fire-walled archives?"

Freya tilted her head. "Only in the governor's mansion, but those were never allowed off the planet and were destroyed in the explosion. Why this line of questioning?"

Magnus took a few steps forward. "You want to keep us around to guard your trinium supply."

"Yes. And?"

"And knowing how much the enemy knows about this place is pretty important if you want us to do a good job. Tell me, if they wanted to raid your refined supply, where would that be?"

"The main aggregate nodes," Freya said. "But their locations are secret top."

"I think you mean top-secret, queen Freya lady person," Cyril said, raising an index finger to make his point.

"Top secret," Freya said, eyeing Cyril like he made a tempting snack.

"Then you're going to have to upgrade our clearance if you want our help," Magnus said. "And if raiders wanted more than just your current supply? If they wanted to take over the whole mine?"

"That is impossible, manservant."

"Humor me."

Freya said. "They would do it from here." She raised a paw toward the command center.

"Then we have ourselves some assets, people," Magnus said to the gladias. "Colonel?"

"We're grateful for you breaking with tradition to show us what few other outsiders have seen, ní Freya," Caldwell said. "But, as Magnus said, we're going to need access to your entire operation if you expect us to do right by you. Cyril?"

"Yeah, yeah, sure. That's gonna have to include a detailed blueprint, access points, power grid overlays, comm relays, supply flow—"

"We're also going to need exact locations of your surface sites," Magnus added.

"Do you think so much is necessary?" Freya asked, turning to the colonel. "Not even the Republic knew so much."

He nodded. "Trust me. I understand your reservations in turning over sensitive information. But I can assure you that you are getting our very best, and what we learn here stays here."

"But how can we be sure?"

Caldwell chomped on his cigar once. "Ya can't, momma. Yer just gonna have to trust us on this one."

Freya seemed agitated by Caldwell's words.

"It's a term of honor where we come from," Awen said as she raised her chin in Caldwell's direction.

The colonel seemed to pick up on Awen's lead. "Sure the hell is."

"Continue," Freya said to Caldwell.

"This enemy of yours—of ours—is a wily son of a bitch, ma'am. In my mind, you can't be too safe, not with what they're capable of."

"He's right," Willowood added, causing Freya's head to snap in her direction. "If Master So-Elku sends a raiding party, there's no telling what they might do."

"And yet we have designed this network to be impenetrable," Freya said. "Even if someone were to learn of its existence, gaining access is impossible, and doing so without flooding a node or exposing people to high levels of radiation is even more so."

"More so than impossible?" Cyril said in a nasal tone. "Haha—that's a redundant statement."

"Can it, Cyril," Caldwell barked.

"Ní Freya," Willowood said, drawing the leader's attention back. "Based on what we've seen, these new Luma are quite capable. If you want to preserve this operation, then you need to give us as much latitude as your conscience permits, knowing that it could be the difference between keeping the enemy at bay and discovering that you were raided while you slept."

"Worse still," Magnus said, pointing toward the command center. "You don't want them taking control of the mine. If that happens—"

"They'll be like a nest of Bormar pigmy chigs that lay larva in your epidermis," Cyril said. "Then those larva lay eggs, and those eggs multiply once every sixteen minutes until your whole body looks like Duke Vladimir's main henchman in *Damnation & Stagnation IV: No Rest for the Dead*, where he throws puss at—"

"Cyril!" Caldwell flicked his saliva-stained cigar nub across the room and struck Cyril in the forehead. The inert munition left a brown splat of wet tobacco on the kid's skin.

"So so sorry, colonel commander, sir. Shutting up now."

A small chirp came from Wobix's in-ear comm, and then he turned away from the group. A moment later, he leaned into Freya and spoke in Sekmitian—or whatever they called it.

"If you'll excuse me," Freya said. She took an offered data pad from one of her servants and then walked a few paces down the hall.

"So what do you think, Magnus?" Caldwell said in a quiet tone.

"I think it's gonna be a pain in the ass to secure," Magnus replied. "But as long as Cyril gets his wish list and we have time to analyze it, we might have a shot at keeping the diaper babies at bay."

"Agreed, but let's not get our hopes up. These pussycats aren't exactly the friendliest, contrary to what Miss DiAntora claimed."

"Speaking of DiAntora," Freya said, rejoining the group. "It seems she has an idea for us."

"What kind of idea?" Caldwell asked. If he felt caught off guard by the Sekmit's eavesdropping on their conversation, he didn't show it.

"One that she and the Neo Republic leaders think might lure So-Elku right where we want him."

"Neo Republic?" Magnus said. Then to Caldwell, he said, "Seems everyone wants to rename their orgs these days."

Caldwell chuckled and then looked to Freya. "Well, let's hear it. We're burning daylight, and I've already tired out all my lady friends."

5

So-Elku didn't even wince when he saw Governor Littleton's mansion explode. The bright holo screens cast his face in white light for several seconds until the cameras in the surveillance recordings adjusted their apertures to account for the sudden change. Then all So-Elku saw was a burning pile of rubble surrounding several craters.

"Incendiary explosives," Lor, So-Elku's intelligence minister, said. He wore his long blond hair in a braid and kept his black belt cinched tight around his green and black uniform.

"Suspects?" So-Elku said, still watching the holo window projected above the dimly lit conference room table.

"All indicators point to the Sekmit, master. Most likely retaliation against the Republic over Littleton's grievous crimes." Lor brought up several videos from the social feeds depicting the governor's murderous tryst.

So-Elku waved his hands. "Stop. Stop it! I've seen it already."

"My apologies, master."

"And any word from Blackman?" So-Elku asked Trinklyn, his newest minister of foreign affairs.

"Unfortunately, no," she replied. "After conferring with Minister Lor, we have reason to believe Blackman was killed in the explosion."

"What a pity," So-Elku said as he steepled his fingers and touched them to his lips. "Your evidence?"

Brodin, communications minister, cleared his throat. "His last comms transmission places him inside the main reception hall a minute before the explosion, and we have no footage from our security cameras of him walking out the main doors."

"The contents of his transmission?" So-Elku asked.

"He summoned the Li-Dain. Said he was under some kind of assault. We have nothing more."

So-Elku sighed. The former senator was a valuable asset, one the Luma Master had fought long and hard to secure. But So-Elku would not let Blackman's death, if it could be confirmed, spoil his mood. The fact that the Sekmit had taken out the Republic's planetary governor, while unfortunate for Littleton, was a stroke of good luck for the LAW. *One less middleman to manipulate*, he thought. Such losses were to be expected when courting suitors in matters of war and peace.

"And my Li-Dain?" So-Elku asked.

The eight ministers around his table shifted in their chairs, the creaks of which echoed through the high-ceiling chamber.

"We have every reason to believe they died in the explosion as well," Brodin said. "I'm sorry, my master."

If there was one thing that could spoil So-Elku's mood, now he knew what it was. He brought a fist down on the table. "We'll retaliate."

"Of course, sir," General Rink-Ba, Commandant of the Li-Dain, said.

"We'll make them pay," So-Elku continued. "Those putrid feral cats." It aggravated him to know that the feline race had bested twenty-four of his prized Nexus champions in a single blow. But how? So-Elku knew the Sekmit were Unity users, but little was known of their abilities. How did the cats lure his Li-Dain into a trap so easily? Surely his followers would have sensed the ordnance and taken precautions. Perhaps this enemy was not to be underestimated. "I want their chiefs—"

"Tribe mothers," Trinklyn said.

"I want them targeted. We'll cripple them and apply so much pressure that they'll beg us to accept their mines out of sheer desperation. All we need is the right inroad."

"Yes, my master," Rink-Ba said, nodding once.

"They will not escape this unscathed. The Sekmit will serve as an example to all of what happens when you bite the LAW's hand."

"There is one more matter to discuss," Lor said. "Concerning Undoria."

So-Elku eyed the fair-haired man. "What about?"

"We've received two unconfirmed reports that Governor Morandu was assassinated inside the Capitol Building yesterday afternoon."

"Assassinated?" So-Elku leaned forward. "But I just spoke with him yesterday afternoon."

"That is correct, master. The timeline places the murder only a few minutes after your exchange."

"The Neo Republic?"

"Nothing is certain. However, those complicit seem to have been among his staff."

"His people?" So-Elku swore under his breath. "Any arrests made?"

"None, master. The firefight left all suspects dead."

"Well, surely they're interviewing others?"

"My information is limited, but I would expect so."

So-Elku drummed his fingertips on the table and stared into the near distance. "They're getting desperate, this Neo Republic. They're like a mortally wounded animal who knows its time is near." He looked up and scanned his council members. "But their self-interest will be costly. Mistakes will be made. And we will be there to exploit them when they happen. Mark my words, my leaders, we will see the Neo Republic fall. For with every stride we make forward, they lose three backward. Their time is drawing to a close."

"Here here," Rink-Ba said, wrapping his knuckles on the wooden table.

"Here here," said the others, knocking the table with him.

When the adulation faded, the communications minister raised a finger for So-Elku's attention.

"Yes, Brodin," the Luma Master said.

"My master, you have an incoming secure subspace transmission, marked urgent."

"From?"

"From Aluross, my master. If the metadata is correct, it's ní Freya, pride mother of the Linux."

A hush fell over the table as So-Elku blinked twice at Brodin. How fortuitous. "I'll take it here."

Brodin typed on his data pad and then swiped the message toward So-Elku. "On your device, master."

So-Elku looked down and allowed his data pad to scan his retina and then his palm. A green Accept badge appeared, and the transmission went live, projected for all to see in the middle of the conference room table.

"Ní Freya," So-Elku said. "To what do we owe the honor of your call?"

"Master So-Elku." She raised her chin ever so slightly, eyes darting left and right. "I see you are in session."

"Easily dismissed." He raised his hands to clap them when Freya waved him off.

"That won't be necessary, Master Luma. What I have to say will need to be shared with your elders anyway. Permit them to stay, if you will."

"Of course."

"I'm sure by now that you have gotten word about Governor Littleton's untimely death."

"We have, yes. A terrible accident."

"It wasn't an accident," Freya said as she leaned back in her chair.

How interesting, So-Elku thought to himself. He titled his head in curiosity. "You suspect foul play then? Any suspects?"

"Of course."

So-Elku raised his eyebrows. "And you're pursuing them?"

"There is no need to, Master Luma. It was me."

The abruptness of her statement caught So-Elku off guard, but he'd long ago mastered the art of suppressing his emotions for the sake of diplomatic progress. Instead, he stroked the thin beard around his chin and examined Freya's calm face, considering his next words carefully.

"It is a just reply for the man's brazen acts against your people," So-Elku said at last.

Freya seemed pleased by this reply as So-Elku thought he heard a soft purr come over the transmission. "He was foolish to take our women for his amusement."

"Quite so."

"And even more foolish to think he and the Galactic Republic could undermine our longstanding trade terms."

So-Elku sat forward. This was an interesting wrinkle. "How so? If you don't mind me asking."

"I will permit it. In light of the recent events on Capriana Prime, the governor sought to renegotiate the price of trinium."

So-Elku knew that Aluross's trinium mines were a well-kept secret. But he also knew that Freya's watchful eyes were examining him and might detect a lie. So he took a chance, as all negotiators must, and gambled that Freya wanted him to know since she herself brought it up. "It is always unfortunate when the powerful take advantage of the"—So-Elku was about to say weak when he decided to choose his words more carefully—"of supposed friends for the sake of their own gain."

Freya's cheek twitched, showing the barest glint of her teeth. "Indeed."

"Begging your pardon, but why are you coming to us with this?"

"The Order of the Luma have long been advocates for those who have been taken advantage of. As such, we hope that you might stand as the intermediary between us and any system seeking trade."

So-Elku wanted to smile—to pour himself a glass of aged bratch and revel in the cosmos's favor on his life. Instead, he stroked his beard some more and forced his heart rate to stay low. "Surely this is something you can manage yourselves, ní Freya. The Luma are not in the business of, well, doing business."

"But times are changing, Master Luma. Without your help, I fear we will be overrun once the quadrant learns of Aluross's resources. Not only do we lack the ability to manage so many requests for trade, but I fear we lack the infrastructure to resist an attack should a suitor decide to become aggressive."

"You fear for your safety?"

"We do. Having the Luma as our official representatives would go a long way in preserving the peace and financial security of our people."

How fortuitous. And yet, things that seemed too good to be true most often were. So-Elku had to assume that he was being played. Freya wanted something beyond what she was saying. Revenge, perhaps? Surely this was connected to the Li-Dain and the governor's mansion. So-Elku's mind raced with the possibilities.

While the idea of trading with the Sekmit was a promising prospect, who was to say that friendly negotiations were the only route to obtaining trinium? After all, he was determined to make them pay for what they did; he would avenge his fallen Li-Dain. This was just the in road he needed. So-Elku's eyes narrowed as he began devising ways around the Sekmit leader's rouse.

"And, I might add," Freya said as if picking up on So-Elku's hesitation. "We will make it worth the Luma's time."

So-Elku pursed his lips and narrowed his eyes. "As fortune would have it, ní Freya, we here on Worru have been working on something that you may find rather interesting. For, you see, you are not the first to approach us about such things. And yet you epitomize the reason for our new course of action. Aluross and the Sekmit would rise to the very forefront of our attention and merit the width and breadth of our aid."

Freya dipped her head perhaps no more than a few millimeters, which So-Elku took as a good thing. The Sekmit, he knew, could be a finicky species, and one needed to tread cautiously when dealing with them.

"Might I suggest we take this up in person?" So-Elku asked. "Perhaps on Aluross, where we can speak more freely and examine the particulars of what we are discussing in detail?" He hoped she could read between the lines of his statement.

"You are welcome on Aluross in four days, Master Luma. We will be happy to greet you."

So-Elku looked at his data pad and pretended to examine his calendar. Instead, he was reviewing subspace jump times—twenty-two hours at level one, but eleven hours at Epsilon level two. "Unfortunately, I'm busy in four days' time and will be occupied for the next week after that. It must be tomorrow."

Freya raised one bushy eyebrow. "I'm afraid that—"

"As I said, ní Freya, you are not the only world in need of aid, but you will be the first, if you wish it."

There was a moment's pause as the pride mother considered the timeline. "Very well. We will receive you tomorrow. My pride will send arrival coordinates and docking procedures within the hour."

"We look forward to them."

"Tomorrow, then," Freya said.

So-Elku bowed. "Tomorrow." When the transmission closed, he steepled his fingers. "We're in."

"I WANT the Li-Dain coming with us, Commandant," So-Elku said to General Rink-Ba.

The man blinked once. "All of them, master?"

"Yes, all of them."

"Begging your pardon, master," Trinklyn said. "But won't the Sekmit see that as aggressive action?"

"Not if it's kept a secret," So-Elku replied.

"But if they find out"—the woman paused, her eyes searching something in the near distance—"who's to say they don't kill us all? We don't know what kind of powers they have. At the mansion, they decimated our—"

"They got lucky," Rink-Ba interjected. "Nothing more. And it won't happen again." He turned to So-Elku. "Your orders?"

"Freya wishes us to be their broker in the quadrant, something the LAW is only too willing to do. Her coming to us saves us the time of having to woo the Sekmit, which means half the work is already done for us. But if the terms are unfavorable? If lady Freya fails to see the bigger picture?" So-Elku tapped a finger on his lips. "The Sekmit will find themselves in an unfortunate situation."

"You mean to threaten them?" Lor asked.

"No, I mean to take the mines for ourselves."

"Take over the mines?" Rink-Ba said. "But, my master, begging your pardon, we would need detailed schematics of their entire operation and weeks of planning."

"Well, you have a detailed schematic." So-Elku pulled a small data card from inside his green and black robes and slid it across the table to the commandant. "And you have"—So-Elku checked his data pad for the time—"nineteen hours to come up with a plan."

The Li-Dain leader looked a little pale.

"Come now, Rink-Ba," So-Elku said. "It's moments like these where our mettle is tested, and we rise to new heights."

"My master," Lor said, loosening his uniform around his neck with two fingers. "Might this line of action be, I don't know, perhaps a bit hasty given the unknown variables and the accelerated timeline?"

"Hasty?" So-Elku said, eyes widening. He glanced at the rest of his council members and could tell by their sheepish expressions that they were siding with the intelligence minister. If So-Elku didn't nip this in the bud, their nearsightedness could undermine the very spirit of the LAW.

"Let's review, shall we?" So-Elku leaned back and rested his hands on his chair's arms, taking a moment to inhale through his nose and exhale through his mouth. "The so-called Neo Republic is teetering on the edge of oblivion. They are scraping and clawing just to remain relevant in the sector—this *sector*"—he tapped the table for emphasis on how small a territory that constituted—"and are losing allied systems by the day. One of which is perhaps the largest producer of trinium in the known galaxy. And instead of branching out on their own, where do they come?"

So-Elku glanced around the table. "This isn't a rhetorical question, people," he said with a raised voice. "Where do they come?"

"To us," Lor replied.

"To us," So-Elku shouted, his spittle landing on the table's middle. "To. Us. And they will not come again. They *never* will come again. This is it. Which means we *will* take Aluross one way or another. Because if we don't do it now, the next time we try, they will be allied with some other system, and our efforts will be incalculably more costly. Never again will they invite us to their table. Never again will they allow us to inspect their operation. And never again will we be able to send our forces into the heart of the beast. Which means, if or when the time comes, we can squeeze their veins. And if they still don't comply?" He looked around the table, and then he made a fist and struck the table once more. "Then we strangle them and take it. We take it all."

A quiet resolve followed the speech as each member nodded to themselves and then looked to one another. *Good*, So-Elku thought. He wouldn't need to relieve anyone of their duties today.

"Where did you get these plans?" Rink-Ba said, holding up the translucent data card.

"Governor Littleton's office," So-Elku said.

"But I was under the impression they were keyed to Aluross's surface."

"A security measure easily broken."

"Littleton risked his life for the exchange with you?"

"Not with me. With the late senator. And it seems Louis was only too willing."

Rink-Ba studied the clear card. "So Blackman threatened him and then transmitted the data off-world."

"He didn't have to threaten him, general. Blackman just had to make him the right offer. And with so many vices, it was an easy deal to strike." So-Elku looked to Admiral Porampus, director of fleet operations. "Ready the needed vessels, Admiral. We will leave as soon as you're ready."

"Yes, my master," Porampus said.

"Dismissed."

So-Elku retired to his private study in an effort to calm himself over the pending operation. But after several minutes of pacing around the floor, he decided to try a different route of relaxation. So he descended to the Grand Arielina's basement spa, disrobed, and entered one of the spring-fed hot baths. He was pleased no one else was present to bother him.

"A drink for you, Luma Master?" said a familiar voice.

So-Elku opened his eyes to see Nants standing over him. *How did the young man enter so quietly?* So-Elku wondered. The novice was growing in the arts. "Fetch me some bratch. Whatever the spa has at its disposal."

"Yes, my master." Nants turned and disappeared through the bathhouse door.

So-Elku slid down until the water touched his lips. He closed his eyes again and savored the heat as it eased his muscles. A few minutes of this, and then perhaps a massage would do wonders for him.

This time, when Nants returned, So-Elku was ready for him and blindly reached to take the glass just as the novice bent down to offer it. "Thank you, Nants."

"You're welcome, my master. Will there be anything else?"

"No. That will be all."

Nants bowed and then left the bathhouse.

So-Elku sipped the amber liquid and savored the burn as it slid down his throat. The water surged around his body, shaking the tension from his muscles. Meanwhile, the white noise of a waterfall along the far wall lulled him toward relaxation. The thought of having hot water beat against the top of his head made So-Elku push away from the underwater seat and float toward the falls. He took one more sip of the bratch and then set it poolside.

The naturally heated water cascaded over So-Elku and consumed his senses. It plunged him into a world of roaring sound and prickling flesh. The Luma Master rolled his neck and let the torrents beat against the base of his shoulders. With his face down, he opened his eyes and saw a shadow move in the pool.

So-Elku's heart skipped a beat as he realized someone was in the bath with him. He pushed off the wall and emerged from the waterfall, eyes blinking the water away. But when he looked around, he saw nothing. He was still alone.

A presence flitted behind him. So-Elku spun toward the waterfall. But, again, there was nothing there.

"Get ahold of yourself," he said, then he reached for the glass of bratch. But his hand grasped only air.

The sound of glass shattering on the floor came from somewhere behind him. So-Elku swished around to see the bratch and broken crystals spread across the tile. His heart raced.

"Who's there?" he said, and then decided he'd had enough. From within his second sight, So-Elku searched the Unity for whoever was trying to play a trick on him. But as his otherworldly vision searched all around, there was no one to be found. "Come out! Show yourself."

"Hello, Teerbrin," said a low voice.

The sound of his first name startled So-Elku almost as much as the imposter's voice. The Luma master leapt from the Unity and turned around to see Nants in the waters with him.

"Nants! What in the name of Tavid's stars are you doing?"

"The boy is gone, Teerbrin."

So-Elku was about to switch to his second sight when the intruder cut him off.

"Don't bother. You won't see me there any better."

"Who are you?" So-Elku asked. There was something dark about the novice's eyes, as if something possessed him. "How do you know my name?"

"Both adequate questions," the body said, its jaw and head twitching and jerking as he spoke. "And yet not the most pertinent."

So-Elku backed up and neared the pool's edge. He needed to protect himself and then get out of here. But he also needed to be careful. Whoever had taken over Nants's body would probably be able to defend themselves. "And what's the most pertinent?"

Nants's head stuttered and then locked at an odd angle. "The question should be, what do I want."

So-Elku knew this voice. Not Nants's, but the one beneath it, layered somewhere in the darkness. "And what do you want?"

"You, Teerbrin."

"And who are you?"

Nants's body convulsed as he let out a peal of stuttering laughter. "You do not sense me? Are we not familiar with one another?"

So-Elku's adrenaline wasn't letting him think clearly. Whoever this person was, they were powerful. And yet no one he knew could take over a body from afar like this. Unless…

"Yes, there it is," the intruder said. "I can feel you discerning the matter."

So-Elku squinted. "Moldark?"

Nants's head jerked in a quick succession of nods followed by a bleating of high-pitched giggling. "Shall we dance?"

So-Elku sensed it before he saw it—a dagger-like thrust of Moldark's ethereal presence shooting toward his chest. The Luma master drew power from the Nexus, let it pool around his forearms, and then swept his hands through the water and across his torso. The dagger deflected into the pool wall and turned a patch of stone to dust. The water surged to fill in the void, pulling So-Elku backward.

A second thrust from Moldark shot at the Luma master's head.

So-Elku ducked and plunged his head underwater. When he resurfaced, a third shadowy dagger swept across his belly but missed as So-Elku sucked in his gut. Now it was the Luma master's time to go on the offensive.

So-Elku summoned more power from the Nexus, pressed his wrists together, and then drove his palms forward. The energy blast shot from his hands like lightning, striking Nants in the sternum. The novice's body surged backward through the water, causing a wave to spill over the pool's edge. So-Elku fired a second blast, but Moldark forced the young man's body underwater. The pool's edge exploded and sent chunks of tile and stone into the ceiling and walls.

A shape darted toward So-Elku underwater. He moved to block Moldark's lunge, but he wasn't fast enough. As soon as the novice's hands touched So-Elku's thighs, it felt like red hot firebrands touched his skin. So-Elku cried out in pain and then fought to shove the enemy's hands away. But the novice squeezed tighter and tighter as Moldark's presence began sucking the life from So-Elku's body.

The Luma master tried to distance himself from the pain and focus on the Nexus. He drew another line of energy from the deep place, knowing it may very well be his last attempt, and then reached for Nants's head. The moment So-Elku's hands touched him, the novice let go of So-Elku's thighs. Nants's body convulsed and retracted as the Nexus energy left So-Elku's body.

Free of Moldark's dark umbilical, So-Elku turned and hoisted himself out of the pool. He made it only three wet steps before something wrapped around his ankles and caused him to land flat on his face. Blood filled his mouth as he strained to look down at his feet. A shadowy tendril of darkness had So-Elku and was pulling his body toward Nants, who still stood in the water. The Luma Master's fingers searched for something to latch onto, but everything he tried was too slippery as his body slid across the tiles. Suddenly, his left fingers caught on a small ledge around an inset stairway leading into the water.

"There's no use fighting me," Moldark said in a sweet-sounding tone.

So-Elku wanted to reply, wanted to say something vengeful, but between the pain in his legs, the sense of his soul being sucked out, and the effort it took to keep his hand on the ledge, he couldn't think of anything to say.

"Just let it go, Master Luma," Moldark said.

"Never," So-Elku replied. But his grip was weakening, and Moldark's power was strong. So-Elku cast Nants a glance. The novice's eyes had gone completely black and seemed to have a reverse-glow about them—as if they were a void of light instead of a reflection of it.

"Let me ease your suffering," Moldark said as he sent a new wave of pain coursing up the Luma master's legs. "Let go!"

At that moment, So-Elku realized he had one last attempt to save his life. And he would let go. His fingertips flooded with as much power as he could summon in so little a time and then he let go. As So-Elku's body slingshotted toward Moldark, the Luma master thrust his hands down and aimed his fingers toward Nants. Moldark pulled with all his might but was too late to do anything about the oncoming attack.

So-Elku's supercharged digits drove into Nants's face and plunged into the novice's brain. At the same moment, So-Elku released the energy in his fingertips and obliterated the novice's cranium. Blood and bone sprayed across the bathhouse and pelted the waterfall as Nants's corpse shot under the surface.

At once, the grip on So-Elku's soul vanished, leaving the Luma master to collapse in the bloody water. He struggled to swim toward the edge, eager to get as far away from Nants as possible. *No*, he corrected himself. *From Moldark*. Even as he climbed over the side, gasping for breath, So-Elku felt his adrenaline ebbing and a sense of dread taking its place.

The Luma master rested his head on the side of the pool and stared at Nants's body, which was floating face down in the water. Swirls of scarlet mixed with the blue waters as the current whisked the blood toward a vent. So-Elku's fear suddenly turned to rage as he cursed the Paragon leader's audacity—that the enemy thought he could come here, unannounced, and make an attempt on the Luma master's life?

"You will not best me," So-Elku said and then coughed against the tile. However Moldark had managed this—whatever *this* was—So-Elku knew the monster of a man would be back. He would try again. But next time, So-Elku would be ready.

6

MOLDARK GASPED as his consciousness returned to Kane's body.

"Are you alright, Mithriel?" Psykon said, staring down at the dark lord's face.

Moldark brushed the man aside and sat up. The hum of the supplicants had stopped, but its echo still reverberated around the massive chamber. "I'm not sure," Moldark said as he touched a hand to his chest. "Something, something happened to me."

"Yes, we saw that So-Elku resisted you."

"But something about this encounter—" Moldark couldn't explain what had happened. And as he thought about it, he wasn't sure how much he should divulge to Psykon. Something *had* happened to him when So-Elku killed Nants. Even with the small amount of life force Moldark sucked from the Luma master, Moldark still felt as though he'd been—*been what?* he asked himself. *Wounded?* But only mortals could be injured. The very idea that Moldark could be harmed was absurd.

And yet he still wondered whether or not something had hurt him.

Moldark eyed Psykon. Did the man know? Did he suspect something? Or worse, did he know something but was not divulging it?

"I'm fine," Moldark said at last.

"Good," Psykon replied and offered his hand.

Moldark refused and slid off the stone table himself. "We have tried confronting him your way from afar and failed. Now it is time I deal with him in my own way. I will collect my ships and be done with this place."

"And we thank you for trying," Psykon said and offered Moldark a small bow. "We have learned much from you even if we have not accomplished our tasks. And now we will make good on our promises."

"Where do we begin?" Moldark said.

Psykon spun around and walked toward the sanctuary's entrance. "Follow me. This way, Mithriel."

THE STONE ESCARPMENT that led up to the ship's hull took almost twenty minutes to walk. The mammoth angular starship sat at the end of it like a crow on the tip of a branch, ready to take flight. But unlike a bird, the ship was not balanced on the end of the tree limb. Instead, it hovered in place without the sound of repulsors or engines. According to Psykon, it was the Unity alone that held it in place, and the Unity that would return it to orbit when called upon.

The ship itself resembled the same type that Moldark saw from onboard the *Peregrine*, or at least, so he thought. The black starship's triangular shape was pointed at the bow and blocky at the stern.

Meanwhile, the decks that extended above and below the centerline were staggered like cliff faces. The entire thing resembled a misshapen spearhead fashioned from coarse stone. But unlike the Bull-wraith sized ship that assaulted him over Oorajee, this vessel reached almost twice as long as one of the Republic's Goliath-class Super Dreadnaughts.

"What do you call it?" Moldark asked as they stepped into the beast's shadow.

"We do not name our vessels according to the nomenclature you have become familiar with," Psykon said. "Only that it is classified to us as a Leviathan. This one, in particular, destroyed your ships, so we believe it will be of special interest to you as your new flagship."

"This one?" Moldark was not expecting delivery of a ship so soon. "Now?"

"Does this displease you, Mithriel?"

"No. And I did not realize the ship was so large when it attacked us."

"And neither will your enemies when you converge upon them." Psykon motioned Moldark forward. "Come. Let us proceed."

Once inside, Psykon led Moldark down several glossy black-stone hallways that held doors every seven to eight meters. Dim grey lighting filtered from the ceiling while the pathway's edges gave off a faint red glow. And as their feet clopped down the corridor, Moldark detected the musty smell of wet stone.

They eventually came to a massive chamber that resembled the sanctuary back in the city. But instead of a central circle and table, this hall had an elevator bay on the far end that looked to be hewn from the face of a cliff—at least he thought it was an elevator bay. Moldark craned his neck and looked into the vast space above. The wall eventually towered out of site.

"This way," Psykon said as he began leading Moldark across the hall.

Along the floor, Moldark noticed lines cut in the stone, each eventually leading to the central elevator shaft. "What is the significance of these lines? Of this place?"

"It is where we first summon the ship to life and imbue it with the power that will sustain it throughout its service."

"And the elevator?"

"We will ride it to the bridge. The main wall you see is, in fact, the cornerstone of the entire ship, and it's filled with enough energy to last into the next millennium."

"Interesting," Moldark said. He did not claim to understand biologics or their ways, much less deranged ones who used the Unity to alter their bodies' systems and maintained an epoch's long vendetta against a group of robed mystics. But he did find this particular accomplishment unusually impressive. To forge an entire starship out of rock and then suffuse it with the Unity was an impressive feat. In fact, it was the closest thing to his natural state of existence that Moldark had ever encountered, which brought up another question.

"Tell me, where did the Obscura learn these ways?"

"Which ways are those?"

Moldark gestured toward the giant stone face that stretched up into the darkness. "The Luma do not fashion such things from the ground, nor do they instill power within them. How did you come across such skills?"

"It was a matter of necessity," Psykon said. "When you have so little for so long, you learn to make do."

"And this skill, one of making the raw elements host of your power, this is your own creation?"

"Hardly."

Moldark slowed while Psykon approached the elevator.

"We observed the Unity within all things. Ours was merely learning to imbue the inanimate with more than it ever knew."

"And it was the Unity that inspired you?"

"It is as I have said." Psykon pressed his palm to a bare spot of stone beside the elevator doors. A thin red outline appeared around his hand, and a low hum vibrated in the ground. A second outline appeared around the doors themselves moments before they parted to reveal a large chamber lit in red and white. "Come, let us rise."

Psykon stepped inside, followed by Moldark. The exterior doors closed, and the elevator surged upward as the rock wall glided down the pod's open face. A small circular cluster of red indicators on each sidewall indicated the lift's progress. However, Moldark could not decipher the strange patterns' meanings as individual dots blinked on and off, seemingly at random.

The pair of men rode in silence until long openings in the tower's face gave Moldark a strobe-like view of the sanctuary floor far below. At one point, the lift passed what Moldark suspected was some sort of perch—a landing from which a speaker might address a crowd below—but it passed by so quickly it was hard to know for sure. The windows to the sanctuary vanished, and the sliding rock face returned as the lift continued to rise.

Eventually, the elevator slowed, as did the blinking red dots on the walls. When the lift came to a stop, the doors opened onto a wide balcony that looked down onto a lower command bridge filled with blocky black tables. An equally dark glossy wall wrapped 180° around the three-story-tall theatre.

"This is your bridge, Mithriel," Psykon said. "From here, you can helm the vessel with the touch of a hand."

Psykon walked to a small black panel in the middle of the balcony's railing. As soon as he placed his palm on the stone, the bridge came to life. Moldark felt a low hum under his feet while every glossy surface, from the large wrap-around wall to every table along the lower floor, burst to life with projected holo images of the ship's systems, including what Moldark suspected were diagnostics, navigation, and communications. While the Obscura runes made deciphering each station's purpose difficult, the geometric compositions on several more advanced readouts looked like weapons, targeting, and shielding.

The most amazing display of all, however, was the panoramic view of the ship's surroundings. Not only did it offer a look at the ship's bow, but 180° of the planet's horizon. The gray sands and black rock clusters spread out under the dim sky so clearly that Moldark felt as if he could step out and walk across them.

"Remarkable, isn't it?"

Moldark nodded. "I have never seen a display like it among the fleets of this galaxy."

"Nor will you. Unlike manufactured screens and holo projections that utilize digital pixels to deceive the eye into thinking an image is real, what you see here *is* real. The Unity makes it so."

"Impressive."

"But there's more. Watch." Psykon placed his palm back on the balcony's stone, a surface that glowed with red and white outlines and markings, and moved his hand to the left. As soon as he did, the wrap-around wall's view shifted to port. Moldark felt Kane's body grow unsteady and instinctively reached for the railing. Psykon slid his hand to the right, and the perspective moved to starboard.

"You try," Psykon said, stepping away from the panel.

Not to be outdone by the strange mystic, Moldark reined in his vertigo and placed his hand on the pedestal. He found that the image was so connected to his touch that even the slightest movement caused the view to shift. Moldark slid his palm side to side and watched the screen mimic the motion. He made wider sweeps and then moved his hand down, which caused the view to shift up. A dim field of stars filled the screen as Moldark looked into orbit. Surprised at the freedom of range, Moldark moved his hand up, which brought the perspective down. The view swept through a cross-section of the ship's decks in a second and then stopped on an image of the sands beneath the vessel when Moldark pulled his hand back.

"Your view is limited only by your imagination," Psykon said. He tapped the screen once to center the view and then used his fingers to zoom in on the sun until it filled the screen. The image was so clear that Moldark made out individual spouts of fire that leaped into the void. "At least to a degree. Even the Unity has its limits."

"And the vessel is powered by?"

"By the energy we've imbued it with, as I've said. To move, simply will it."

"Will it?" Moldark looked from Psykon to the screen to the pedestal control panel.

"Observe." Psykon centered the view once more and placed his hand on the glossy surface. All at once, Moldark felt the ship surge forward—by how much he could not say. Inertia dampeners were designed to mitigate the effects of changes in motion, and this ship would no doubt have the equivalent.

"How far did we move?" Moldark asked searching the various data lists for some indication of distance traveled or coordinate differentiation, but all the text was in Psykon's runic language.

"Try this," the Obscura leader said. A beat later all the runes changed to galactic common.

Moldark searched a subwindow on the main display and felt his mind jar. "We moved twenty-five point five seven kilometers?"

"Indeed."

"But that's—"

"Impossible? Perhaps, according to your Republic standards."

"They are not my standards," Moldark interjected.

Psykon raised an apologetic hand and clarified. "According to the Republic's standards. But, as I expressed earlier, we are not using conventional means of propulsion."

"Nor weapons, I might add. At least judging by how you dispatched my remaining starships."

"An unfortunate loss, we admit, but one worth taking, especially in light of your potential gains. A show of overwhelming force was the only way to secure your attention; were we wrong?"

"No." He looked back to the main display and then searched out what he thought was the weapons station.

"Ah, you wish a demonstration of the ship's attack capabilities."

Moldark nodded.

"Come." Psykon motioned for Moldark to follow and then led the way down a staircase to the main floor. They crossed to the weapons station, and Psykon rested his hands on the pedestal's surface. Targeting reticles of various shapes and sizes fluttered across the main display, locking onto dozens of features from rock clusters to ridges on the horizon to the sun itself. "Which do you wish to destroy?"

Moldark looked between the screen and Psykon. "That group of rocks there"—he pointed to the far right where a cluster of boulders sat at the base of a dune—"by the low rise."

Three red dots appeared on the rock formation, and then a blast of red energy streaked across the plain and struck the target. The ensuing eruption sent a torrent of fire and a fountain of sparks into the sky, followed by a shockwave that rippled across the sand. When the light faded, Moldark saw a smoking crater in the ground.

"What about the rest of those targets?" Moldark asked, pointing to the dozens of reticles still locked on points of interest around the screen. "How long does it take to recharge the—"

Blasts of energy shot from the ship and streaked toward the remaining targets—including the planet's sun. While the star wouldn't register the impact, all the points on the planet's surface did, exploding at various intervals according to their distances relative to the ship.

Moldark was spellbound. It was—well—*glorious*.

"You are pleased, Mithriel?" Psykon asked.

"I am." But with so much power, several new questions presented themselves. "However, I wonder why you expect me to fare any better than you when confronting the Luma? You said their power in the Unity prevented you from attacking them in the past."

"A worthy question. The short answer is, we don't."

"But I thought—"

"The Obscura recognized a mutual disdain for a common foe, and together we attempted to assail So-Elku with our combined powers from afar. The attempt fell short, and now the Obscura are making good on our promise to you. What you choose to do with it is up to you. We advise you, however, not to employ our Unity-powered vessels in a direct assault on Worru, lest you fall prey to their defenses."

"And you're sure they can thwart even this?" Moldark gestured to the entire bridge. This ship was indeed a force to be reckoned with.

"Nothing is ever certain, Mithriel. But, yes, we believe a direct assault would be unwise, which is why we spent so much time courting you."

"And what will you do now that your attempts to mimic my abilities have failed you?"

"A legitimate question," Psykon replied. "But one that requires a level of allegiance to our order that I assume you are not willing to pledge."

"How convenient for you."

Psykon seemed to consider a different answer and then said, "We will abide in the dark until a new alternative presents itself."

"And yet, with so much firepower, why not raze every species within the galaxy?"

"Those who threaten our existence we do."

"And the rest? Surely you could destroy them without so much as a flick of your hand."

"Again, if they pose a threat. But as you are not a member—"

"Neither will I be a recipient."

Psykon nodded. Then he straightened his back—a move that seemed to suggest he wished to change topics. "As to our agreement, do you find this ship's systems to your liking?"

"I do. How many can you produce?"

"How many crew and squadrons do you anticipate hosting?"

"That all depends on the personnel you promised to introduce me to."

Psykon spread his hands apart. "Those resources are more than you could ever exhaust. Rather, the questions surround your ability to command—"

"I can command whatever I will," Moldark said with a sharp tone.

"I said nothing to the contrary. I only meant to suggest that the size of your crew will be contingent upon your ambitions, nothing more."

Moldark stared at Psykon for a moment. "This ship. How many does it hold?"

"Nine thousand souls."

Moldark couldn't help but raise an eyebrow. That was twice as many as a Super Dreadnaught. "So many?"

"Indeed. And up to five squadrons of starfighters, at least according to your Republic definitions."

"You have designed a starfighter?"

"The Abeyant-class, yes. It is within the scope of the Republic Talon. Fifteen to a squadron."

For a non-ambitious people, they sure had enough ingenuity and resourcefulness to wipe out entire systems. Which got Moldark thinking—*how many species have they wiped out with no one the wiser?* Where other governments or terrorist organizations rushed to claim attacks in the hopes of bolstering their efforts publicly, Moldark imagined that the Obscura would be far more content to recede into the darkness.

"Then I will take nine Leviathans," Moldark said. "One for each member of the circle who wronged me in this universe. And the five squadrons for each, loaded within their bays."

Psykon noted these numbers with a nod of his head.

"There is, of course, the matter of where I will take delivery of my vessels, assuming my legions are not here on X."

"They are not. We will ferry your ships into metaspace."

"My home universe?"

"Is it not your desired destination, Mithriel?"

"It is." The convenience felt too fortunate. "But my military?"

"Also found within your home universe."

Moldark's eyes widened. "How can this be?"

"All in due time. For now, take this ship for you and your crew. While the vessel will tend to your bodies' more primitive requirements, you will need to secure food and water at your earliest convenience. We will summon you upon the completion of your new fleet."

"Understood. And what about instructions for operating this vessel?"

"My people will provide your crew with tutelage at once."

"Excellent."

"Is there anything else we can do for you, Mithriel?"

"Yes." Moldark glowered at Psykon, still trying to see under the brim of the man's hood. "Never use my name again and forget you ever heard it."

"As you wish."

Less than two hours later, the *Peregrine* was safely secured within a large hangar bay in the Levithan's aft sections, starboard side. Shortly after that, ten Obscura led the ship's crew to the bridge. Moldark could tell that his Paragon team members were unnerved by the hooded figures. Ellis, Porteous, Yeager, and the other forty or so crew seemed to keep their distance. They gave the Obscura sideways glances while never turning their backs on them for a second.

During a break in the training, Moldark asked Ellis what kind of progress they were making.

"As good as can be expected for learning to helm a completely alien ship," Ellis replied. "Though it's far more intuitive than I would have thought."

"Anything you see as a potential problem?"

Ellis hesitated and scratched his sideburn.

"What?" Moldark asked. "Speak."

"It's more a matter of what *isn't* there, my lord," Ellis replied. "As in things like life support, including waste management, water reclamation, air treatment, and pressurization systems. They're simply not present."

"Overseen by the Unity."

"As far as I can tell, yes."

"You're hesitant," Moldark said, sensing the captain's anxiety.

Ellis moved his hand off his face and scratched the back of his neck. "It's just that if a system fails—if something goes down, I mean—we have no way to troubleshoot it. I can't even tell you how it works."

"And aside from those systems?"

"Well, that's just it. I can steer the ship. We can acquire and fire on targets. We can even enter planetary atmospheres without so much as flicking on a thruster. It's mind-boggling."

"But?"

"But I can't tell you how any of it works. And that doesn't boost my confidence in choosing this as a fighting platform. There won't be any repairing it."

"But it will fly and fire? It will suit our purposes?"

Ellis sighed. "As a short term assault carrier? Sure. But we're going to need to make some massive retrofits if you want a crew to stay alive for more than a few days at a time."

"Then it will do," Moldark said. "Resume your studies, and then brief me in full when you're through, Captain."

"Yes, my lord." Ellis made to turn away but then stopped. "Sir?"

"What?"

"What will you call this one? Just out of curiosity."

Moldark hadn't thought about it. Ship naming conventions seemed a tedious exercise to him. However, he had to admit that naming a ship made from a planet's hide, as it were, was far more in line with his heritage. The Norxük could have easily inhabited the lands that comprised this vessel, and were they not worthy of names? Suddenly, Moldark had an idea.

"I will call it *Norxük's Revenge*."

"I'm not familiar with Norxük. Which conflict did he serve in?"

Moldark frowned at Ellis and considered whether or not to end his life on the spot. But the captain would be too useful in helming the *Revenge*, so he refrained. "A very old one, Captain Ellis. Before your time."

"Understood, my lord."

"Dismissed."

Ellis saluted him and then returned to the tutelage of the Obscura.

Moldark climbed the stairs to the command overlook and then spread his hands along the railing and looked down on his Paragon crew. They took notes on their data pads and asked endless questions of their teachers. Every answer brought Moldark one step closer to departing this awful planet and returning to metaspace. He would find the Novia Minoosh's singularity on Ithnor Itheliana and then destroy them once and for all.

But another matter plagued Moldark, that of his unfinished business with So-Elku. Their confrontation in the bathhouse was like a Cephormith tick-fly bite. The more you scratch it, the more it itches. Thus, there were only two ways to get it to stop: gouge out the infected flesh or, if the poison went too deep, cut off your hand. And Moldark wasn't about to remove a limb.

Psykon's warning not to go after the Luma only served to irritate matters more. The fact that some ephemeral being had told Moldark what to do made his blood boil. He was an Elemental, after all. What were the constraints of mere mortals to him? Nothing but momentary setbacks. And with more ships on the way and the promise of a quantum tunnel back to metaspace, what did it matter if Moldark lost one vessel? Especially if it meant killing So-Elku once and for all. If Moldark was lucky, he could take out the Luma's capital city too.

"No," Moldark said to himself as he looked toward the horizon. "You will not see me coming, So-Elku. And by the time you realize your life is over, it will be too late to do anything to stop me. I'm coming for you, Teerbrin. The darkness is coming for you."

7

"The meeting is set," Freya said as she closed out the call on her data pad. "The Luma Master will arrive tomorrow."

"Yeah, heard that," Magnus replied. He sat beside Caldwell and Awen inside of the pride mother's private office back in the capital city of Meesrin Pin. "I'm not a big fan of the pressure this places on the team." DiAntora's plan of luring So-Elku to the negotiation table was a good one, but not on such a tight schedule.

"Yet this is only a meeting." Freya sat back in her chair and put her paws together. "Your people will capture him, and DiAntora's people will take him into custody as planned."

Magnus cleared his throat. "Right, so the whole 'as planned' thing tends never to go *as planned*, your loftiness."

"Are you saying you are unable to set an adequate security detail, manservant?"

If she calls me that one more time—

Easy, Adonis, Awen said from inside his head. *I'm doing my best to keep your thoughts hidden, but you've got to keep yourself calm.*

Roger that, he replied. "All I'm saying is that if a guy like So-Elku is coming here, he's not coming just to chat. He lost troops at the mansion, and he's going to want revenge of some kind."

"I have to agree with our manservant on this one," Caldwell said, giving Magnus a cockeyed grin. "While it may only be a simple chit chat, we need to go into this expecting that So-Elku's bringing a fighting force."

"Like those undeveloped fecal producing offspring you keep referring to?"

"Golden-robed diaper babies?" Caldwell chuckled. "Like those, yes."

"But our orbital defense systems will be sufficient to ward off an assault, based on the limited number of ships the LAW has access to."

"True." Caldwell moved his cigar to the other side of his mouth. "But they're not going to risk an outright confrontation."

"They're not?"

"No. For one simple reason."

"And that is?" Freya said, her eyes searching the colonel's face for any hints of a clue.

"If every ship that your intelligence officers have determined is under So-Elku's command showed up right now, do you think you could take them out?"

"It is probable, yes."

"Then that's why he won't come at you head-on. It's too early in the game for the LAW to make such a brazen move. So-Elku needs to appear in command—the guy needs to appear stately. Remember, he's trying to court a hundred other worlds like Aluross that have felt disenfranchised by the Republic."

"So you're suggesting he'll operate covertly?"

"Exactly," Magnus said. "If he wants your trinium, he'll go for it behind your back."

Freya examined Magnus. "But you've seen our mine. You understand firsthand that such a feat would be—"

"Impossible?" Magnus didn't mean to be rude, but it was precisely this kind of naive thinking that caught plenty of worlds with their pants down and left them on the wrong side of history. "Like people saying it was impossible that the Akuda would surface and threaten the Caledonians? Like the Simikon would invade Limbia Centrella? That Capriana Prime would fall?" Magnus picked at something between his teeth with his tongue. "No disrespect, your highness, but nothing is impossible, especially when we're talking about the Luma and planetary negotiations. The last 'peace talks' I was a part of"—Magnus used two fingers on each hand to emphasize the term—"ended with a king's throne room getting bombed to splick. What Caldwell is suggesting, what we're all suggesting, is that we need to be ready for anything, especially a covert operation."

Awen nodded and then spoke up. "But with only a day, we must hurry to make the most of it."

"Then you have a plan?" Freya asked her.

"Not yet. But we will. And we'll need your full cooperation. That includes Wobix and his narskill, access to your facilities, the mines, everything."

Freya worked her jaw. "Very well. If this enemy is as cunning as you say, then we would be foolish not to stop him at our very first chance."

"Now you're talking, queeny," Magnus said.

"Excuse me?" Freya's lips curled back to reveal her teeth.

Awen placed a hand on Magnus's chest. "What Magnus is

trying to say is that he believes your sentiment is wise—a proper response becoming someone of your stature."

"I do not need his affirmation to know it is so," Freya replied.

"No, of course you don't. But it is customary among our warriors to confer affirmation out of respect."

Freya seemed to consider Awen's explanation and then concealed her teeth. "Very well. I accept the praise. But barely."

"Barely works fine for me," Magnus said, hoping to help ease the tension. But both Freya and Awen gave him a hairy eyeball. If Magnus and the Gladio Umbra could pull this off, it would be a miracle. But it was the best idea anyone had that accomplished several goals at once. For one, the galaxy would be rid of Master So-Elku once and for all. Two, the LAW uprising would most likely be quelled within weeks of its start. Third, the Sekmit would be free to sell their valuable trinium supply—free of both the Repub and Neo Repub constraints. And, most important of all, four: Magnus could finally get his damn vacation.

"You have access to whatever you need," Freya said at last.

She snapped the nubs of her paw, and a second later, the doors to her office slid apart. Wobix entered the room and conversed with Freya in a fit of Sekmetian words that finished with her giving him a soft hiss. Wobix bowed.

"Wobix and his warriors are now at your disposal," Freya said.

"Thank you, ní Freya," Caldwell replied as he stood. "We will keep you apprised of our progress."

"As will Wobix," Freya said.

Caldwell glanced at the warrior. "I'm sure he will."

Since the Gladio Umbra's purpose on Aluross had changed from shore leave to a capital defense operation, Caldwell ordered the entire battalion out of Fînta and to head to Meersin Pin. Any promise of R&R would have to wait for another day, but Magnus already figured as much when the mission at the governor's mansion went sideways.

In the meantime, Caldwell gathered the company commanders and a few additional leaders to go over his and Magnus's working plan. At the same time, the rest of the leadership oversaw the battalion's move. Sootriman, Ezo, TO-96, and Rohoar hovered over one end of a spacious holo table, while Abimbola, Zoll, and Wobix sat at the other. Freya allowed the command team access to her dimly lit war room within the capital building and provided refreshments for all. Accordingly, the Sekmit leader provided several files that Cyril had asked for.

Last but not least, Caldwell called in Azelon via a hardlight emitter positioned on the table. To the uneducated, it looked as though Azelon stood in the flesh—or the metal?—a meter from the colonel. "How do you read us, Smarty Pants?"

"Like the text on an ancient Novian stone tablet," Azelon replied.

Magnus laughed. "I believe she just called you ancient."

"Didn't need you to point it out, son." Caldwell blew a mouthful of smoke in Magnus's direction. "All right, folks. Let's get down to business. We've got a splickton of work to do in a short amount of time."

Heads nodded, and Wobix sniffed the air.

"Bixy, you wanna start?"

Wobix reeled at the sound of his new nickname. "Who are you referring to?"

"Amended names are indicators of trust," Azelon said.

Wobix looked back and forth between Caldwell and Azelon before looking the colonel in the eyes. "Yes. I have the requested schematics, Smokey."

Caldwell's bushy white eyebrows went up higher than Magnus had ever seen them.

"Smokey?" Caldwell said.

"Ha," Magnus bellowed and then clapped his hands. "I like your style, Wobix."

"Thank you, Maggsy," Wobix replied.

Magnus's glee vaporized. "Hey, now wait just a second—"

"He can dish it, but he can't take it," Caldwell said under his breath. Several people laughed before the colonel regained control of the room and nodded at Wobix. "Getting back to business."

Wobix waved a hand over the table, and a holo display appeared. The narskill warrior began batching root files together and swiping them over to Cyril's data pad. The code splicer confirmed receipt of each packet and then went to work opening and sifting through the mountain of data. Magnus was always amazed at just how fast the kid could navigate through an operating system. But he supposed Cyril was gifted with code the same way a skilled Marine could put a tight grouping on target at five-hundred meters.

"Uh-huh," Cyril said to himself. "Yeah, I see you. Mmm-hmmm." Holo window after holo window appeared over the table as Cyril moved them around the room, flicking them left, right, and up. The faster the kid's fingers danced through the air, the more noises he made. "Yup, yup, snap dink-a-do. A little flipdee-flop, annnnd—"

"Cyril," Magnus said. "Is that necessary?"

"Is what necessary, Mr. Commander Lieutenant, sir?" Cyril asked without taking his eyes from his work.

"All that talking to yourself."

"But I don't talk to myself, sir."

Magnus chuckled. "Oh really?"

"I think I would know if I talked to myself, sir." Cyril's fingers moved even faster as detailed plans spread out across the table. They included images of Meesrin Pin, maps of the streets, multiple layers of the Trinium Mines of Neptali, and even cross-sections of the planet. Cyril began beatboxing as he worked—at least that's what Magnus figured it was. But between all the spittle and missed beats, Magnus wondered if Cyril wasn't bludgeoning the imaginary drum set to death. "*Btss-dip-puh'cha—boots-ship'a-wah'wah—ptts-dibby—*"

"Cyril?" Magnus asked.

Cyril looked up. "Yes, your commandship?"

"You almost done?"

The kid nodded. "Just… about—got it. All ready for you, sir."

"Good. Now wipe your mouth and tell us what we're looking at."

Cyril apologized and wiped his lips with the back of his sleeve. "Weird. I must've drooled on myself—haha. Anyway, Mr. Wobix here has provided what I believe are the most necessary schematics in order for us to stage an adequate defense of Meesrin Pin as well as the mines. And if there's something you don't see that you want to see, like, if you wanted exact metrics on mine airflow volumes over, say, a forty-nine-minute period beginning at the post-midnight hour of 0256, and then overlay that with the oxygen saturation levels of nodes found in section 4-B21, I can draw correlations between the power substation and resulting air density resistance patterns, which would provide a—"

"Cyril?"

The code slicer hesitated. "Was it—was that too much?"

"A tad," Magnus said. "But we're all blown away."

"Ha ha. Thank you, sir."

"All right people," Caldwell said. "The first order of business is engaging So-Elku's convoy upon their arrival in orbit and escorting them to the surface. We won't know his exact ship composition until they arrive, but they'll be expecting a Sekmit welcome wagon, so it shouldn't be out of the ordinary."

"We'll take care of that," Wobix said.

"Good." Caldwell toked on his cigar. "What we need to keep an eye out for is an advanced team or a separate contingent of ships. Azelon?"

"I am able to facilitate deep space scans with the *Spire*, Colonel. Additionally, I will monitor for any attempts to use the Unity to hide the vessels in and around Aluross's gravity well."

"Can you do that?" Magnus asked, looking at Awen and then Willowood. "Cloak ships with the Unity, I mean?"

"Theoretically, yes," Willowood said. "Though it's never been done before, for several reasons. The most obvious of which is that the Luma would never conceal themselves, as that goes against the Order's code of ethics. The point is to serve star systems openly, not subvert them."

"Well, I think it is safe to say their code of ethics has been thrown out," Abimbola noted.

"Agreed," Willowood said.

Awen put her elbows on the table. "Before, So-Elku would have lacked the power to conceal a starship. That's a rather large undertaking for any Luma. But given his access to the Nexus, and what we've seen of the Li-Dain already? I wouldn't be surprised if he has the capability now."

"Would you?" Magnus asked Awen. "Be able to conceal one, I mean?"

"Given what we know about the Nexus now?" She glanced at Willowood. The two seemed to arrive at some sort of silent agreement. "In a word, yes. It depends on the size of the vessel, how long you'd want it hidden for, and how thorough an investigation it needed to hold up to, but, yes. We could do it."

"Then early detection will be important," Caldwell said to Azelon. "Ricio, I want you and all of Fang Company working with her and the other members of Drambull and Raptor Companies to create a net over the planet. If an asteroid so much as farts, I want to know about it."

"Understood, Colonel," Ricio said.

"Next, we'll need to secure a perimeter around So-Elku's landing party and determine the most likely routes between his LZ and the meet point." Caldwell pointed to a map of Meesrin Pin, made a fist in the air, and pulled the window toward him. Then he zoomed into the city's capital district. "Cyril. Can you outline all viable routes between So-Elku's hangar and the capitol building? Include secondary routes that might be used as contingencies."

"Sure, sure. Right away, Supreme Leader, sir."

"It's just Colonel, son."

"Right, right, totally. Sorry." Cyril's fingers prodded the air, pinched in and out of the map, and ran along streets. In less than thirty seconds, five different routes were outlined. "Zippidy-zap, there it is, Colonel."

"Good work, son."

"There are two more possibilities," Wobix interjected. All eyes turned toward the Sekmit.

"What did I miss?" Cyril asked with a tone of genuine curiosity.

Wobix took control of the map and separated the street level view from two subterranean views. Almost as soon as he did, Cyril let out a soft, "Of course."

"One route would be here," Wobix said, highlighting a path that followed some of the main streets but also crisscrossed beneath buildings. "This tunnel is part of the city's energy and communications network. And this one"—Wobix outlined a second course on a layer below the first—"proceeds through the city's sewer system."

"Mystics, please not the sewers again," Magnus said to whatever ethereal spirits may have been listening to him.

"Good work, Bixy," Caldwell said. "I want you setting up checkpoints along each of those street routes. Place sentries in the sublevel routes as well. Nelson, I want gladias supplementing Sekmit forces in those tunnels. But keep them out of sight until absolutely necessary. By all appearance, I want this to be a Sekmit-led operation."

"Got it."

Caldwell took another drag on his cigar. "My hunch is that while So-Elku is being escorted to the capitol building, he'll want his own security forces moving incognito along these additional routes. Willowood, I want some mystics posted at each location as well."

"Absolutely."

"If you see anything, you call it in." Heads nodded, and Caldwell forged ahead by looking at Wobix. "The meeting itself will be entirely under Sekmit oversight. We'll have gladias there to back you up, but again, we must stay out of sight."

Caldwell looked at the capitol building's blueprint, expanded it, and then moved through the floors until he found Freya's massive reception hall that doubled as a throne room.

Right then, Magnus had a curious thought. While Freya's title of pride mother of the Linux seemed to indicate that she was one of many tribal leaders serving under the queen, there didn't appear to be any other halls in the capital as significant as the one allocated to her. Likewise, Magnus hadn't met or heard mention of any other tribal leaders that were her equal, nor had he met the queen. In fact, it seemed strange that So-Elku was meeting with Freya and not Queen Nishti herself—whoever she was. This could've been a matter of coincidence, of course. Then again, Magnus couldn't help wonder if Freya was more important than everyone thought.

Caldwell pointed to two anterior chambers behind Freya's throne. "I'm thinking we'll want the Neo Repub forces staged in here. Nelson, you'll also oversee our end of things and help ensure General Lovell gets what he wants."

"Will do, Colonel."

"Willowood, I'll need you and whoever you can spare from Paladia Company waiting in the wings too, ready to assist the Sekmit and the Marines in capturing So-Elku. I don't expect him to yield without a fight."

"Nor should you," Willowood said. "He'll be on his guard, and we'll need to keep everyone well hidden in the Unity. We can't keep it up indefintiely, but it will buy us the time we need."

"The Sekmit can assist you there," Wobix said. "While we are not as skilled as your gladias, our abilities in the Unity are not to be underestimated, nor is our prowess in combat."

While Magnus had never seen a Sekmit fight, he didn't doubt Wobix's claims in the least. From those Magnus knew who had seen the feline-like warriors fight, they were ferocious, on par with the Jujari, as far as he could tell.

"Thank you." Willowood raised her chin. "We'll need to work together."

Caldwell sucked his lips clean of tobacco-stained saliva. "If all goes well, we'll take So-Elku here, and the Neo Republic will get him back to Minrok Santari for trial. Now, let's turn to what happens if things get six ways from Tuesday." He nodded at Magnus. "Lieutenant?"

"First off, I think we can expect So-Elku and the Li-Dain to raise hell inside Freya's throne room once they're engaged. The faster we can take them down, the better, so speed will be important. That will be up to Wobix, Nelson, and Willowood's companies. Meanwhile, we have to assume that So-Elku is going to make a play for the trinium."

Magnus pulled up the map of the mines, which took up the majority of the Leonï Ocean. Truthfully, Magnus couldn't believe the operation's scope when he saw it on a map. It extended north and south, almost to each pole, and west to the Olpandian continent. The undertaking must've taken decades to create and untold trillions to fund. *Which I guess isn't so hard when you're mining and selling trinium*, Magnus thought.

"According to our Sekmitian friends, the best locations to acquire the most trinium in the shortest amount of time are the aggregate nodes." Magnus made a few taps on menus, selected the categories, and then watched as the map highlighted several dozen points along the ocean floor. He knew there were going to be a lot, but not as many as the map displayed.

"So many?" Willowood said.

"There must be hundreds," Awen said.

"192, to be exact," Wobix said.

"I can confirm the Sekmit's count," TO-96 said.

"How are we going to defend so many?" Forbes asked Magnus.

"We aren't. First off, we don't have the numbers. But neither do they."

"We're both underpowered," Awen said.

"Yup. But more importantly, I believe we need to make two assumptions. The first is that So-Elku will try for a power grab."

"He is going to press hard for Freya's allegiance," Sootriman said. "Force her to comply."

Magnus nodded. "And then, if he can't get Freya to align with the LAW, he'll either try and take as much trinium as he can, or…"

"He's going to try and take over the mine," Awen said, staring into the near distance.

"Take over the whole mine?" Wobix said. "But I thought you said he doesn't have the numbers for that kind of maneuver."

"He doesn't, in my opinion. But that doesn't mean he won't try. Especially if he suspects that the Sekmit may double-cross him."

"You think he suspects that we may assassinate him?" Wobix said.

"Would you?" Magnus replied.

The narskill commander scowled. "If he plans to harm our people or steal our trinium? Of course."

"Well, there you go. So he's going to use the mines as leverage—at least that's what I would do."

"So you think his Li-Dain will either head for the most profitable aggregate nodes or to the main command node?" Willowood asked.

Magnus nodded. "Either Freya complies with his wishes, or he's going to leverage the mine against her."

"Or blow it up," Awen said.

Everyone turned to her, most likely as surprised at her fatalistic pronouncement as Magnus was. He motioned her to continue.

"He lacks the resources to take over Aluross as a whole," she said. "So if he can't get what he wants, why not keep the Sekmit from getting what they want too? He could bide his time and come back later to sort things out."

She had a point, Magnus admitted, albeit a dramatic one. "It's certainly within the realm of possibility. That said, I'd bet Bimby's entire poker chip manufacturing plant on the diaper babies setting up shop in the command complex before doing that."

"You mean to tell Rohoar that Abimbola makes the poker chips himself?" Rohoar turned toward Abimbola and laid his ears back. "Is this true?"

Magnus looked between the two giant warriors and realized he had just made a sizable misstep. "What I meant to say was—"

Rohoar started speaking in Jujari—expletives if the tone was any indication. Abimbola replied in Jujari, raising his voice at Rohoar. Within seconds, the two were shouting at each other and their faces got closer.

Then a piercing whistle ripped through the air and silenced the room. Everyone looked at Willowood. She removed her thumb and index finger from her mouth and eyed the two men. "We done here, boys?"

Rohoar's shoulders relaxed as he let out a long sigh. "We shall discuss this later, Miblimbian. Perhaps over a skralggrit."

"Should I even ask what a Scralagrit is?" Magnus said as he looked between the two warriors.

Awen spoke up. "It's a traditional Jujari feast where the offended party is paid back by slow roasting and then eating the one who offended him."

"Seems fair," Magnus said and cast Rohoar a smile.

"You see?" Rohoar said to Abimbola while raising a paw at Magnus. "Our Magnus agrees."

"Whoa, whoa." Magnus pumped his hands. "We have an op to run first."

"Not to worry, buckethead," Abimbola said in a dismissive tone. "Most Jujari business transactions involve yelling and threats. It's all for show."

"Rohoar may still eat you, Miblimbian."

Abimbola chuckled. "How about we survive this first, and then you eat me?"

"Rohoar is fine with this, yes."

Caldwell blew out a long stream of smoke. "Well now that we got that incredible splick-show out of the way, mind unbunching your undies and focusing?"

Abimbola and Rohoar nodded to each other and then at the colonel.

Caldwell gestured for Magnus to continue. "Back to you, son."

"All right then." Magnus cleared his throat. "While I'm not as fatalistic as Awen, sabotaging the mine isn't out of the question. However, given the constraints of our timetable and the number of assault options, we need to group threat possibilities into a cascading hierarchy."

"In galactic common, please?" Awen said.

Cyril spoke before Magnus could explain. "So, so, it's, like, basically saying that we can account for all the enemy's possible targets if we nest them within one or two possible defense trees."

"Yeah, that made it worse." Awen looked back to Magnus.

He sighed. "While they might intend to blow up the mine, we remove that possibility if we focus on keeping them out of the mine altogether. The side effect is that in keeping them out, we also stop them from doing twenty other things that we're not thinking of."

"Got it," Awen replied. "Back to Willowood's question, you think they'll either head for the most profitable nodes or to the main command complex?"

"I do." Magnus expanded the mine's holo map until he focused on the most central aggregate node. "But I want to make the choice for them. According to the data, it looks like this is the largest consolidation point. Can you double-check me on this Wobix? Cyril?"

"Yes," Wobix said first. "That is node 4.721-1."

"Let's call it Zulu One," Magnus replied.

"It serves as the central distribution point for the core nodes."

"And you transport the refined trinium to the surface, how?"

Wobix took control of the holo map. He rolled the display sideways to show a cross section of the seafloor, Zulu One, and the ocean's surface some four klicks above. Then Wobix made a subcategory visible—one marked Transport. Not only did a sizable oceanic hydrofoil freighter appear on the surface, but so did dozens of small underwater craft.

"These are automated submersible mineral carriers," Wobix said. "The Repub officials who knew of them referred to the vehicles as ASMCs. They are responsible for moving the trinium from the seafloor to the surface and delivering it to the freighter."

Cyril let out a long whistle. So long, in fact, that Magnus figured the code slicer totally misunderstood the purpose of whistling at something he found amazing. That or the kid was off in one of his holo game worlds again, daydreaming about whatever it is that brainiacs dream about.

"Something you find interesting, Cyril?"

"No," Cyril replied.

Magnus raised an eyebrow at him.

"I mean, well, sure. But it's more just, you know, haha—"

"What is it, Cyril?"

The code slicer leaned forward and pulled up a secondary window containing multiple schematic views of the ASMCs. The vessel looked like a sleek underwater dart with fins and four counter-rotating spiral propellers in the aft. "Um, so. This thing is fast. Ha ha. I'm not sure how familiar everyone is with fluid dynamics, because, wow, let me tell you, this puppy exceeds anything else in its class. It's three times as fast as the Festoonial black marspin. Have you ever seen the footage of those? Cause I have. Once, there was a whole school of them, and they actually used their snouts to harpoon a Telderine giant sea mammoth. Went so fast they drove straight through the beast and cut it to ribbons. You know, you can download the uncut version on—"

"Hey, Cyril?" Magnus said.

"Yeah?"

"Can you maybe stick to telling us about the ASMCs and why you think they might be pertinent to our mission?"

"Oh, sure, sure. Sorry about that. So, the Sekmits' submersibles are supercavitating—that's where the fluid pressure behind an object drops below the liquid's vapor pressure, thus reducing drag and allowing it—"

"Cyril?"

"It goes fast, Lieutenant. And since it doesn't require a biological pilot, it can get by all of the pesky pressurization issues that, you know, tend to kill people like us."

"So you're saying the ASMCs can get a lot of trinium to the surface relatively quickly."

"Yes, sir. At an average floor to surface speed of 270 kilometers per hour, covering a distance of 4.23 kilometers, they can make the one-way trip in about one minute."

Okay, so now Magnus understood why Cyril had whistled. "Damn."

"Yeah, exactly, sir. Damn. Even double or triple damn, depending on the corollary. The design is ingenious for several other reasons too, namely that inboard water cooling allows the trinium to remain stable. And, without a biologic driver, there is no risk of death should the element destabilize. Likewise, any meltdown is absorbed by the ocean with little to no fallout for the planet."

Magnus had to hand it to the Sekmit: they were crafty little cats. "And they can carry how much trinium?"

"Up to twenty-six metric tons, sir," Cyril said as he brought up a cross section of the ASMC's cargo hold.

Now it was Magnus's turn to whistle, and then he looked at Wobix. "Quite an operation you've got going on here."

The narskill warrior nodded but did not reply.

"If the quadrant only knew," Magnus said.

"Which brings up another point," Cyril added. "As far as I can tell, the Sekmit only use one OHF at a time."

"OHF?" Magnus asked.

"Oceanic hydrofoil freighter." The code slicer brought up a second vehicle holo window, this time featuring an elegant multi-story mono-hulled ship with massive hydrofoils stemming from its belly.

"Looks like a boat that missed its calling as a ski champion," Forbes noted.

"Ha ha, something like that, Mr. Forbes, yeah." Cyril ran an animation sequence that showed the OHF opening underwater bay doors in the aft to receive an ASMC, followed by a second set under the bow to release the delivery ship. "Once the trinium has been deposited, the OHF's unique hydrofoil design allows it to speed across any ocean condition to the mainland where it deposits its cargo."

"Why only one?" Ezo asked. "Move more product, make more credits."

"Credits we have," Wobix said. "But security, we do not."

Magnus nodded at the Sekmit. "You keep the surface-level trinium radiation down by only moving one batch a time."

Wobix gave a single nod. "Discretion is as valuable as trinium, and we have learned to cultivate both."

A plan was forming in Magnus's head. It wasn't a great one, but he didn't have time for great. Instead, the Gladio Umbra would have to settle for the "let's hope it works so we don't get screwed" kind.

"Bixy? Azie? What are the chances that So-Elku knows about how much trinium the planet can produce?" Magnus waved the question away as soon as he'd spoken it. "What are the chances that they've observed the mine's normal output as it pertains to Zulu One?"

"I can answer your first question," Wobix said. "As it's been mentioned to you, the agreement specifications on file with the governor's office do outline the production expectations of our long-standing contract with the Galactic Republic. What they do not do, however, is detail the scope of our entire operation."

"So even if So-Elku somehow got his hands on that contract, he'd only know what the Repub knew, not what you do."

"Correct."

"I can attempt to answer the second question," Azelon said. "Given the Sekmit's faithfulness to limit the mine's apparent production capacity, I expect So-Elku has observed what any other long-range sensors sweep has observed."

Magnus jabbed a finger toward her and then clapped his hands once. "And that, Azie, is exactly what we're going to bank on."

"I'm not sure I follow, sir."

"His objectives can be rather difficult to discern at times," TO-96 said to her. "As you have no doubt experienced before."

"I have, yes. Thank you for your consideration, Tee-Tee."

Magnus looked at TO-96. "Did she just give you a nickname, 'Six?"

"Yes, sir. It had been in place for several thousand milliseconds."

Magnus folded his arms. "Well I'll be."

"You'll be what, sir?"

"Impressed, 'Six. I'm impressed. Keep it up, you sly dog, you."

"Sly dog?" TO-96's head turned back and forth between Azelon and Magnus several times before Azelon spoke up.

"Difficult to discern, yet again," she said, pointing at Magnus.

He ignored them and moved on with explaining his plan. Magnus moved the top map window and the oceanic hydrofoil freighter window until they were side by side. "Wobix?"

"Yes, manservant with military-grade tactical knowledge?"

Magnus snickered. *I kinda like the sound of that.* "I wanna pack this OHF so full of trinium that it's gonna wanna sink."

"Sink, manservant?"

Magnus pointed to the ship's diagram. "We're gonna make this sucker glow so bright that So-Elku's forces won't be able to resist it."

Cyril was nodding so hard Magnus worried the kid was going to snap his neck. "Yeah, yeah, yeah. That would group all possible assault scenarios under one action tree quite well. That said, Mr. Magnus, what is your plan if the Li-Dain choose to go for the command complex?"

"Easy. We disable the hovertrain."

Cyril smiled. "Ah. Simple yet effective."

"I'm glad you approve." Magnus looked at Azelon. "And Azie?"

"Yes, Magnus?"

"We're gonna need some new armor and submersible toys. Time to warm up those 3D printers of yours."

"I'm way ahead of you, sir."

Magnus's curiosity was piqued. "You are?"

"Ever since your sudden decision to plunge to the bottom of Capriana Prime, I've been working on a submersible platform should you ever wish to repeat the episode."

Magnus balked. "My decision? Azie, our shuttle was hit by a shockwave from an orbital round."

"And were you prepared for it? No. I take that personally." Magnus couldn't be sure but it seemed like Azelon straightened her back a little. "You may wish to make future modifications, of course. But I have already begun production, and I think you'll be pleased." She turned to TO-96. "In order to finish more quickly, I'm going to need your help, you sly dog."

TO-96's eyes warmed to a soft orange glow. "I'll be on my way as soon as this meeting is concluded."

"Why, Ninety-Six," Awen said. "Are you blushing?"

The bot shrugged. "As I am no longer conversant with Azelon

inside the Novian singularity, it makes our absences that much more"—he cocked his head sideways as if searching for the right word—"angst-laden."

Magnus couldn't help but laugh at the fact that the bot was apparently trying to describe sexual tension, though TO-96 lacked all the required "systems," as it were.

"So it sounds like we have a plan then," Caldwell said, reining the meeting back in. "Ricio, Azelon, you're in charge of early detection, orbital defense, and tracking."

"Copy that," Ricio said as he gave a half-salute to Azelon.

"Felicity," Caldwell said, using Willowood's first name. "You and Nelson will oversee the capital operations with DiAntora."

"Understood," Willowood and Nelson both replied.

"And Magnus, you and Forbes have the mines."

"Aye aye, boss," Magnus said.

Forbes touched his index finger to his forehead and waved at Caldwell.

"Feared Aggressor," Wobix said. "Ní Freya has ordered me to assist you beyond the planning phase."

"Don't sound so excited about it," Caldwell replied. "You might go around giving people the impression that you actually want to help us."

Wobix looked puzzled. "But I don't."

Magnus laughed with Caldwell at this brutally honest confession. If Wobix could fight as well as he could offend, then he was going to make a good asset outside the wire.

"Be that as it may, we don't want to disappoint Freya now, do we?" Caldwell asked.

"I would sooner castrate myself."

The colonel grimaced. "No need to go crazy on me, Bixy. Let

me ask you: of the three units we've formed, which do you think could use your expertise the most?"

Magnus had a feeling Bixy was about to provide another giant helping of honesty.

"Magnus's work with the trinium operation," Wobix said. "He has clearly taken on far more than he is capable of handling and will most likely expose himself and his team to high levels of radiation before the day is through."

"Thanks for the vote of confidence," Magnus said.

Wobix eyed him. "I have very little confidence in you, manservant. I am not sure why you wish me to vote on the matter."

"Very well," Caldwell said. "You will assist my manservant and Captain Forbes."

"Really?" Magnus said to Caldwell, remarking on the title and then thumbing toward Forbes. "But he gets Captain?"

"Nicknames," Caldwell said with a shrug. "Amazing how they can stick."

8

AZELON LIVED up to her claims that Magnus would be pleased with the new submersible armor system. Christened the Mark III MANTA armor, the red-tinted suit featured an ultra-resistant shell capable of withstanding water pressure at depths up to fourteen kilometers—not that Magnus ever intended to go anywhere near that depth. Substantial servo assistance provided greater dexterity when submerged, and the high-intensity multi-spectrum emitters and sensor suite gave operators a wide variety of optical and audio options with which to navigate.

"You've really outdone yourself this time, Azie," Magnus said, submerged thirty-four meters under the Leonï Ocean. He and the rest of Granther Company had deployed directly over waypoint Zulu One from a shuttle to acclimate to the new suits. They were waiting to rendezvous with Wobix and the oceanic hydrofoil freighter within the hour, which meant everyone had about thirty-five minutes to get their sea legs.

"Thank you, sir," Azelon said from a comms window in

Magnus's HUD. She stood onboard the *Spire's* bridge along with TO-96. "You are enjoying yourself, I take it?"

Magnus gave a little laugh. One of the perks of being an elite warrior was getting to play with equipment civilians could only dream of, and this experience was no exception. "Azie, you've made my day."

"Happy to hear that, sir. There are several more features I'd like to make your company aware of, not the least of which is the radiation shielding that will help reduce your exposure to trinium should you experience any unprotected events."

"Robillard experiences unprotected events every weekend," Bliss said.

"Wouldn't you like to know," Robillard replied.

"Easy, boys," Magnus said.

Azelon went on to explain that the telecolos-capable suit made use of submarine ballast tech but in miniature, allowing the operator to flood or clear a network of cavities. Not only did this let a gladia obtain neutral buoyancy but also attitude—pitch, roll, and yaw. Moreover, the system was tied into the Novia biotech interface, which meant all an operator needed to do was *think* about the position they wanted to be in and the suit would do the rest. This included movement too, as two EDF thrusters on the hips and eight contact thrusters mounted around the suit's limbs and torso provided multi-directional motion.

Of course, not everyone found it as easy to use as Magnus. Rohoar's voice barked over comms as his suit shot forward and bounced off two other gladia's before smacking into Abimbola's side.

"You want to start the skralggrit early?" Abimbola said, rotating his suit to face Rohoar.

"Rohoar does not want to do anything but learn how to swim," the Jujari replied without any attempt to hide his nervousness.

Likewise, Bliss seemed to be having a hard time getting himself to stay right-side up.

"Your other left, dammit," Robillard yelled to his fellow fireteam leader.

"I am!"

"Now you're just cartwheeling yourself in circles."

"Well, maybe I want to," Bliss said.

"Nah, you don't," Robillard replied.

"Shut up."

Azelon spoke over the company's VNET channel. "If you ever find yourself in a situation you can't get out of—"

"That's Bliss every weekend," Robillard said under his breath.

"I heard that," Bliss shouted back.

"—you can either *think* or *say* 'stabilize,' or simply call out to me, and I'll be happy to override your orientation controls."

"Sounds good, Azie," Magnus said. "Again, the suits are great."

"TO-96's assistance was indispensable over the final few hours," she replied, looking over at her counterpart. "I'm only sorry we could not provide more SUBCATs for you."

When the gladias needed to get somewhere in a hurry, Azelon designed the SUBCAT—the name no doubt an ode to the Gladio Umbra's feline hosts. This multi-purpose transport vehicle could carry up to six fully-armored MANTA gladias and equipment at speeds of up to 150 kilometers per hour. The four tube-like power plants fixed to the base looked like torpedo bays, though Azelon assured Magnus they were just there to provide vectored thrust.

"We only had time to manufacture two SUBCATs," TO-96 said

over VNET. "So the rest of you will be pulled along on state of the art tow cables."

"State of the art?" Magnus asked.

"Synthetic rope with loops tied along its length. Unless, of course, you wish the manipulators to conduct you along."

Magnus laughed. "The rope will do just fine."

In addition to the SUBCAT's high-speed transportation abilities, it also made use of two heavy-grade arm manipulators as well as a crane extender mounted on the roof. Together, these three instruments could pick up, pry, drill, crush, hammer, or twist just about anything worth investigating. And if they couldn't do the job? That's where the real fun began.

"Let's talk about weaponry," Magnus said to the bots.

"With pleasure," TO-96 said. He turned to Azelon. "After you."

"No," she said. "After you."

"But I insist."

"And I counter insist."

"Hey, guys?" Magnus said. "Can one of you just give us a rundown?"

"I think you should explain these," Azelon said to TO-96. "They are more analog than I am used to anyway."

"As you wish," TO-96 replied, and then turned to face Magnus and the rest of the gladias. "As you probably know, underwater warfare makes all but the most powerful energy weapons inert—I mean, who wants to schlep an LO9D cannon around on their back? Am I right?" TO-96's head bobbed back and forth as if he was expecting a laugh from a studio audience.

"Is he okay?" Awen said on a private channel.

Magnus chuckled. "Sure is starting to loosen up a little. Betcha it's that woman of his."

"You say that like it's a bad thing."

"It's always a woman," Magnus mumbled to himself.

TO-96 recovered from his applause-less bit and forged ahead. "As I was saying, the SUBCAT and the MANTA suit make use of more conventional weaponry. Together, Azelon and I crafted—"

"Mostly you," Azelon said.

TO-96 rotated his head to look at her. "But I couldn't have made them without your help."

"'Six," Magnus said. "We're burning time here."

"Yes, of course, sir. Azelon and I crafted two similar weapons of differing sizes. The first is the weapon you all find maglocked to your suits at present. If you will all please remove them for inspection."

Magnus did so, pulling the rifle from his thigh. The black weapon had a short stock, thick upper receiver, and a drum-like front end around the barrel. The bulkier magazines had far more mass than energy mags and inserted through the bottom of the main handle.

"Excellent," TO-96 said. "This is the BT16, also called the bolt-torpedo 16mm diameter variable warhead delivery platform. We've tried to combine traditional underwater munitions with the variable ordnance detonation system. The traditional rifle-style weapon can fire a single chemically accelerated torpedo bolt every 0.28 seconds. Once fired, the bolt can travel guided or unguided to its target. You can choose from a variety of impact modes, including inert—where the munition will act as the antiquated slug throwers of the last millennium, which still proves fatal to most biologic life forms when aimed properly—to omni- and hyper-directional shaped charges, scattered-round burst, and armor-piercing deep-penetration."

Dutch whistled over comms and cradled her BT16 lovingly. "Would you get a load of that."

"Nice work, 'Six," Magnus said. "And the SUBCATs?"

"They have an identical mounted platform, only with 80mm rounds, sir."

"No kidding," Magnus replied.

"You're damn straight I'm not kidding," TO-96 said. He placed his hands on his hips and looked at Azelon.

Magnus couldn't help but laugh. Over his private channel with Awen, he said, "See. Told you it was the woman."

TO-96 addressed the company again. "All modes and weapons data, including targeting assistance, system integrity, and ammunition levels will populate in your HUDs like normal. Please keep in mind, everyone, that this weapons platform is far more limited in the number of rounds you can deploy. Each magazine only holds ten bolts, and you have been preassigned seven magazines, three on each thigh for your convenience, and one in the chamber."

"He means this ammo's going fast, people," Magnus said, knowing he'd need to reiterate the bot's point. "Gotta make every round count."

"La-raah," said a few gladias over comms.

"I would like to point out one primary cause for concern, if I may," TO-96 said.

"Go ahead, 'Six," Magnus replied.

"Please pay attention to the proximity of your targets as well as your fellow gladias, particularly when using the omni- and hyper-directional shaped charges. Since you are immersed in a dense liquid environment, the concussive power of all explosive rounds will be far more damaging than were you to be in a normal atmosphere."

"That means keep your distance," Robillard said as he shook off Bliss's desperate handhold around his elbow. "And watch where you shoot."

"Precisely, Mr. Robillard," TO-96 replied. "In addition, since you are facing Luma adversaries with stronger shielding capabilities, as per Magnus's observations when encountering the Li-Dain in the governor's palace, we have taken measures to maximize each round's payload delivery using a quantum algorithm that we believe will attenuate the Li-Dain's harmonic resonance so that—"

"Boil it down for us, 'Six," said Magnus. "Easy terms."

"You won't require as many shots to reduce their shields as you needed with the BATRIGs."

"That wasn't so hard, was it?"

"No. But I fear that if you don't understand it—"

"These things can kill Li-Dain, right?"

TO-96 pulled his head back in surprise. "Of course, sir. When used properly."

"Then that's all we need to know."

TO-96 nodded. "I suppose it's worth informing you that NOV2s' firmware has been updated with a similar algorithm to help with the advanced shielding as well, not that you have any NOV2s on you now. But the rest of the battalion does. Azelon and I do hope that these upgrades help to offset your exposure."

"What kind of exposure?" Magnus asked.

"Well, your telecolos technology is not as effective against Unity users as you might wish it to be."

"You're saying they can still see us."

The bot nodded. "In a manner of speaking, yes. We have worked to conceal you as best we can, but having the mystics hide you in the Unity is always the best option—that is, when they can afford to."

"Got it. Anything else, buddy?"

"One more thing, yes. Should you find yourselves transitioning from underwater to land combat, the suit's more cumbersome components can be jettisoned. While a far cry from the stealth and mobility of the Mark I and II systems, the MANTA will provide more than sufficient protection, navigation, and communication. That is all, sir."

"You both have done a bang-up job, 'Six."

"Why, thank you, sir. That is kind of you to say."

Azelon nodded. "If you have any questions, please don't hesitate to inquire."

"Likewise, we'll be monitoring your progress during the entire operation, as always," 'Six added.

"Copy that," Magnus said.

"Speaking of which," Azelon said. "The OHF is in-bound, headed to your present location. ETA three minutes."

"Everyone topside," Magnus said.

"Colonel, this is Ricio."

Caldwell transferred the call to his data pad and placed the unit on Freya's desk so she could be privy to the transmission's contents. He knew that part of any successful joint operation was not only the sharing of information but the *eagerness* to share it. Such efforts paid long-lasting dividends—assuming both parties survived the op. "Go for Caldwell," he replied and looked at the pride mother.

"Colonel, we might have something up here," Ricio said. "We're detecting several anomalies over the western hemisphere just north of Aluross's equator."

Before Freya even saw the coordinates light up on the holo map, she seemed to draw the connection. "That's above 4.721-1."

"You think they're Luma?" Caldwell said to Ricio.

"Well, if they are, sir, they're certainly not trying to make their approach subtle—minus the cloaking, of course."

"It would have been better if they'd approached from the far side and traversed under our sensors," Freya said.

Caldwell's cigar drooped as he gave the pride mother an impressed pout. "Well said, ní Freya." He looked back at Ricio. "Investigate for a closer look, but do not engage. We need So-Elku to make his meeting, so we can't afford to go scaring him off."

"Hard copy. I'll keep you apprised."

"Caldwell out." The comms channel closed, and the colonel retrieved his data pad. "Seems So-Elku sent an advance team over the mine."

"So he is interested in the trinium," Freya said.

"Did you ever doubt it?"

"No. I just thought he might go about securing it more diplomatically. But this"—her eyes studied the holo map for a moment before continuing—"this violation of sovereign space means he intends to take our resources by force."

Caldwell nodded. "And here I was hoping for a leisurely evening on your capitol office's terrace."

"No you weren't," Freya said without blinking. "You want to kick Luma ass butt."

Caldwell chuckled at the blunder and blew a puff of smoke. "Something like that. Guess it's time to get this Paglothian pigmy pony saddled and ready to shoot."

THE OHF ARRIVED an hour before sunset and snuck up on Magnus like a ghost stalking an unsuspecting victim. Were it not for his bioteknia eyes' advanced augmented reality tracking tech or the low-energy vibration in the water, Magnus would never have known the OHF was coming until it was right on top of him. The craft's blackout security measures even spoofed the MANTA's sensor array, which was surprising given how advanced Azelon's tech was.

"These kitty cats sure know how to stay out of sight," Magnus said to Awen as they rose and fell with the ocean rollers and watched the ship head toward them.

"My HUD didn't pick them up until ten seconds ago," Awen replied.

For as large as the vessel was, the freighter balanced miraculously atop several fin-like arms that slid through the waves. Beneath the surface, two massive hydrofoil wings not only supported the ship but housed the ship's twin trinium-drive propulsion systems.

Magnus activated his helmet's strobe light for a few seconds until the freighter's captain acknowledged him with a double flash from the boat's bridge-mounted searchlight.

"The captain sees you, Magnus," Wobix said over comms. Azelon had patched the Sekmit's military frequencies into VNET for ease of use.

"And aren't we grateful for that," Magnus said as he watched the multi-ton monstrosity slow and then sink into the sea swell. Granther Company propelled themselves around to the ship's stern like Volpine crap gnats circling the tail end of spotted Nimber elk. A hatch opened above the water, and Magnus recognized Wobix's face.

"Good to see you, manservant," the Sekmit said. "And all dressed up for the occasion too."

"Something like that," Magnus replied over his helmet's external speakers.

Wobix reached down and helped Magnus climb onto a landing platform. When Magnus had stabilized himself along a railing, he called out over comms.

"Alpha and Bravo Teams with me. Charlie and Delta, you're staying wet."

Everyone acknowledged the orders in the HUD's chat window, and then Magnus worked with Wobix to help the rest of First Squad out of the water and onto the freighter. According to the mission plan, Abimbola's and Zoll's fire teams were tasked with supporting Wobix and an elite unit of narskill warriors with defending the OHF. Meanwhile, Bliss's and Robillard's fireteams would stay in the water in support, looking for any and every opportunity to take out ships or swimmers who decided to hijack the ASMCs or find other ways down to Zulu One.

Once inside the freighter's aft crew compartment, Magnus and the rest of First Squad detached their main thrusters and removed the extra ballast weights from their armor. The result was a far more agile suit than Magnus would have anticipated, though still a far cry from the Mark I armor. Magnus flipped up his blaster-proof windowplex visor so he could speak to Wobix open-air. "Mind showing us where to set up?"

Wobix twitched his nose and then turned toward a bulkhead door. "This way."

First Squad followed the cat commander through several massive cargo holds, each complete with catwalks and dollied cranes and hoists. Further down in the holds, Magnus noticed rubberized tracks that he assumed were for the ASMCs to ride in, unload, and then speed out the ship's bow. Massive shielded containers on either side of the track were no doubt for the trinium.

Wobix eventually emerged on a top deck where the smell of salt-water filled Magnus's head with seaside memories along Capriana's shores—and some less pleasant memories on Caledonia's. He smelled something else on the air too.

"Storm's coming in," Wobix said before Magnus could get the words out.

"I see that," Magnus replied. Far to the west, the soon-setting sun was turning red as it sank into a low lying mass of dark clouds. "How big?"

Wobix considered the wispy cloud straight overhead and then sniffed the air. "Very big."

"Perfect."

The Sekmit warrior studied Magnus for a moment. "Many of your words don't make sense to me, manservant. This one especially."

"You'll catch on if we work together enough."

"Then I will not catch on."

Magnus let out a sharp laugh, even surprising himself. "You're all right, Sekmit. You know that?"

"Yes. And I don't need your reminder either."

Magnus laughed some more and then pointed ahead to a sleek command tower toward the bow. "That the bridge?"

"Yes. Come."

Wobix led the teams into the command structure and gave them a quick tour. For being such a utilitarian vessel, the ship was substantially advanced, technologically speaking. The glossy control surfaces and multi-layered holo displays must have cost a small fortune. The well-appointed cabin was also trimmed out in leather and teak, and it was capable of holding at least a dozen personnel comfortably.

"The command staff will continue to remain at their posts," Wobix said as he brought up a holo schematic of the ship. "My warriors will provide support on the bridge, as per your terms. The rest of my units will be stationed throughout the ship at locations, again, as per your recommendations." Two dozen blue markers lit up across the ship, mostly inside the hull.

But Magnus couldn't help detect a note of dissatisfaction in Wobix's tone. "You sound disappointed. Something the matter?"

Wobix raised his chin. "Your glandies."

"Gladias."

"They are to stand sentry around the ship's gunwales."

Magnus nodded. "A defensive perimeter along the outermost rails, yes."

"Wobix does not like that you will have first contact."

Magnus looked at Wobix in surprise. This guy had the attitude of a real fighter. "I can assure you that it's for your own safety, Bixy."

The cat hissed. "We do not need protection."

"I didn't say that you needed protection. I said safety. Meaning, if anyone is going to lose their lives in this op, we want it being us, not you."

"And this is not a fair balance of sacrifice."

Magnus eyed the catman. He'd never heard this term before. "Balance of sacrifice?"

"If you glandies—"

"Gladias."

"—lose more warriors in this fight than the Sekmit, then it was not the Sekmit who defended our home. It was your—"

"Gladias."

"Yes."

Magnus sighed. "Listen. I can certainly appreciate that attitude. But part of our ethos is the mantra 'Dominate. Liberate.'"

"I heard someone say this, yes."

"And part of dominating the enemy is making sure that the people we are helping liberate don't suffer more than they already have."

Wobix's eyes narrowed. The cat seemed to consider Magnus's words for a moment before speaking again. "I see this. And it is noble of you. However, Wobix also requests that we, as fellow warriors and liberators of our own planet, be allowed to share the sacrifice."

"I think you're going to have many more opportunities to—"

"Share the sacrifice out there," Wobix said, pointing a clawed nub toward the exterior railing. "And wherever the enemy may seek to bring harm."

If this guy wanted to die for his people, then Magnus wasn't going to be the one to stand in the way. Hell, it was pretty noble of the cat—if not incredibly stupid. Their armor was little more than a few hardened leather plates and similarly fashioned helmets. Besides the Thørzin power bow, the most imposing thing about the narskill were their teeth and claws, and Magnus doubted those would be much use against the Li-Dain. Then again, he knew that underestimating any civilization's desire to defend itself was unwise.

"Very well," Magnus said at last. "You're welcome to divvy up your warriors as you see fit, so long as you keep the interior bays guarded."

"I thank you for this," Wobix said. He placed a fist on his chest and raised his head.

Magnus did the same, hoping to honor the Sekmit properly. It felt weird, but Wobix seemed pleased. In his head, Magnus heard Awen say, *I'm proud of you.*

Thanks, Magnus replied. *Felt awkward.*

But he got the message, and you probably just made a new friend.

'Cause that's what I was really hoping for.

Awen gave a small laugh behind Magnus's left shoulder.

"Magnus." It was Caldwell on the company channel. "You copy?"

Magnus pulled up Caldwell's face in his biotekina eyes while the other gladia's viewed the colonel's face in the HUD projected on their bubble visors. "Go for Magnus."

"Ricio's picked up some anomalies inbound on your location."

"Ships?"

"That's what we think. Azelon thinks they're Unity cloaked."

"Is So-Elku even planet-side yet?"

"Negative," Caldwell said. "And that's the rub. We can't engage until he's in the meeting. Any premature movement, and he'll know it's a trap."

"But you don't think he'd risk negotiations with a premature assault of his own, do you?"

Caldwell's shoulders rose and fell as air whistled through his mustache. "I'd hope not. But this one's a strange bird, as you well know. Just get in position, keep your heads down, and keep your fingers off the trigger until I say. I'll be monitoring your feeds."

"Copy."

"And Magnus?"

"Yes, Colonel?"

"I don't need to remind you that if things go nova, we want it to happen at sea."

"I understand."

The colonel pushed his lips under his nose and gave Magnus a quick nod. "Caldwell out."

Magnus turned and looked at the rest of his squad. "We might be in for a tense encounter. No matter what, I don't want a single round going off until I give the order. Is that clear?"

Everyone assented on the chat window and gave head nods.

"Good." Magnus addressed Wobix. "How soon can you fill the ship with trinium?"

"Twenty minutes, and it will be glowing bright enough for sensors in the next system to see."

"Then let's get a move on. We need to give our guests something pretty to look at."

9

Lani DiAntora's gut had been tight ever since the news broke about the explosion of Governor Littleton's mansion, and that was saying something because it took a lot to make her uneasy. Still, she'd been able to keep her emotions under control, both in front of the chancellor and the rest of CENTCOM. But now that she was alone in her quarters on a confiscated Sorellian heavy freighter, just moments from landing on her homeworld, DiAntora wanted nothing more than a martial arts gym full of laser targets.

Commending the Gladio Umbra to ní Freya's care had been a deliberate move to help her people escape the burden of Republic control. It was Freya's intention all along to ask the gladias for assistance in dethroning the philandering overseer. Littleton had long been a bane and embarrassment to the Sekmit. But ousting him was more than a matter of national pride—it was a national opportunity.

Aluross's trade deal with the Galactic Republic, while beneficial in the early years, had eventually become a source of great contention. As the demand for trinium increased, so too did the Republic's price for the precious commodity. And yet the Sekmit were not making any more per gram of trinium than they were fifty years prior.

The Republic trade ambassadors spouted lines of rehearsed excuses that cited everything from distribution costs and market uncertainty to trade deficits and ever-increasing security measures. But when it came to the Sekmit voicing their concerns and looking to meet their own needs, the Republic swept their protests aside, saying that things would be addressed "eventually" and that "now was not the time."

DiAntora wasn't sure if Aluross would ever be free of the Republic's stranglehold—*at least not in my lifetime*, she thought. Not without an all-out war. But the fall of Capriana Prime, as unspeakably tragic as it was, created an unprecedented opportunity to be rid of the alliance once and for all. Like Freya and the rest of the pride mothers, DiAntora knew that the Republic would never allow the Sekmit to back out of the relationship. Once you were in the Galactic Republic, you could never get out. And with the Republic ailing from one of the most significant assaults in recorded history, the limping government would cinch down even tighter on controlling its resources—which was precisely the right time to strike.

With decimated fleets and senate, DiAntora knew better than anyone that the Republic would not be able to counter an uprising. Whereas just a few weeks before kicking a governor off-world would have been met with swift and decisive retaliation, now it was simply added to the ever-growing list of uncontrollable partnerships unraveling in Capriana's wake. Granted, she had not expected them to blow up sovereign property. But even still, the results mattered little.

The point was that the Republic—Galactic or Neo—was powerless to do anything about it.

What they could do, however, was attempt to keep the trinium supply from falling into the hands of a rival. And, if Chancellor David Seaman played his hand right, earn a way back into ní Freya's and the Sekmit populace's good graces. While the Republic would never enjoy the steep profits it had seen in the golden era, Seaman would need trinium to rebuild.

Not that DiAntora cared for the Republic anymore. She'd learned too much in her years of service—seen just how deep the economic injustice against her people went. She didn't blame David, at least not fundamentally; some of her feelings toward him were genuine. But the more the Neo Republic scrambled for security, the more DiAntora realized he was just another cog in the machine. Gaining his trust and affections had paid off when he'd agreed to let the Gladio Umbra take refuge on Aluross.

Regardless of where her heart stood toward Seaman, her plan had worked. Both the Sekmit and the Neo Republic were going to get what they wanted: So-Elku and the LAW out and away from the Aluross's trinium production. Seaman had been quite vocal about how, if this operation were successful, it would mean the Republic would have a front-row seat in renegotiating a trade deal with the Sekmit. She, on the other hand, knew that her government would never again trade directly with the Republic. If CENTCOM or a new senate wanted Alurossian trinium, they'd buy it through a third party—*and at a premium*, if DiAntora had anything to say about it.

"Admiral DiAntora," said the shuttle's captain over comms. "We are preparing for orbital entry."

"Thank you, Captain," DiAntora said. "I'll be up momentarily."

"Understood. Bridge out."

DiAntora looked at herself in the mirror, smoothed her traditional Sekmit tunic and breeches, and took a deep breath. How long had it been since she'd donned these garments? *Too long*, she concluded. Then she glanced at the folded uniform on her bed and wondered how much longer she would be allowed to wear the Neo Republic colors. *No*, she thought. The real question was how much longer she would allow herself to wear those colors.

SEEING Aluross from the air calmed DiAntora's nerves. With so much time abroad, it often felt as though her homeland was nothing more than a dream, and that all her long planning to help free her people was spent on a fictional place. But seeing the oceans wrap around the lush jungle-strewn continents brought her back to the heartbeat of why she'd sacrificed so much of her life.

"But it wasn't a sacrifice," she whispered. "It was a privilege."

"What was that, sir?" Captain Nedrow asked.

Had she said that out loud? "Nothing," DiAntora replied, and then she scolded herself for letting her heart get the best of her.

"Must feel good to be back home," Nedrow said.

DiAntora let out a soft purr. "It does. Though I have grown so accustomed to space-faring that it hardly seems like my home anymore, and I'd just as soon be back on a Super Dreadnaught. Wouldn't you?"

Nedrow hesitated. "Yes, of course. I just thought—"

"Keep those to yourself, Captain."

"Yes, Admiral." Nedrow responded to a chirp on the instrument panel. "We've been granted docking permission at hangar bay four."

"Not the best parking spot, but not an insult either."

"Yes, Admiral."

"Take us in nice and easy. We don't need any unnecessary attention today."

Nedrow nodded and then resumed his focus on helming the ship to port.

The landing sequence went smoothly, and it wasn't long before the command bridge ramp extended and DiAntora took her first deep breath of Alurossian air in over five years. She'd missed this place more than she admitted out loud. Contrary to her admonishment, Nedrow was right: it did feel good to be back home.

A security gate opened on the hangar's far side, allowing a phalanx of green-robbed narskill to file into the bay. They formed two lines, twenty Sekmit deep, punctuated by tall staves and curved Thørzin bows. As one, the warriors turned outward to establish a center aisle and struck the stone floor with their poles. When the percussive echo faded, DiAntora saw ní Freya ap Liuix appear at the column's end dressed in a white gown and a translucent red shawl.

DiAntora and Freya raised their chins and crossed the distance in short order with DiAntora descending the ramp and Freya emerging out of the security passage's shadows. They met in the middle of the phalanx and crossed necks, tails whipping to and fro.

"Ní Freya, is it good to see you again," DiAntora said.

"And you. I trust your trip went well?"

"It did."

"Any unwanted attention I should be concerned about?"

DiAntora shook her head. "Our Republic merchant manifest lists Sorellian seafood, as purchased."

Freya gave a soft hiss. "Not the best quality, but also not the worst. And how is your cargo?"

"Ready for your guests, pride mother. Just say the word."

"Good. I've arranged for private transport." Freya clapped her paws once, and a detachment of narskill broke away from the line. The four warriors crossed to a large double-wide access door and opened it. A moment later, four hover freight-trucks drove into the hangar, circled to the ship's aft cargo hold, and slowed to a stop.

DiAntora looked back to Nedrow, who stood at the top of the bridge ramp. "Captain, make sure that our merchandise is properly loaded onto the royal transports."

"I'll see to it personally."

DiAntora looked back to Freya. "And the rest of your banquet preparations? How are those going?"

"Rather well, I'd say. My staff has been hard at work, and the guest list has been finalized."

"Arriving shortly, I presume?"

Freya nodded. "I think we'd better get you back to the kitchen. I'd like you to meet the banquet coordinator."

"I look forward to it."

THE TRIP from the spaceport to the capitol building was uneventful. DiAntora rode with Freya in her private pod and kept her eyes out for anything unusual, but things in the city looked to be flowing just as they'd been the last time she was here. The sidewalks bustled with early evening pedestrian traffic while the roads overflowed with hover vehicles commuting home from work. Skyscraper lights began to replace the sun's glow as the brightest things overhead, rivaled only by the neon hovertrains as they surged through the translucent tube lines.

Up ahead, the narskill used the command modules on their hoverbikes to change the traffic lights, clearing the way for the freight trucks. To any onlookers, this was just one more special delivery heading to the capitol building. Little did they know that Freya herself was at the head of this particular convoy and that its contents were anything but the Sorellian seafood listed on the manifest.

The convoy passed two mid-city security checkpoints, which DiAntora noted were new. But the gates were raised well in advance, allowing the vehicles to pass through without stopping.

"Added security for the event?" DiAntora asked.

"For the safety of our guests," Freya replied.

"Of course."

It took less than twenty minutes to reach the complex's rear security gates, and another two minutes to back the trucks up to the underground cargo bays. By the time DiAntora had gotten out of Freya's pod and walked to the back of the vehicles, her black-clad security forces were already filing into the basement led by a contingent of narskill.

"This way," Freya said, gesturing to a secondary side entrance. The pride mother's personal bodyguards kept step with the two women as they entered the building and proceeded toward a private elevator that required a biometric scan of the lead warrior's paw and eye to activate. Once inside, Freya pressed the button for the main hall. Fifteen seconds later, the doors parted. DiAntora followed Freya and the narskill down a private hallway and through a final set of old wooden double-doors.

As DiAntora emerged into the Great Hall of Queens, a surge of emotion flooded her chest. She fought to hold back tears, but the effort was unsuccessful as at least two droplets left her eyes and seeped into her fur. She hoped Freya wouldn't notice.

Blood red drapes sailed down from the hall's upper reaches, alternating with floor to ceiling windows that shot toward the room's domed heights. White and black marbled columns with bases carved to depict Aluross's queens lined the main thoroughfare, while a lush red carpet led to and covered the elevated dais. And there, upon it, sat the throne of Aluross.

"It's been so long," DiAntora said in a whisper. "And yet, it feels like yesterday."

"Its power transcends time," Freya said, turning to look at DiAntora. "And we are pleased to have you back."

DiAntora pulled her tunic down and composed herself. "And it's good to be back."

"Come," the pride mother said. "This way. They are eager to brief you."

DiAntora followed Freya down the hallway to a small anteroom behind the dais. Inside was Caldwell, the white-haired rogue Marine Colonel who DiAntora recognized from their ship-to-ship holo negotiations. There was also someone new—an older wiry-haired woman with so many bangle bracelets on that DiAntora wondered how she held her arms up. Beside her stood one more man dressed in sophisticated armor, the likes of which DiAntora had never seen.

"DiAntora," Freya said as she commenced introductions. "I present Feared Aggressor Caldwell, Lady Willowood, and Captain Newton."

"It's Nelson," the man replied as he shook DiAntora's hand. Freya glared at the gladia.

"But Newton also works," he added.

"I'm pleased to meet you." DiAntora looked at Caldwell. "And to meet you in person, Colonel."

"The pleasure's mutual, Admiral," Caldwell replied.

DiAntora tilted her head. "You heard of my promotion?"

"Word of changes within the Neo Republic is traveling faster than a sex scandal in an election year," the colonel replied. "I would offer my congratulations, but we both know the added responsibilities you've assumed."

"Quite so," DiAntora replied. "You'll no doubt appreciate the gratitude of the Neo Republic for your willingness to help us apprehend a certain soon-arriving guest."

"And, for what it's worth, we're grateful for you sticking your neck out and making inroads for us to find sanctuary here."

"My pleasure, Colonel. Though word has it, you've been busier on Aluross than you would have liked."

"Nonsense. A couple of days down and some warm grub I think will fix the troops up just fine. Plus, any good fighting force gets lazy if they're kept out of the action for too long. And the way I see it, the Sekmit and the Gladio Umbra are creating ourselves a solid track record of mutually beneficial operations."

"Agreed."

Caldwell pulled his cigar from his mouth and looked around. "Welp, seems to me we should get this shindig wound up before someone's gun barrel rusts out."

"I have no idea what you just said, Colonel, but I believe I agree with your sentiment," DiAntora said.

"This way," Freya replied, gesturing toward a prepared table with a panoramic view of the complex's northern gardens.

Everyone took a seat as Freya called up a holo window and

projected it over the table. The pride mother reviewed the plan in detail, giving DiAntora specific instructions on where Republic, Sekmit, and Gladio Umbra forces would be set up. Using their superior Unity abilities within the Nexus, the majority of gladia mystics under Willowood's command would work to conceal Sekmit units as they neutralized So-Elku's security detail throughout the building. Meanwhile, Nelson's and Willowood's remaining squads would work with DiAntora's forces to subdue the Luma Master in the Great Hall.

"Then you will conduct So-Elku back through the city to the Sorrellian heavy freighter and rendezvous with your in-bound Republic command ship," Freya said to DiAntora.

"A sound plan," DiAntora said. "Assuming it all goes accordingly."

"Which we know it won't," Caldwell said as calmly as if he'd been commenting on the inspection of some green cadets. "The key will be how well we work together when the splick hits the spud slicer."

"Agreed." DiAntora addressed Willowood. "How confident are you in going up against these Li-Dain?"

Willowood seemed to consider her response for a moment, which was something DiAntora appreciated. "I think we all know never to underestimate the enemy. Given what I know of So-Elku, of the Li-Dain and the Li-Loré arts, and of the order's recent access to the Nexus, I believe we'll be able to keep most of our activities concealed, at least for the first phase of the operation. Subduing So-Elku himself, however, will prove the most difficult. That said, we have the element of surprise as well as greater numbers."

Willowood took a deep breath and rested her palms on the

table. The older woman wasn't through yet, and DiAntora knew better than to interrupt a sage when they were speaking.

"No matter what, this opportunity certainly constitutes our best and only chance to capture So-Elku, and so we must try. He must be stopped. The LAW poses a serious threat not only to us but the entire quadrant. So if we fail today?" She shook her head. "Well, we must not."

"Well spoken, Madame Mystic," Freya said. She'd hardly finished speaking when there was a trill from the room's main door. "Come."

It was a narskill warrior bearing a captain's sash. "Ní Freya, we have been hailed by a LAW vessel requesting docking permission."

"If you'll excuse me," Freya said as she stood. "It seems our most important guests have arrived. I'll leave you to your final preparations."

The other members stood, and then Freya exited with the captain.

Willowood looked at DiAntora with keen eyes. "Is everything okay, Admiral?"

DiAntora wondered what, if anything, the sage had seen. "Of course. Why do you ask?"

Willowood seemed like she was about to explain herself but then changed her mind at the last moment. "Nothing." The mystic sighed. "Just nerves, I suppose. That or I'm getting too old for this sort of covert work. Shall we get ready?"

DiAntora nodded, wondering how close she'd just come to being discovered. "Of course. Lead the way."

10

"This usually takes place while underway," Wobix said to Magnus as they stood over one of the trinium cargo holds inside the OHF. "But we're going for quantity today, not speed."

Like Magnus, Wobix had donned his own armored suit that protected him from the high levels of radiation now coursing through the ship. Three of the dart-like automated submersible mineral carriers stretched out along the rubberized conveyor belt. Robotic arms removed trinium cubes from the ASMCs' holds and stacked the containers in the wells on either side of the hull.

"You're saying the submersibles drive into the ship while you're moving?" Magnus asked to better understand the tech.

Wobix nodded from inside his green and black mech-like suit. "It means the ASMCs don't need to waste time slowing down, and it keeps anyone watching in deep space from getting an exact location on our operations."

"Smart. Efficient. I like it."

Wobix let his eyes linger on Magnus for a second longer before looking back at the unfolding operation. Magnus wasn't sure if that was a good look or a bad one, but he'd hoped his praise won at least a little more goodwill with the frosty narskill leader.

"So, you ever do anything like this before?" Magnus asked Wobix.

"Lure an enemy toward a freighter overloaded with trinium?" Wobix gave Magnus two elevated furry eyebrows. "Never. We've always had the Republic to fend off predators."

"Makes sense. You feel good right now?"

Wobix stared at Magnus. "Are glands always so talkative before missions?"

Magnus chuckled. "Well, some of us *glands* like to chat to stay loose just before something big goes down. Helps break up the tension, you know?"

"No. I don't."

For as much as the Sekmit and the Jujari truly embodied the old idiom of "like cats and dogs," Magnus suspected they had far more in common than either party knew, if only they were to take the time to get to know one another more. *And there's Awen rubbing off on you again*, he thought.

What am I doing to you? she asked from inside his head.

Splick. I mean—didn't realize you were, you know.

I'm just messing with you, Adonis. "Here, we can talk like this if it makes you feel better," she said over their private comms channel.

Nah, Magnus replied in his head. *I kinda like having you this close.*

Fair enough.

"Looks like you're animated, sir," TO-96 said over VNET. "We're detecting multiple pings inbound on your location."

"Roger that, 'Six," Magnus replied. "And it looks *alive*, just for the record."

"Ah, yes. That is more concise."

Magnus looked at Wobix and spoke over their inter-team channel. "Seems like they took the bait."

"Yes? We have incoming?"

Magnus nodded and then pulled Caldwell in. His face appeared beside TO-96's. "We've got company, colonel."

"How many?" Caldwell asked.

"It appears to be six vessels, sir," TO-96 replied. "Though it is hard to be entirely certain given the source noise."

"Cloaking tech?" Magnus asked.

"Indeed, sir. Though Azelon and I must caution you against jumping to conclusions. Since we are only monitoring proton displacement trails, there may be more ships flying in tight formation in order to hide their wake patterns."

"Fancy new powers, same old story." Caldwell eyed Magnus. "We're still waiting for So-Elku here, so remember—"

"Fingers off the triggers."

Caldwell smiled. "I'll be in touch."

The colonel's window blinked out, and Magnus looked to Wobix. "We'll be right here if things go sideways."

"I do not understand all your talk of things turning on their sides. You must be used to operating in low gravity."

"Something like that." Magnus activated chameleon mode and knew his suit blinked out of existence.

Wobix's eyes went wide. "Queen's claws, manservant," he exclaimed. "You vanished—but I still see you in the Unity."

"And hopefully not for long."

Wobix's eyes widened even further as Awen concealed Magnus in the unseen realm. "You are truly a powerful manservant. Wobix respects you."

"Thanks, buddy," Magnus said over comms. "Feeling's mutual. Now act busy."

Wobix nodded to the empty space, face still filled with wonder, and then headed for the bridge.

From the foredeck, Magnus and the rest of Alpha Team watched as the horizon pulsed with strange apparitions that moved like heat waves rising from the desert floor. Just as TO-96 had said, Magnus counted six anomalies and tagged them on his HUD for the rest of the team.

"What's your guess, buckethead?" Abimbola asked Magnus.

"I think they're going to stay concealed as long as possible until they get word from So-Elku on how the meeting goes. Why, what do you think?"

"I say they board and assume strategic positions around the vessels in case they need to act quickly."

"No way," Magnus said, waving the Miblimbian off. "Way too risky. Plus, they know the Sekmit are Unity users."

"They are also proud," Abimbola said. "You want to make a wager?"

"Are you guys seriously betting right now?" Awen asked.

"Hey, I want some of that action," Bliss said over comms from inside his SUBCAT. "Deal me in for 100 creds on Abimbola's plan."

"Way too dangerous," Robillard said from the other submersible. "100 on Magnus."

"You are all unbelievable." Awen's hands were on her hips.

"Rohoar would bet too," said the mwadim. "However, all he has are Abimbola's poker chips, and they are not worth nearly as much as what he claims they are to be worth, and so they are, in fact, worthless."

Bliss raised an eyebrow, presumably meant for Rohoar. "We need to work on your insult skills, buddy."

"No. This was insult enough to make virtuous men cry and feel ashamed."

"Yeah. I'm not so sure about that."

"Look at him," Rohoar said pointing at Abimbola. "Rohoar can see his eyes in the HUD and can determine that he is crying in shame."

"Pretty sure he's trying not to laugh," Bliss said.

"I'll spot you some credits," Zoll said from Bravo Team's position in the ship's stern. He was clearly stifling a chuckle of his own. "Pick your side, Fluffy."

"Magnus's," Rohoar said. "Though only out of principal. Rohoar agrees that they will board the ship and remain hidden."

"Damn," Bliss exclaimed. "You're a crazy one."

Rohoar grunted in a way that made his chops flip outward for a second and then crossed his arms. "Rohoar is not crazy. He is merely appreprensive."

"What?" Bliss asked.

Something caught Magnus's eye in the distance. "Heads up, guns up." He drew his BT16 and pointed it toward the horizon. The evening air wavered as thrusters from an incoming shuttle flared about one kilometer off the OHF's port bow. The Li-Dain's cloaking abilities needed improvement, but Magnus doubted the freighter's captain would have noticed the aberration without being told where to look.

What caught Magnus off guard, however, was the complete lack of sound. The enemy shuttle gave off no repulsor whine, no vectored thrust burn. Instead, Magnus heard the whipping of wind over the waves and the crack of distant thunder from the storm front.

The team watched as the target lock indicators in their HUDs followed the anomalies across the horizon and toward the OHF's stern. The enemy vessels, whatever class they were, came within 500 meters of the freighter, held the position for several seconds, and then backed away.

"Son of a bitch, Bimby," Magnus said.

"I am pretty sure that is an amphibious deployment," Abimbola replied.

"Well they're not on the boat yet."

"Give it time, buckethead."

Alpha Team moved to the back of the ship, where Bravo Team was standing guard.

"I'm making out bodies in the water," Awen said.

"Me too," Wish added.

"So they're hanging out in the rollers until they get orders," Magnus said. "Pay up, Bimby."

"Not so fast, Adonis," Awen said, pointing out to sea. "They're swimming in."

"Mysticsdammit." Magnus sighed and then brought up the inter-team channel. "Everyone in position. Looks like we're in for an early boarding, and I'm out 100 credits."

By the time the first Li-Dain slipped over the transom, Magnus was standing next to Wobix on the bridge overlook on the ship's starboard side. The rest of Alpha Team was spread around the ship's bow tower while Zoll and Bravo Team took up defensive positions along the stern. As for Awen and Wish, the two teams' mystics, Magnus had ordered them to stay concealed; without their protective Unity shielding, both now and in the event of combat, Magnus worried this might be a lopsided fight, and not in the gladia's favor.

"Remember to act natural," Magnus said to Wobix as the catman looked to the horizon.

"Why is this something I need to remember? I don't even know how to act anti-natural."

"Just act like you don't see the enemy."

"But that is not natural."

"I don't think he understands the nuances of your speech, sir," TO-96 said.

Magnus laughed. "Copy that, 'Six. Mind giving him some lessons later?"

"It would be my pleasure, sir."

Magnus felt his gut tighten as the first group of LAW warriors approached Bravo Team's position at the stern. "Nice and easy," Magnus said in a calm tone.

"We're really going to let them walk on by like this, sir?" Rix asked from near Zoll's location.

"We are," Zoll replied. "Magnus, we've got ten tangos aboard so far."

"Copy." Magnus watched as ten target tags popped up on his HUD, care of Wish. He raised his weapon and sighted in on the lead enemy.

"And it looks like another twenty in the water, at least," Bliss said from his SUBCAT. "Telwin's saying there might be more, but they're too heavily concealed."

"He's right," Awen said in a tight voice. "They're impossible to see further out. Working hard to keep themselves hidden."

"But we're working harder, right?" Magnus said.

She grunted. "Something like that."

The good news was that the Li-Dain walked right past Bravo Team's position. The bad news was that Granther Company's mystics were tagging more and more Li-Dain every second. The enemy spread out along the outer decks like a virus and infected the inner decks. Magnus knew it wouldn't be long before they contaminated the heart of the beast and flooded the bridge.

"What is this?" Dutch said. "A family reunion?"

"Nobody make a move," Magnus said again for good measure. "Wobix, please remind your narskill to—"

"Act anti-natural," the Sekmit warrior interjected. "I already have."

Magnus gave a half smile. "Good."

The narskill were scattered around the ship, posing as a regular security detail. Of course, the Li-Dain didn't know that Wobix's particular force was composed of some of Aluross's most fierce warriors. Nor did they know that an OHF normally staffed a quarter of the security that Wobix had brought. And nor did they know that regular security guards didn't wear combat mech armor, only radiation shield suits. But why should they? No one but a Sekmit had ever been allowed on an OHF before. So as far as the Li-Dain were concerned, this was business as usual.

"I want to strike them down," Wobix said in a whisper.

"I know you do, Bixy." Magnus tracked two Li-Dain moving up the starboard stairwell less than eight meters from his position. "I promise you'll get your chance." Three seconds later, the two Li-Dain were topside and moving toward Magnus, Wobix, and Awen.

The starboard bridge door was a meter and a half off Magnus's right shoulder.

"I've got two on the port side, top deck," Haze said from the other side of the bridge.

Magnus turned his helmet and saw the target tags superimposed on his HUD. "Leave them be."

"Roger."

Everything in Magnus screamed at him to open fire. Memories of encountering the diaper babies in Governor Littleton's mansion flashed in Magnus's head. He knew what the Li-Dain could do and how much destruction they'd rain down when confronted. Still, Granther Company had the element of surprise—*at least for the time being*, he thought.

And we'll keep it for as long as we can, Awen said.

Copy that. Her words weren't much, but he tried to take them to heart. His pessimism only increased as more Li-Dain climbed over the stern.

"Count is up to thirty-eight," Zoll whispered.

Splick.

It was time to call the colonel.

"Go for Caldwell," the older man said in the HUD frame.

"We've got thirty-eight tangos on board," Magnus said.

The look on Caldwell's face said the same thing Magnus was thinking, but neither vocalized it. *Damn.*

"Any sign of So-Elku?"

"His shuttle just landed."

Magnus squinted at Caldwell. "You mean—"

"Meeting won't start for another twenty minutes at least."

"You've gotta be splicking me."

"Sorry, son," Caldwell said while he removed his cigar. "Looks like yer gonna have to cuddle up between your Aunt Martha's milk-shake mountains and get comfortable. Do not make a move until I give the order—I don't care how awkward it is. That clear?"

"Crystal." Magnus looked at Wobix. "And if they start attacking the Sekmit?"

Caldwell perched the cigar under his mustache again. "Let's hope that's a decision you don't have to make."

"Splick, sir."

"Splick indeed. Caldwell out."

Magnus kept his weapon trained on the two closest Li-Dain who were stacked on the bridge door. Their golden robes dripped with salt water, leaving dark stains on the teak deck. But Wobix ignored the enemy, choosing instead to keep his eyes fixed on the horizon. Magnus knew this had to be hard for the narskill—hell, it was hard for Magnus and it wasn't even his ship. Sure, it took courage to run headlong into a firefight, but it took nerves of steel to keep from firing on the enemy when they were right under your nose.

The security pad beside the bridge door beeped as a series of numbers were entered by an invisible hand. A second later, a red Access Denied badge appeared.

"Damn diaper babies are trying to enter access codes," Haze said from the opposite door.

"Same over here," Magnus said. "Listen, if we can't take them without risking the op in the capital, they can't take the ship without risking whatever So-Elku has planned too."

"You sure?" Awen said.

"Pretty sure." Magnus took a breath. "Wobix, go ahead and act like you notice the sounds. But don't engage."

"Finally," Wobix said. He turned and innocently examined the access pad. The two Li-Dain backed away from the door, giving the narskill plenty of room. It was just as Magnus suspected. They weren't willing to hijack the ship—not yet.

"We're at a standoff," Magnus said to the teams. "Everyone sit tight, and don't do anything stupid. But let's keep the bridge secure."

"I will see to it," Wobix said. Then he leaned his back against the bridge door, crossed his arms, and started whistling.

11

"How many checkpoints is this?" So-Elku said, looking up from his data pad. He rode in the back of a finely appointed luxury hovercar provided by ní Freya's tribe. The black and tan leather was soft, and everything about the vehicle said it was brand new—that, or hardly used.

"This is the third one, my master," Lor said. "Standard Sekmit procedure, based on what we know." He sat beside Trinklyn, head of foreign affairs, Brodin, the communications minister, and General Rink-Ba, Li-Dain Commandant. The only other significant members of So-Elku's inner circle not present were Admiral Porampus, who remained in orbit, and Yon-Mornick, the LAW's Trade Minister who rode in the next vehicle back.

"Seems a little much, doesn't it?" So-Elku asked.

"We would do the same," Rink-Ba said. "Were the roles reversed."

So-Elku looked out the window as two Sekmit security guards

passed along the vehicle with handheld scanners. Or was it paw-held scanners for them? "I suppose we would. How many more?"

"Our orbital scans show two more, sir," Lor said.

"Two?" So-Elku was tiring of all the delays. And yet, by day's end, he would have control of Aluross, so what did it matter how slow their approach to the capitol building was? He craned his neck behind him to look at the rest of the vehicles in their group. Sekmit inspectors were going over them too, asking for credentials and scanning cavities. His cohort was forty persons in all—a size that suggested ample strength but not overwhelming dominance.

There was another reason for his desire to get out of the cramped vehicle and away from his staff.

Moldark.

Images of Nants's possessed face haunted So-Elku. The encounter in the bathhouse had rattled him more than he cared to admit. How the dark lord was able to get close to So-Elku was unnerving the Luma Master. What was worse was just how close Moldark had come to ending his life.

All will be well, So-Elku tried telling himself. But he questioned the legitimacy of his own counsel. His eyes flicked between the other occupants of the vehicle as he wondered which of them might be the next to host Moldark and attempt an assassination.

Stop this, Teerbrin, he told himself. But even the sound of his first name had been tainted by the way Nants had said it.*No, by the way* Moldark *had said it.*

Pull yourself together, So-Elku said inwardly. He needed to stay focused—he couldn't afford any distractions. Not now. Plus, unlike the bathhouse, which had been mostly unguarded, at least in the ways that could have kept out a Unity intruder, his presence here on

Aluross was well covered by sentries both in the vehicles and in orbit. There was nothing to worry about.

The sun had set, and the city's lights were growing brighter by the minute. So-Elku took a moment to study the strange architecture, noting how it seemed to bridge the gap between ancient Sekmit tradition on the one hand and more modern stylings on the other. Even the lighted signs and street lamps were a mix of old and new. "Quaint," he said to himself, noting just how nice it would be to add the feline world to the LAW's portfolio.

"What's that?" Trinklyn asked.

So-Elku gestured toward the city outside the hovercar. "It's quaint, don't you think?"

The foreign affairs minister nodded. Trinklyn was, without question, the LAW's leading authority on the Sekmit, having majored in the culture and history in observances. But between Aluross's tight connection with the Galactic Republic coupled with the fact that they remained to themselves as a species, Trinklyn's major was of little use to anyone—until now. The fact that she had ventured into other fields of study certainly helped broaden her usefulness, making her a natural choice for the LAW's foreign affairs minister. But it was her knowledge of the Sekmit that made her genuinely indispensable for this mission, even if it meant putting up with some of her more eccentric aspects.

The glow of neon signs and street lamps reflected off Trinklyn's eyes. "They have a long history."

"Which makes today even more historic, don't you think?" So-Elku said.

The woman seemed hesitant.

So-Elku scowled at her. "What is it?"

Still, Trinklyn seemed caught between whether or not she

should speak. And after their last few meetings, she was right to. Her resistance to many of So-Elku's ideas and plans was wearing on him to the point that he was beginning to second guess her appointment to his counsel. *Those damn eccentricities*, he thought to himself again. "Out with it," So-Elku demanded. "Speak your mind."

"We are taking a large risk on this endeavor, my master. The Sekmit are notoriously slow movers when it comes to trade negotiations, as Yon-Mornick can attest. Begging General Rink-Ba's pardon, I think it premature to have the attack force so eager to deploy. Perhaps hold them back a little farther until we know for certain what the Sekmit intend to do with our offer."

Rink-Ba seemed to bristle at this, but So-Elku raised a hand at the general. The Luma Master would take the objection head-on himself. After all, the plan was his, not Rink-Ba's, so he knew that Trinklyn was only targeting the general because she was too weak to confront So-Elku to his face.

"So the Sekmit decide to take a few weeks to consider our proposal," So-Elku said. "If they accept, then we all win. But if they come back to us, after we're long gone, and say no?"

"You've explained your reasoning before," Trinklyn said. "It's just that—"

"That you don't like the use of force, now that we're here, is that it?"

The foreign affairs minister didn't reply. But she didn't need to. Non-violent action was the Luma way, and So-Elku had fought it for years. He had even fought it in himself. He'd been raised on Worru by parents who taught him to memorize the ancient texts long before he was tested on them during observances. He knew the Luma tenants. *Better than anyone*, he thought. *And where have they gotten us?* "Tell me, minister, is the galaxy any more united than it was before?"

Trinklyn furrowed her brow. "I'm not sure I—"

"In the last 1,000 years, has our Order succeeded in fostering peace in the galaxy?"

"We've made strides in saving countless worlds, my master."

"Strides, yes." So-Elku stroked his beard. "And yet, I ask again, have we created lasting peace? Do those who rule themselves, as well as those who were ruled by the Republic, exhibit evidence of peace?"

It was several seconds before Trinklyn answered. "No," she said.

"No," So-Elku repeated as he folded his hands and placed them in his lap. "It is more broken than ever, its pieces scattered across the stars. And all because those who *were* strong enough to stop it decided not to. And why?" He leaned forward. "Because it would have required something our predecessor was too weak to demonstrate."

"And what is that?" Trinklyn asked.

"Power." So-Elku dropped a fist into his open palm. "True power."

A chime sounded on General Rink-Ba's data pad. He touched the screen, and a holo display appeared over the tablet.

"General, sir," said a Li-Dain commander dressed in gold. "Cadres one through three are onboard the target freighter now. Four through eight are standing by for deployment. The rest of first battalion is providing overwatch, and their comms are being jammed."

"You're ahead of schedule," Rink-Ba said.

"Things went better than expected."

"And your presence is still undetected?"

The commander nodded. "Affirmative."

"Excellent. What about second and third battalions?"

"They are in place and awaiting your signal, General."

Trinklyn looked at So-Elku. "Second and third battalions? I wasn't aware that we brought—"

So-Elku waved her off. "No one was."

Trinklyn worked her jaw and took a deep breath before sitting back in her seat. "Begging your pardon, sir, but if I'm going to be head of foreign affairs, I think it important that I know—"

"Only what you need to know, minister." So-Elku glared at her until the woman was forced to look away.

"Order all units to prepare for phase two," Rink-Ba said to his commander.

"Yes, general."

Rink-Ba closed the transmission.

"We will not be the weak ones this time," So-Elku said to the vehicle's passengers. "We will finally do what all those before us never could. And you"—So-Elku leaned forward and bent his head to catch Trinklyn's eye—"are either with us or against us. Is there a problem, minister?"

She shook her head. "No, my master."

"Good. Anyone else?"

Ní Freya sat upon her elevated tribal throne at the far end of the royal hall while a phalanx of no less than fifty armed warriors lined either side of a red carpet that stretched the room's length. The only thing she wore was a semi-translucent red shawl that draped from her shoulders and cascaded down her lithe body to her feet. For a fleeting second, So-Elku wondered if the lack of clothing was as salacious to the Sekmit as it would have been to more human species.

So-Elku was also surprised to see so many guards, given that the Sekmit had invited him to the negotiating table. Then again, they were a warrior race, and he'd learned long ago not to take such displays of strength personally. If anything, he was the one in the dominant position. *Finally*. It was only a matter of time before the Sekmit understood that too.

"Wait until she waves you forward," Trinklyn said from behind him. "If she stands to meet you, raise your chin. It's a sign of honor."

So-Elku gave her the slightest of nods but kept his eyes pointed straight ahead. Someone proclaimed something in the Sekmit's native tongue and then announced the LAW visitors' arrival in broken galactic common. So-Elku couldn't see the speaker but heard the echo of his or her voice ringing throughout the hall.

A beat later, Freya raised a paw and motioned So-Elku forward.

"Here we go," Trinklyn said.

So-Elku led the way down the carpet, aware that all the Sekmit warriors were watching him. They held staves in one paw and rested the other on bows slung over their shoulders. Given the fact that these warriors were Unity users of some level, So-Elku guessed the weapons were mystically powered and, most likely, were quite deadly. The Luma frowned upon the Unity's use for violence—at least according to the old ways. Today, however, So-Elku would be sure to inquire about the Sekmit's technology should this meeting end favorably. Then again, even if it didn't end well, he would still find a way to acquire the weapons' schematics. Like the city itself, the power bows and staves were a quaint mix of things both old and new.

As So-Elku neared the dais, Freya stood. As Trinklyn had instructed him, the Luma Master raised his chin and kept his eyes fixed on the pride mother. She did the same and then descended the stairs to stand before him. While So-Elku didn't find the Sekmit attractive, he had to admit that the scantily clad female was somehow alluring—perhaps even disarming.

"Master So-Elku of the Luma, welcome to Aluross," she said in an assertive voice.

"Thank you for the invitation," So-Elku replied. "The honor to meet you is made even more delightful by doing so on your beautiful homeworld."

Freya tilted her head by maybe a centimeter. "What have you seen of our planet that is beautiful?"

So-Elku hesitated for less than a second, smoothing his surprise with a fluid hand motion and a slow blink of his eyes. "Why, our journey from the spaceport to here, of course."

"Either you are attempting to flatter me, or you need to get out more. Both are sorry conditions."

So-Elku raised an eyebrow. He was not used to such frankness. Trinklyn had warned him before, but he was not prepared. Rather than try to defend himself, however, he thought it best to press on. "In any event, I must say that I was very pleased to receive your request for a meeting."

"Why *must* you say it?"

Again, So-Elku felt caught off guard but recovered even more quickly than the first time. "Because I wish to be candid with you and express the sincere appreciation I feel toward this potentially momentous occasion."

Freya's facial features relaxed by a degree. She was a study in poise and precision, and not someone he wanted to cross. At least, not to her face. Everything the LAW had set up behind the scenes was, by its very nature, a grand double-cross. As So-Elku studied her micro-expressions, he wondered—*does she suspect us?*

When Freya spoke next, her voice felt more relaxed, as if the initial frost of their first minor exchange had warmed under the sun's morning rays. "I imagine you and your entourage must be hungry or thirsty. May I interest you in something to nourish you?"

Again, Trinklyn had warned So-Elku against declining Freya's hospitality, noting its offensive nature. His advisor's words came back to him now, along with an unexpected emotion: the shame of acting two-faced toward her. On the one hand, he valued Trinklyn's counsel about the Sekmit; on the other, he felt her skepticism of the operation was repugnant and found himself questioning her loyalties. But intergalactic negotiations were morally ambiguous by nature, so why should he be surprised that such tensions wouldn't exist in his own staff?

No. What bothered So-Elku, he realized, was that he was troubled by this matter with Trinklyn at all. It was a distraction. *She* was a distraction. And So-Elku could not support it. He needed his inner circle to be entirely for him or not at all. And so he determined he would deal with her when this was over. Her usefulness to him at the moment, after all, was too important to dismiss prematurely.

"We would be delighted by some refreshments," So-Elku said with a quick raise of his chin.

"This way," Freya replied as she turned toward the dais and motioned with a paw.

So-Elku and his entourage followed her to a small receiving hall adjacent to the throne room. It contained two dozen standing tables adorned with clear vases of exotic flowers. Appetizers and drinks lined several lower tables in the room's middle. Comfortable looking pieces of furniture and short-legged tables sat in clusters on one side of the room while the other side opened to a veranda that welcomed the smells and sounds of the night. So-Elku thought he smelled the scent of rain on the breeze—a storm perhaps. *How fitting.*

"Your people may help themselves," Freya said as she walked between the tables and continued across the room.

So-Elku passed the instruction on to his senior staff and then watched his retinue of forty file into the reception hall. They accepted the offerings with smiles and hushed comments to one another. As So-Elku observed them, he wondered which of them might be a spy—who might be possessed by Moldark. The black eyes, the foul soul. Who might be a confidant one moment only to turn on him the next.

"My master?" Trinklyn's voice summoned So-Elku back from the daydream. "Is everything all right?"

"Yes, of course."

Trinklyn nodded toward Freya, who was headed across the lounge area toward a set of wooden double doors. "I said, you need to follow her."

So-Elku looked after the Sekmit leader and thanked Trinklyn.

But the woman caught him by the elbow and lowered her voice. "If she invites you to her table, you will be allowed to summon four of your advisors. And be careful: the drink she's going to offer you is very strong."

So-Elku wondered if the woman's eyes might suddenly turn black. But he shook the notion from his head, thanked Trinklyn again, and then stepped away to follow Freya.

The Sekmit leader slowed in front of the doors and accepted two narrow wine glasses from an attendant, then she offered one to

So-Elku. "Kyreethsha?" she asked as she held up the glass. When So-Elku hesitated, Freya raised it a little higher. "The Sekmit cup of welcome. Do not be afraid."

So-Elku accepted the flute and examined the clear pinkish fluid. Even before putting it to his nose, he smelled lavender and some sort of sweet citrus fruit. He also smelled alcohol and wondered how much might be too much for him to consume.

But that wasn't his only reason for making a quick examination of the fluid in the Unity. If it contained poison, he would be ready to take Freya's life and activate the Li-Dain.

"To the future." Freya raised her glass.

"To the future," So-Elku replied when he determined the drink was clean, and then the two of them sipped. So-Elku found it rather delightful. He also noticed the near-immediate effects of the shockingly potent cocktail.

"Most humans find it too strong for their liking," Freya said.

So-Elku could have sworn he saw a satisfied glint in her eye as he blinked to clear his vision. "It's more *flavorful* than I would have expected."

She narrowed her eyes as if deciding whether or not to accept the statement. "It is said that one sip of kyreethsha reveals the truth of a person's words."

Had So-Elku not been reeling from the strong drink, he might have faltered then. As it was, however, he managed to give only an unsure half-smile.

Freya grinned and let out a purr-like laugh. "*Flavorful.* I'll have to remember that one. Come." She turned on her heel, which caused her shawl to billow in her wake, and headed for ornate doors.

Two attendants opened the entrance to reveal a round dinner table prepared for ten. While the table boasted elaborate place settings of fine silverware and multicolored ceramic plates, it was devoid of any tall centerpieces that might keep the participants from seeing one another's faces. Floor to ceiling windows gave the room a spectacular view of a grand lower garden, as well as to the Sekmit sentries who patrolled the grounds. The scene's many paths and pools were lit by lights that fought to keep the darkness at bay.

"It would be my pleasure to host you and four of your advisors for dinner, Master Luma," Freya said.

"And I am honored by your invitation. Thank you." Before the words were even out of his mouth, So-Elku slipped into his second sight to examine the immediate vicinity. Two side doors on either side of the dining room led to service hallways—one that opened to a sizable kitchen bustling with food service staff, the other to a maintenance corridor and laundry. Several side rooms branched off from the main hallways, but they were empty of occupants. So-Elku wasn't sure what he was searching for exactly—a concealed group of elite Sekmit warriors perhaps—but that seemed foolish given how many guards were already on hand. Nothing seemed out of place. Everywhere he looked, Sekmit busied themselves with the various duties of hosting a state dinner.

Freya summoned one of the two attendants at the door. "Have the Luma Master's staff brought in." She looked at So-Elku with an upturned paw as if expecting a gift of some sort.

"The names are Lor, Yon-Mornick, Rink-Ba, and Trinklyn," So-Elku said—half the list spoken to Freya, half spoken to the attendant. He almost invited Brodin, his communications minister, instead of Trinklyn. But the foreign affairs minister had already proven too invaluable. He might need her in these deliberations, and Brodin could always be debriefed later.

The servant raised his chin and then turned out of the room with his tail whipping through the air after him.

"Please," Freya said, indicating one of the chairs. "Be seated."

For a moment, So-Elku wondered if this was some sort of Sekmitian test. Would the warrior-leader judge him according to the seat he chose? But then So-Elku noticed nameplates at each position and spied his at the setting closest to the double doors. Meanwhile, Freya walked around the table with her long shawl trailing behind her. The remaining attendant followed Freya and pulled out the chair closest to the glass windows.

A third attendant appeared from one of the side doors and pulled So-Elku's chair out, inviting him to sit. The Luma Master thanked the servant and then made himself comfortable. He took another sip of the kysreethsha but was quick to try and offset the drink's inhibitive side effects with some subtle resistance in the Unity. If Trinklyn hadn't warmed him, he would have assumed the pride mother was attempting to intoxicate him on purpose.

So-Elku placed his glass on the table and studied Freya. Her incredible stillness betrayed either a supreme self-satisfaction, in which she felt no need to fill the silence with small talk as other world leaders might, or an immense amount of self-discipline so as not to begin important deliberations until the rest of her advisors were present. If So-Elku were a lesser man, he might have balked at the deafening stillness that pervaded the room. Instead, however, he matched her motionless form and piercing gaze.

Two can play this game, he said to himself, making sure to conceal his thoughts in the Unity.

Neither person looked away until the sound of footsteps announced the rest of the dinner party. So-Elku's four advisors entered the dining room, followed by four of Freya's staff. Attendants pulled out chairs and offered to top off everyone's drinks. Nodding their appreciation, the humans unfolded napkins and placed them in their laps while the Sekmit withdrew long metal files and began sharpening their nails.

Freya looked up after a long pull of her rasp. "Shall we begin?"

12

"HATE TO BOTHER YOU, COLONEL," Magnus said over comms. "But we could use some good news right about now."

"Everyone's just about to sit down to dinner," Caldwell replied. "Willowood says So-Elku needs to take a few more sips of his cocktail."

"Can't you tell him to hurry it up any?"

Caldwell smiled. "Why? Aunt Martha's twin chest pillows giving you the willies?"

Magnus gave a soft chuckle and then studied the situation unfolding in front of him. "Wobix and his guards are keeping tight to the bridge access doors, but we've got a handful of tangos who seem intent on busting through the windowplex any second."

"And the rest?"

"They're scattered throughout the ship. Engineering, drive core, navigation, and sensors array hubs. Damn diaper babies have this place locked down cold."

"Sirs," TO-96 interjected. "If I may."

"Whaddya got, Ballsy," Caldwell said.

"It appears that several more cloaked vessels are entering Aluross's atmosphere above Granther Company's current location."

"How many is several?" Magnus asked the bot.

"Fifteen to twenty, sir. However, please be advised those numbers are guesses."

"Mystics," Zoll said. "How many damn ships do they need to take a single freighter?"

That's when the severity of the situation dawned on Magnus. "This isn't a raid. It's an invasion."

"Rohoar does not understand what the enemy has to gain by congregating over a single ship," the Jujari said.

"Neither do I, Fluffy," Magnus said. "Which is why I have a bad feeling about this."

"Rohoar also has bad feelings inside of his lower intestines. Perhaps also more bad feelings applying pressure around his chest. He wishes to be rid of the bad feelings quickly."

"Don't we all." Magnus focused on the colonel's screen. "Please tell Willowood I'm not sure how much longer we can keep this box of thermal detonators from going nova. Get that man good and drunk, cause if my gladias don't pick a fight soon, the narskill sure as hell will."

Willowood looked at Piper, who sat on a plush leather couch, holding her knees to her chest. The child wore her Novian power suit with some additional slender pieces of plate armor added as *incidental protection*, as Awen liked to call it. Willowood's granddaughter looked so peaceful with her eyes closed—*so the reflection of your mother*, Willowood thought. But this was no time for sentiment. They were in the middle of an operation that would stem the growth of the LAW's tyranny if successful.

After conversing with Caldwell, Willowood sat beside Piper and stroked her soft blonde hair. "How is everything, my child?"

"Good, Nana," Piper said, eyes still closed tight. "I'm keeping everyone hidden, just like you said."

"Wonderful. Thank you. And you're feeling?"

"Maybe a little thirsty?"

"Of course." Willowood waved one of the Sekmit attendants over.

"Can I have more of their orange drink?" Piper asked. "It's super yummy."

The attendant raised his chin at Willowood and then moved toward the bar lining a far wall.

The command team was set up inside a large meeting room one level above Freya's formal reception hall and private dining room. Mobile workstations lay across tables and end tables, while senior members of Nelson's Hedgebore Company and Willowood's Paladia Company hovered over the holo displays, coordinating unit movement throughout the building. Not only that, but they were in touch with Captain Forbes's Taursar Company, who were stationed at all the main hovertrain entrances to the mines, as well as Ricio's Fang Company, who was patrolling in orbit. If Caldwell couldn't be in the *Spire* to oversee this op, Azelon had made sure this mobile command center was the next best thing.

"Felicity," Caldwell said over Willowood's shoulder. "A moment?"

Willowood nodded but spoke to Piper. "I'll be right back. Keep it up, okay?"

"Copy hardly, Nana," Piper said in a broken attempt at military comm-speak.

Willowood stroked her hair one more time and then rose to follow Caldwell to a corner of the room. "Something come up?"

"Magnus is asking to accelerate the timeline," Caldwell said. "He's worried things are going to fall apart on the ship."

Willowood crossed her arms. "I'm not sure we can make him drink any faster. He already seems to think that Freya is intentionally trying to intoxicate him as it is."

"How much more does he need?"

Willowood sighed. "Maybe three more sips? It depends on how hard he's resisting the sedative."

Caldwell gave Willowood a mischievous look. "Think I've got something."

"Careful, William," she said, placing a hand on his arm. "If he even suspects for a moment—"

"I know." Caldwell patted her hand. "We're gonna get this son of a bitch."

So-Elku eyed the still-moving appetizer of Sorellian tarantula squid while doing his very best to hide his abject disgust. The Sekmit ate the seafood raw, which meant the already pungent taste lingered even longer than it did when it was cooked. This was due to the fact that the creature excreted a potent solution of acid as a self-defense mechanism while sliding down the throat. The Sekmit loved it, but So-Elku found it repulsive. He looked for anything to wash the foul flavor away, but there was nothing besides the kyreethsha.

"Pardon me," So-Elku said while raising a hand toward one of the attendants. He felt Freya's eyes settle on him, but it didn't matter. If he didn't get the rancid taste off his tongue, he was going to vomit.

"What are you doing?" Trinklyn asked in a forced whisper.

"I need something else to drink," So-Elku said out of the corner of his mouth.

"It's an insult, my master."

"I don't care."

Trinklyn's next words came in a hurried jumble that raced against the approaching attendant. "It suggests that you feel their hospitality lacking and assumes that anything else they present, including trade proposals, will be refused."

"How may I be of service?" the attendant purred to So-Elku, bending down.

The Luma Master worked his jaw, trying his best to ignore the rising bile in his throat. He could feel Freya studying him, and he knew Trinklyn would never let him hear the last of this if he made such a glaring social misstep. But anything was better than the raw squid—*even if it means ordering the attack prematurely?* he thought. No, he wouldn't go that far.

"May I be so bold as to order another round of kyreethsha for the table?" So-Elku said. He reached for his glass and then gave Freya a warm smile. "A toast, in good faith, to the first of many meetings between our people." So-Elku almost choked on his last words, doing his best to keep the violent seafood at bay. But as the strong drink overpowered the taste of raw tarantula squid, he felt his gastrointestinal anxiety melt away—aided in part by the extra-long draft of the liquor. Everyone else sipped as well, including Freya, who seemed to offer a genuine smile. Whether the merry smirk came at So-Elku's expense, because the pride mother surely knew how repulsive the tarantula squid tasted to humans, or at So-Elku's pleasure for showing a sign of goodwill, the Luma Master couldn't be sure. But he'd successfully routed the Sorellian terror, and that was its own victory.

"And to that end," Freya said, still holding her flute aloft. "I would like to propose that the first year of *exclusive* trade with the LAW, should final negotiations be to our mutual liking, come with a thirty-eight percent savings to our guests."

Everything up until this point had suggested that the night was going to be a long one, fraught with point and counterpoint exchanges that would demand So-Elku's constant attention. But this? This had taken him completely by surprise. The quadrant's largest trinium mine, at sixty percent for the first year? This meant he could grow his empire as he'd dreamed. It would forge the way for negotiations with hundreds of worlds. This was more than he could have hoped for, presuming it was true, of course. But he had no reason to doubt the Sekmit's words. They were, after all, a notoriously blunt species. That, and Freya's statement, was witnessed by the heads of both councils. Then again, So-Elku was feeling a bit light-headed. Maybe this whole thing was too good to be true.

"We are honored by your proposition." Then So-Elku raised his glass high. "Here is to a long and mutually prosperous relationship."

"Here here," everyone said and toasted one another.

So-Elku touched the glass to his lips and took another long sip, this time savoring the liquid just as he did his good fortune. For the briefest moment, he felt happy. The memory of Moldark's attack faded from his mind, as did the image of Nants's headless corpse floating in the water. The kyreethsha also pushed away other memories—those of the attack on Capriana Prime, of the Luma resistance and the meddling rebels led by the treacherous Willowood and her protege Awen. He even started to forget about the child, Piper, who he'd come so close to pulling into his fold. Yet even as those memories faded, dulled by the effects of the Sekmit drink and the euphoria of the initial trade proposal, So-Elku found himself sifting them as they slipped through his fingers, searching for ingots of gold within the disappearing sand. He felt something there, hidden in the granules. As more and more sand sifted through his fingers, the object's form took shape, until finally, So-Elku's mind settled on something that startled him. It was more surprising than Freya's initial summons, more remarkable than her offer of thirty-eight percent. In the hands of his mind, now empty of sand, So-Elku could see a person. A single tiny person.

He pulled his kyreethsha flute away from his lips and stared at it. "Piper." Within the Unity, So-Elku searched the immediate area once again, looking down the hallways and side rooms and into the kitchen. Everything seemed normal. But that was just it: where there should have been extra staff and supplies for hosting forty guests for a state dinner, there was *nothing*. As if—*as if what is there is being concealed*.

In a flash, So-Elku focused on the reception hall with its standing tables and finger foods. The rest of his entourage was gone. Even the throne room was empty.

So-Elku returned to his body and looked across the table at

Freya. Her eyes were not concerned, nor were they curious. Instead, they were cold and calculating.

This wasn't a trade negotiation. This was a trap.

"All teams, move in," Caldwell yelled over comms. "Magnus, you're up!"

13

"Let's light 'em up," Magnus said over the joint task force comms channel. Wobix purred in reply, and several other gladia spoke the Dominate Liberate mantra into their helmets. It was go time.

Magnus had been holding a bead on the nearest Li-Dain warrior for the last several minutes. Were it not for the servo assist in his MANTA's suit, his arms would have been shaking too wildly to take the shot. Instead, his TB16 remained steady, lined up with the enemy's unprotected head. Magnus squeezed the trigger and fired a single 16mm round.

Since the Li-Dain weren't expecting a surprise counterattack, they failed to shield themselves in any significant way—a critical mistake. As a result, Magnus's torpedo bolt penetrated a fragile Unity film—most likely meant to conceal noise than protect against a high-powered kinetic round fired two meters away—and punctured the Li-Dain's temple. A microsecond later and the variable warhead, set to omnidirectional expansion, exploded and covered the bridge's exterior windows with blood.

Before the body hit the deck, Wobix spun away from the bridge door that he'd been leaning on for the better part of ten minutes, grabbed his closest target's head with one paw, and then drove the man face-first into the bulkhead. Magnus heard the victim's forehead cave in as the Sekmit repeated the action twice more. As soon as Wobix retracted his claws, the Li-Dain's body fell away from the Sekmit's paw and crumpled in a heap on the ground.

But Wobix was far from finished. He unslung the Thørzin power bow from his shoulder, extended the grip in one hand, and pulled back a shimmering strand of light in the other. The bow's segmented pieces, held together by a glowing blue light, seemed to generate an electrical arrow that began at the grip and raced back to the translucent string. When Wobix released the projectile, it streaked through the bridge windows without cracking a single one and intercepted a Li-Dain on the far side observation balcony. The enemy's body flew backward, slammed into the railing, and flipped over the side. If the broken back hadn't killed him, the blackened hole in his chest certainly did.

"I need to get myself one of those," Magnus said.

"Stick to your blasters, manservant," Wobix said. "You're not strong enough to bend this bow."

Magnus would have contested the accusation were it not for two Li-Dain spinning toward Wobix's position from opposite sides.

"Go right," Magnus said, hoping the Sekmit would catch his meaning. Meanwhile, Magnus turned left and fired another 16mm bolt at the Li-Dain approaching from the stern just as Wobix drew and released one of his electrical arrows at the Li-Dain toward the bow. Again, both enemies were unprotected and fell to their deaths. Magnus's victim spun sideways before the warhead embedded in his chest expanded violently, while Wobix's target toppled over the bridge railing and landed on the foredeck.

"Nice shooting," Magnus said.

"They go down too easy," Wobix replied.

"Yeah, but that won't last long."

As if emphasizing his point, Abimbola's voice broke over comms. "A little help here, someone?" It was the first time Magnus had ever heard the Miblimbian giant sound stressed.

Abimbola crouched below the bridge on the main foredeck, taking cover behind an anchor housing near the bow. His TB16 fired four torpedo bolts every second in a steady drum-like rhythm as the enemy advanced on his position. But instead of killing the enemy, the torpedoes detonated against an invisible shield, showering the foredeck with fire.

The uncloaked Li-Dain, undeterred, returned fire. Apparently, the diaper babies couldn't be both cloaked and shielded at the same time, at least not to any degree of success. Bright streams of yellow energy burst from the warrior's hands and streaked toward Abimbola. And wherever the Unity power met a torpedo bolt, the resulting explosion bathed the ship in orange and white light. The concussive sound of incarnating ordnance shook the ship's decking and traveled up through Magnus's feet.

Before Magnus could shoot, Wobix sent an electrical arrow atop of the Li-Dain's head. But the effort was only partially successful, reducing the size and shape of the enemy's personal shield but not penetrating it. For the moment, the fire on Abimbola's position stopped as the Li-Dain turned and looked up at Wobix.

"Well don't stop now," Magnus yelled at the Sekmit captain and then aimed his weapon down at the enemy. Together, they fired on the golden-robed Li-Dain, raining down electrical arrows and torpedo bolts in quick succession. Abimbola joined the volley and drilled the enemy in the back.

The volume of firepower was too much for the enemy. His shield collapsed, and his body vaporized under the three withering streams of weapons fire.

"Thanks for the help, buckethead," Abimbola said from below.

"It'll cost you," Magnus replied.

"We'll see about that."

"Four down," Wobix said to Magnus.

"And a splickton more to go," he replied.

"I do not know this measurement of splickton," Wobix said as he turned toward the sound of footsteps coming up the interior stairwell.

"I'll let you know when we reach it." Magnus fired at the head of the emerging Li-Dain. But before the bolt hit its target, the Luma warrior leapt five meters into the air and somersaulted overhead. Magnus tracked the robed figure until his arms and head bound up, forcing him to pivot. The Li-Dain landed behind Magnus and Wobix. Then, with glowing hands, he reached forward, grabbed the defender's weapons, and yanked them past his sides.

Magnus knew better than to let go of his firearm—years of Marine training had conditioned him for that. But as the move took him off balance, he wondered if maybe it wouldn't have been better to release the gun and take a swing at the Li-Dain.

As Magnus's exposed neck and back flew past the warrior, he felt heat erupt above him and then drive his face down into the deck. He imagined that the Luma had just elbow dropped him between the shoulder blades. His helmet smacked against the teak, but he still managed to grip his TB16, and his HUD didn't register any armor damage. Magnus pulled the weapon in close, rolled to his side, and fired a bolt through the back of Li-Dain's calf. It was a gamble to think Magnus was within the Luma's protective radius, but a risk worth taking. The bolt struck bone, and the mini warhead ruptured, blowing Magnus backward and sending the one-legged Luma cartwheeling overboard.

When the smoke cleared, Wobix lay across from Magnus, apparently having suffered the same elbow drop to the shoulder blades. "You good, Bixy?"

"My moral alignment has not changed in the last few moments." Wobix sprang up to his feet. "Is this a common issue with your kind?"

"What?" Magnus stood up as well. "I mean, are you hurt?"

"No." Wobix looked toward the ship's stern. "Come. I think we must fight to keep you from converting to evil."

Magnus chuckled and then gestured for Wobix to lead the way.

Zoll and Rix had seen plenty of combat together on Oorajee. Defending the Dregs had been a full-time job, and they were two of Abimbola's best. At least, that's what Zoll thought. Rix had signed up to help Magnus rescue the Marine hostages from the Selskrit, and Zoll had been one of the first to volunteer for Abimbola's attempt to aid the Gladio Umbra. Now, here they were on the backend of a super freighter, overloaded with trinium, working with a joint task force of alien species, and fighting off golden robed martial artists. "What is the universe coming to?" Zoll asked no one in particular.

"Crazy splick, that's what," Rix replied from beside Zoll.

The two gladias took cover behind a vertical deck support and fired on several advancing Li-Dain. The enemy continued to pour over the stern but had done away with their invisibility nonsense, opting instead to put up some sort of Unity shield. Fortunately, the gladias had their own defensive measures, thanks to Awen and Wish. Were it not for them, Bravo Team would have been out of the fight already, as far as Zoll figured. The Li-Dain had numbers and seemed to wield the Unity in powerful ways.

Zoll used the biotech interface to line up his TB16's sights on a Luma trying to advance from the transom. Zoll couldn't risk sticking his head out to aim down the sights, so he let his HUD do it. As soon as he had positive target acquisition, he squeezed the trigger and emptied his current magazine on the enemy. The first several torpedo bolts struck the Luma's shield and billowed out in plumes of fire, sparks, and smoke. But Zoll's aim was steady enough that the rounds eventually drilled a hole through the defense. All it took was for one warhead to explode inside the enemy's bubble to incinerate the Luma.

"Hell yeah," Dutch said. She gave him a quick salute from the port side where she'd obviously seen the kill. "Keep it up, team lead."

"I plan to." Zoll swapped out for a fresh magazine and then racked the first torpedo bolt.

He rolled out to fire on his next target when Rix grabbed the back of his collar and yanked him behind the pillar. "Look out!"

A massive yellow orb of energy slammed into the column and bent it inward. The deck groaned beneath Zoll's feet. Then he looked up to see the metal support glowing red-hot. Were it not for Rix's actions, Zoll would have surely lost his head.

"Thanks," Zoll said.

Rix nodded and then leaned back out to return fire. "Those diaper babies sure know how to throw a tantrum."

Zoll opened the channel to his unit. "Bravo Team, I want concentrated fire on the transom. We have to keep any more from getting on deck." The rest of the team acknowledged the order, followed by a renewed wave of torpedo bolts streaking toward the aft.

From atop the ship's communication array, Silk had a clear line of sight to almost every part of the upper decks. The only spaces out of her reach were those hidden by overhangs as well as the very aft of the ship. From the sounds of it, Zoll could use her help, but so could Alpha Team. Abimbola was busy fighting Li-Dain at the bow while Magnus and Wobix were keeping the little buggers from getting inside the bridge. Additional narskill fought along the port and starboard decks, engaging in violent close-quarters combat when needed but choosing to use their power bows wherever possible.

Silk tracked two Li-Dain making their way toward Magnus's position, and the LT seemed busy with a Luma of his own.

"Just where do you think you're going?" Silk said as she aimed down her TB16e—the E standing for Extension, a barrel modification that Azelon had given the snipers in Granther Company. Like most weaponry, the extended barrel meant her torpedo bolts had a faster muzzle velocity and were more accurate—facts that played to her advantage as she lined up the enemy fourteen meters below. It also meant the weapon kicked more as the chemically accelerated bolts leaped from the barrel and tore across the blackness, leaving a red streak in the air.

The first round detonated against the top of the Li-Dain's shield; the second complimented the damage of the first. But it was the third round that punched through and exploded inside the bubble. For a split second after the Li-Dain's body ruptured, the Unity shield stayed in place, appearing as a red ball from the victim's blood. Then as the power blinked out, the carnage fell apart and splashed on the deck.

The second Li-Dain slowed at the sight of her counterpart's destruction and looked up. Silk wasn't sure if the Luma could see her in the comm's array, but she wasn't waiting around to find out. She placed her targeting reticle on the Luma's bubble and squeezed, depressing the trigger for an eight-round burst that spanned two full seconds.

Unlike the Luma Silk had dispatched a moment before, this enemy must have diverted more energy to the wall above her head. The torpedo bolts did not punch a hole in the shield as they had before. At least, not at first. It took seven rounds to burrow through the Luma's bubble, and it was the eighth that decapitated her.

"Saw that," Magnus said over VNET. "Thanks, Silk."

"Just doing my job, LT."

Rohoar worked through the ship's inner decks, where the tight corridors lent themselves to his natural skills in close quarters combat. Unfortunately, the tiny golden cherubs were also skilled in paw to paw combat. Rohoar stepped through a bulkhead door and onto a suspended catwalk when one of the Li-Dain charged him from the right. The Jujari ducked under an energy bolt and then stood upright to catch the enemy's fist as it sped toward his head.

Had anyone but a Unity user caught the blow, it would have obliterated their hand—at least that's what Rohoar thought, given the amount of energy he absorbed. Instead, the punch succeeded in pushing his paw back a quarter of a meter before Rohoar clamped down on the enemy's hand and began crushing it. The tiny person screamed and thrashed in his bathrobe as bones broke.

A roundhouse kick came straight for Rohoar's head. He raised his left forearm and blocked the blow, allowing the stored Unity energy to dissipate along his armor. A second kick came up from the opposite side, but Rohoar didn't release the Luma's fist to block it. Instead, he leaned into the strike with his shoulder and absorbed the energy—both physical and ethereal.

Rohoar could tell he was frustrating the little fighter with how he deflected each assault. And the Jujari would have gone on like this for a while, infuriating the Li-Dain for sport, were it not for the fact that the gladias needed to put an end to this assault quickly.

As the Luma wound up for another side kick, Rohoar raised his free hand in a fist and then pulled the Luma's head into it using his grip on the Li-Dain's broken hand. The human's neck snapped back under the impact, and the body went limp.

"Should have had a helmet," Rohoar said while rapping his knuckles once against the side of his head. "Stupid."

The next Luma appeared on the far side of the bay and raced along the catwalk in a flurry of swirling hand motions and glowing orbs. Rohoar tried tracking the movements, but they were too fast. Also, the Li-Dain was screaming in some loud tone that Rohoar suspected was meant to instill fear in him. But it only made him laugh in a way that his jowls fluttered over his gums.

Just as the Li-Dain drew within striking distance, Rohoar put both his fists together, summoned all his strength, and then drove his paws forward. The lateral piledriver of unstoppable force caught the Luma square in the chest and sent him on a reverse course. The sudden shift in inertia ruptured organs and snapped bones, killing the Li-Dain instantly. His body landed in a heap—legs and arms twisted and unmoving. "Also stupid."

Movement far below caught Rohoar's attention. The Jujari leaned over the railing and spied three Li-Dain working around the ASMCs and the trinium bays. But Rohoar couldn't tell what they were doing from this distance. He could have used his HUD's zoom feature to examine the enemy's activities more closely, but where was the fun in that? Magnus hadn't brought him into the Gladio Umbra to do *recognizing*—or whatever it was called. He had called upon Rohoar to do what Rohoar's did best: smash things.

Rohoar gauged the distance, ensured his suit's servos were operational, and then vaulted over the catwalk's railing. His massive armor-clad body whistled as it picked up speed, covering the twenty-meter jump in seconds. When he landed, an enormous *thud* reverberated through the ship.

The Li-Dain around the hold looked shocked, probably noticing his wavering image with their natural and supernatural sight, just as the others had seen. They stopped whatever it was they were doing and then came at him.

The first Li-Dain, who Rohoar considered the bravest if not the most stupid, leaped forward in a flying kick. Rohoar had plenty of time to deflect the blow and parried the Luma's glowing foot as he might bat away an annoying Oorajeen gull-winged vulture. What Rohoar wasn't expecting, however, was the blow to his lower back that came from a second assailant. What energy Rohoar could not absorb in the Unity was absorbed by the suit. Still, enough got through that his HUD registered minus fifteen percent battle damage to the lumbar area.

Rohoar spun around and swept his arm like a club. But the Li-Dain ducked and then punched at Rohoar's side. Again, the Jujari managed to absorb some of the glowing Unity energy, but not as much as before. The suit took the rest, as well as more damage—another fifteen percent loss. Rohoar sensed something sting his flesh and cause an ache in his bones.

"I will end you," Rohoar said and then licked his chops. He lunged at the nearest Li-Dain and succeeded in grasping the man by the head. As Rohoar began to squeeze, the Luma shrieked. The other warriors turned their attention to the invisible hand that held their partner aloft and began beating Rohoar's arm. But the Jujari's grip was too sure, his strength too much. In a second, Rohoar had crushed the top half of the Li-Dain's skull and tossed the limp body away like a rag doll's. Then he turned to the remaining two Luma and spoke over his external speakers. "Come here, small babies in robes."

14

The first blow came from Freya.

She'd fired a blaster pistol that she'd pulled from under the table. So-Elku saw the bolt cross the tabletop as if in slow motion. At first, he could hardly believe Freya had fired on him—it felt surreal. He was, after all, at a state dinner to negotiate a peaceful trade deal. But then again, when had anything he'd ever been a part of been normal? His entire leadership life was one of covert dealings and dark escapades. This was simply another episode in a long and sordid rise to the top of the galaxy's food chain.

The blaster bolt struck So-Elku's Unity shield but not without piercing the skin of his left pectoral. Something had slowed his reflexes. As soon as the bolt seared his flesh, So-Elku raised his hands and struck the five Sekmit on the opposite side of the table. Their bodies flew into but did not break the blaster-proof windowplex wall that looked over the garden. Again, his powers seemed limited, and he wondered why the victims had not been launched over the garden.

The rest of So-Elku's leaders raised their hands, ready to fight alongside him in the Li-Loré arts. Conventional weapons had not been permitted in the capitol building, but everyone knew that was merely a formality—a vestige of the Republic era.

With Freya and her leaders incapacitated, So-Elku made to step around the table to finish the job.

"Master," Trinklyn said, grabbing his arm. "You're hurt."

So-Elku looked down at the blood seeping through the smoking hole in his black and green robes. Then he pulled his arm free. "It's manageable." He continued around the table until he stood over Freya's unconscious form. "A pity we could not have been business partners." Then So-Elku opened the flat of his hand and made to annihilate the traitorous leader.

The doors on all three sides of the dining room burst open. In stormed Black-clad Neo Republic Marines, other figures dressed in white and grey armor, and a host of narskill warriors—their weapons trained on So-Elku and his staff. The LAW leaders raised their hands. All, that is, save So-Elku. He knew the universal sign of capitulation was all for show, and his captors should have too. To a Luma, it didn't matter where their hands went.

The fools, he thought.

"Put your hands up," said one Marine; it was hard to tell who spoke. Then again, it didn't matter.

"Or what?" So-Elku chuckled as he looked around the room at the mixed group of warriors. "You're going to try and stop me? What, with your little weapons? Is that it?"

"No," came a familiar voice from back in the reception hall. "But we will."

So-Elku watched in amazement as Willowood strode forward. She was dressed in the same sort of form-fitting suit that Piper had worn when she first appeared to him. This time, the outfit looked different. Rather than the yellow and blue colors, the suit's translucent conductors glowed with the magenta fire of the Nexus.

A volcano of anger stirred in So-Elku's gut. *Willowood* had been behind this. *She* had conspired against him with the pride mother. And he scolded himself for not deducing it sooner.

"What is it you want?" So-Elku said. "Have you come to kill me?"

"That's up to you," Willowood replied.

"So you're going to arrest me?"

"Not me." Willowood gestured toward the Marines. "Them."

So-Elku couldn't help but laugh. "Them? The *Neo Republic*? You can't actually be serious."

But Willowood said nothing in reply.

So-Elku laughed hard enough that it was a struggle to get the words out. "They lost, Willowood." He repeated the words in a defiant shout. "They. Lost. Capriana is no more, the senate is no more, and their alliances are falling by the day. And who did they lose to?" So-Elku looked around at the warriors, offering them a chance to answer the question. "To me, dear lady Willowood. To. Me."

"They are taking you into custody to stand trial."

"Trial?" So-Elku bellowed and looked to his right and left. "What trial? Before what judge and jury? They're finished, Willowood." He turned to glare at some of the Marines. "You hear me, bucketheads? You're all finished."

"They seem to think otherwise, So-Elku. And I happen to agree with them."

"You." The Luma Master sneered at Willowood and took a step toward her. But every weapon in the room tracked with him, and

So-Elku was reminded of the pain in his chest. With whatever Willowood had done to him, he doubted he could survive so many opponents at once. He needed to get out of here. "You're just an old woman now. A shadow of your former self. What can you possibly expect to do against me?"

Willowood nodded, acting as if she were impressed.

But So-Elku knew better. She was up to something.

"I may just be an old bag of bones. But, you see, my granddaughter is not."

A tiny girl popped out from behind Willowood. "Boo," Piper said.

The pestilential child actually startled him, which only made her giggle.

"I think you'll find that the kyreethsha has rather tamed your more miraculous abilities," Willowood said, using her fingers to flicker through the air when she said the last two words.

"I've had enough," So-Elku said.

"And so have we," Willowood replied. "Come peacefully, and we will guarantee the safety of your entire retinue back to Minrok Santari."

"You"—So-Elku had to pause for a bout of laughter—"you will guarantee our safety?"

"Please, master," Trinklyn said. "I think you should listen to—"

"Silence!" So-Elku backhanded the woman, causing her to tumble into a chair. Then he glowered at Willowood. "We will *never* submit to you." And with that, So-Elku sent a shockwave through the room that knocked the Marines off their feet.

Willowood shielded Piper from So-Elku's blast, though she hardly needed to. The child was everything Willowood was and then so much more. So-Elku's impudent attempt to thwart capture also revealed just how much the sedative had worked. It wouldn't inhibit him for long, of course, but it should be enough for Piper to rein him in.

While the Neo Republic Marines faltered, the members of Nelson's Hedgebore Company did not. Paladia Company, whose mystics were hidden strategically throughout the building to multiply their effectiveness, had made sure to reinforce the gladias' Mark I armor with ample support in the Unity. They'd also succeeded in subduing the other members of So-Elku's entourage during the dinner's opening moments. Therefore, as soon as So-Elku's initial energy wave passed, Nelson gave the order to activate chameleon mode, and the gladias blinked out of sight. Then they leveled their NOV2s and fired stun rounds at So-Elku's position. But as Willowood suspected, the Luma Master ensconced himself in a Nexus shield and grinned as the rounds dispersed in the light of his magenta-colored bubble.

"Go ahead, Piper," Willowood said, tapping the child on the shoulder.

"Okay, Nana." Piper flipped down her helmet's dark visor and then gathered the Nexus's strength. Her suit began to glow, casting the reception hall and the dining room in a deep red color. Even So-Elku seemed to pale in the mounting light. Then Piper lowered her head as a pool of liquid red light passed through So-Elku's defensive bubble and wrapped his body.

"Hello, Mr. So-Elku, sir," Piper said. "You hurt a lot of people, and we're not going to let you do that anymore."

So-Elku fought against the grip that constricted his arms and legs. Even his mouth seemed unable to open. Only the terrified expressions in his eyes betrayed any emotion.

In all her years of knowing Teerbrin—from the small boy who'd sat under his father's tutelage to the proud new Luma leader in Elder's Hall—Willowood had never seen the man so afraid as he was in this moment. She would have been lying if she said it didn't make her smile too. The fear in his eyes made him look insignificant and weak, as if being overcome by a child were a fate worse than death.

"Good, Piper," Willowood said. "Now set the bonds."

"Yes, Nana." The red light around So-Elku swirled, dotted with white motes, and seemed to form bands that interlocked around So-Elku's body. The master's own advisors backed away as their hair whipped in the wind. Even the Marines seemed unsure what to do with the child's unexpected display of power. Finally, the bands of light seemed to sink into So-Elku's body until the wind subsided, and So-Elku stood as stiff as a dried out corn husk.

Freya pushed herself off the floor and accepted a narskill warrior's assistance to stand. The pride mother knew the risks of this operation. Fortunately, however, she didn't look injured. Freya gave Willowood a quick nod and then looked past Willowood to a Sekmit woman in the reception hall. Willowood stepped aside to let DiAntora enter the dining room.

"Teerbrin Vanick So-Elku," the admiral said, stepping forward in her officer's field uniform. "Under article four of the Neo Republic Charter of Intergalactic Law and section nine of the Valdaiga Accords, you are hereby arrested on suspicion of treason, murder, and the formation of an illegal governing body."

If So-Elku was struggling against Piper's bonds, there was no way to tell. Only the pulsing blood vessels in his temples, bloodshot eyes, and furrowed brow gave onlookers any hints that the Luma Master's fear had turned to rage as he listened to DiAntora's pronouncement. But the man had it coming.

For her part, Willowood had to admit that it felt good to finally have So-Elku in custody. The man had lost his way, and she sensed it was only a matter of time before his vision of personal grandeur caught up with him.

"Now, call off the attack over the mine," Caldwell said to So-Elku. When the man didn't reply, the colonel asked Willowood if Piper could loosen her stranglehold on the prisoner.

Piper nodded and closed her eyes for a moment.

"I will do no such thing," So-Elku said in a foul-tempered tone. "If you think for one moment that—" So-Elku's voice broke off.

Caldwell looked down at Piper.

"He's really kinda annoying," the child said.

"I agree." The colonel addressed the LAW master again. "If you comply, we'll go easier on your people."

So-Elku gave the colonel a deep scowl. It seemed unlikely the man would yield. Still, Caldwell invited Piper to lift her restraint.

"Go to hell," So-Elku said. He made to spit at the colonel, but the saliva just ran down his chin, thanks to Piper.

"He's got a dirty mouth," Piper added.

"Indeed he does. And I know dirty mouths."

"Yeah." Piper smiled at the old man. "Yours is pretty bad, Mr. Colonel, sir. But I think it's funny."

"Thanks." Cadlwell looked back to So-Elku. "Tough break, So-Elku. My people are gonna have your attack locked down any minute now. Should've taken the deal."

DiAntora shifted her focus to So-Elku's counterparts, all of whom still had their hands raised. "As for you, you are also arrested according to article four of the Neo Republic Charter of Intergalactic Law and section nine of the Valdaiga Accords on suspicion of aiding and abetting a known enemy of the state, as well as conspiracy to commit treason." DiAntora looked to her captain and pointed at the LAW reprobates. "Take them away."

The Marine captain nodded at DiAntora and then looked to one of the narskill warriors. The Sekmit, in turn, gave an order for his men to place plasma binders on the four accomplices.

"They're all yours," Freya said to DiAntora.

"Thank you, pride mother," the Neo Republic admiral said as she raised her chin. "We will keep you apprised of their trial date. You will be summoned to testify, if you would."

"Of course."

DiAntora looked to Willowood and then to Caldwell. "Thank you, both."

"It's our pleasure," Willowood said.

"We're only too happy to assist the Galactic Republic, Admiral," Caldwell added.

Willowood couldn't be sure, but she thought she heard a hint of regret in the old colonel's voice. She cast him a sideways glance but tried to underplay her curiosity.

"*Neo* Republic," DiAntora said to Caldwell. "Which means we will look for new ways to overlook past grievances. Should parties be interested."

Caldwell looked at Willowood.

But DiAntora wasn't through. "In the wake of all that has happened, we have need of competent leaders, Colonel. Please keep that in mind."

Willowood couldn't tell what Caldwell was thinking, and she resisted the urge to intrude upon his inner thoughts—she respected him too much for that. Still, based on the wistful air that seemed to wash over his face, she wondered if the old coot wasn't going soft. Would he actually consider a return to the Republic after all he'd been through? Perhaps Willowood didn't know him as well as she thought. Then again, the Corps had been his home for the majority of his life. So she supposed she couldn't blame him for wanting.

"I'll keep that in mind, Admiral. Thank you. Now, if you'll excuse us, we still have—"

"We've got a big problem, Colonel," Magnus's voice said over Willowood's VNET earpiece.

Willowood looked at Caldwell, who immediately pardoned himself and took Magnus's call. "What is it, son?"

15

Magnus and Wobix led a unit of three narskill warriors in defending the OHF's bridge while Abimbola worked just below them on the foredeck. Magnus had cycled out to his second magazine by the time the initial charge against the enclosed pilothouse slowed. He'd taken out three more of the golden robed assailants, while Wobix and his men had killed five.

"Do you think that's it then?" Wobix asked, his power bow aimed at the port-side stairwell.

"I wouldn't bet on it," Magnus replied, circling the bridge toward the starboard stairwell. Something felt off about the momentary lull. He didn't like the storm nearing from the west either—the winds had picked up, stirring the waves into a froth. Magnus called for a SITREP over the company channel.

"We're still busy keeping them off the stern," Zoll reported. "Another eight tangos down."

"I've tracked at least five more headed below deck," Wish said from her perch in the comms array.

"And Rohoar is still delivering justice to these perpetrators in cherub's cloth," the Jujari said.

Magnus double-checked Rohoar's location and saw that the Jujari was deep in the hull with the trinium. Then he brought up Rohoar's camera feed and saw the mwadim taking on one Li-Dain after another, pummeling, pounding, and punching his way through a steady line of enemies. The enemy going for the trinium before they'd secured the bridge seemed like a failure to prioritize. The cargo meant little if they couldn't unload it. So Magnus chalked it up to poor mission planning and the fact that the LAW wasn't made of tacticians. *Just diplomats with attitude problems.*

He didn't have time to think about the issue long, however, as four enemy combatants flipped over the starboard railing and landed on the deck in front of Magnus.

"Splick," he said and brought up his TB16. "The enemy got wise about using the stairs!"

"Over here too," Wobix said from the opposite side of the bridge.

Magnus fired on the nearest Luma. His first three rounds struck the woman's shield and billowed out in fiery plumes. Magnus knew he couldn't handle four all at once, so he backed around the front of the bridge for cover. But this also meant giving up the starboard-side entrance. He decided to pull a VOD from his hip, set it to a compass-bearing disbursement pointed away from the wheelhouse, and then rolled it under the oncoming Lumas' feet.

When the VOD detonated, two of the four enemies were blown sky-high. Their dismembered bodies twirled through the night air and cleared the ship's decks to land somewhere in the turbulent sea. The remaining two, however, diverted energy toward the explosion and managed to stay on their feet. The woman in the lead summoned red orbs of energy around her hands and pointed them at Magnus. He ducked around the windowplex just as twin streams of light flashed past his helmet. The power was so strong that it reduced his shield's power by twenty percent without even hitting it.

"Somebody's pissed," he said. Then he dropped to a knee, aimed at the woman's abdomen, and held the TB16's trigger. A total of six torpedo bolts streaked from the barrel, the first three of which were flash-incinerated by a second burst of Luma energy. But the last three punched a hole through the shell and exploded point-blank, turning the Li-Dain's torso to a pulp.

The fourth enemy jumped away from the explosion, stepped off the railing, and somersaulted over Magnus's head to land square in front of the bridge's command window. Magnus spun but felt his weapon knocked aside even before he brought it to bear on the Luma. A second blow caught him under the chin and forced his head back. It felt like this enemy's hands were made of steel.

Again, Magnus tried bringing his TB16 up, but the Li-Dain was too fast, hammering it to the deck with a quick downward thrust to the top of the barrel. Magnus was forced to let go of the weapon but used the opportunity to throw a punch of his own. His fist landed against the side of the Luma's head, throwing the man into the bridge's window. On anyone else, the servo-assisted blow would have fractured their skull and probably killed them instantly. But this was no ordinary enemy.

The man touched his lip and pulled away a fingertip tinged with a smudge of red saliva. Then the Luma smiled at Magnus.

Faster than Magnus could think, the man lunged with one fist outstretched, the other held behind him ready for a punch. Magnus wasn't sure which hand to concern himself with, as the hand around his throat felt like a vice clamping down on his windpipe while the other fist flashed bright red. So Magnus decided to fall back and use the assailant's momentum against him. The pair rolled along the ground, and Magnus used his legs to kick the Li-Dain up and away. A blow to the man's elbow loosed his grip around Magnus's neck and sent him hurtling into the railing. The enemy yelped as something cracked—a bone or two, Magnus hoped. But the man recovered quickly and raised his hands, both glowing with the otherworldly red light.

Magnus looked for his weapon, but it was too far away. He thought about using his VP2 but remembered he hadn't brought it since the pistol was worthless in water environments. All he had left was his NCK combat knife and three more VODs—those, and his hands.

But the Li-Dain charged before he could withdraw his knife. Magnus parried a blow meant for his head, feeling the energized hand graze his armored forearm with white-hot pain. The HUD registered another twelve percent reduction in shield power. Magnus knew enough not to try to catch one of the Li-Dain's punches, imagining his hand exploding as a result. The most he could do would be to deflect the blows until he got his window of opportunity. The enemy threw three more successive jabs before Magnus found a hole in the Li-Dain's defense and punched him in the sternum. Again, the servo-assisted strike was overwhelming—at least it would have been against an ordinary combatant. Instead, the Luma flew back into the railing but managed to stay upright.

"You've gotta be splickin' me," Magnus said. He didn't have time to keep entertaining this guy. Magnus needed a weapon, but his TB16 was still too far away.

In the split second before the assailant charged again, Magnus thought of how he'd used the VOD's compass direction mode to protect the bridge's door while dispatching the enemy. He brought up a detonator, activated the compass mode, and then maglocked the ordnance to his chest plate, hoping to all the mystics that he'd set the right direction. Then, as if in complete disregard for his own life, Magnus threw himself, arms outstretched, at the enemy.

The Li-Dain's oncoming punch glanced off the top of Magnus's helmet, and the resulting energy explosion helped propel Magnus forward. His shoulder caught the enemy under the chin and knocked the Li-Dain's head back. All the while, Magnus continued to rush forward, driving hard toward the railing. The VOD's three-second fuse felt three times as long as Magnus waited for the kick. He carried the Luma up and over the fence and joined the enemy in a midair freefall.

A blinding flash of light seared Magnus's bioteknia eyes. His pain receptors shut down just before the force of a runaway hover truck walloped him in the chest. He swore, sure that the instantaneous change in momentum had flattened all his organs, and sensed his body shoot skyward. For a moment, Magnus endured the horrible sense of falling and not having anything to hold on to. He felt like a child who'd been thrown out of a moving vehicle, grasping for something to save him. Then he saw the ship's bridge flip over the top of his vision and the deck rush up to meet him.

The sensation of landing on the ground felt more like a fluffy pillow when compared to the VOD's kick. He gasped for air and then registered his HUD deploying the suit's nanobot tech. It was calling for adrenaline supplements and minor tissue repair. But aside from that, and the forty percent loss in shielding, Magnus was relatively okay.

"Are you completely crazy?" a voice said over comms.

He fought the intense pain that the voice produced in his head, but the nanobots would help alleviate that too. Then a hand touched his back. Magnus thought maybe it was an enemy, but he was too groggy to do anything about it.

"Have you gone insane?"

Magnus rolled sideways and looked up. "Awen. Boy am I glad to see you."

"You're such an idiot, pulling a stunt like that."

"It was the only thing I could—" But Magnus cut himself short when another four Li-Dain appeared over the blown apart railing. "Look out!"

Awen was relieved that Magnus was moving. From inside the bridge, she watched in horror as Magnus used the VOD to defeat the enemy Luma, and then she saw him fly back onto the deck. The stunt was stupid and would have ended a lesser man. Then again, a lesser man would never have attempted such a ludicrous feat. She wanted to kill him and kiss him all at the same time.

"Look out," Magnus yelled, pointing past her to where the VOD had blown apart the starboard deck. Four golden-robed Li-Dain assumed Li-Loré fighting positions and summoned Nexus energy into their fists. She looked back at Magnus, but he'd need another minute before he was in any shape to take on these combatants. *And I don't have that long.*

So she was just going to have to do this herself.

While the Nexus-powered Li-Dain outnumbered her, they did not possess Azelon's suit tech, which helped harness, shape, and amplify the Unity's power. So Awen formed a protective sphere around her body and then increased the shield surrounding her

Novian power suit. This would at least keep their ranged attacks at bay, forcing her opponents to use hand-to-hand combat instead. Then Awen flipped her helmet's visor down and took up her fighting position. *Let's do this*, she said through the Unity.

The first man to come at her looked vaguely familiar. Then again, that wasn't saying much. She'd probably bumped into all of these warriors on Worru at one point or another. Once upon a time, they'd been pledged together in service of the same Order—sworn protectors of peace, defenders of species near and far. But now a veritable ocean of differences separated them. They were kin no more, and Awen knew she had to do what needed doing despite the reservations she had about killing.

The man's hands rolled over one another as he sought to distract Awen from his intentions. When the first punch flew toward Awen's face, she bent right. The second punch came at the same speed, but she sidestepped left. As the third punch was thrown, Awen ducked under it and then struck the man in the belly. A flash of magenta-colored light radiated outward like a solar flare. Awen even winced, shocked by just how powerful her attack had been. The man flew backward and struck a Li-Dain in the chest. The two passed through the crater in the deck and disappeared out of sight.

Awen looked at her hand, surprised at whatever new resource she'd tapped into. Then again, she hadn't exactly fought in a situation like this before. She didn't need to store up Nexus energy in her firsts as the Li-Dain did—her power suit took care of that. All she needed to do was direct the flow, much like a mythical god creating a riverbed along a valley floor. What surprised her was how much more quickly the ability was coming to her. Perhaps it was just adrenaline.

The next Luma to come at Awen was a large man nearly three

heads taller than she was. That wasn't saying much, Awen knew, as Elonian stature wasn't something anyone bragged about. Still, comparatively speaking, this enemy was a mountain of a man. He threw two quick jabs and then kicked at Awen's head. But she avoided each strike and ducked beneath the leg's deadly arc in time to punch his inner thigh. The man grunted and hopped back, favoring his opposite leg. But he raised his fists—far from out of this fight.

The assailant stepped toward Awen, throwing two jabs again, but then finished with an uppercut to her face. Awen barely avoided the blow, shuddering to think what it may have done had it connected. A beam of red light shot straight up into the blackened sky and disappeared among the stars.

As Awen recovered, she threw a right hook. But her enemy caught her wrist and yanked her sideways. Awen fell and dangled from the man's iron grip. Holding her up like a punching bag, the man threw several punches at Awen's side. While the blows didn't penetrate her suit's shield, she watched the capacity drop in her HUD. Every hit took it down by almost twenty percent. By the fourth strike, her force field registered less than ten percent.

As the fifth and what may have been the final strike came toward her ribs, Awen pulled herself up and flipped her body out of the way. Her legs wrapped the assailant around the neck just as his punch met empty air. Then Awen flowed with her body's momentum, redirected Nexus energy into the movement, and squeezed her legs around the man's head. Her body swiveled around his neck like a ring spinning around a dowel, and then she wrenched him sideways. The man flew off his feet, and his head drove into the teak deck, splitting around the right eye socket. He screamed, but Awen knew he wouldn't be getting up.

She rolled to a crouch just in time for the fourth Li-Dain, a woman in her early thirties maybe, to bounce back and forth on the balls of her feet. Rather than hold her fists up, the woman let her arms dangle at her sides as if this was just another relaxed sparring match. She even used a forced breath to blow a few wet strands of her short brown hair from her eyes. "You ready for me, Awen?" the woman asked.

Rather than provide some snarky movie line that Cyril would no doubt be proud of, all Awen could think to say was, "Don't act like you know me." Instead, something like "I was born ready" or even just "Bring it on" would have been so much cooler. But Awen wasn't thinking about being cool. She was thinking about protecting her unit and serving the Sekmit. So, "Don't act like you know me" was all the woman was going to get.

Without giving the enemy a chance to respond, Awen stepped forward and brought her arms up. The other woman continued to bounce from side to side.

"I never thought I'd see this day," she said. "Name's Clair, by the way."

"Don't care," Awen said. Then she threw a punch at Clair's head. The woman avoided it and adjusted her feet.

"I sat behind you in inter-quadrant economics and developing star systems."

Awen threw another punch, but Clair dodged it just as easily as the first.

"You were always such a bitch. You know that? A real teacher's pet."

Awen circled with the woman, looking for an opportunity to strike. She didn't remember Clair, but she knew the type. They didn't attend observances to learn or to better the galaxy; they were there because daddy had an in with a senator who made a few calls and secured an academic seat. There was never any intention of serving out their time as an emissary or volunteering on one of the Luma's sanctioned missions. Instead, people like Clair used Worru for the educational credentials, the night clubs on the west end, and the connections it secured them. Meanwhile, people like Awen, who wanted to learn and do good in the cosmos, suffered under their incessant bullying.

"But now look at us, Awen," Clair said. "Ironic, isn't it? I finally get to do what I always wanted to, and you're not even a Luma anymore. And you know what the best part is?"

If Clair thought Awen was going to try and answer the rhetorical question, the woman had another thing coming.

"The best part is that they've asked me to kill you." A smug look crossed Clair's face as she finally brought her fists up.

Awen threw her left hand forward and drove a beam of energy into Clair's chest. But the woman crossed her forearms and blocked the shot. Instead, the force pushed Clair backward, and her feet slid toward the hole in the deck.

"Whoa-huh-ho," Clair said once Awen's assault had ebbed. "Somebody's developed a temper. You know, you data whores are all the same, acting all prim and proper. But inside, you've got just as much rage as the rest of us. Probably more. Because unlike us, you don't talk about how everyone hurt you. You just bottle it up until—"

Awen fired again. She was getting tired of Clair's ramblings.

But instead of blocking the shot, the woman jumped aside to avoid the still-smoking crater. "Until you snap, just like that."

Awen turned to face Clair when the woman—fast as lightning—ran up and across the side of the bridge tower and then jumped toward Awen, foot extended in a kick. The move impressed as much as surprised Awen, but she managed to put her arms up in time to block most of the kick's power. Still, her HUD advised her that her personal Unity shield was now depleted. This wasn't a big deal, of course, as Awen could quickly summon more shielding; however, it would take concentration, whereas the suit's job was to handle that on its own. And given how fast Clair was moving, Awen didn't have the mental resources to give to shielding; she was already assisting Alpha Team as it was. She needed to stop this woman before anyone else got hurt—before *she* got hurt.

Clair threw several punches, all of which Awen managed to avoid. But the woman was driving Awen toward the bow railing, and if she didn't do something fast, Clair might just pin her down.

That's when Awen decided to do something risky. But if Magnus was allowed to, why wasn't she? Awen turned away from Clair, ran up the railing's rungs, and then dove into a backflip. She saw Clair appear upside down, gauged the distance, and then scissor-kicked her legs into her head and shoulders. Combined with a release of Unity energy, the effect dropped Clair to the ground in a heap. She didn't let out so much as a yelp.

Awen stood over Clair's body, relieved at knowing the battle was over and disgusted that she'd killed a former classmate.

"SHE'S RIGHT, YOU KNOW," Magnus said, still on his belly. "You can be a real bitch."

"Shut up." Awen offered him a hand and helped him stand. "You okay?"

"I'll be fine. Just need another minute." Magnus looked at the two Luma that Awen downed, and then nodded toward the crater where the two other had fallen through. "You did good work."

"Thanks. It's just a shame that—"

"We can worry about all that later." Magnus placed a hand on her shoulder. "Right now, we need—"

"Magnus, this is Rohoar who speaks to you."

Magnus chuckled. "I can see that, pal."

"Rohoar believes there is a serious problem down here in the lower trinium containment areas where Rohoar has been dispatching diaper cherubs."

"And what's that?"

Rohoar switched out his face camera for a view from his helmet. There, attached at half a dozen points along a trinium bay, were several bag-looking lumps with blinking lights.

"Oh, splick," Magnus said.

"Yes." Rohoar zoomed in on one of the bags. "If we were on Oorajee, you and your Marines would call these IMTBs, Rohoar believes."

Magnus nodded and then looked at Awen. "We've got to get everyone off the ship."

"What? Why?"

"IMTBs—improvised multi-trigger bombs. My gut says that's trinitex."

"That is also Rohoar's intestinal sensation on the matter," the Jujari replied.

"All units, all units," Magnus said over the all-unit channel. "Get off the ship. I repeat, abandon ship. She's rigged to blow." Then as Magnus led Awen to the side railing and looked into the water, he opened a line to Caldwell. "We've got a big problem, Colonel."

"What is it, son?"

But Magnus was slow in responding. Something unusual caught his attention. Even amongst the growing waves stirred up by the storm, he noticed splashing in the distance—the same kind that signaled the Li-Dain deploying from their shuttles.

"What is it, Magnus?" Awen asked.

"But that doesn't make any sense," he said, more to himself than anyone else.

"What's going on there, son," Caldwell said. "Need you to talk to me."

"They've rigged the OHF to blow, colonel. Trinitex."

"Damn." Caldwell pulled his cigar out. "What are they thinking?"

"I don't know." Magnus watched as more Li-Dain appeared to make water entry along the horizon. "But they're deploying reinforcements into the water, which doesn't make sense if they're just planning to scuttle the ship and blow the trinium."

Into the water. Even as he repeated his own phrase, something dawned on him.

Magnus brought up Captain Forbes. The man's face appeared in a window next to Caldwell's. "Heard you're having all the fun without us, Maggs."

"Daniel," Magnus said. "Where are you and your men?"

"Stationed as planned. All hovertrain entry points are locked down."

"And the mines?"

"Emptied as per emergency protocol. Why? What's this about?"

Magnus glanced at Awen, then the OHF, then the ocean. "They only wanted this trinium as a distraction."

"What are you talking about?" Awen asked.

"I second her question, son," Caldwell said.

"They wanted to make a statement. Maybe even take a city out if they could've gotten close to shore. But they're not after the freighter. They're going after the whole damn mine."

"We accounted for this," Forbes said. "You called it, and we've got it covered."

"No," Magnus said. "We don't."

16

A LIGHT as bright as the sun lit the western horizon and flooded the dining room. It lasted only a second, but the dark mushroom cloud and massive fireball that began rising west of the mountains blotted out the stars. Willowood watched Caldwell study the cataclysmic event, noting how his cigar went limp in his lips. Everyone in the room seemed spellbound by the trinium explosion—all but So-Elku, who was facing the wrong direction.

"What was that?" Piper said.

"Nothing that Magnus doesn't have under control, my love," Willowood replied and placed a hand on Piper's head. The older woman hoped her granddaughter didn't detect the white lie. The truth was, the VNET transmission had been cut just before they saw the explosion. Neither Caldwell nor Willowood knew what had happened to Granther Company and Wobix's narskill, and it would be several minutes before comms were back up. "You just stay focused on keeping So-Elku bound."

"Oh, that's not hard."

Willowood smiled at the child's natural confidence then turned to Admiral DiAntora and motioned her out of earshot from So-Elku and his four secured officers. "We're ready to move when you are, Admiral."

"Understood," DiAntora replied. But she looked through the windowplex to the west. "Is everything okay?"

CALDWELL STEPPED in to answer DiAntora's question. He didn't want Piper to have to hear any more half-truths. "It seems our guests may have bitten off more than they can chew." Then he turned to Freya. "I'm only sorry that it seems you just lost a sizable load of trinium."

Freya studied the billowing mushroom cloud. "It is of little consequence. We have plenty more where that came from, and it was a calculated risk worth taking, so long as my warriors and your team are safe."

"We have reason to believe that all made it off the ship before it exploded, but I am still waiting for confirmation on that." Caldwell was acting extremely optimistic, given the circumstances. Willowood wondered if that was a defense mechanism, a trait he'd picked up from his years in the Corps, or a way of keeping the Sekmit at ease. The fact was, they needed to get So-Elku off the planet, and from what Magnus said, there was going to be an attempt on the mines.

Freya turned to face Caldwell. "Hearing from your team will take time, given that the radiation noise must settle."

"Indeed," Caldwell said with a nod. "I am more concerned with how this will affect your people. Your planet."

Freya waved what seemed to be a dismissive paw through the

air. "You think this is our first meltdown? Please. There is a reason we harvest in the middle of the ocean, Colonel. In addition, the Sateem Mountains protect our continent from any fallout."

Caldwell took a deep breath and then looked between Freya and DiAntora. "What we need to be concerned about now is getting So-Elku and his people to your ship, Admiral. And, ní Freya, we suspect your mine may still be a target."

"But we have the hovertrain lines under close watch," Freya replied.

"We do. But I'm afraid our resources may be in the wrong place, I'm sorry to say."

"The wrong place?" Freya looked from Caldwell to Willowood. "I don't understand."

Caldwell blew out a puff of smoke. "The last thing Magnus offered before we lost contact was his suspicion that the Li-Dain were going to take the mine somehow."

"Again, I fail to see what his suspicions might be."

"I have to imagine that it's something he's seen at sea, something out there." He pointed to the still billowing clouds stretching toward orbit.

"Are you suggesting the Li-Dain mean to dive on our operation?" The rising of both bushy eyebrows emphasized the surprise in Freya's voice. "I can't imagine that being an easy nor rewarding endeavor."

"Nor can I," Caldwell replied. "But we're not dealing with a conventional enemy. If Magnus had doubts, then they're well-founded, and we'll need to follow through on them. Ní Freya, if it pleases you, I'd like our combined forces to enter the mines and see if they can't stage some sort of defense."

"But the mine is vast. How will we even begin to know where to send them?"

"I, uh, I'm probably the best one to help with that," Cyril said, walking out from behind a door in the reception hall. He'd been hunkered down behind a wall of holo displays and work station terminals, helping Caldwell and Willowood monitor both operations. Seeing him come out from the makeshift command room and blink through his goggles was like watching a Quinzellian mole rat emerge from hibernation. "I mean, well, I should probably correct that statement. Azelon and I are the best to help with that." He ran his fingers through his messy hair. "Wow, I'm so excited. What about TO-96? Of course. So what I really should have said was that Azelon, TO-96, and myself are—"

"How can you help?" Freya said.

Cyril snapped out of his stream of thought. "We can triangulate the enemy's estimated surface locations and then deduce a map of suspected entry points based upon the most likely routes, taking into account the current strata, thermal declination, and—"

"You can narrow down the potential nodes they might try breaching?"

"Uh, ha ha, yes, My Lady Freya Queen."

Freya hissed once at Cyril and then turned on Caldwell. "We will abide by whatever data you provide, Feared Aggressor."

"Then we'll get right on that." The colonel snapped his fingers at Cyril and gave him a smile. "Back inside your cave, Blinky."

"Yes, yes, of course, Mr. Commander, sir. Copy and over roger."

"Pride mother," DiAntora said, addressing Freya directly, but still choosing to speak in galactic common for reasons Caldwell didn't know—perhaps to just keep the rest of the team in the loop.

"Given the severity of the situation, would it not be wise for Neo Republic forces to assist you in defending the mines?"

"No," Freya said. "Your priority is returning So-Elku to Minrok Santari. And even as we speak, their starship is, no doubt, awaiting word from them. It won't be long before So-Elku's silence raises suspicions, and your chances of departing the system unscathed will only decrease. So you must be on your way."

Caldwell felt DiAntora's request was extremely odd. Why would a Neo Republic Admiral offer to divert from her mission directives to engage in combat she and her team were not ready for? Secondly, the idea of the Republic—Galactic, Neo, or otherwise—offering to aid a planet who they'd only just broken faith with days before seemed both distasteful and unprofessional. The only reason Caldwell could think of for any of this was that DiAntora was still Sekmit—naturally, she would want to aid her people and protect their interests. But her willingness to breach Repub protocol and divert from her directives was—*well, it's downright astounding*, the colonel thought to himself. In any other moment, this would have gotten her a court-martial and a discharge from the Navy.

DiAntora raised her chin at Freya and then looked to Willowood. "In light of the enemy's activity above the mines, are you and your granddaughter still willing to help us escort the prisoners?"

Willowood looked at Piper. "What do you say?"

"Uh-huh," the girl replied. "Sounds exciting."

"Very well," DiAntora said.

"And you still have the rest of Paladia and Hedgebore Companies at your disposal," Caldwell said. "Until we get more details about the unfolding situation at sea, we continue as planned."

"We are most grateful for your cooperation, Colonel."

"The transports are in the palace basement, as discussed," Freya said. "I also took the liberty of upgrading them to something a little more comfortable than a seafood truck."

"We are grateful, pride mother," DiAntora said with a lift of her chin.

Caldwell couldn't put his finger on it, but DiAntora seemed to take on a sentimental air as she studied Freya's face and then looked around at the other Sekmit. With how much the Repub had been shaken over the last several weeks, it didn't surprise Caldwell that someone like DiAntora, or any member of the Repub for that matter, would long for home. He'd seen some of his best Marines come to tears when talking about family, friends, favorite foods, and local hotspots, especially in between firefights. Caldwell didn't scorn them for it either, so long as it didn't distract them from the mission. Hell, a deep love for home was a strong motivator when it came to pushing through a lousy op. Still, DiAntora's behavior was unbecoming of a high ranking officer. Perhaps the woman was at a breaking point? Maybe things were worse among the Neo Republic's leadership than anyone knew?

DiAntora straightened and looked Freya in the eye. "We'd better be on our way then. Thank you for your assistance in helping bring So-Elku to justice."

"It has been our honor, Admiral."

Colonel Caldwell paced outside an armored personnel carrier in the basement level while his units assisted the Repub forces in securing the prisoners. Each APC was a late model Advanced Galactic Solutions DS9 hover truck, boasting twin drive cores, reinforced repulsor beds, and top-of-the-line inertia dampeners. The matte-back angular body panels were made of duradex fiber weave and used armor resonance disruption technology, which made the vehicles nearly impregnable by conventional weapons.

For firepower, each DS9-APC came with a MUT50 ultra torrent tri-reticulating blaster mounted above the driver's compartment. Its 50mm rounds delivered the distinct banshee-shriek that meant "get the hell out of the way" to anyone unlucky enough to hear them. Just above the rear doors, the DS9s sported a modified 70mm RBMB, or really big missile battery, that replaced the sentient operator with a digital one, making the entire system AI controlled. This not only freed the DS9 operators up to take care of the mission, but the vehicle's onboard AI was damn good at identifying and taking out targets on its own.

Orange trim and glossy black insignias rounded out the DS9's matte black body—a badass, no-nonsense physique that alluded to the vehicle's pedigree. Caldwell knew from experience that these particular "dark spec" trucks had been made exclusively for Shadow Ops by Advanced Galactic Solutions. While the manufacturing plant on Capriana Prime was no more, limited numbers of these war machines were scattered throughout the quadrant. How Freya had come to possess the twelve that stretched out in a line under the palace was curious, but Caldwell guessed it had something to do with the lucrative trade deal with the old Republic.

Each assault vehicle held twenty passengers, composed of gladias from Hedgebore Company and narskill from Freya's personal guard, plus up to eight detainees. Piper's oversight and the support of several dozen mystics from Paladia Company in the adjacent APCs meant the convoy would be the most secure prisoner escort detail Caldwell had ever seen. But this was no ordinary set of prisoners.

Colonel Caldwell cradled his Mark I helmet under his arm and checked his wrist comm for the time. It had been ten minutes since the trinium freighter detonated.

"Any word from Granther Company?" Caldwell asked TO-96 over VNET.

"I'm afraid not, sir," the bot replied. "Our spectrometers are still reading substantial interference patterns such that all communications within the blast radius are disrupted."

"Keep trying. I want to know the second we reestablish contact with Magnus."

"Affirmative, sir."

"We're ready to move, Colonel," said Nelson over comms. Seated beside a Sekmit driver, the captain would be commanding from the front of Caldwell's APC, slated sixth from the lead vehicle.

The colonel acknowledged the ready-up hail and then climbed into his DS9. Willowood, Piper, DiAntora, and a purposefully mixed security detail of gladias, Sekmit, and Neo Repub guards—fifteen in all—sat behind a metallic containment cell that contained Master So-Elku himself. The crate's dark shade of green was so deep it almost appeared black. Beveled corners, double-reinforced doors, automatic emergency lockdown systems, and prisoner incapacitation protocols made the chamber an inescapable and, when necessary, highly lethal vault.

"How you feeling, little lady?" Caldwell said to Piper.

"I'm a little hungry," the child replied. "But I think that's just because I'm excited to go for a ride in this truck. I get hungry when I'm excited. But I also get hungry when I'm nervous too, so, I'm not sure what I am, I guess, Mr. Colonel William." Piper's eyes went wide. "Oops. I'm not supposed to use your first name. I'm so sorry."

"You can use my first name, Piper. I use yours, right?"

She nodded and widened her eyes.

"And we'll get you something to eat." Caldwell snapped his fingers at one of the gladias under Nelson's command and ordered a protein sup bar from a ration crate. "Your big job now is—"

"To keep Master So-Elku in this box."

"Right," Caldwell said with a smile. "Think you can do that?"

Piper waved a hand in front of her face. "Easy peasy, Mr. William, sir."

"Good." Caldwell glanced up at Willowood as if looking for confirmation.

"Everything's set on our end," she assured him. "All prisoners are bound and being overseen by our mystics. We're powering up the containment fields of each modular cell block as planned. DiAntora will have more than enough time to get the units back to Minrok Santari."

"And we are grateful for your extra efforts," DiAntora said.

"Any word from Magnus?" Willowood said to Caldwell.

The colonel shook his head. "Still too much distortion."

"That's to be expected, I suppose." Willowood sighed. "For what it's worth, I still sense Awen's presence."

"Me too," Piper offered with a wide smile.

"Well, that's something," Caldwell said.

"But not conclusive," Willowood said. "It could just be an after-event, like a reflection of—" Willowood looked at Piper and seemed to think better of finishing her sentence.

"Understood." Caldwell gave Willowood a knowing look and held her eyes for two seconds. He found it hard not to get sidelined by her beauty. Why the woman never remarried after Kane was beyond him. That Caldwell would be so lucky to have her affections, newly budding as they were, made him feel like one lucky son of a bitch. "Time to get rolling." Caldwell called up to Nelson. "Let's get moving, Captain."

"Right away, Colonel."

THE CONVOY EMERGED from tunnels in the palace's side lawn some 300 meters to the east. As the vehicles turned south and entered traffic, Caldwell watched through a portal on the APC's left side. Bright neon signs, street lights, and headlights raced by as the convoy picked up speed. Beyond the city's skyscrapers lay a field of stars set against the deep blackness of the void.

The colonel was tempted to revel in So-Elku's capture but knew better than to celebrate any op's success prematurely. It was still a long way back to Minrock Santari, but that was up to the Republic to figure out. The Gladio Umbra's part was nearly over.

Caldwell watched Sekmit battle bikes pull up along both sides of the convoy—not that the DS9s needed any protection. But no one ever got points off for being overly cautious, and Caldwell didn't mind the extra support.

"Streets are clear to the spaceport, Colonel," Nelson announced from the lead vehicle.

"Copy that," Caldwell said. He turned to DiAntora. "Looks like Freya's provided some additional armor."

The Repub admiral nodded. "Can't be too cautious."

"Agreed."

Caldwell studied one of the armored battle bikes that pulled even with his DS9. The two-seater escort vehicle's black armor panels created a sleek cockpit for the driver and Thørzin power bow gunner. Unlike the personal weapons that the narskill carried on their shoulders, the hoverbike boasted an enlarged crossbow version ensconced in a turret enclosure. The soft blue glow of the energy bolt meant the operator had the weapon charged and ready to fire.

"Your people are ready for action," Caldwell said over his shoulder to DiAntora.

"Without the Republic's assistance, vigilance is even more important to ní Freya and our people."

"Can't blame her."

Caldwell was just about to remark on the Thørzin crossbow iteration when Nelson's voice hailed him.

"Colonel, we've got something ahead. Twenty-two hundred meters and closing."

"Patch it through to my HUD." Caldwell pulled his cigar out and slapped his visor down as a live camera feed from Nelson's helmet appeared. "What the hell is that?"

"It seems to be some sort of energy barricade."

A band of yellow light about four meters high stretched from one side of the street to the other.

"Felicity, you seeing this?" the colonel asked.

"I am," replied Willowood. "My guess is that it's more Li-Dain."

"Eighteen hundred meters," Nelson announced.

"More Li-Dain?" DiAntora stood and brought up a camera feed along one of the DS9's side holo consoles. "How is that possible?"

Caldwell could think of several reasons for the miscalculation, but they didn't have time to debate them. "Doesn't matter. Bottom line is we underestimated them. Willowood, I need unit strength and composition. DiAntora, any chance we turn around and have your vessel make a pick up from the palace?"

"Negative. There's not enough room. And even if there was, the palace lacks the equipment to move the mobile cell blocks. It would take several hours if not a day to get everything there."

Caldwell grunted. He minimized the camera feed in his HUD and then looked at Willowood. "Estimates?"

"It's hard to say. They're covering themselves well. But if I had to guess, I'd say over 300."

"That's a lot, right?" Piper asked.

"Yes, my love," Willowood confirmed. "That's a lot."

"But not more than we can handle," Caldwell said. "And that's the important thing."

"Fourteen hundred meters," Nelson said.

Caldwell turned to DiAntora. "Sekmit air support? Additional ground support?"

"Freya would never allow fighters over the city, and more ground units would never get here in time. She thought this would be enough."

"Then it will be. Do you have access to monitoring that can tell us about the civilian population? If we engage the Li-Dain out here, we're talking—"

"Significant civilian casualties," DiAntora said. "Yes. Stand by." The Sekmit woman's paws danced across the holo terminal as various screens filled with data. Several new live-footage windows appeared displaying street views. "Looks like all pedestrians have been driven back, as has vehicular traffic. There are a few apartment buildings in the vicinity, but the majority are commercial, and it's well after hours."

"One thousand meters, Colonel," Nelson said.

Caldwell heard the rising tension in his captain's voice. It was time to act. "Nelson, get this convoy in attack formation. We're punching through."

"Roger that," Nelson said.

"Everyone else, hold on." Caldwell looked at Piper. "This might get bumpy."

17

"Everybody off, now," Magnus roared. He grabbed Awen's arm and thrust her toward the bridge deck's railing. "Jump!"

"But, Magnus, I—"

There wasn't time. Magnus maglocked his TB16 to his back and then used both arms to launch Awen off the OHF. The servo-assisted MANTA suit amplified his efforts, sending her ten meters out—more than enough to clear the lower deck's outside railing. He watched as she hit the water and then slipped beneath the surface.

"Everyone off and dive!" Magnus looked around to see if anyone else needed help. The Sekmit bridge crew, as well as all his gladias, were abandoning their posts and headed for the side railings. His HUD showed Rohoar climbing up an interior stairwell, five meters short of the main deck.

"Move it, Fluffy," Magnus yelled over comms.

"Rohoar is moving it," the Jujari said, out of breath.

Magnus jumped through the blown-out crater leftover from his

VOD body attack and landed four meters below on the main deck. His suit absorbed the impact effortlessly. Then he turned to line up his bioteknia eyes with Rohoar's HUD tag. The Jujari stepped outside and looked around.

"About time," Magnus said and thrust a flat hand toward the freighter's side. "Let's go!"

The two gladias leaped off the OHF and plummeted toward wind-whipped waves. Magnus folded his arms and straightened his legs seconds before the sea enveloped his body. As a world of bubbles whirled through Magnus's field of view, he engaged his suit's thrusters and flooded the MANTA's ballast cavities with water. The suit responded like a high-performance hovercar—albeit one slowed by a highly dense fluid. Still, Magnus watched his depth gauge drop as his body plunged toward the ocean floor.

"SITREP," Magnus demanded.

"Alpha Team descending," Abimbola said.

"Bravo Team accounted for and descending," Zoll added.

"Watching you all head our way," Bliss added from inside his SUBCAT. "We're twenty-meters and holding."

"No," Magnus said. "Do not hold! Dive, dive, dive."

"Copy that," Bliss said. "Charlie Team, diving."

"Delta Team, diving," Robillard said from the other SUBCAT.

"Wobix?" Magnus said. "What's your status?"

"My narskill are following right behind you, manservant. What are your intentions?"

Magnus watched his depth gauge pass thirty meters. They needed to get deeper. "My intentions are not to get us all killed from a trinium detonation."

"This is a good intention."

Magnus smiled, but barely. They were passing meter marker thirty. "Everyone, brace for—"

A light from above turned the ocean depths into a whiteout. Magnus's bioteknia eyes and his HUD were both slow to dim and sent pain shooting through his optic nerves. A second later, a subsonic concussion made a gargantuan *kuh-thunk* as it sped toward the ocean floor. Magnus's body felt like it was on a blanket's hem as someone shook it out—head slamming against the inside of his helmet. His ears popped, followed by the sound of emergency indicators blaring in his ears. He winced against the pain and then studied new warnings that flashed on his HUD: Suit Fracture Detected, Port Leg; Suit Fracture Detected, Starboard Elbow; Main Ballast Valve Inoperable, Aft; Helmet Seal Integrity, 19%; Suit Integrity 34%; Location Sensors Array, Offline; Intercommunication Bio Relays, Disabled."

Of all the warnings, it was the last one that concerned Magnus the most. With the bio connection broken, Magnus wouldn't be able to see real-time vitals on his units.

"SITREP," he yelled, but between the ringing in his ears and the warnings, he could hardly hear his own voice. So he yelled the order one more time just to make sure the word got out. When no one responded, Magnus shouted it a third time.

Bliss's voice was the first to break over comms. "Splick! Still here. But barely." The background noise of klaxons and warning chimes flooded the channel. "Sustained heavy damage."

"Us too," Robillard said. "Almost cracked us like an egg. But we're still seaworthy."

That was good news. But Magnus wasn't as concerned with the SUBCATs as he was with the gladias in open water. And, so far, no one was talking back.

"Mysticsdammit, people!"

"I'm here," Awen said. "I'm good, Adonis."

Magnus felt a wave of relief warm his chest. Of all the gladias, Awen was the most important to him. But her safety didn't lessen the growing sense of urgency he felt for the company and the mission.

"Everyone else?"

"Magnus, some comms may be down," Awen said.

Right. Magnus changed gears. "If you can hear my voice and your status is nominal, ping the chat window with an affirmation icon."

Within seconds, green badges raced down the side of the respective HUD frame. Magnus connected the status updates with the gladia names and felt his anxiety begin to lessen. So far, seven of first squad's ten members replied positively. But two former Marauders, Haze and Rix, as well as Longchomps, were unresponsive.

"Does anyone have eyes on Haze, Rix, and Longchomps?" Magnus said. A burst of static fizzled through his biotech interface, coming in and out with someone's voice. A speaker tag blinked to life. It was Zoll.

"...see...chomps. Looks...helmet...now."

"Zoll," Magnus said. "Do you read me? Zoll? Come in!" When Zoll didn't reply, Magnus swished about in the water, hoping his suit would get a fix on Zoll's locator beacon. But the damn location sensors array was still offline. That's when Magnus decided to use the most tactful, state of the art practice he could think of to try and reinitiate the system: he made a fist and clocked the side of his helmet.

"Location Sensors Array rebooting," said a sampled recording of Azelon's smooth female voice.

"When in doubt, knock it out," Magnus said to himself. Two seconds later, compass bearings, unit positions, and vectors returned in Magnus's HUD. He spun himself 110° and found Zoll's tag. The gladia was moving toward Longchomps's location. But unlike the other bodies Magnus saw, the Jujari wasn't moving.

"Come on," Magnus said in a forceful whisper, willing the Jujari to be okay. Zoll closed on Longchomps's location.

More static burst over the comms, followed by the last part of Zoll's sentence: "…unconscious, but looks to be alive."

Magnus hadn't realized he wasn't breathing until he released a pent-up breath. "Stay with him," Magnus said to Zoll. "What about Haze and Rix?" Even as Magnus spun around to search for the two unresponsive gladias, he heard Wish's voice come over the channel.

"I'm closing on Rix," she said. "Still sensing his life force."

The brute of a man had jumped in the water toward the ship's stern and was beyond Magnus's sightline.

"Nearly there," Wish added. "Stand by."

Again, Magnus sensed that he was holding his breath and forced himself to breathe normally. He hated to think that any of his team would die all because he failed to anticipate an act of sabotage.

"He's okay," Wish said. "He's pointing to his helmet. Comms are down."

That only left Haze with Alpha Team. Magnus seemed to recollect that the gladia had jumped amidships, not too far from where he, Awen, and Wobix had entered. Magnus turned his head in the direction he thought Haze might be and then noticed his HUD's vector indicators pointing in the same direction. "I see him,"

Magnus said. He activated his thrusters, but there was no change in his suit's direction. Magus swore under his breath.

"What's wrong?" Awen asked.

"Thrusters are unresponsive," he replied.

"Negative," Abimbola said. "I can see them from here. They seem fine. But you are sinking, fast."

Sure enough, Magnus's depth gauge was spooling out of control. That's when he recalled the damage report list from his suit's AI: the explosion had disabled the MANTA's main ballast valve. If he was sinking, that meant the cavity along his back, the largest of all, was flooded.

"Somebody get to Haze, stat," Magnus said, emphasizing his order by pointing up to the gladia's body. Haze's blackened form hung silhouetted against the light of a massive fireball that billowed far above the ocean's surface some fifty meters overhead.

"I am approaching," Wobix said. Magnus noticed how swiftly the Sekmit propelled himself through the water in his cat-like mech suit. For a feline, the narskill leader sure knew how to navigate in the water.

Magnus watched the two digital identifier tags meet as Wobix closed the distance. A moment later, Wobix reported with a solemn tone: "Your warrior is no more."

Magnus cursed over comms, then he swore again.

"What's the plan, buckethead?" Abimbola said. "You are not getting any lighter from the looks of it."

Magnus was nearing 100 meters of water and falling. He wanted to wait a moment to lament Haze's needless death. But there wasn't time. *There is never enough time.*

"Buckethead?" Abimbola asked.

"We've still got an enemy to engage," Magnus said. "And, unless I'm wrong, they're headed for the mines."

"And it doesn't look like you have a choice anyway," Zoll added.

"Hard copy. Get Longchomps swapped out with someone in the nearest SUBCAT."

"On it."

"You're closest to us, Zoll," Robillard said. "Any volunteers, Delta Team?"

"I'm up to get wet," Reimer said. He was a good choice. The gladia was a sniper, which meant his specialty would come in handy in the event of ranged engagement.

Magnus looked between his feet and saw the faint glow of mine nodes several kilometers below. It was at that same point that he noticed some strange flutters in his HUD. He locked on to a group of the anomalies and then populated it over VNET. "Is anyone else seeing this?" Several affirmation icons popped up.

"Looks like Li-Dain," Awen said. "The water and maybe the pressure are destabilizing their cloaking abilities."

"They are headed for the nodes," Abimbola said.

"Then so are we," Magnus replied. He needed to get word to Forbes about the change in plan and cursed that he had not been faster to contact the captain before abandoning ship. But Magnus didn't have actionable intel at that point, only suspicions.

He pulled up a private channel with the captain. "Forbes, this is Magnus."

Static filled the line.

"Forbes. Come in."

More static. The fallout was most likely messing with the signal strength. "Wobix," Magnus said.

"Yes, manservant."

"Is there any way for you to communicate with your forces at the hovertrain stations? Those with Captain Forbes and Taursar Company?"

"I suspect not. The trinium detonation will disrupt transmissions for several minutes still."

"Right, but what about through the mine nodes? Maybe an internal system?"

Wobix paused long enough that Magnus suspected he'd just given the Sekmit something to think about. "Yes, I believe I can access the intra-mine relay network and ping my captains."

"Try it. Send word of our approximate location and the enemy's intentions."

"Right away."

"Then I need to know how the hell we gain entrance to the mine without flooding the damn thing. 'Cause whatever it is, we can make a bet that the enemy is going to be one step ahead of us. Which means we're going to need an alternate plan."

"Understood."

It took moments for Wobix to report that he was unable to get through to his counterparts on the mainland. That meant defending the mine was going to come down to the forces Magnus had on hand. By his count, that was nineteen gladias in MANTA suits, the two SUBCATS, and twenty-five narskill with Wobix.

Not knowing the enemy's numbers made it impossible to determine if the defender's unit strength would be enough. But at this point, it didn't matter. They had to try. If So-Elku's forces obtained control of the command center, he controlled the planet. He could leverage the mine for anything he wanted, including getting the Sekmit to leave Aluross. And if they didn't? No more Aluross.

As Magnus continued in his out of control plummet toward the ocean floor, he shuddered to think what someone like So-Elku would be capable of if this world fell into his hands. It was no wonder the Republic had kept the find such a secret. Now, however, the responsibility of protecting the Sekmit and saving the galaxy from an emboldened LAW had fallen to Magnus. And he'd be damned if he was going to let the golden diaper babies beat him tonight.

"There are airlocks at the base of each node," Wobix said over the company-wide channel. "Always to the north and south. The codes for entry rotate daily and are generated by a master key system located in the command center."

"The Li-Dain won't have those, will they?" Robillard asked.

"I do not perceive so," Wobix replied. "However, given that they seem confident in the mine's layout, it may be safe to assume that they obtained Governor Littleton's files, which included a master key code."

"Like an override used for VIPs?" Awen asked.

"Correct. In which case, they do not need the rotating security codes to make entry."

"And you know these codes?" Zoll asked.

"I do. However, I would be suspect of the entry points if the enemy thinks we are in pursuit."

"Which, right now, doesn't seem to be a problem," Magnus said.

He'd no sooner said the words than two orbs of yellow light appeared some five hundred meters below him.

"You were saying?" Awen said.

"Aw, splick," Magnus said. "That can't be good."

The orbs expanded until their energy was redirected toward the surface, straight at Magnus's position.

"Look out," Awen yelled. But Magnus was helpless to redirect the negative buoyancy that drove him further into the depths.

It took less than two seconds for the beams to cross the distance. Awen rammed Magnus's MANTA armor and drove him aside. The rays streaked past them both, superheating the water in a flurry of bubbles.

"Wish," Awen yelled. "We need shields on our forces!"

"Got it," the other mystic replied.

More orbs formed in the deep.

"Target those origin points and lock on to any energy patterns you find," Magnus ordered. He de-magged his weapon from his back and brought it around. "Time to see what these TB16s can do underwater."

"Dominate," Bliss yelled.

"Liberate," everyone else replied.

"Obliterate," Wobix added.

Magnus looked in the narskill's direction and smiled. "Nice one."

"What is *nice one*?"

"Ha—I'll explain later." Magnus used his helmet's sensor's array, or what remained of it, to sweep a small sector where the last orb strikes originated from. His HUD showed a cubic meter of water where the temperature was one degree above ambient. Whether residual from the blast or the presence of a Li-Dain, Magnus didn't know. But no time like the present to find out. Plus, the enemy needed to know this wasn't going to be a one-way fight. The weapon's system targeted the region, calculated distance and trajectory, and then prompted Magnus to fire within a rather large operating window—so large, in fact, that when Magnus squeezed the weapon's trigger, he was several degrees off target.

The torpedo bolt exploded from the TB16's barrel with a bright blast of light followed by a blizzard of bubbles. Magnus even felt the recoil push him back in the water, but not enough to thwart his non-stop plunge to the bottom. He tracked the tiny missile as it sped off into the darkness, backlit only by the neon green glow of the closest node. For a few seconds, Magnus wondered if the 16mm round had gotten lost, or maybe there hadn't been an enemy there to begin with—what a waste of a perfectly good shot.

A bright orange explosion billowed, accompanied by a deep *whomp* sound. "Whaddya know," Magnus said.

"Got another one," Silk shouted as a second *whomp* came from an explosion several degrees to the east.

"Scratch one for Rohoar," said the Jujari. "Rohoar does not like being in the water, but he definitely likes this destructive weapon."

"You want us to deploy our units?" Bliss asked Magnus. Each SUBCAT held the rest of Charlie and Delta Teams.

"Negative," Magnus replied. "Sit tight, but put your TB80s to work."

"La-raah," Bliss replied.

The SUBCAT pilot opened fire on several targets at once, but the enemy wasn't taking the assault lying down. More orbs started appearing in an area much more extensive than Magnus expected. Seconds later, at least ten lines of yellow light streaked toward him and the rest of his units.

"Watch out," someone yelled over comms. Magnus felt his body jar to the left as an explosion shoved him off course. He rotated his arms to see that the energy blast had detonated against a Unity shield.

"Thanks," he said to Awen.

"The things I have to do for you." She probably would have said more, but she seemed too focused on keeping everyone else safe.

Magnus found another positive lock on a thermal variant, this one larger than before. In the hopes that maybe he had discovered two targets, he squeezed off two rounds. The torpedoes leaped from the muzzle, one after the other, and tracked toward the target area. Three seconds later, a massive double *whomp* blew shrapnel and what Magnus could have sworn were body parts in a short-lived fire cloud.

"Scratch two," he announced.

As successful as Magnus's efforts had been, he noticed that many more of the gladia's torpedoes were missing than not. For a counterattack, things were not going well. That and the Sekmit had yet to fire on anything. Wobix and his narskill lacked the targeting tech that Azelon had built into the MANTA and TB16 platforms.

I have an idea, Awen said to Magnus privately. *But you're going to need to cover me, and our gladias will be exposed for a moment as I need all three mystics' help.*

Does it mean we get to kill more bad guys? Magnus asked inside his head.

That's the plan.

"Everyone, stay sharp," Magnus said over the channel. "Seems Awen has something she's working on, but it means we won't have shielding. Wish, Telwin, and Finderminth, you're up."

Awen's mystics acknowledged and then went silent. Meanwhile, Magnus watched dozens of torpedo bolts speed toward an ever-widening field of possible enemy positions. Some bolts exploded, taking out the enemy, but more than half did not. The SUCBATS were the most efficient, however, using their four TB80s and advanced sensor suite to violent effect. Just one of the 80mm rounds was enough to produce a concussive force capable of knocking a handful of Li-Dain from their cloaks, several of which died in the process. But even as more maimed bodies appeared, suspended in whirling patches of blood, Magnus was beginning to suspect that the enemy far outnumbered his forces.

"There you are," Awen said over comms.

Magnus turned to look for her, but there was too much commotion between energy streaks and torpedo strikes. Suddenly, from a position over his left shoulder, Magnus saw a bright shaft of magenta light shoot down and strike a space in the water. The resulting flurry of body parts and golden cloth led Magnus to believe she'd successfully hit a Li-Dain. He never doubted that she'd find whatever it was she was looking for. What he hadn't been counting on, however, was the sudden appearance of hundreds of Li-Dain.

"Ho-ly-splick," Robillard said from inside his SUBCAT. "Is everyone else seeing this?"

"I'm counting 100 enemy targets," Silk said. "Make it 200."

"Splick, 300 and counting," Dutch added.

"Someone care to tell me what just happened?" Reimer asked.

"I played a hunch," Awen replied. "Figured they might have one or two mystics in charge of shielding like we do. So, if you take them out—"

"You expose the rest," Magnus said. "Great work."

The plus side to Awen's quick thinking was that the gladias and narskill no longer had to guess at target locations; the downside was realizing Magnus and his units were outnumbered almost eight to one.

"Finally," Wobix said. "Fishies we can see."

The Sekmit's locator beacon put him just over Magnus's right shoulder. Magnus looked up and watched as the mech-encased feline charged his Thørzin power bow and drew back the blue strand of light. Spread along a line to Wobix's left and right, more shafts of blue light appeared between the paws of the other twenty-five narskill.

"Goodbye, little fishies," Wobix said, and then he loosed his dazzling Unity arrow into the abyss.

18

RICIO TAPPED the combat spatial display's holoprojector lens to make sure it wasn't shorting out. Not that he doubted the integrity of Azelon's craftsmanship. But every system needed maintenance, no matter how advanced the manufacturing civilization was.

"Is something the matter, sir?" Azelon asked.

"You spying on me again, Azie?"

"I simply noticed that you are tampering with your CSD's lens. That, combined with a slight increase in blood pressure, would indicate that you fear an element of your Fang is failing you in some way."

"So, you're spying on me."

"Are my suspicions correct, though?"

Ricio sighed. "You know, having an ultra-intelligent AI as a wing-woman can really be intimidating."

"I'll take that as a compliment, sir."

"Figured you would." Ricio sat back in his seat and motioned toward the malfunctioning CSD in exasperation. "It's this latest sensor sweep. I'm getting a huge dead zone in the reading."

"Dead zone, sir?"

"Yeah." Ricio set ident parameters around the region and zoomed in. He and the rest of Fang Company were spread out over Meesrin Pin, silently patrolling the LAW's Battleship-class equivalent, *Enduring Vigilance*, when Ricio noticed a strange readout. *Or lack thereof*, he noted to himself. He forwarded the exact coordinates to Azelon.

"Reviewing now, sir," she replied. After only one second, she said, "It does appear that your sensor array is experiencing some unknown issues, sir."

"So I'm not going crazy," Ricio said with some measure of satisfaction.

"That remains to be seen, sir."

"Cute."

"Be that as it may, I'm going to ask you to return to the *Spire* for full diagnostic review."

"Copy that."

"In the meantime, I will run a scan from the *Spire* to ensure that —" Her voice cut out.

Ricio frowned. "Azie? You all good?"

"It appears that the *Spire* may also need full diagnostic review," she replied after a moment.

"So you're seeing it too?" Ricio straightened in his seat. "That's not good."

"Agreed, sir."

"I beg both your pardons," TO-96 interrupted. "But it appears we may have an urgent issue onboard the oceanic hydrofoil freighter."

"Magnus's?"

TO-96 canted his head to the right. "Mr. Ricio, I fail to see how this particular OHF belongs, as it were, to Mr. Magnus. Rather, it is the property—"

"I mean the one Magnus is on."

"Why, yes. Of course, sir."

"Oh dear," Azelon said, turning to TO-96. "Yes, that does appear to be an urgent issue. Perhaps a catastrophic one at that."

"Would someone please tell me what the hell is going on?"

As if in answer to Ricio's question, a bright light flashed somewhere to the west, bathing the entire Leonï Ocean in white light. Ricio's windowplex shield dimmed. The light vanished, replaced instead by a brilliant fireball that seemed to rise from the water's skin like an irritated boil. Racing to all points on the map, a ring of energy shot away from the epicenter, bowing the blue surface in an ever-expanding circular trench.

"Great mystics," Ricio whispered. "Was that what I think it was?"

"If you were thinking, 'My, that looks like it was a solar flare,' then the answer is no," TO-96 said. "Likewise, if you were thinking, 'It was more like a meteor strike,' the answer is also no. Likewise, if you—"

"Was that trinium? Was that Magnus's ship?"

"Initial sensor readings confirm your suspicions, sir," Azelon said. "I am sorry."

"Was he on it?" Ricio could feel the restraints digging into his chest as he strained to watch the massive fireball rise from the planet's surface.

"A review of Magnus's last communications with the Colonel is inconclusive, commander," TO-96 said.

"Well"—Ricio waved his hands around like it would whip the two bots into action—"can't you find out? Review video? Something?"

"Yes, of course, sir," Azelon said. "However—"

"Was that Magnus's ship?" Ezo said as his face appeared in Ricio's HUD.

Sootriman's entered next. "Please tell me that wasn't Awen."

Ricio threw a frustrated hand at the holo image of Azelon and TO-96. "I'm trying to get these bots to give me something useful."

"What's the holdup, Tee-Oh?" Sootriman asked.

"Your elevated worshipfulness, as I have inform Commander Ricio, we are endeavoring to—"

"I've got something," Azelon interjected.

A beat later, Ricio's HUD filled with a first-person view camera feed shot from someone's helmet onboard the OHF. Based on the identifier in the corner, it belonged to Magnus. A second smaller video window appeared atop the first, giving Ricio a top-down view of several gladias on the ship's outer decks. "You seeing this, you guys?"

"Ezo does," Ezo said.

"Me too," replied Sootriman.

The gladias didn't appear to move at first.

"Do you have audio on this?" Ezo asked.

In the feed, they could see Magnus grab a slender looking gladia and throw the person off the side of the ship.

"That's Awen," Sootriman said with a relieved tone.

All at once, Magnus's voice came over the recording. "Everyone off and dive!" A second later, he added: "Move it, Fluffy!"

"Rohoar is moving it," Rohoar replied.

Magnus appeared to leap down to a lower deck, where he

waited for the Jujari to emerge from inside the ship. "About time. Let's go!"

Then the two gladias hurled themselves overboard. Magnus's camera feed filled with bubbles and then was consumed with an inky blackness. There were several seconds of static-filled chatter, and then the feed went blank. Meanwhile, the orbital view washed out.

"Sacred songs of Melodeon," Sootriman whispered.

"I don't know what that means," Ricio said. "But I'm with you, sister."

"Any further communication from them, 'Six?" Ezo asked.

"Negative, sir," Azelon said. "But even if they tried, the fallout will most likely knock out communications for several minutes."

Those next several minutes came and went as Ricio, Ezo, Sootriman, and the bots discussed what to do next. Their plans to sweep the ocean for life signs were interrupted by an incoming call from Colonel Caldwell.

"Any word from Granther Company?"

"I'm afraid not, sir," TO-96 replied. "Our spectrometers are still reading substantial interference patterns such that all communications within the blast radius are disrupted."

"Keep trying. I want to know the second we reestablish contact with Magnus."

"Affirmative, sir."

No sooner had the colonel ended the transmission than Ricio noticed something else strange on his combat spatial display. "Um, is anyone else seeing a squadron of Talons leave the *Enduring Vigilance* right now?"

"What?" Ezo said. He leaned toward his dashboard to double-check his displays. "Since when did the LAW get starfighters?"

"Can you confirm, Azelon?" Ricio said, his tone becoming all business.

"I can, sir. What you are seeing are fourteen Galactic Republic Talons."

"It looks like they're headed for the surface," Sootriman said.

"Extrapolate possible targets based on current trajectory," Ricio said to the bots.

"They're headed toward the capital," TO-96 replied.

"Not if we have anything to say about it," Ricio said.

"Would you like me to scramble the other two squadrons, sir?" Azelon asked.

Normally, Ezo commanded Blue Squadron, but Ricio had pulled the pilot and his wife into Red for the support op. Ricio liked having the pair with him and counted them as some of the best pilots he'd ever flown with.

"Negative, Azie. We can take 'em, so long as they haven't figured out a way to start shooting Unity blaster bolts or some splick." Ricio offered Ezo and Sootriman a crooked smile, but they returned half grins that lacked any of the confidence he hoped his quip might inspire. *'Cause they haven't figured out how to do that, right Ricio?* he thought. "Your new cloaking concoction still working?"

"By cloaking concoction, do you mean the telecolos skin we applied to your Fangs?"

"Sure do."

"Then yes, it is *still working*, as it was only applied a few days ago. It should keep your visual identifiers to a minimum, though even with my new particle modifiers on your engine systems, you will still be somewhat visible via multispectrum sensors scans."

"Understood. Every little bit helps." Ricio kissed his fingertips and then touched the printed photo of his wife and son for good luck. Knowing his family was safe and sound on Aluross's surface meant the world to him; it also said he'd be damned if he was going to let these fighters enter the planet's atmo. "Time to get our hands dirty, kids."

"Targets populating your CSDs now," Ricio said as he accepted and sent Azelon's tracking data across Red Squadron's fourteen Fangs. Numerically, this was going to be a one-to-one matchup against the LAW's Talons, but that didn't concern him. Not only were the Fangs a superior fighting platform, but Ricio had the element of surprise—something the enemy could have had too if they'd used the same cloaking tech on their fighters as they used on their drop shuttles. Instead, the Talons were out in the open, which meant they didn't have a clue that they were being hunted. *Just the way we like it*, Ricio thought to himself.

"Fangs, prepare to engage," Ricio said to his pilots as he started double-checking his ship's weapons systems and shielding.

"Red Two, standing by," Ezo said.

"Red Three, standing by," Sootirman replied.

The remaining eleven Fangs sounded off as Ricio double-checked everyone's positions and target assignments. "Be ready for orbital defense fire from the *Vigilance* once they triangulate our locations from our engagement. Remember, the LAW just invaded Aluross, tried to take over a Sekmit trinium freighter, and then torched it, all of which are acts of war. The fact that a whole lot of our friends were underneath it too should fuel your resolve, but don't let it shake your aim either."

"Understood, Rick," Ezo said.

Ricio eyed Ezo's image in the HUD's comm region. "You mean Ricio?"

"Nah, Ezo meant Rick. When you get all business, your voice changes, and you're a real son of a bitch for a little bit. That's Rick."

Ricio chuckled. "Whatever makes you shoot better."

"Oh, it does." Ezo stretched his neck side to side. "It certainly does."

The fourteen Talons were spread out in a loose diamond formation, diving toward Aluross. They looked like glimmering jewels set against a black mat as if some gargantuan jeweler was about to scoop them up for examination under a loupe. Hundreds of kilometers below lay the sparkling Sekmit cities. But even the brightness of Meesrin Pin, whose street lights and hover lines glowed against the dark continent, was dwarfed by the still-burning fireball that loomed over the Leonï Ocean.

"Accelerate to attack speed," Ricio said. He took a deep breath and then slowed his breathing.

Ricio's combat spatial display showed the enemy squadron six kilometers away—extremely close as far as void engagements went. He focused on the Talon assigned to him and watched as the targeting reticle narrowed, reducing the chance of a missed shot with each nanosecond that passed. Faster and faster the Fangs flew as the distance closed to less than two kilometers. Red Squadron was practically on top of the Talons when Ricio gave the order. "Weapons free. You are clear to engage the enemy."

Through his Novian biotech interface, Ricio coaxed his Fang to fire both its NR45 primary blasters and NX90 secondary heavy cannons on the unsuspecting Talon in the middle of the enemy formation. It was hardly a fair fight. But then again, neither was blowing up a trinium freighter. The blaster bolts leaped from Ricio's Fang like wide-open spigots of hellfire, as they did from the rest of Red Squadron's starfighters, and met every enemy target in the blink of an eye.

The fire effect would have been stunning. It would have lit up the night sky for hundreds of klicks. It would have—had the enemy Talons been where the targeting systems said they were. But they weren't. And Red Squadron's blaster rounds passed straight through a Talon group that blinked out of existence.

"Red Squadron, evasive maneuvers," Ricio yelled. He'd barely gotten the words out when the Fangs started taking enemy fire from behind.

19

CALDWELL VISUALLY INSPECTED Piper's harness as he heard the DS9-APC's drive core spool up in a loud whine. Every one of his gladias knew the risks they'd signed up for, but if anything happened to the kid, he'd never forgive himself. Plus, if she went down, he knew So-Elku wouldn't stay put for very long. Caldwell winked at Piper through his HUD, and she winked back.

"Hold tight, little one," he said.

"You too, big one."

Caldwell grinned then populated his field of view with numerous exterior camera feeds to track the oncoming carnage. Nelson's DS9 had taken position just in front of Caldwell's, while a third took point. From there, the other vehicles spread away from the tip like an arrowhead, enveloping Caldwell's DS9 to shield it from assault both in front and behind.

To the formation's exterior, the Sekmit battle bikes surged forward and focused fire ahead of the lead APC. Their Thørzin crossbows charged and released in a steady cadence that Caldwell could feel in his chest. The brilliant blue blast bolts sizzled across the gap between APCs and Li-Dain, smashing into the enemy's Unity shields with explosions of yellow and cobalt sparks. But the Sekmit's concentrated fire carved a small hole in the defensive wall. The shots that followed blew Luma off their feet, sending them a dozen meters skyward.

"Hell, yeah," Caldwell exclaimed as he watched the enemy line give way. Then he caught himself and looked at Piper. "Sorry."

"Hell, yeah," she replied through a broad smile and with a raise of a tiny fist.

"Piper," Willowood said in protest, but any further rebuke was cut short as the convoy took return fire.

Bright golden streaks of light leaped from the defensive line and collided with the lead APC. Fortunately, the beastly vehicle's shields absorbed most of the energy in stride. Caldwell glanced at the DS9's status metrics and saw its forward shields drop by twenty-eight percent. Some of the Sekmit battle bikes weren't so lucky.

The colonel watched as one bike to the left took a direct hit in the front repulsor, a blow that sent the vehicle cartwheeling through the air. Fire and smoke covered the battle bike behind the first, forcing the driver to swerve. When the Sekmit did, however, the action put the second bike in a line of fire that drilled the crossbow gunner in the chest and head. A third Luma round struck the driver, and the battle bike lurched to the right. Without a pilot, the vehicle pitched under the nearest DS9 with a loud *crack* and was spit out the back, chassis pulverized from the gravity compression field.

"Escorts taking heavy fire," DiAntora said as more incoming Luma rounds strafed the roadway and collided with the battle bikes.

"Where the hell is our return fire?"

"Coming online now, Colonel," Nelson said. "Takes a sec to cycle up."

The high-pitched shriek of the MUT50 above Caldwell's head couldn't have come any sooner. "'Bout damn time." He watched as the ultra-torrent tri-reticulating blaster fire washed across the enemy's front line, further widening the gap now less than 600 meters ahead. Not to be outdone by the forward cannon, the rear-mounted RBMB, or really big missile battery, started coughing out its 70mm guided rounds to either side of the new lane that emerged amidst the sea of Li-Dain.

"Tell those bikes to get behind us," Caldwell yelled just as the convoy was about to punch through the enemy line. "Everyone, hold on."

To the colonel's surprise, the first DS9 drove into the narrow gap in the Li-Dain wall, with only minimal damage to its already ailing shields. The next APCs, however, were less fortunate. Running three abreast, the armored vehicles on either end clipped the enemy shields, causing the units to pitch up precariously. The DS9 on the right bucked like it was jolting over rough ground, while the one on the left nearly rolled over.

But Advanced Galactic Solutions wasn't in the habit of fabricating garbage for its most valued client. Side-mounted repulsor panels built into the chassis flared in a bright blaze, righting the perplexed APC. The blasts caught one unlucky Li-Dain off guard, boring through his Unity shield and flash-incinerating the man. The vehicle continued over the remaining Unity shield wall like it was skimming across elevated terrain and then dropped down the backside to return to the blacktop.

Next, it was Caldwell's turn.

The Sekmit driver floored the APC, and the colonel felt the

drive core rumble under his feet. The sensation brought back a slew of memories from systems across the quadrant—the wars of his younger years, as he called them. *If we'd only been so lucky to have a rig like this back in those days*, he thought. He grabbed the handholds on either side of his headrest and braced for impact while watching the camera feeds in his HUD. For the briefest moment, his eyes focused on Piper, who sat across the aisle from him. Had they been mad to include her in all of this? Wasn't she just a child?

No, he thought. *Piper's not* just *anything.* Without her, they'd have been dead already. She was as much a part of this fight as his wrinkly old ass—*just a hell of a lot cuter.*

The MUT50 overhead fired on full auto as the APC crossed the enemy threshold. The DS9s to the right and left learned from those who'd gone earlier and slowed to pull in behind Caldwell's vehicle, sparing themselves a world of hurt and upheaval.

As the long line of APCs and battle bikes piped through the central corridor they'd carved, the Li-Dain pummeled the convoy's sides with proximity blows. Caldwell watched an aerial view, shot from some sort of drone, as the line of vehicles shot through the gauntlet. Bright explosions of yellow light blossomed on each side, rattling the APCs and those inside. His own bag of bones shook against the seat—helmet smashing left and right in the headrest.

But the Li-Dain weren't the only ones close to their targets. Half the concussions rocking the DS9s were blowback from their own ordnance. 70mm missile rounds detonated point-blank against the enemy phalanx while the MUT50 clawed their way through the hordes. Three Li-Dain lost their shielding to an RBMB round, only to be cut down a split second later by a solid stream of blaster fire. Bits of body burst apart and showered the shields of their fellow warriors.

And then, just like that, Caldwell's DS9-APC was out the other side. "Keep the heat on those bastards," Caldwell barked. "I want them to think twice about following us."

But even as Nelson complied with the command, the aerial feed showed the Li-Dain break formation and follow the rear-most battle bikes. To their credit, the Sekmit fought fearlessly. Their crossbows lined up on several Li-Dain who had not redirected their shields toward the now-fleeing convoy. One Thørzin charge ended up piercing through no fewer than five enemy warriors stacked in a line. The blue energy round punctured their chests in such quick succession that the enemy took a while to register the blows before falling like Paglothian dominos.

But that was the last lucky shot the Sekmit would get.

Li-Dain shields radiated against the barrage of blaster fire as the convoy accelerated away. Up ahead, Caldwell could see the space-port rising above the buildings; it was still six klicks away, but at these speeds, they'd be there soon enough—just had to hold off the enemy pursuit.

"They appear to be closing on us, colonel," DiAntora said.

"The hell they are." Caldwell stood up and looked out the rear-facing windows. At the same time, he kept one eye on the drone camera feed. "Well tickle my Temarian julip berries." Sure enough, the little robed bastards were riding some sort of light-based hover-cycles. "Willowood. You know about these?"

Willowood stood up and joined Caldwell to look out the back windows. "They're using the Nexus to conduct their bodies through physical space. It's theoretically possible, of course, but I've never seen anything like it."

"Well, believe it, 'cause they're coming fast." He got Nelson back on the line. "Tell the convoy to be ready for—"

Three sequential blasts struck the APC's left side, knocking Caldwell off balance. He felt the vehicle drift right as he reached out to steady himself.

"To be ready for that," the colonel finished. Fits of light flickered as the MUT50 returned fire on two Luma cycles that pulled alongside their APC. Caldwell hesitated to call the red and yellow looking cycles "vehicles" as their lines were too far blurred to constitute solid mass. Still, the riders leaned into energy like any person might ride a regular speed bike.

"We need to shake those," Caldwell said.

"Hold on," Nelson said.

No sooner had the colonel grabbed a ceiling-mounted handhold than the DS9 lurched to the left. Willowood was knocked off her feet, but Caldwell caught her around the waist. "Gotcha."

She probably would have said something smart in reply, but the APC slammed into the two Luma cycles. The force jarred Willowood and Caldwell, causing his Mark I's servos to whine. The passenger compartment's other crew member's heads bounced around like the spring-loaded noggins on those damn dashboard toys.

"Oh, no you don't," Nelson said, probably more to himself than anyone on the channel. The DS9 rolled right and then shot left again, slamming against the Luma riders. This time, one of their shields gave way, and the light bike vanished out from under the Li-Dain. The man face-planted so hard into the pavement that Caldwell thought he saw the victim's head flatten in a spray of red. But it was there and gone before he could process it.

The remaining Luma pulled in close and latched onto the APC, well under the MUT50's reach.

At first, Caldwell thought his eyes were playing tricks on him. "You seeing this?" he asked Willowood.

She looked above Piper's head and must've seen it too because she unlatched the child's safety harness and pulled her out of the seat. The wall glowed red hot, and Caldwell's suit temperature gauge rocketed over 480° Celsius in no time flat.

"I've got this," said a small voice. Piper pulled herself out of Willowood's grip and threw her fists down to her sides with stiff arms. Through the left-side windows, Caldwell saw the Luma and his light bike blast toward the nearest building and then explode in a burst of fire that raked the sidewalk.

"You need to stay focused on So-Elku," Willowood said as she assisted the girl and helped her buckle in on the opposite wall.

"Though we're grateful for whatever that was," Caldwell said, thumbing over his shoulder toward the still-glowing armored wall. A moment later, however, more light cycles pulled up alongside the APC and started firing at the same place.

"Uh, I hate to be the bearer of bad news, Colonel," Nelson said. "But we've got more Li-Dain."

"Splick from a whale whore's nether regions, son. Where?"

"Dead ahead, sir."

Caldwell called up the DS9's forward-facing cams and saw another street-wide roadblock just like the last one. "Hell, we can't do that again. Cyril, you read?"

"Sure, sure, poppa alpha. I read you loud and crystal clear, ten by ten-twenty, Colonel, sir."

"We need another way to the spaceport, stat."

"Yeah, sure. No problem. Ha ha. This is so much like *Wheels of Hellfire: Battle for Nova Centari*, where you have to reroute Egon's war carriage through Simbiant City without running into Hammer Lord's death squads."

"Do you die in real life if you lose?"

"Ha ha, of course not, Mr. Colonel alpha male." The code slicer paused for a second. "But you do in *Vexus III* if you opt for the black market bio-interface module."

"Is that so? 'Cause that's the same thing we're looking at here, kid."

"You got an MX25-B? Do you have any idea how—"

"I need a damn route, Cyril!"

"All set, sir. Already patched it to Mr. ex-Marine Nelson's nav comp."

"Got it," Nelson said.

"You're a gem, son," Caldwell said to Cyril. "Keep playing those video games."

"Technically, sir, they're not video games. Rather, they are complex multi-path architecture—"

"Sounds great, son. Tell me more later, copy?"

"Copy, big roger daddy."

"I know I sound like a broken disk drive," Nelson said. "But everyone's gonna wanna hold on here."

The APC broke from the pack and turned hard right, throwing all the passengers to the far left wall. Caldwell's feet hovered over the red patch of metal as he held onto the ceiling-mounted hand-hold. That's when he heard Willowood let out a wild yell that was somewhere between a cackle and a scream. For a second, he thought she was hurt; instead, she was holding onto the right side window above Piper's head and smiling as the vehicle turned onto the side street.

"Think they'll let me drive next?" she said to Caldwell when he asked if she was okay.

"You're one wild momma. You know that?"

Willowood winked at him through her HUD cam. "Wouldn't you like to know."

"You guys are gross," Piper said.

Any mirth from the moment was shattered when more Luma fire burst against their DS9 and sent it sliding against the nearest building. Rather than bind against the structure, the APC pushed away using the side repulsors and accelerated down the side street that Cyril had picked. Caldwell pulled up a live topo map and saw that the lead APCs had done an about-face and were following the rest of the convoy down the detour.

Seconds later, four Sekmit battle bikes pulled up alongside Caldwell's vehicle and raised their helmeted faces toward the blackout windows. The colonel wasn't sure if they could see him, either through shared HUD transmission or with the cats' powers in the Unity, but he saluted them nonetheless—just in case.

The escorts' Thørzin crossbows charged new energy bolts and then shot them back down the street where Luma cycles were no doubt in pursuit. Caldwell called up the aerial cam again and overlaid it with the topo map so he could keep track of the ident tags in real-time. He stopped counting at twenty Luma cycles following them down the corridor. "Damn bastards aren't taking this one lying down," Caldwell said to anyone listening.

As if to emphasize the point, more Luma energy streaked along both sides of the lead APC. Caldwell pushed Nelson to return fire, but the captain said the convoy was blocking all targets. Instead, it was left to the Sekmit escorts, who had much better sightlines. However, that also meant they were in harm's way.

One Sekmit cycle to the right suffered a direct hit that struck its drive core: the bike detonated in a trinium explosion that rocked the APC side to side.

"Shields at twenty-nine percent, Colonel," Nelson reported, but Caldwell already had the vehicle's stats pulled up.

"Keep our cat driving!"

The other Sekmit bike to the right took several rounds before folding into the street in a blaze of shrapnel. Within seconds, three Luma cycles took its place. Then there were several loud *thuds* on the APC's roof.

"Left turn," Nelson yelled.

Caldwell leaned with the turn this time as their armored personnel pushed them to the right. The Luma bikes pressed against the sides, and at least one Li-Dain touched the wall, turning it red hot.

"I've got this one," Willowood said as if telling Piper to stay put. She tucked her fists underneath her armpits, which attracted swirling motes of light that drew toward her hands. Then Willowood shot her palms forward with a shout. The energy in her hands passed through the APC's wall and struck whoever was on the other side. The victim sailed away from the carrier and blew through a bodega.

"Remind me never to make her mad," Caldwell said to Piper in an attempt to keep the mood light.

"Yeah," she replied with a mischievous smile. "She can totally take you."

Caldwell laughed—because he knew it was true.

The APC's metal superstructure began creaking overhead as the ceiling turned red.

"These cockroaches just won't leave us the hell alone," the colonel said.

The MUT50 turret gunner screamed over VNET, followed by the sound of a loud crunch and then an explosion that sent smoke and fire billowing through the passenger compartment.

"They've taken out our 50," DiAntora yelled.

Caldwell de-magged his NOV2 from his back and raised it with one hand, all while stepping in front of Piper. "We've got these," he said to Willowood, indicating the intruders. "You and Piper keep any more from hitching a ride."

"You got it, handsome," Willowood said.

Caldwell, along with DiAntora and the rest of the gladias, narskill, and Repub Marines, raised their barrels toward the gaping hole in the roof. The moment someone saw a foot enter the gap, weapons started spitting blaster bolts from every angle. Caldwell actually pitied whoever had followed some LAW officer's orders to breach the roof and enter. He'd seen plenty of higher-ups give suicide orders in his day; he was just glad to be on the opposite end of the bone-headed directives for once.

It was also at that moment that Caldwell learned something else about the enemy—something critical. For all their superpowers and mystical arts, the Li-Dain were not tacticians. To the unlearned, waging war was all about who had the most numbers, the most guns, and the most ammo. But in real life, winning came down to tactics, patience, and supply lines. And in this case, the Luma demonstrated that while they may have mastered a lethal craft, they did not know how to take out an armored vehicle.

Instead of dropping a VOD through the hole in the APC's roof—a literal application to the oft-quoted "fire in the hole" phrase—the Li-Dain warrior opted to jump down feet first. The Luma was drilled with so many blaster rounds that his body wasn't even recognizable by the time it landed on the deck in ribbons.

In response, the Marines took up firing positions to cut off the enemy's angle of attack and made plenty of floor space just in case some Li-Dain decided to drop a detonator through the hole. In that case, the Marines could quickly grab the ordnance and toss it out—a crude and risky practice, but one they were trained for. The most effective defense was often the simplest defense.

The next Li-Dain got smart, choosing to fire an energy round into the APC before edging toward the smoking hole. But that was only one step below stupid as the defenders had a clear sightline to the enemy's head, which they wrested from the woman's shoulders with three-round bursts. Her body flipped backward and disappeared off the vehicle's side.

Caldwell looked to one of Hedgebore Company's gladias. "Pop a VOD and mag-lock it."

The man nodded, removed a detonator from his hip, and adjusted the setting. Then he tossed it up through the hole. The device made it less than a meter above the roof when its magnetic resonance pads drew it sideways and stuck it to the reinforced metal decking. Caldwell heard the telltale *clunk* that gave any Marine who'd seen combat the willies. A beat later, the VOD detonated and rocked the roof.

As long as the assailants hadn't put up any shields, that should have done the job. Caldwell flicked his sensors to thermal and upped the sensitivity to deep scan. The only thing he saw on the roof was the radiant glow of the armor plating. Apparently, the sticky VOD had worked. That, and it had given off an unusually bright energy burst.

"What'd you put in that, corporal?" Caldwell asked the gladia who'd tossed the grenade. "Some of your nana's private pouch of pootang?"

"Negative, Colonel," the man replied, looking through the hole. "That came from orbit."

Caldwell chanced a glance toward the night sky and saw small motes of light flitting about. The colonel knew an orbital dogfight when he saw one, and someone had just gone nova. "Let's just hope it wasn't us," he said. Caldwell was about to check in with the bots to make sure everything was okay when Nelson yelled over comms.

"Another hard left."

"You heard him," Caldwell said as he pointed to the webbed slings that lined the ceiling. Hands shot up and grabbed a fistful of the black weave just as the APC lurched sideways.

The colonel looked out the window and saw more Sekmit battle bikes pull up alongside the Luma cycles. They attacked one another, exchanging crossbow bolts and streaking orbs of light. The cityscape whizzed by, adding to the visual chaos like someone had thrown neon screens and holo displays in a blender and hit purée.

One Luma cycle seemed to be doling out an unusual amount of damage. Caldwell noted it to Willowood, who then passed instructions to Piper. The child smiled and then lowered her head as if in prayer. Caldwell wondered why Willowood gave the task to the girl, but there wasn't time to inquire. All Caldwell could do was watch in amazement as the Luma cycle blinked out from beneath the rider, sending him face-first into the blacktop.

Piper's eyes opened, and she smiled into her HUD cam. "Like that, Mr. Colonel William?"

Caldwell chuckled. "That'll do, little lady. That'll do just fine."

"Colonel," came Nelson's voice. "We're approaching the spaceport."

"'Bout damn time." Caldwell opened the company channel for the entire convoy. So far, they hadn't lost a single DS9, and he intended to keep it that way. "Listen up. We've gotta assume the enemy's dug into the hangar bay. We're gonna clear the spaceport one section at a time until we reach the Repub's ship, bay…" He looked to DiAntora.

"Twenty-nine," she offered.

"Bay twenty-nine," Caldwell said with a nod. "I want snipers on the rim, topside. Anyone runs into a nest, tag it and wait for support. I'm not doing funerals for solo heroes. La-raah?"

Confirmation icons raced down the chat window even though he knew not everyone would be familiar with the Gladio Umbra's verbal cue. But if the fighters had any doubts as to what it meant, Caldwell's no-nonsense delivery made it clear. For the Marines present, however, he added, "Own the field," to which they replied with "OTF" badges in the HUD.

"How close can you get us to bay twenty-nine?" Caldwell asked Nelson.

"Not as close as you're gonna like, colonel."

"Do your best, captain."

"Copy that."

Nelson ordered the convoy into a concave formation with orders to defend the rear as the APCs approached the monolithic spaceport. MUT50s and RBMBs continued to spew defensive fire at the chasing Luma cycles. Fiery explosions momentarily enveloped whole sections of the enemy pursuit only for the radiant bikes to reemerge into clear air. But still, there were enough Li-Dain flooding the streets that Caldwell feared his convoy might be overwhelmed when they stopped.

"Willowood," he said as he turned to her. "Think Paladia Company can build us a wall? Buy us some time?"

"We can come up with something, yes," she replied.

"Just don't sacrifice the support of Piper and the prisoners."

"Right."

Caldwell felt his APC decelerate. He glanced outside to see each vehicle begin to rotate, prepping for the ramps to drop toward the spaceport. Simultaneously, all roof-mounted weapons, at least those that hadn't been blown off, pivoted to keep the enemy at bay. "Let's give 'em hell." He was just about to walk down the APC's ramp when large-caliber blaster fire chewed up the pavement. A beat later, he heard the unmistakable engine whine of Talons in a diving run.

20

To Magnus's astonishment, he watched Wobix's Thørzin bolt streak through the water and slice through no less than three Li-Dain in a row. The energy seemed to curve as it followed an unconventional path through the enemy bodies. Magnus blinked twice just to make sure the watery depths weren't playing tricks on him.

"Can your weapons do that?" Wobix asked as if picking up on Magnus's dismay.

"They most certainly can't," Magnus replied. But he wasn't about to let the cat have all the fun. Even despite his non-stop descent to the ocean floor, Magnus targeted one enemy after another and used his bioteknia eye in collaboration with his MANTA's HUD and sensor suite to fire on the Li-Dain. One torpedo bolt detonated prematurely—set off by one force or another—and managed to knock three Li-Dain out, rupturing shields and tearing through soft tissue. Magnus looked at Wobix's face in the chat windows and forwarded him a video loop of the carnage. "But they can do that."

"You got lucky," Wobix replied.

"Maybe."

"Definitely lucky."

Magnus didn't have time to continue bantering, however, as he had a far more pressing issue to attend to, that of surviving his breakneck fall. Assuming he didn't crack his suit, get shot, or a combination of both, then he needed to figure out how to walk toward a mine airlock without being ground into the ocean floor.

Even as he descended past them, Magnus continued firing on the Li-Dain. Several enemies looked from inside their protective bubbles, their faces filled with surprise. But they were too busy defending against the bulk of the gladias and Sekmit further above to pay him heed, which was fine by Magnus. He fired three more torpedo bolts at the enemy before sinking past them and into the clear. The only thing below his feet was a dark expanse dotted with ever-growing mine nodes.

Magnus did his best to calculate his trajectory—a feat made difficult by the cross currents and random nature of an object slipping through water. Fortunately, however, there seemed to be a green-glowing node rising to meet him. From what his MANTA's onboard AI told him, if he angled his body slightly ahead and to starboard, he should be able to land on the node.

"Wobix," Magnus said. "Looks like I'll be reaching one of those airlocks before everyone else."

"I would advise against doing what I believe you are suggesting you do," the Sekmit replied.

"Not securing the lock before the enemy?"

"Correct. You will be one against their whole number upon infiltration. Rather, I suggest you land atop the nearest node's dome and await our arrival. I have a plan."

"But if the Li-Dain gain access to the dome before we do—"

"That is a statistical inevitability, manservant. Let them continue on their course. We will adapt."

"I'm trusting you, pal."

"As you should."

Magnus aligned his body with his nav computer's suggested descent angle and watched as he slowly adjusted course over the dome. The underlying superstructure would absorb his impact without breaking, and his suit's servos would keep his legs from crumpling into mush—at least, that's what Magnus hoped would happen. He found himself holding his breath as he neared the green dome, readying himself for the impact.

Two things dawned on Magnus in the seconds before he struck the structure. The first was just how massive the edifice was. He'd already been impressed with the underwater environments during the Gladio Umbra's tour of the command facility. But this dome seemed even more massive than the command one, at least by a factor of four. Just when Magnus thought he was about to collide with the surface, the building kept growing larger and larger until it eclipsed any view of the ocean floor beyond.

The second thing that struck him was just how fast he was traveling. Since losing his aft ballast tank, his body had turned into a veritable missile, one that streaked toward the dome with a death wish.

"Awen, any chance you're able to, I don't know, keep me from drilling this node like a human torpedo?" Magnus asked.

"Whoa," was all Awen said, as if noticing his velocity for the first time since the battle began.

Magnus watched the distance to impact close, sure that he was about to die in one of the least heroic ways imaginable. He'd closed to within twenty-five meters of the node's summit when he felt his body decelerate, made evident by the way his stomach dropped into his boots.

"Hold on," Awen said, her voice tight.

"To what?" Magnus replied through gritted teeth.

Even with Awen's help, he was still closing the gap way too fast. "Awen?"

"You're too far," she shouted.

That was the last thing Magnus heard before the jolt knocked him out.

Magnus followed the sound of warning trills back toward consciousness. When he finally opened his eyes, he lay flat on a green lawn that glowed from with the brightness of a full moon. Only the yard wasn't composed of soft grass; instead, it was hard. And it had hurt him. Bad.

"Magnus? Do you read?" It was a woman's voice. Someone he knew. "Magnus!"

"Splick," Magnus replied. "You don't have to shout."

Awen sighed. "Mystics, you're all right."

"If this is what all right feels like, I'd hate to know what not all right is."

"Stay put. We're about a minute out from your position."

"Doesn't look like I have too much of a choice." Among the several HUD indicators that jockeyed for his attention was a center-most one, flashing the words Hull Failure: Breach Imminent. Between the impact's force and the crushing pressure at this depth, his MANTA suit declared, in no uncertain terms, that it had had enough. And he didn't exactly blame the armor. If anything, he wanted to give it a love pat and a well-wish for its next life—assuming he could get out of the thing.

The node's curve swept out and away from Magnus's position. True to its projections, angling his body in the final half klick had put him square on top of the dome. And thanks to Awen's help, he had avoided both drilling through and being pancaked on top of the surface. Though, given the pain that wracked him, he doubted if he wasn't less pancaked than had he hit at full speed. His HUD read that the MANTA's nanobots had already been deployed, attending to some minor organ repair and multiple capillary hemorrhages.

"Bless you, tiny bots," Magnus said as he continued to take in deep breaths—which drew his eyes to the next most prominent warning: Oxygen Levels: Depleted. "What did you say your ETA was, Awen?"

"Forty-five seconds," she replied.

That was just under the sixty-second breath-holding limit he tried to maintain as a frequent traveler in the void. One never knew when one long breath might save your life. Granted, he knew he had had at least another minute of oxygen in his blood before his brain went sour, but he'd rather things not come to that if possible.

"And how long before you think you can get us inside, Wobix?"

"As I said, I have a plan. Not more than a few minutes, perhaps."

"Why?" Awen asked, her voice betraying the fact that she'd picked up something behind Magnus's question. "What's going on, Adonis?"

"Oh, you know, low oxygen levels and failing suit integrity. Nothing major—if you're a bottom-feeding crustacean."

"What about picking you up in our SUBCAT?" Bliss said.

"Not at this depth, you're not," Magnus said.

"He's right," Robillard said. "These things aren't rated for that kind of onboarding."

"You have one more problem to face first, buckethead," Abimbola said.

Sensing he knew what they Miblimbian meant, Magnus pulled up the combat overlay and noted the hundred-fold enemy tags between him and the rest of Granther Company.

"There is no way those tiny robed babies see him," Rohoar said. But as if the great mystics themselves wished to protest the Jujari's shortsighted assertion, several Luma sent energy blasts careening toward Magnus.

"Are they crazy?" he yelled, doing his best to roll away from a round that exploded against the dome. "They break this thing, and the mine's going to flood!"

"No, just that single node," Wobix replied. "The others will engage in emergency containment protocols. Do not worry."

"Oh, that really helps, Bixy."

Magnus felt his vision growing fuzzy, signaling the end of the suit's oxygen. He took one last breath and held it before rolling away from a second blast that nearly took off his head. From on his back, Magnus raised his TB16 and fired at a cluster of Li-Dain who seemed intent on smearing him across the dome like a bug across a windshield. He squeezed off one, two, three, four torpedo bolts and watched as they zipped toward the enemy. Then, uncertain if he'd survive long enough to use the rest of his ammo, he opted for a sustained trigger-press. Over the next several seconds, Magus drained his magazine as two dozen 16mm rounds streaked toward the enemy and erupted in just as many explosions.

The fire and waves broke his comms connection with the rest of his team, allowing only fragments of Awen's voice to reach his ears. Concussive waves from exploding ordnance rippled toward him and then pinned his body to the dome. He imagined the force rupturing the node and sucking him inside, only to be dashed across the mining equipment in a violent death. But the breach never came, nor did Magnus's suit succumb to the catastrophic assault. Instead, a series of flashes farther above lit up the dim depths like a fireworks celebration.

Those enemies who did not yield to Magnus's last-ditch effort to protect himself fled to the node's north and south edges, making a run for the airlocks. Meanwhile, the rest of Granther Company and the narskill descended toward Magnus's position.

"We're almost to you," Awen said, her comms connection fully restored.

The most Magnus could offer in reply was a confirmation icon in the chat window, followed by a thought-turned-text that read, "No oxygen left."

"We've got to get him inside," Awen yelled, presumably at Wobix. But Magnus couldn't be sure: the edges of his vision were starting to close in. That last breath he'd taken must have been mostly bad air.

Motes of light danced toward Magnus, each in the shape of a person. They floated toward him like angels, wreathed in a soft glow. Magnus fought the involuntary reflex to gasp for breath as he knew there was no air to fill his lungs. The violent muscle spasms wracked his diaphragm, and he tried to focus on the face coming into view.

"We're gonna get you inside," Awen said. Her voice sounded

distant and hollow, like it was passing to his helmet from another room.

Magnus winced against the sudden appearance of a wall of bright light in his helmet. The shock temporarily diverted his attention from the fire that burned in his lungs—the one that screamed at his brain to take a deep breath. He blinked and tried to focus on what seemed like a small bubble forming around his body, and Awen's face just beyond it. Perhaps this was it: the afterlife. This was the veil separating him from the living. At least his last moment would be spent staring at the face of the woman he loved.

Until she passed through the veil and grabbed his armor with both hands. "Brace yourself," she said, as if in slow motion.

The dome under his back rumbled, shaking his body and sending a wave of pain through his skull. Whatever adrenaline Magnus had left shot through his veins and startled him awake. His vision returned enough for him to see the green-glowing dome's surface pass by either side of his head. Then the sensation of free-fall made his stomach flip over as he dropped below the glowing trusses that gave the giant dome its shape.

Above him was Awen's ever-watchful face, cradled in the soft glow of her MANTA helmet. Her hands held his chest plate as his body dragged her down with him. They fell through the open air, accelerating toward whatever dire end awaited them. Perhaps it was best that he did see his fate—to enter the afterlife unaware and devoid of fear. But knowing that she had joined him in the death plunge was something he would regret for eternity if indeed a long forever was what awaited them.

I've got you, Awen said inside his head.

Her voice so startled Magnus that he convulsed.

Easy Adonis.

All at once, Magnus felt his suit press against his back. He was slowing down. And with the peace that he would not, in fact, be impaled on some piece of Sekmit industrial equipment came a return of his deoxygenated blood and the tunnel vision that swept away his consciousness.

"Get up," she screamed above him.

Magnus felt something hard sting his cheek.

"Get up now!"

The sting hit him again.

"Adonis!"

As the hand flew toward his face a third time, he caught the wrist. She looked at him with wild eyes, and he knew something was wrong.

The good news was that he was breathing. Despite the pain behind his eyes and the burning sensation that ran down his chest and limbs, he was alive. The bad news was that Awen looked frantic. That and the sound of TB16s firing all around him meant the enemy was close.

Awen and someone else offered him their hands. He grasped them and rose to his feet. His helmet lay on the ground, its visor cracked, as did many dismembered parts of his MANTA suit. Someone had taken the liberty of detaching the non-essential components for land operation. But he still had his TB16 in hand.

Magnus looked up to see that he stood amidst a looming latticework of trusses, crane arms, bucket loaders, drilling rigs, and freight containers. The architecture formed the guts of a large mining town, if not a small city, while overhead lay a bright emerald sky.

"We're inside the dome," Magnus said, barely recognizing his slurred speech.

"Yes," Awen said through her helmet's flipped up visor. "And right now, we need you to shoot!" She pointed across the town to dozens of Li-Dain who were stepping out of an airlock.

Magnus wanted to ask how the gladias had gained access to the dome without using the airlocks, and just how he'd survived. All he had were bits and pieces—fleeting memories that did little to quench his curiosity. But right now, none of that mattered. He needed to return fire on the enemy and take stock of whatever units remained under his command.

As if underscoring these needs, a barrage of Li-Dain fire peppered a ground mover just behind Magnus. The sudden wave of heat made the hairs stand up on his neck and sent a chill down his body. It was go time.

Magnus leveled his TB16 and found that his bioteknia eyes picked up the weapon's sight picture instantaneously. He spotted a Li-Dain running for cover behind a metal crate and then led the enemy with his weapon. He was a split second from firing when an armored paw pushed his weapon's muzzle skyward.

"No," Wobix yelled. "Trinium!"

Holy splick, Magnus thought. He hadn't even put that together.

"Very big boom, manservant."

"Right," Magnus replied. Apparently, he'd missed the briefing while he was, you know, trying not to die. "Thanks, Bixy. Any other tips?"

"You may shoot anything but the crates and the open mine shafts."

"Got it."

Magnus brought his weapon back up and targeted two Li-Dain

who were hunkered down behind a small forklift. The area seemed clear of trinium containers, so Magnus fired. A single torpedo bolt sped through a crisscross corridor of cranes, cables, and corrugated steel before striking the lift. The small vehicles leaped off the ground and blew apart, showering all those Luma in the vicinity with molten bits of its frame as well as pulp from the two intended victims.

"Yes," Awen said. "Like that. Do that some more."

"Yes ma'am," he said, suddenly feeling more like himself.

Magnus aimed at another Li-Dain, who bolted for cover behind a cluster of boulders that formed an elevated makeshift picnic area. Some Sekmit had even gone to the trouble of erecting a small table. Magnus led the Luma and then fired. The torpedo bolt met the man two meters before he would have found cover, spraying the table with food for whatever scavengers lived in these domes.

Magnus took a moment to survey his team and prompt his NBTI to reconnect with the company network now that his helmet was out of commission. He also chanced another glance at the ceiling, over a hundred meters up, noting a few dark holes in the structure where, presumably, his team had dropped through. There also seemed to be two larger holes surrounded by shadow—probably from the SUBCATs. Several long cables, no doubt remnants of the MANTA's shoulder winches, dangled from the punctures, encircling his current position.

Magnus's bioteknia eyes registered the unit's ident tags and positions relative to his location. From the looks of it, everyone had gotten through unscathed except Haze. That was good. What was bad was that the Li-Dain seemed to be exiting through a corridor on the dome's northeast side, directly adjacent to the northern airlock. Meanwhile, the gladias and the narskill were occupying the center of the dome and pinned down by enemy fire.

"Where are they going?" Magnus asked Wobix.

"The same place we need to be going: the command center."

"Splick."

Wobix nodded. "If this is a word used for cursing, then yes, very splick."

Magnus smiled, aimed at one of the Luma looking to make a run for the exit, and fired. The round popped against the Li-Dain's shield, leaving the enemy to flee in peace. Frustrated, Magnus looked at his weapon and double-checked the upper receiver.

"It's not the weapon," Awen said. "That one's a true blood."

Magnus hadn't heard the term in a while—perhaps since he'd heard it used about Piper and Awen. "They're special. Like you."

"Yes," she said, pausing to send a shaft of energy toward the back end of a bucket loader. The resulting explosion sent two Li-Dain cartwheeling through the air. "They access the Unity more easily. Harder to put down."

"Any way for guys like me to tell?"

"Nope. But I'll try and tag them when I see them."

Just then, Magnus noted a new black tag float over the fleeing Li-Dain's head as he disappeared into the corridor. It read True blood in red letters. "Got it. Thanks."

"You bet."

Magnus turned to the narskill leader. "Well, Bixy, you have any bright ideas for us?"

"Yes." The cat-man pulled up from firing on an enemy position and faced Magnus. "It involves lots of shooting and chasing, that we might get to the command center before the enemy does."

Magnus felt his jaw go slack ever so slightly. "You're kidding."

"Never."

Magnus nodded, slowly at first, and then called in his team. "Listen up, Granthers. We cannot let those little bastards get to the command complex. We've got to run faster, shoot better, and think smarter. Because if they get there before us, then they will control the whole mine."

"Yes," Wobix said. "And gain control of the auto defense turrets."

"The what?" Magnus blinked at Wobix.

"The mine's auto defense turrets."

"You have point defense turrets *inside* the mine?" Abimbola asked.

"Of course," replied Wobix. "Would not you have the same?"

Abimbola shrugged and gave the cat what looked to be an acquiescent nod.

Magnus didn't need to tell any of his team just how bad things would get if the Li-Dain got access to point defense turrets, especially inside of a trinium mine. He wanted to ask Wobix what the hell the Sekmit were thinking, but he knew the line of dialogue had nothing to do with the task at hand and would only satisfy his momentary desire to be pissed off at shortsighted defense engineers.

"But, how would they know about those turrets?" Zoll asked as he took out another Luma.

"Blackwell," Awen replied. "They got all the plans from Blackwell, who got them from Littleton. We've been over this."

Magnus brought up a topo map of the mines in his bioteknia eyes. "Bixy, is there any way for us to cut the Luma off? Beat them to the punch?"

"We only deflect and return punches, not beat them. As for the command complex, the Li-Dain are choosing the best route. It is five nodes to our north and east."

"But there are multiple ways there, right?"

"Yes, but each longer than the next."

Magnus took a deep breath. "Longer on foot. But what about hover trains or—"

"Trinium carts?"

Magnus thought trinium carts sounded promising. "What are those?"

"The system by which we move trinium."

"Of course they are." Magnus chuckled to himself. "And they move fast?"

"Very."

"Enough to get us to the command node before the enemy?"

Wobix gave what seemed like the Sekmit version of a shoulder shrug. "I think so."

Magnus nodded—he was beginning to like where this was going despite a growing pit in his stomach. "But there's something you're not telling me."

"The carts, they are not good for you, manservant with no helmet." Wobix pointed to Magnus's head. "Too much concentration of trinium radiation. Out here in the open? You are fine. But in those cars? Your weak hairless flesh will melt."

"Easy with the compliments, Bixy. You're gonna overwhelm me with kindness." Magnus looked back to his helmet that lay a few yards away on the ground. Even if the visor wasn't cracked, he still lacked oxygen reserves or an air filtration system.

"Also, we will most likely lose your Veesey-NETs connection for some moments."

Magnus raised an eyebrow. "It's just VNET. And I figured as

much." Magnus didn't like the idea of being out of comms range from the team, but sending them on alone would give the Granther's the edge they needed to beat the Li-Dain to the command node. "Let's do it. And I'll pick up the rear."

"By yourself?" Wobix asked.

Magnus was already nodding when Abimbola interjected. "We will stay with you, buckethead."

Magnus made to protest, but Awen, Rohoar, and Silk seconded the team leader's announcement. There would be no turning them aside. "Fine. Zoll, you have Granther Company."

"Copy that," Zoll said.

"I'm coming with you too," Rix added. "You're down a demo engineer and medic without Haze."

"That's a good idea," Zoll said.

As before, Magnus wasn't going to protest the idea, both because he could use the extra man and because he knew he wouldn't win the argument. Magnus looked at Zoll and the rest of Bravo, Charlie, and Delta Teams. "Stay close to Wobix. We'll be right behind. If anything, maybe our presence at the back will keep them from guessing that you're trying to outflank them. Questions?"

Heads shook.

"Dominate," Magnus said.

"Liberate," everyone else replied. And then, as if guessing what the Sekmit might say, the gladias joined with the narksill in an awkward smattering of, "Obliterate."

"See you at the command complex," Magnus added. "La-raah."

21

Ricio's Fang flipped around and leveled its weapons systems on two squadrons of Talon-class starfighters that had appeared out of thin air—*or thin space*, he mused, noting how his brain attempted to alleviate the danger with irony, *as space can't be thin, now can it, Ricio.* Behind the starfighters sat the *Enduring Vigilance*, which hadn't looked imposing, up until twenty-four FAF-28 attack fighters framed it with their heavy NR330 blaster cannons and their secondary T-100s.

Despite Ricio's Fang's inertia still speeding him toward Aluross, having the planet to his stern was advantageous. Atmosphere in a low-orbit dogfight could be a powerful weapon in the hands of the right pilot. Right now, however, he and Red Squadron needed to lay down as much weapons fire as they could to send an important message.

"You may have gotten the jump on us," Ricio said as his brain danced with the targeting systems. "But that's all you're going to get." He prompted his gunship to attack and watched the Fang's primary NR45 light blasters spray the nearest Talon with a withering barrage of high-rate fire. Simultaneously, the Fang's NX90 heavy cannons pounded a second Talon, knocking out its forward shields and punching a hole right through the cockpit. Meanwhile, the NR45 assault shredded the first Talon, cutting it in two.

While the LAW pilots may have caught the gladias by surprise, they were not ace pilots, and therefore no match for Ricio and his squadron. Still, the Talons did manage to land a few shots against Ricio's forward shields.

"Warning: Forward shields at eighty-five percent," said an automated voice in Ricio's head.

"Yeah, yeah, yeah," Ricio replied. "Don't act like it's the end of the world." Then, just before turning away from the planet, he commanded the Fang to fire two HPGM Ball Buster missiles. "Birdies one and two, away." Even though the Fang could carry up to six VDM Angle Fire missiles or four medium-payload guided munitions, it could only stock two of the larger missiles, which is what Ricio had asked to be outfitted with before leaving the *Spire* on this sortie.

The twin heavy-payload guided munitions that Ricio had recently nicknamed ball busters lurched from the Fang's belly and rocketed toward their targets. The trinium-tipped warheads could light up enemies even if missile defense systems took the weapons out ahead of a target. "Just busting their balls," Ricio had said to Azelon after watching her prototype demonstration.

And the weapons did not disappoint.

The first HPGM ran into a stream of anti-missile fire from two Talons still gunning for Ricio's retreat toward Aluross. The ordnance detonated in a blinding white flash. But it was the missile's reinforced housing that redirected the energy, focusing the trinium's destructive payload into the oncoming enemy.

An unfortunate Talon was caught dead-to-rights in the middle of the particle wave. The energy ripped the fins and armor plating from the starfighter in the blink of an eye, while newly liberated electrons tore through the drive core and blew it apart. The spectacular explosion forced all remaining Talons to disengage.

All but one.

The Talon to catch the second HPGM became the epicenter for a light show that Ricio guessed could be seen on the planet's surface. As soon as the warhead detonated against the fighter's shield, the Talon's fuel cell went nova, creating a cataclysmic event that even engulfed the first target's explosion. Ricio raised his hand against the light of the twin star-like energy bursts and let out a whistle over comms.

"That'll knock the crust from your dingus," he said over VNET while he flipped his Fang around and pulled away from Aluross's thickening atmosphere. As Ricio negotiated the tight turn, ever riding the line between blacking out and overtaxing the inertia dampeners, he checked on the rest of his squadron.

Red Two and Three, Ezo and Sootriman, had already wrapped around the enemy and pressed their left flank, all while avoiding auto turret fire from the *Vigilance*. They worked in tandem to coax two Talons out of formation, wearing them down like culling Bormithan bull cubs from a herd. Fiery eruptions and fits of sparks signaled the two enemy's demise; flames, fuselages, and ident tags blinked out just before Ezo and Sootriman returned to the enemy pack to hunt for more victims.

Red Four and Five, veteran Repub fliers Gill Quo and Dye Vallon, anticipated the enemy's offensive response following Ricio's initial HPGM strikes. Within moments of the bright flashes, Quo and Vallon dove after three Talons attempting to target Ricio. The gladia's sustained blaster fire punched holes in one enemy ship's shield and clipped its port-side wing. The control surfaces were only meant for in-atmo maneuvering, of course, but in the void, the stabilizers became target planks that could spin a Talon out of control. And, being as familiar as they were with the Talon, it was apparent that Quo and Vallon knew just what they were doing when the first starfighter rolled to the left and cartwheeled into the second ship's fuselage. The two enemies blew apart and sent a debris field hurtling toward Aluross.

The third Talon raced ahead to close on Ricio, but Red Four and Five paired their NX90 fire and punched through the aft shields with precision-based fire control. The ship blew apart and added its remains to all those fragments burning up in the planet's mesosphere.

"Thanks, Red Four and Five," Ricio said.

"Just doing our job, Red Leader," Quo said in reply.

Despite the early gains, the LAW squadrons still had the advantage of numbers and the *Vigilance's* fire support, which made the second moves harder than the opening ones. Ricio doubled back to follow three Talons taking refuge in the battleship's shadow. As long as Ricio stayed directly behind the fighter's formation, the turret defense fire wouldn't be a problem. But the moment they split up—*like they are right now*, he noted—then he'd be an open target for the support ship.

Ricio tracked the Talon that rounded the *Vigilance's* bow and then rolled over and pulled back toward the stern. The Talon dodged left and right, slaloming between cannon emplacements in the hopes of shaking the pursuing Fang and exposing it to defensive munitions. Ricio's Novian-based platform was far more agile than the Talon and allowed the pilot to input tighter turns. The result was a nearly unshakable pursuit, giving Ricio the upper hand. As the pair crossed amidships, Ricio got a positive target lock and fired both large-caliber NX90 blasters simultaneously. The result pitched the Talon forward and drove it into the *Vigilance's* hull, showering the battleship with molten shrapnel and ashes of the pilot's incinerated body.

"Mr. Ricio, sir," TO-96 said over VNET. "Please be advised that the bulk of the Talon squadrons appear to be heading for Aluross's surface."

"But for real this time?" Ricio asked. Sure enough, the combat display showed that most of the enemy had resisted following the Fangs and maintained their course heading toward Meesrin Pin.

"Yes, sir. For real this time. I believe this would be classified as sardonic, would it not?"

"Something like that, yeah." Ricio brought up the squadron channel. "Looks like our new friends have lost interest in the void game and are taking their ball to another playground."

"We're tracking," Ezo replied. "Time to see what Azelon's little winged chariots can do in-atmo."

"Oh," Ricio replied with a hearty chuckle, thinking back to his original impromptu mission over Worru. "Just you wait, my friend."

As Ricio burned toward Aluross's stratosphere, diving straight after the Talon group, he felt his pilot's seat cinch tighter around his shaking body. Even with Azelon's advanced shielding and composite armor plating, the Fang still rattled as friction threatened to rip the starfighter apart. *There are only so many physical laws you can break before one of them eventually catches up with you*, Ricio thought. But as his altitude continued to plummet, smoother air returned, and with it, the Fang's terrifying scream as it streaked across the sky.

"We can't let them reach the city," Ricio said to the squadron. Everyone registered the ultimatum with green icons and then followed Ricio's push for maximum thrust. It was always an exhilarating feeling to point the nose of any aircraft directly into the center of a planet at full burn. In this case, the Fangs closed on the Talons as they were the faster of the two platforms. But not before the enemy fired into the city some forty kilometers below.

"Splick," Ezo yelled over comms. "They must be desperate!"

He was right. The hasty shots from so far away were evidence that the enemy feared they might not accomplish their mission before being blown out of the sky. Then again, Ricio had made accurate shots from farther away with the Talon; the platform's targeting system was reasonably robust. Plus, he wouldn't be surprised if the Luma pilots somehow managed to use their Unity powers to direct their blaster fire. Either way, he and the rest of Fang Company couldn't afford to let the assault go on.

There was only one problem.

There had to be millions of Sekmit living around the spaceport located just to the south of the city's center. This meant disabling any Talons here made them fireballs down there. But as every second ticked by, the threat of civilian casualties increased exponentially, both from enemy fire and enemy shrapnel.

"We've got to steer them away from the capital," Ricio said as he fought off the G-forces pressing him into his seat. "And if you take one out, you'd better be damn sure it's in a million pieces." What he wouldn't give for just one more HPGM missile.

That's when his eyes noticed Sootriman's load-out data. *She* had two HPGMs onboard!

"Sootriman," he exclaimed. "I want both your ball busters deployed, stat!"

"Can do," she said.

"Everyone else target the debris fields, but reduce your blaster range to five klicks."

"Birdies one and two, away," Sootriman yelled.

The twin missiles rocketed away from the Fang squadron and blew out the aperture of every HUD in the fighter group. Ricio watched the ordnance tags on the CSD as the two birdies closed the gap. The Talons were still firing around the spaceport when the trinium tipped warheads detonated, bathing the enemy squadron in light. Unlike the void the explosions in-atmo clipped the audio sensors of every Fang in the squadron, followed by a concussion wave that knocked Ricio's starfighter off course.

The good news was that the twin munitions had taken out almost eight fighters at once, pulverizing their fuselages. The bad news was that the Fangs had been blown wide of their desired target window, delaying attempts to take out the larger fragments before they reached the city. That, and there were still five more Talons firing toward the spaceport.

"I want those fighters out of here," Ricio bellowed.

"On it," Ezo yelled. He and Sootriman took Red Five, Six, and Seven on a run that swooped in front of the remaining Talons. It was a gutsy move, especially since the five Fangs stayed their weapons—most likely in the hopes of presenting themselves as easy targets. Ricio picked up on the tactic and fired non-lethal shots around the Talon formation in the hopes of pressuring the enemy to follow the more convenient targets.

"They took the bait," Ricio said. "Get them out of here, but watch your sixes."

"Copy," Ezo replied.

"Everyone else, we've got some cleanup work to do." Ricio led the remaining Fangs in blasting through the debris field, beginning with the largest Talon scrap first. Precise NZ45 fire tore through the metal, shredding the wreckage into molten rain that cooled long before it sprinkled across Sekmit buildings far below.

But not *that* far below. The spaceport was coming up fast, and there was still half a Talon fuselage hurtling toward the streets.

"Come on," Ricio said with a grunt, willing himself to make the shot. "Where're those ace skills at, Reece?" He lined up his NX90 reticle on the boulder-sized chunk of flaming metal. If he missed, this round wouldn't stop short of the city like the curtailed NZ45. But he couldn't rely on the smaller weapon to get the job done. He only had one shot—literally.

Ricio ordered the starfighter to fire.

A single NX90 round spat from under the Fang's nose and struck the stray hulk, reducing it to a red-hot cluster of plate fragments. "And not a moment to spare," Ricio said to himself. He'd stopped watching his altimeter to focus on the shot. As a result, he began pulling up with less than five kilometers to the deck—which seemed like a lot unless you understood the physics of traveling at 2,100 kilometers-per-hour and making the turn in less than six seconds.

Ricio felt the blood drain from his head as the inertia dampeners pegged out. Warning indicators for proximity alert, high-speed stall, and inertia maximus all blared in Ricio's biotech interface. But he was committed, and none of those alerts mattered as long as he stayed conscious enough to complete the ninety-degree turn over Meesrin Pin.

Darkness crept in from the sides of his vision and blotted out the cockpit's interior. Ricio willed the Fang to keep raising its nose as he watched the city's lights speed beneath him. The tunnel vision constricted even further when he noticed the shape and height of buildings that loomed ahead. An open area outside the spaceport was filled with armored personnel carriers and infantry elements engaged in a firefight. For a split second, Ricio wondered if those were friendly forces, but the thought was there and gone. Instead, he became possessed with the task of rolling his Fang between two skyscrapers and pulling out of the turn.

Ricio grunted in conjunction with his flight suit's pressure bladders to force his circulatory system to keep him from blacking out. But whether he was out of shape, getting too old for this, or had finally picked a line that was too steep, Ricio couldn't keep himself away from the darkness. The last thing he remembered was the adrenaline boost from releasing the controls, and the emotion of knowing he was about to die.

22

WILLOWOOD FELL as Caldwell shoved her back inside the APC. She looked around his body to see fountains of broken pavement shoot into the night sky. The ground churned like an angry black ocean, disturbed by blaster fire that cascaded down from above. And then there were the banshee shrieks that rattled her head inside her helmet—the sound of an unholy summons for the living to join the dead.

Caldwell's body lay across Willowood's as bits of blacktop peppered those inside the APC. She could feel the vehicle shudder as more blaster fire tore up the ground outside. Willowood reached for Piper's hand; her granddaughter was curled up on the floor an arm's length away.

Everything's going to be okay, Willowood said through the Unity.

I know, Nana, Piper replied.

Willowood looked across the floor to see Piper smile through her tinted visor. Outside, the howls still came, and the lights still flickered, but the pavement had settled.

It's safe to move, Piper said. *I've covered us.*

"William?" Willowood said to the man who still pinned her down. "I know you're probably enjoying this as much as I am, but we've got to move. Piper has us covered."

Caldwell pulled his head back to stare at Willowood. "Did you say you're enjoying—"

"Get off me, old man," she said, and then she threw him aside with only a little Unity assistance.

Caldwell rolled onto his back. "Everyone make for the spaceport. And, so help me mystics, if I catch a single one of you millpy loafer gas totes taking your sweet time, I'm gonna grind your biscuits and feed them to my Aunt Thelma's pet bunions." He paused to look in Piper's direction. "Sorry you had to hear that, darlin'."

"I want a pet bunion," Piper replied, climbing to her feet.

"No you don't," Willowood said, pulling Piper close.

"You two stay together," Caldwell said to Willowood.

"We'll be just fine, William. Lead the way."

Caldwell was first out of the APC, his weapon raised skyward. As soon as Willowood cleared the ramp, she looked up too, amazed to see a translucent golden dome protecting them from incoming starfighter fire.

"Are those Talons?" she asked Caldwell.

"Looks like it."

"But why would—?"

A bright light flashed overhead, filling the sky like the sun at high noon. Willowood instinctively shielded Piper even though she knew the girl didn't need protection. The sound of a thunderous *boom* struck the convoy seconds later, followed by multiple *cracks* that signaled drive cores tearing through the sky like jars of lightning splitting apart.

"What is going on?" Willowood asked.

"Your guess is as good as mine," Caldwell replied.

"Those are Galactic Republic Talons," TO-96 said over VNET. "Re-tasked by the LAW and piloted by Li-Dain, as far as we can tell. Commander Ricio is currently in pursuit, though Azelon and I strongly suggest you take cover within the spaceport as—"

"We're on our way," Caldwell interrupted as he pushed Willowood forward with a hand on her hip.

"Careful, Colonel," she said with a quick look at his choice of hand placement.

"Just get inside. And make sure Piper can maintain a connection with our prisoner while the crew unloads him."

"I've got him," Piper said but pointed overhead. "But I do need to let the big shield down."

Caldwell nodded. "The worst is over. Now get inside." He'd no sooner said the words than Luma fire erupted from the street behind their position. "Ah, splick." Caldwell pushed past the two females and raised his NOV2 as he made for the APC's side. The rest of the units were taking cover behind the vehicle. But not before two gladias and three sekmit were struck down while walking in the open.

Willowood couldn't leave Caldwell and the rest of the warriors like this. The Li-Dain still outnumbered them, and who knew how many more lives would be lost in the attempt to cross to the spaceport. She turned to Piper and then pointed to a wide freight entrance. "I want you inside that port, understood?"

Piper nodded. "But what about you?"

"I'm staying here to help," Willowood replied. "Now go!"

Piper turned and ran for the spaceport, but not before more blaster fire sounded overhead. Willowood looked up, expecting to see more Talons streaking toward her position.

"No need to worry, Madame Willowood," TO-96 said over comms. "Our Fangs have routed the enemy fighters. That sound is simply Mr. Ricio and his squadron attempting to break up the debris field before it crushes anyone in the city below."

"Thank you, Ninety-Six," she replied. "Though it does appear that one fighter is coming in awfully fast." Even as she said the words, she noticed herself involuntarily bending her knees as if to shy away from the incoming Fang.

"That would be Mr. Ricio, Madame. Statistically speaking, he has a high probability of pulling out of the dive he's in."

Another bright flash filled Willowood's HUD as a large Talon fragment exploded, leaving only the sight of a single Fang barreling toward the convoy. Willowood looked to Piper: she was twelve meters from being inside the blast-proof building.

That's too far, Willowood thought as she looked up to see the Fang rocketing toward them.

Ricio wasn't pulling up.

"I wish to amend my previous statement," TO-96 said. "Mr. Ricio's chances of survival are plummeting." The bot paused and then added, "Did you notice my play on words, Madame Willowood?"

"Not now." Willowood charged across the open ground and summoned her strength in the Unity. She thought of trying to project a shield similar to what Piper had done, but she doubted it could withstand the force of the speeding Fang. Willowood glanced up one more time to see Ricio's ship attempting to pull out of the steep dive. The whine of the star fighter's drive core felt as though it tore the air in two, sending a fearful chill through Willowood's limbs. There was only one thing to do. She reached out in the Unity and shoved Piper forward, throwing the girl into the spaceport.

At the last second, Willowood's feet tangled amongst some rubble, and she sprawled across the ground. The screaming sound of the Fang shook her body, and Willowood was sure this was the end. She covered her head and resigned herself to her fate.

But it was a fate that would wait for another day.

Ricio's engine thrust slammed against Willowood's side and sent her spinning across the plaza. She tried to stop herself from spiraling away, but the force was too much. That is, until she steadied herself in the Unity and managed to plant her feet on the ground. Willowood leaned forward, pitched against the vectored thrust, and stared the Fang down as it skimmed a side street not more than five meters above the deck. Several hover cars, bikes, and even shuttered street vendor carts flipped away from the starfighter as it darted between buildings and narrowly avoided a catastrophic end.

But Ricio wasn't out of the woods yet. A large office building stood at the end of his course, and he was far from being able to fly over the structure.

"Come on," Willowood said as if willing the man to pull up. "You can do it, Ricio!"

But still, the fighter seemed bound to hit the ground. If anything, she sensed the ship falter, as if the multiple forces of gravity had been too much for the ace pilot.

"Ricio," Willowood yelled. But there was no use. Even if he could resume control, there was no time to dodge the skyscraper.

"I'm sorry, Madame Willowood," TO-96 said. "But Mr. Ricio has lost consciousness."

Willowood's heart sank as the starfighter careened toward the building.

"I, however, have not," said the bot.

The Fang rolled right and slipped through a gap between buildings that was so small, Willowood hadn't even noticed it. She blinked once, and the ship was gone, swallowed by the city.

"Is he—Ninety-Six, did he—"

"Mr. Ricio is fine, your wiseness."

She blinked again. A small black shape with a trail of light surged up from the skyline and darted toward the starfield. "Oh, Ninety-Six, I could kiss you right now."

"Excuse me?" Azelon said as she stepped into TO-96's holo frame.

"She meant it metaphorically," TO-96 said to the other bot with a reassuring tone.

"No I didn't," Willowood said. "I'll show you when we're together again."

"Felicity," Caldwell yelled.

The urgency in his voice snapped Willowood's attention back to the conflict at hand. "What is it?"

"You and Piper safe? HUD says you're—"

"She's secure."

"Secure enough for you to lend us a hand?"

Willowood looked to Piper, who stood inside the entryway.

I'm okay, Nana, Piper said in the Unity. *Go save your big strong man.*

Willowood smiled. *You stay put, okay?*

I will.

When Willowood joined Caldwell at the front line, she realized why none of the team had made entry into the spaceport as he'd ordered: the enemy fire was simply too great. Were the convoy's forces to break ranks and fall back from the APCs' cover, Caldwell's units would be overwhelmed. It seemed that every Li-Dain they'd passed on the street had rallied to the fight here and was giving the battle-hardened colonel a run for his credits. So heavy was the fighting, in fact, that the prisoner escort team hadn't even moved the jail crates from the APCs.

"Nice of you to join us," DiAntora said from beside Caldwell. The two military leaders crouched behind one of the mobile barricades deployed from the APC's side.

"What's going on?" Willowood asked, but thought she had already worked out the problem.

"Our blaster fire is holding them back, but that's about it," the colonel said. "Can't risk making a run for it without letting up, and that—"

"Would cost lives," she said.

He nodded.

"Think your mystics and the narskill can level the playing field?" DiAntora asked.

"We can do more than that," Willowood replied. "Just get ready to make a run for it." She opened the all-unit channel. "Paladia Company and any available narskill, we're taking the fight to the Li-Dain. Everyone else, we need covering fire to get us past the enemy's defenses. On my mark."

"Be careful," Caldwell said to Willowood.

But she shook her head. "It's 'be dangerous,' William. Get it right." Then over the company channel, she said, "Now!"

WILLOWOOD VAULTED the barricade and raced forward with a Nexus shield projected a meter in front of her. The magenta-colored wall became the Li-Dain's new target as Luma fire concentrated on Willowood's position. But her powers were up to the task—at least for a few seconds.

More gladias jumped forward, followed closely by Sekmit in their cat-like mech suits and wielding their Thørzin power bows and wooden staves. The mystics' personal shields created a phalanx that surged toward the Li-Dain, forcing the enemy to rethink their assault. Moments later, Caldwell ordered a renewed counterattack, targeting specific pockets of Li-Dain that he marked on the company topo map. Willowood saw the targets as strategic posts for her to navigate between, knowing she needed to keep her forces away from friendly fire. She complimented Caldwell's efforts and surged toward the holes in the enemy line. Within seconds, Willowood had crossed the open ground and drove toward three Li-Dain warriors whose eyes widened in shock.

Willowood summoned more Nexus power around her fists, jumped into the air, and then loosed the pent-up energy at the enemies. Rather than emanate as two beams, however, the blast shot out in a fan pattern, slicing through the enemy's wall and knocking all three Li-Dain on their backs.

As Willowood sailed over the bodies, she drove a shaft of light through each of their heads. She noticed, then, just how young they were, and it grieved her. But they had made their choice and had pledged their service to So-Elku and the LAW. It saddened her to know they had so passionately aligned themselves with the sinister master. *Did they even know?*she wondered. *Did they know how devious his* *character, how dark his plots?* And, for their sake, she chose to conclude: *No. They merely thought themselves freedom fighters who would be found on the right side of history*. Somehow, assuring herself of their naiveté helped ease the burden she felt in killing them. Not because it made her feel any better about her lethal use of force—nothing could mitigate that regret. But because it meant they might find easier passage into whatever afterlife awaited them as unwitting victims of war.

Now that she was within the enemy's shield wall, followed by a dozen gladias and Sekmit, Willowood started to chew through the Li-Dain's bulk. A golden-robed mystic to her right threw a punch at Willowood's head. The older woman leaned back from the blow meant for her temple and then shot a right-handed jab at the man's chest, meeting his sternum with her super-charged knuckles. The Luma flew backward with a scorched hole in his rib cage.

Another Li-Dain charged at Willowood's left flank. The young woman threw a roundhouse kick that sailed over Willowood's head. From her crouched position, Willowood lashed out with another fury-bound fist and punched the woman in the knee. The sudden release of Nexus energy detonated the joint like one of Azelon's VODs had gone off from inside the bones. The Luma woman fell screaming, and Willowood ended her suffering with a stroke to the woman's head.

Two more Li-Dain came at the elder gladia head-on, their fists extended in a brazen effort to knock Willowood back. But she somersaulted forward, whipping her outstretched legs over her head with a half twist, and landed behind the men at the same time that she drove her palms into the base of their necks. The Li-Dain fell forward and hit the ground as corpses.

"Did you know she could do that?" DiAntora asked Caldwell.

"Negative," he replied. "And it reminds me never to piss her off." Caldwell stood and waved his forces back. "Let's haul ass to the spaceport, people. Move out!"

Caldwell dropped behind his APC and monitored the prisoner escort detail as they unclamped So-Elku's armored crate and began sliding it across the floor. The low-power repulsor pads made moving the one-tonne container a breeze; the slightest touch could set the smart-box on its way, and the operators could raise or lower the inertia sensitivity. But Caldwell could tell the officer in charge was already too careful with the unit.

"We're not giving him a guided tour, Lieutenant," Caldwell said to the detail's OIC, a woman named LaMaster. *How fitting*, he noted to himself, given her role over overseeing the Luma dictator. "You can dispense with the niceties."

"Your orders, not mine," LeMaster said. "Stand clear." Caldwell stood back from the ramp as the lieutenant swiped up on the crate's control pad, raising the assistance level to maximum. Then she leaned back and gave the transport a hearty kick.

The armor-plated cell flew out the back of the APC like someone had just hurled a spaceball at a goal. Caldwell even had to keep one Repub Marine from losing his head by throwing an arm in front of the overzealous warrior. "Easy there, Sergeant."

The Marine reared away from the jettisoned prisoner transport and then looked at the colonel. "Thank you, Colonel."

"Get your units inside."

"Right away."

LeMaster jumped out of the APC with her team and continued pushing So-Elku's box toward the spaceport. Caldwell thought about hailing Piper again, just to see how she was doing, but thought better of it. He didn't want to distract her from her work. Plus, the fact that So-Elku hadn't burst out of the container in some flurry of lightning yet meant she was still okay. "Just keep it up, little lady," he said to himself as he looked toward the spaceport.

Caldwell reviewed the topo map and saw that all his forces had dropped back to the spaceport and taken cover behind the building's multiple defensive offerings. From café seating, marble fountains, and lighted walkways to vendor booths, storefronts, and security stations, the spaceport's wrap-around exterior was a small city unto itself. In the middle of it all was the northside main entrance where Piper was hidden.

With the APCs' roof-mounted weapons on remote and the defenders in better positions, Caldwell told Willowood to fall back. "We'll cover your tail from here."

"I bet you've been waiting to say that all day," she replied.

He laughed. "Come to think of it, I hadn't. But I can repeat it if it makes you—"

"Save it for later, Colonel Caldwell."

"Yes ma'am." He didn't know what she meant by that, but living long enough to find out gave him one more incentive to not die today. "Let's give 'em hell, people!"

Caldwell helped cover LeMaster's retreat into the spaceport's main entrance, making any Li-Dain think twice about even considering a run on the prisoner. Several other gladias and Sekmit saw his efforts and stepped up to assist. The narskill, in particular, amazed him with their power bows and, to his surprise, their staves.

When one Li-Dain got too close for a big cat's liking, the narskill warrior whipped his staff around and struck the Luma on the side of the arm. Where Caldwell thought the enemy might simply deflect the wooden weapon, the staff released a bright blue charge of energy that sent the enemy flying across the pavement. Slits along the staff glowed a soft blue and then dimmed until the weapon looked like just another walking stick again.

"Hey, you," Caldwell said to the Sekmit. "Keep that up, copy?"

The narskill nodded once and then turned toward the enemy.

Caldwell elbowed DiAntora while he put down a Li-Dain running between APCs. "Think you can arrange for me to get one of those? Pull a few strings with Freya?"

"Assuming we make it out of here, I'll see what I can do," the admiral said, then she returned to firing her Repub MC90 on a pair of Li-Dain.

"Colonel Caldwell, sir?" came TO-96's voice over comms.

"Go ahead, son."

"Azelon thinks she has detected an unknown ship inbound on your location."

"Thinks?" Caldwell lowered his NOV2. "What do you mean she thinks?"

"Oh my. Have you not known she is sentient this whole time?" TO-96 placed a hand on his chest. "I feel as though I am to blame for this."

"Focus, bot. Why can't you give me more intel?"

"Because the ship is attempting to cloak itself, sir."

"So it's hostile."

"We're not sure."

Caldwell forced a breath through his nostrils. The bots were getting on his nerves. "Well, if it came from the *Vigilance*, then you can be sure it's hostile."

"But that's just it." TO-96 called up a space map to replace his headcam in the HUD feed. A red square reticle zeroed on a section of space just above Aluross. "Can you see the incoming map?"

"I see it, Ballsy. Just a bunch of empty space."

"This was the first place we noticed the vessel."

"Jump point?"

"We don't believe so, Colonel. It is far too close to Aluross's gravity well. As you know, an object emerging from subspace cannot—"

"I understand FTL mechanics, bot. What I don't understand is why you and miss Fancy Pants can't give me more on this ship. Can't your girlfriend take over its systems or some such business?"

"That's just it, sir. Azelon's is attempting to infiltrate the vessel's command architecture but is so far unable to gain any substantial footing."

Caldwell looked up, trying to see if he could notice anything moving against the stars. "You at least have an ETA?"

"That is also hard to determine."

"Of course it is." Caldwell brought his weapon up and fired at a Li-Dain who was getting a little too close for comfort. The NOV2's first three-round burst punched a small hole in the warrior's shield, but only because additional blaster fire from elsewhere had weakened it. Caldwell's second three-round burst knocked the man back, flipping his feet over his head. "Can't you send Ricio to intercept?"

"We've initiated that very order, sir, but they're having trouble finding it despite its size, and he doesn't want to risk inadvertently ramming into it. As you know, an object traveling at a high rate of speed that suddenly collides—"

"Oh, for your sister Sally's bra collection, quit with the tutorials already." Caldwell chomped on his unlit cigar and then fired four shots as a Li-Dain charged his position. "Just keep me posted on anything else you get on this mystery ship."

"I will, sir. And I hope you—"

Caldwell sank a final shot into the charging Li-Dain's head. "Die, you son of a bitch."

"I'm not exactly sure how to respond to that, sir."

"Not you, bot. Just talking to the enemy."

"Ah, very good. Well, keep it up, sir. I'm sure they need a good talking to."

Caldwell chuckled and then kicked the body just to make sure the Luma was dead. "They most certainly do, Ballsy. They most certainly do."

23

Magnus and the rest of Alpha Team had pursued the Li-Dain out of the mining node that they'd landed in and into a second node using the northeasterly tunnel. Each connecting corridor that radiated from a given node was up to five kilometers in length—some even longer—which meant, without vehicular assistance, Alpha Team had a lot of running ahead. Magnus still felt it was odd that the Li-Dain had chosen to move on foot, given how much they knew of the mine's layout. Then again, maybe the Luma were just as afraid of free electrons as anyone else and could not protect themselves in the mine carts without heavy armor.

The node Magnus and Alpha Team fought through was much like if not identical to the first. Large crane booms crisscrossed one another in a competition to reach the dome's upper reaches. Meanwhile, mining equipment, including excavators, drilling rigs, and dump trucks, sat dormant around giant pits gouged from the ocean floor.

Luma forces fired Unity bolts across the vertical mine shafts, pinning Magnus and his fireteam behind cover. The best the gladias could do against such overwhelming numbers was wait for breaks in the enemy assault.

Sensing one such reprieve, Magnus leaned out from a steel crate, targeted a Li-Dain, and squeezed off a round. Clearly, the Luma had not expected the shot as the blaster bolts punctured his shield with minimal effort. The man spun as three bolts struck his side and shoulder. Then he lost his footing and fell into the nearest pit, screaming as he dropped.

"You are so lucky, buckethead," Abimbola said over external speakers. "That, or you cheat."

"Cheat?" Magnus said, feigning offense.

"Yes. Your bioteknia eyes tell you when their shields are down. That, or bedding this Luma"—Abimbola pointed at Awen—"grants you mystical powers to see those Luma"—he gestured to the Li-Dain.

"Abimbola," Awen yelled, hands on her hips. "I'll have you know that Magnus and I—"

"No, no, Awen," Magnus said with a raised hand. "He's got a point."

"I knew it," Abimbola said. "Cheater."

Magnus sensed Awen was about to let him have it, so he fired on several more Li-Dain who maneuvered toward the next corridor leading away to the northeast.

"Magnus," she hollered.

"Sorry, can't hear you."

How about now?

"Mystics," he exclaimed, pulling himself behind cover. "You can't do that while I'm shooting."

"Tell him," she said, pointing at Abimbola.

"Tell him what?" Again, Magnus put on a show and offered Awen an innocent expression.

Clearly frustrated, Awen turned toward Abimbola and was about to set the record straight when a salvo of enemy fire blasted against the steel container at their backs.

"Get clear," Magnus roared as the massive crate rocked toward them. He thrust Awen out of the container's shadow and then made a run for it. Over his shoulder, he could see the object chasing him down. It let out a low moan as the steel ground against the rocky floor. Magnus dove clear, and the giant box slammed against the terrain producing a plume of dust.

Fortunately, the giant metal box still provided ample cover as before, just from on its side. Awen had rolled into a crouch and stayed out of harm's way.

"You good?" Magnus asked her from on his stomach.

"Yeah, thanks," she said. "But don't think that bought you any favors."

"Now why would I think saving your life would do that?"

"I could have saved myself, you know."

Magnus winked at her. "And yet you wanted me to."

"You fight like a mating couple in heat," Rohoar said.

"We—wait, what did you say?" Awen glared at Rohoar.

"I said, you fight exactly like—"

"Belay that, Fluffy," Magnus said, then pointed to the enemy. "They're heading down the next tunnel. Let's go."

Magnus led the way around the node's perimeter and then slowed as the fire team approached the corridor heading to the next node. The topo map in his bioteknia eyes showed the tunnel was three klicks long. "Looks like we've got another long run in front of us. Let's move."

They'd made it a dozen paces into the hallway when Luma fire forced Magnus, Awen, and Silk into a structural recess in the left wall. At the same time, Abimbola, Rohoar, and Rix flattened themselves against one in the right. They needed to backtrack and rethink how they were going to pursue the enemy.

"Reminds me a little of Oorjaee, eh Bimby?" Magnus said as he blindly returned fire down the tunnel.

"Did we not almost die in that rescue attempt?" Abimbola replied, sending a short burst toward the enemy. The Li-Dain responded with another round of Unity-powered blasts.

"Almost dying is a lot different than actually dying," Magnus said. "It's one of our things."

"So you say." Abimbola laughed then fired again.

"I agree with the Miblimbian," Rohoar said. "Everywhere Rohoar goes, he seems to follow you into dangerous circumstances."

"And you love every second of it."

"No. There are many seconds Rohoar does not love."

Magnus sent more rounds after the enemy. "But the majority you do."

"Enough, you guys," Awen said. "We can't make good time out in the open like this. And we've got to pick up the pace."

"Agreed," Magnus said. "Can't you make a shield for us or something?"

"I can. But against these guys? It's going to take all my concentration, and I'm not sure you want to carry me around like some portable shield generator."

"That would make shooting a little more difficult," he said.

"Though, you would be the prettiest PSG I'd ever thrown over my shoulder."

"More acronyms," she replied with a wink. "Cute."

"What about this track?" Abimbola said, pointing at a hover lane that ran down the tunnel's center. "Seems like they use it enough to keep it cleared off."

"But I thought the mine cart tunnels are where Wobix is leading Zoll and the others?" Silk said.

"They are," Magnus replied as he scratched his chin in thought. The enemy fire had lessened, and he looked back toward the node they'd come from. "I'm guessing they use these for people and equipment."

"I didn't see any hover sleds back there," Silk said.

Magnus nodded in agreement. "Me either. I'm guessing all transports were used to evacuate the mine. But that doesn't mean we can't come up with something." He turned back toward the node they'd come from and waited for a break in fire. "Come on."

"What are we looking for exactly?" Rohoar asked as Alpha Team sorted through the mining equipment.

"Anything that will allow us to haul your furry ass down those tunnels," Abimbola replied from among a scrap metal heap.

"At least Rohoar's ass is not naked, like you human types. Rohoar has seen some of your asses, and they scare him."

Magnus laughed despite the urgent timeline they were facing. "Just keep your eyes peeled for—"

"Found some scrap repulsors," Rix said from the doorway of a supply shed. He held up four glass-like disks by their wire leads, clenching two sets in either hand. Each repulsor was about fifty centimeters across, sporting a translucent lens in the center and a metallic ring around the outer edge.

"Great," Magnus said. "See if they have continuity and then get them to Awen."

Rix nodded and ran down the steps and headed toward Awen.

"I think we can use this as a base," Abimbola said, picking up a thick piece of sheet metal and hoisting it over his head.

"It's not pretty, but it will do," Magnus replied and then waved him toward Awen.

"And I've got a capacitor," Silk said and then looked at Awen. "Think you can charge it?"

"Bring it over and I'll tell you," Awen replied.

Magnus got distracted by a commotion near some drilling equipment where Rohoar had been. But the Jujari had disappeared, and several of the larger vehicles began rocking back and forth as spits of dust shot up from between them. At first, Magnus had visions of horror holo movies where giant subterranean beasts swallowed unsuspecting people who happened upon their nests. But then Magnus heard a loud *bang*, and Rohoar popped up from behind two excavation rigs.

"Rohoar has something," he announced as he held a massive four-bit drilling plate over his head. The tools were used on the sides of the larger tunneling vehicles to grind away at the walls.

Magnus gave Rohoar a bewildered look and couldn't help but chuckle. "Buddy, what's that for?"

"We mount in on the front to counterbalance our sled and to cover Rohoar's furry ass so Awen does not need to."

It took less than ten minutes for the team to cobble the components together—time they could easily make up if this contraption worked. With Abimbola, Silk, and Rix's experience in building mismatched vehicles in the Dregs combined with Awen's powers in the Unity, which apparently included supercharging electronic capacitors and welding metal together, Alpha Team had a transport cart ready for use.

"It's not pretty," Awen said. "But it'll have to do."

"Rohoar calls it *The Ass Protector*," the Jujari said as he crossed his arms.

"I preferred *The Tiny Terror*," Abimbola replied. "But we can go with yours."

Rohoar back-pawed Abimbola's bicep. "What about *The Tiny Ass Protector of Terror*? You like this, yes?"

Abimbola gave Rohoar one raised eyebrow and said nothing.

"I like it," Magnus said. "Especially if it does what the title suggests. Now let's get moving."

"Just remember," Awen said as she pointed to the scrappy looking sled. "We have no way to slow it down. We can't throttle the capacitor, and the repulsors are mounted at an angle."

"Which means we'll continue to increase speed until we jump off," Magnus said.

"Exactly." Awen stepped onto the base plate and hunkered down behind the drilling wall. "Who's ready?"

Once activated, the repulsors raised the cob-job sled and all six passengers a half meter off the ground without a hiccup. The transport locked onto the narrow blastcrete lane that ran down the corridor and then lurched forward. With any luck, the sled would adhere to the track and move around each successive node's perimeter until Alpha Team caught up with the enemy. That is, assuming everyone could hold on.

"Well, we know it hovers," Magnus said.

"Yeah, but it's already moving kinda fast," Rix replied. "And you're the one not wearing a helmet."

"Don't remind me." Magnus watched as the tunnel's end drew closer. "When we get into the node, everyone lean with the turn. Copy?"

They nodded and adjusted their handholds on the sled's sides. The transport's speed continued to increase, and Magnus grew more apprehensive about not having throttle control; the little contraption was already moving far faster than he anticipated it would. "Here we go."

The blastcrete lane curved left, and the sled followed, tilting so that the repulsors pushed against the direction of inertia. The natural stabilization helped, and everyone did their best to lean into the turn. However, the laws of inertia had a pesky way of interfering with good intentions. Silk lost her grip, slid up the plate floor, and flew over the right side. But not before Abimbola and Rohoar caught her by the wrists and pulled her back on.

"Thanks," she said as she scrambled to regain her handholds as the cart leveled out and tracked along the node's left-side perimeter.

The room's large circumference made for a more gentle turn, which gave Magnus time to look around. But as with the other nodes, there was little new to see—just more industrial mining equipment and massive holes in the ocean floor.

"No signs of the Li-Dain," Awen said from upfront. She clung to the front wall and peeked over the top. "But the next tunnel's coming up."

"And we've picked up speed," Magnus said. "Hold tight."

The broad curve around the node had been deceiving; Magnus hadn't realized just how much they'd accelerated until the little sled banked hard left and jolted the passengers sideways. Fortunately, everyone stayed on, and the cart righted itself as it shot down the next connecting tunnel.

"Rohoar is growing less assured about *The Tiny Ass Protector of Terror's* ability to protect his ass," the Jujari said.

"Just hang in there, Fluffy," Magnus replied. "The more ground we gain, the better."

The wind whipped through Magnus's hair as the cart hurtled down the straightaway. He looked through the tunnel's windowplex walls to see strange ocean life lumbering about in the deepwater currents. The corridor's exterior lights cast everything in a murky green hue, including giant fish with undulating fins, crustaceans in grotesque plate armor, and plant life that looked more carnivore-fauna than flora. Magnus wondered if the sea creatures noticed the small sled streaking by. The underwater life floated in peaceful contrast to the cart and its breakneck speed.

"Here we go again," Awen said from the front, already moving to the left in anticipation of the sharp turn. Silk joined her, practically riding the sled's edge, and the three large men were double-fisting their handholds. Magnus sat in the rear with his left leg draped over the side, ready to ride the tilting sled if need be.

The cart turned left, but it also banked to the left, which drove the passengers into the floor plate. As before, the repulsors were working in line with the sharp turn to push away from the direction of inertia. Still, someone could slide toward the right edge and fly off into the node's center.

When the transport leveled out and banked right around the room, Magnus breathed another sigh of relief when he saw that no one had slipped off. They continued to accelerate, rolled into the next tunnel, and then flew into the following node.

"I thought we would have caught up with the enemy by now," Abimbola said, peering further down the tunnel.

"Copy that," Magnus replied. It was a bit odd that they hadn't encountered the Li-Dain. "Especially with them on foot. Unless…"

"You think they got themselves a sled?" Silk asked.

"Not sure." Magnus stared at the back of Awen's head until she turned to look at him.

"What?" she asked.

"Can the Luma, I don't know, float, maybe?"

Awen shrugged. "I mean, theoretically we—*they*—could move along on some sort of Unity energy flow. It's not really something anyone ever explored."

"To your knowledge."

"Yes," she replied. "To my knowledge."

"But they could if they had enough talent. Like the true bloods."

"We're coming up on the next node," Silk said.

But Awen still looked at Magnus. "The true bloods with access to the Nexus—yeah. They could probably move along on light energy."

"Hold on," Abimbola said.

The speedy little *Ass Protector* shuddered as it careened into the node, and then it doubled back to roll along the outside wall. Now the cart groaned under the G-forces, and Magnus guessed it wouldn't hold together for much longer. Which was fine, as he was pretty sure they were coming up on the command node soon.

"Can you explain moving along on light energy?" Magnus asked Awen as he squeezed the vibrating floor deck tighter.

"Not really," she said. "I've never seen it done."

"But if you were?"

"Next tunnel," Silk yelled. "Hold on."

The cart screeched as it went up on its left side. The improvised vehicle jumped the blastcrete lane and slammed against the tunnel's inside wall. Magnus's chin struck the deck and smashed his teeth together. Amazingly, the cart righted itself and relocated the smooth path.

"If I was," Awen said, looking down the final corridor. "It might look something like that."

"What the hell?" Magnus demagged his TB16 and brought it into high ready position then used his bioteknia eyes to zoom in for a closer look. Another half klick ahead, he saw what looked like the tail end of a hoverbike gang. Only these riders weren't dressed in leather and plate armor and hunched over chrome handlebars; instead, they wore golden robes and seemed to lean over channels of yellow and red light.

"Rohoar wants to knock them off and eviscerate them," Rohoar said.

"I think you're gonna get your chance," Magnus said. While the Unity-powered hoverbikes were fast, the Luma probably hadn't imagined they were being pursued—and certainly not by a *Tiny Ass Protector*.

"We're coming in hot," Rix said.

"No splick," Magnus replied. "Any bright ideas?"

"If you cut the power, we drop hard, right?" Silk asked Awen.

"I'm afraid so."

"Plus, it leaves us way behind," Magnus added. "Which is not good."

"And if we continue aboard," Abimbola said—his face looking as though he imagined the repercussions and how the passengers might fare in the impact. "We will most likely not survive."

"But neither will the enemy," Rohoar added. "Which is satisfying to know."

"Speak for yourself, Fluffy." Magnus gave the Jujari the stink eye. "Then that leaves us with a third option. We jump."

"At this speed?" Awen said.

"You got a better idea?"

Awen seemed to consider the question. "I can probably shield our fall."

"How much is probably?" Rix asked.

"Somewhere between ouch and that's gonna leave a mark."

Rix shrugged. "I can work with that."

"Then everyone get ready." Magnus cradled his weapon, intending to use it as soon as he was back on his feet—assuming, of course, that Awen's shielding was sufficient. But he trusted her.

How magnanimous of you, Awen said in his head.

Sorry, he replied in his thoughts. *Just being honest.*

Yeah, yeah. Let's see you try and form a Unity bubble around six people hurtling through a tunnel at the bottom of the ocean.

Magnus raised his hands in deference and then nodded toward the enemy. So far, the Li-Dain still hadn't noticed them, and with any luck, they wouldn't until it was too late.

"You ready?" he yelled to Awen.

She nodded.

"Everyone else?"

The rest of the team cast furtive glances over the speeding cart's edge, but all gave head nods or a thumb's up.

"On three," Magnus said. "One, two, three!"

It was never natural to leap off a speeding vehicle, even when decked out in advanced alien armor. But it sure as hell was fun. Magnus felt the unmistakable surge of adrenaline shoot through his veins as he did when rushing an enemy stronghold. Unlike what the poets said, he didn't see his life flash before his eyes. But time did seem to slow down, enough that, for a split second, it felt like he was floating. That moment never lasted long though.

When Magnus hit the ground, it was far less soft than he imagined Awen might make it. Somehow, he thought crash-landing in a shielded bubble meant a slow deceleration where he ended up on his feet. Instead, Magnus and the others flipped head over heels, eventually rolling to a stop. It was about as far from the holo movies as he could imagine. *At least we're not dead*, he thought, and then cringed at the rebuke he knew was coming his way.

That's fine, she said. *You can handle it next time.*

Magnus coughed and then rose to his feet. "What I meant to say was—"

"Check it out," Rix said while pointing down the tunnel.

Free of its occupants, the *Tiny Ass Protector* accelerated even faster, catching up to the Luma in seconds. By the time the Li-Dain noticed the out of control drill-fronted transport vehicle, it was too late. The cart slammed into the rearmost Luma riders and threw two aside while trampling over a third in the middle.

Abimbola gave out a baritone victory cry as the sled burrowed its way deeper into the enemy lines. More Li-Dain fell off their gleaming Luma cycles and flipped head over heels along the ground. Several people smacked against the ceiling only to come back down on top of one another. The Li-Dain had made the unwitting mistake of riding far too close to one another so that the cart set off a chain reaction.

"Weapons hot," Magnus yelled. "Let's move!"

Alpha Team ran flat out for two hundred meters before Magnus fired his first round. Those Li-Dain who had survived the repulsor-powered projectile were mostly toward the front of the pack, while at least a dozen Luma in the rear succumbed to their injuries. There was still no telling exactly how many enemies lay ahead, but Magnus guessed it was still well over two hundred, and the bulk of them were, no doubt, entering the command center node.

Several Li-Dain picked themselves off the ground and looked back down the corridor. When they did, a volley of torpedo rounds was headed their way. The tunnel filled with orange flames and the deafening sound of explosions. A beat later, super-heated air whooshed against Magnus's face accompanied by the pungent smell of spent propellant and detonation compound.

"You had better be careful over there," came Wobix's voice over the biotech interface in Magnus's head.

"Wobix," Magnus exclaimed, happy to hear the cat's voice. He slowed the team down with a wave of his hand and then pointed to their helmets to make sure they heard the transmission over VNET. Silk gave Magnus a thumbs up to confirm. "Where you at, Bixy?"

"Next tunnel over to your southeast."

"So you haven't made it to the command node either?"

"No."

That was not good news; it meant the enemy was going to get there first.

"We hear you over there, manservant. You need to cease firing your torpedo rounds. These corridors can only take so much pressure."

"Copy," Magnus replied while lifting his weapon's muzzle. To the group, he said: "Wobix says we've gotta cool it with the TB16s in the tunnels."

"Then what do we have?" Abimbola asked.

"We have an Awen," Rohoar exclaimed, pointing a clawed nub at the mystic. "Come, tiny Elonian. Do your worst against these wretched scum who intrude upon your previous order's sacred lineage and desecrate the Luma reputation with their filthy souls."

"I agree with the Jujari," Wobix said. "Use the Awen, manservant."

"I swear I'm buying you two galactic common lessons when this is over," Magnus said, more for his own sake than anyone else's.

"Yes, but we fight well," Rohoar replied.

"That has nothing to do with—" Magnus pulled himself up short, knowing any further conversation would be a waste of time. He aimed his finger down the tunnel and cast Rohoar an exasperated look. "Point the Awen that way and get her to fire."

Now that comms were back up, Magnus hailed Bravo Team as Alpha Team raced forward under cover of Awen's energy blasts. "Where you at, Zoll?"

"We're moving on foot northwest, about 120 meters from the

command node," Zoll said from the pop-up frame in Magnus's bioteknia eyes.

"We're about 300 meters from the same," Magnus replied, out of breath. "But we've still got a whole lotta robes in front of us."

"So the enemy's gonna get there first."

"Splick's about to get real," Magnus said. "Our only advantage is having them on two sides."

"But without the numbers, I don't—"

"I was trying to be positive, Zoll."

He gave a half-smile. "Copy."

"See if you can gain access to the command center. We'll try and draw their fire."

"See you inside."

Awen hurled energy blasts down the corridor like a Marine with her MAR30 on full-auto.

Truth be told, Magnus admired how hard Awen was working at a discipline that she would have scorned a few months prior. Then again, a lot had happened in that time, and she and Magnus were different people in many regards. To think that this once proud Luma emissary would be casting a barrage of energy rounds at enemy combatants, much less former classmates and leaders, would have baffled the Magnus who rode out of Oorajee on the *Geronimo Nine*.

But in another regard, Magnus felt a strange sense of guilt over breaking Awen. Seeing the light flash against her power suit as she took other people's lives wasn't something he wanted to celebrate. If anything, he wanted it to stop as soon as possible. Of course, what she was doing was necessary—that was the only way he could justify the mystic and her foreboding display of power. But necessary and right were two different things.

The fact was, none of this was right. The violence, the chaos, and the power play—it was all wrong. And Magnus wanted it to end more than ever. He was growing tired of the fighting even though he was good at the killing. And he wanted his friends to be done with it too. If they could hold on just a little bit more, it would be over soon enough.

You just keep telling yourself that, Adonis, he said to himself. After all, hadn't he been feeding himself that same line since Caledonia? *Just a little bit more.*

Yeah, but this time it's different, he said. This time, when So-Elku was captured and Moldark slain, he'd hang his bucket up for good. People, good people, had told him that they couldn't imagine a world without a Magnus fighting to save it. What they didn't realize was that Magnus would never be free of fighting the battles that replayed inside his own head from here to the end of time.

Just a little more.

"Can we use our '16s again?" Rix asked. "Please, oh, please say yes."

Magnus blinked up at the command center that filled the large node. Praise be to all seven of Andromeda's sweet sisters, they'd made it at last.

"Hell, yeah," Magnus said as he pulled his TB16 from his back and took cover behind a security checkpoint hut. But even as he aimed at a Li-Dain who bounded toward the main building, Magus saw something flicker along the dome's ceiling. He focused on the movement and saw four blaster barrels drop out of metallic housings and then rotate 360° in a standard startup sequence. And, unlike standard Repub versions of the point defense turrets, these had shimmering blue shields around them—no doubt care of Sekmit engineering and use of the Unity.

"Son of a bitch," Magnus said as he raised his weapon toward the dome. "They activated the point defenses."

"Yeah, and those aren't the only ones," Silk said, and then nodded behind them.

Magnus glanced over his shoulder and looked back down the tunnel. There, along the spine in the ceiling, he counted three turrets spinning up and gaining orientation. "Come on, really?"

24

CALDWELL FOLLOWED DiAntora through the spaceport's complex systems of hallways, walkways, elevators, and sky trains. Without her guidance, Caldwell feared he'd get lost in what was a half glorified shopping mall, half bridge to the galaxy. Fortunately, the one thing the team didn't have to fight against were pedestrians as Freya had ordered the building clear of public use the day before. It felt odd walking through such a thoroughly empty commercial building, the eateries and boutiques of which sat shuttered like the ocular sockets of some napping multi-eyed beast.

"This way." DiAntora ran toward a hovertrain's wide-open doors. "It's the fastest way to bay twenty-nine."

"But will he fit?" Caldwell asked, thumbing over his shoulder at So-Elku's crate.

"Negative."

The admiral had just confirmed Caldwell's fears. "Then we'll take another route."

"But Colonel, we don't have time. The bay is at least twenty minutes by foot—more if you factor in our numbers, and the fact that the enemy will reengage us as soon as they determine which ship belongs to us."

"She's right, William," Willowood said.

"We are not letting that freak out of his box," Caldwell said, nodding at the prisoner crate.

"I can handle him," Piper replied. She reached out and squeezed Caldwell's hand. "It's not hard. Promise."

"There's got to be another way." Caldwell looked from Willowood back to DiAntora. Then he glanced at Nelson. "I thought I told you to get as close to bay twenty-nine as possible?"

"I did, Colonel. This was it."

All at once, the sounds of shouts and blaster fire echoed through the mall's glossy corridors from someplace farther back.

"We're running out of time," DiAntora hissed.

"If Piper says she can handle him, I say we let her," Willowood said to Caldwell. "It's that, or our timeline gets extended."

"Fine," Caldwell said. "But you're assisting full time."

"Planned on it," Willowood said.

Caldwell motioned to LaMaster and ordered her to unlock the mobile prisoner cell.

She hesitated for a fraction of a second, an act which did little to reassure him of this decision.

"Go ahead, Lieutenant." Caldwell nodded at her with a conciliatory look. "It's all right."

"Yes, Colonel." LeMaster moved to the security control pad and began tapping on the screen. Then she inputted the necessary biometric data and ordered her men to ready their weapons. The fireteam raised their MAR30s to high ready position and aimed at the dark green metallic panels. When LeMaster seemed satisfied, she punched the release button.

Red lights projected from the roof and a warning klaxon announced that the cell's opening procedures had been engaged. Caldwell had seen containment units like this before and always thought the bells and whistles were a bit over the top, created by some overly dramatic engineers. *But not this time*, he thought. This time, the transport cell had every reason to let bystanders know how dangerous it was to open it. Even Caldwell raised his NOV2.

Supercooled hydraulics vented their condensed air streams as the front panels demagnetized. The doors separated like the segmented sections of a Thendarian sea serpent's back, masked in a thin veil of white mist. Combined with the swirling red emergency lights, Caldwell felt this was more akin to something out of a suspense movie than real life. Then again, most of his life in recent days had felt more like fiction than not. *How fitting*, he mused.

The doors separated to reveal a bound and muzzled So-Elku bathed in red light. His dark eyes went from Caldwell to Willowood to DiAntora, and then to Piper. Caldwell wanted to blast the man in the head for even looking at the girl. But that wasn't the mission. *Yeah, but I can make it the mission*, he thought to himself. *Just give me a reason, you fork-tongued son of a bitch.*

"He's secure," Piper said. The natural confidence in her small voice had a way of easing the tension.

"Then let's move," Caldwell replied as the sound of blaster fire grew closer.

"You heard him," said one of LeMaster's security team.

So-Elku cast the trooper a devilish look—at least as much as one could be conveyed with a muzzle over his mouth.

But the trooper didn't flinch. "I said, move it."

So-Elku lowered his head and shuffled through the still-venting ports and into the mall's wide-open space. He looked around and then gazed at Caldwell.

"Undo his feet so he can walk," Caldwell ordered.

LeMaster nodded and touched something on her data pad. The plasma restraints around So-Elku's ankles de-powered and fell to the ground with a *clank*. Another trooper retrieved them and clipped the shackles to his belt. All the while, So-Elku's gaze never left Caldwell's.

"If he does anything you don't like," the colonel said to Piper, making sure that So-Elku could hear him. "Kill him."

Piper laughed. The sound was so innocent, so arrestingly out of place, that So-Elku seemed startled as he studied Piper.

"No problem, Mr. William, sir. That's super easy to do."

So-Elku glanced back up at Caldwell, and the colonel thought he detected the faintest hint of fear behind the Luma Master's eyes. *Hell yeah, you'd better be afraid.*

DiAntora rocked from side to side as the hovertrain slalomed through the underground tunnel. Caldwell was growing increasingly curious about why she'd left Aluross to join the Republic, especially considering the underlying tensions between the two governments. Maybe when this was all over, he'd get her story in full.

"I wanted to know the enemy," DiAntora said without looking at him.

The sudden pronouncement caught the colonel off guard. He flipped his visor up and looked at the woman. "An officer could get themself in a lot of trouble for less."

DiAntora turned to face him. "Listening to peoples' thoughts or calling the Republic my enemy?"

"Both."

DiAntora seemed to consider the pronouncement and then gave a warm smile of acceptance. "I figured that if I was going to do my part in liberating my people, I needed to know what I was up against."

"How ambitious. Though it seems you got distracted along the way."

"Distracted?"

"If I'm not mistaken, you're an admiral, Miss DiAntora. A lifer. Could have taken your shot against the Repub a long time ago."

"And who's saying I'm not now?" she said with a wink.

Caldwell chuckled. She certainly had balls. But then there was something about the way DiAntora replied that reinforced his original curiosity. Not that he suspected she was malicious or anything; he didn't feel she was dangerous to him or the gladias. But there was more to her story than she was letting on.

"Here we go, people," DiAntora said over her in-ear comm's device. "Stay sharp."

A platoon of Marines and Sekmit filed out of the train car and set a perimeter in the receiving hall. Caldwell stepped beside Piper as DiAntora motioned So-Elku out. Then all the squads rejoined and followed the large directional signs that read Bay 29.

"Colonel?" came TO-96's voice.

"Go for Caldwell."

"We have more news on the mystery ship, sir."

Caldwell flipped his visor down so he could see the bot in his HUD and maintain privacy. "Talk to me."

"Well, sir, it seems to be heading right for your position."

"We've been over that," Caldwell replied.

"No, no—I mean, your specific position at docking bay twenty-nine."

"But DiAnotra's ship, it's presence is—"

"Private. We know, sir. That's why it concerns us."

Caldwell looked to DiAntora. His imagination could cast her as a mole; she certainly had the means. But the motive seemed unclear. If this was about killing or capturing So-Elku, she was already on point for those things. No, this wasn't her doing. Plus, there wasn't an organization alive that could spoof Azelon this bad, at least none that Caldwell knew of.

"How much time do we have, 'Six?"

"Two minutes is our best-revised guess. The vessel is tough to track. And, sir?"

"What?"

"It's big."

Caldwell led the team into the open air of docking bay twenty-nine. If something was hunting them, he wanted to see it first. A light flashed above the hangar's rim, followed by a thunder crack that sounded in the distance. The storm was upon them, and it would be raining soon. Caldwell ordered everyone to secure the hangar and told Piper and Willowood to keep a close eye on So-Elku.

The Repub's disguised shuttle sat in the middle of the space, bathed in beams of light swirling with flying insects; a docking bay crew swept the blastcrete floor and tidied up charge lines; and a spaceball match played out over a holo screen within the security office on the bay's far side. Everything was strangely and uneasily as it should be.

Caldwell looked skyward, but there was nothing to see there either. No engine burn, no repulsor waves, not even the stars. The colonel was about to call TO-96 back and let the bot have it when something odd struck him.

Caldwell froze.

The stars.

As he studied the darkness, the colonel realized that the only stars he could see were just above the hangar's upper rim—and even they were disappearing. Fast.

"We've got a ship inbound on our position," he yelled over the company channel and started running for cover along the inside wall. "Twelve o'clock high!"

"But Colonel," Captain Nelson replied. "There's nothing—"

Nelson's voice was drowned out by the painful sound of stone on metal as something crashed into the Repub shuttle's raised tail. A second later, the lights along the bay's upper rim exploded, bathing the shuttle and the floor in sparks. More hellacious noise sounded as the entire bay's circumference compressed like the rim of an aluminum cup. Electrical explosions popped, and metal plates flew out to strike the Repub ship. The shuttle itself was being driven into the blastcrete, using its emergency lights and sirens to protest its demise.

Caldwell wanted to shoot something, but now that a deep blackness had closed in on them, there was nothing to see but small fires and a few interior lights from inside the spaceport.

"SITREP with anything intelligent?" Caldwell asked with a clipped tone.

Nelson's nervous voice broke comms silence first. "It's like the sky just caved in on us, sir."

"I said something intelligent, Captain." Caldwell was pissed. No, furious and pissed. He opened the channel to the *Spire.* "What in Patty's pants are we looking at, Ballsy?" Caldwell waited for a beat for the bot to reply, but the channel was silent. "You've got to be kidding me right now." He switched back to the company channel. "All units, fall back to—"

A horizontal red line three meters across appeared somewhere above the crushed Repub shuttle. Then two vertical shafts plunged away from the ends until Caldwell realized he was looking at a ramp door. The platform came down without the sound of hydraulics or winches—just a smooth and steady *whoosh* as it swept through the air. As the leading edge lowered, Caldwell saw a black figure appear, silhouetted by an intense red light that sent long tendrils into the haze-stricken underworld.

For several long seconds, silence filled the space as both the figure and Caldwell's forces remained in place, weapons at the ready, fingers resting on trigger guards.

"What is this?" Nelson finally said. "And who the hell is—" The captain's words were cut short by the sound of him gagging.

Caldwell glanced at the captain and then back to the silhouette in the ship. There was only one person Caldwell could think of that would do this. "Light him up," he roared over VNET.

The closed hangar space exploded in a frenetic display of blaster fire and Unity energy bolts. One-hundred eighty degrees of light streamed into the opening accompanied by a deafening wail. With nowhere to go, the energy build-up shook the ground in protest of its containment, but still, Caldwell let the assault continue.

When, at last, the colonel didn't think the target could take any more, he gave the order to cease fire and raised his hand.

His eyes were slow to readjust to the dim light, but when they did, he saw the same figure standing in the same place as before. "Son of a bitch."

Just then, a gravel-strewn voice sounded from the silhouette, loud enough for Caldwell and everyone else to hear.

"Are you finished?"

Caldwell raised his NOV2 and fired one last round. He couldn't be sure, but he thought he saw the figure flinch. "There," Caldwell said over external speakers. "Now I'm finished. At least for the time being."

The silhouette nodded and then started walking down the ramp. Caldwell wondered how far the man would venture into the hangar; clearly, some sort of force field had kept the enemy protected.

"Nelson," Caldwell said. "You still with us?"

The captain's voice came back in a groggy whisper. "Yeah, but I could use a stiff drink."

"We'll get you squared away in a bit."

"Copy that, Colonel."

"William," Willowood said over a private channel.

"Whaddya got," Caldwell replied as he brought her face up on his HUD.

"I'm sensing something strange about this ship."

"Can you elaborate?"

Willowood shook her head. "Not at the moment. But I'm working on it."

"Well, let me know just as soon as you know. Copy?"

"I will. And, you do know who that is, right?"

Caldwell gave her a half-smile. "I might be a little slower than I used to be, but I know a parasite when I see one."

She pursed her lips and gave him a nod. "Just be careful."

"Don't you mean, be dangerous?"

She winked at him and then closed out the channel.

By the time the enemy stopped at the ramp's bottom, Caldwell had stepped clear of his cover but kept his weapon pointed dead ahead. "Looks like you need a few lessons in basic piloting, Moldark."

"Colonel Caldwell," the enemy said. "How nice of you to parley with me."

"What do you want, Blacky? Cause last I checked, you weren't sent an invitation to this party."

"No," Moldark said, wringing his gloved hands; the squeak they produced made Caldwell's neck hair stand up. "No, I wasn't. Which is a shame, because I think I could have spared you so much unnecessary work."

"And how's that?"

"Well, you're taking great care to protect someone I want."

Caldwell instantly thought of Piper. After all, the child had been forcefully removed from the Admiral's clutches on the *Black Labyrinth*.

"Which I, of course, appreciate," Moldark continued. "But I no longer require your assistance in preserving him."

Caldwell balked. "Him? You mean So-Elku?"

"Well done, Colonel." Moldark clapped his hands slowly and then offered one palm up. "Now, if you don't mind, I'd like my prize."

Caldwell was about to decline the bastard's offer when Moldark interjected. "And before you refuse me, I'd like to point out that my ship and my crew are quite happy to exact payment upon the

Sekmit and their charming capital city, as you, no doubt, remember that I'm fond of doing, mmmm, Colonel?"

The sick bastard was talking about Capriana, of course, and it took everything in the colonel not to blast Moldark in the face—not that it would do any good. *But it sure as hell will make me feel better*, Caldwell thought to himself.

"So here's what I'm going to do," Moldark said. "I'm going to give you, let's say"—he glanced at his wrist—"ninety seconds to think it over, and then I'm going to take action on whatever answer you give me—or don't give me, that's up to you."

"Well, I can tell you where I'm gonna put your ninety—"

"We need to talk," Willowood said over his comms. "Now."

Caldwell pressed his tongue against the inside of his cheek. He couldn't believe he was going to take this monster up on an invitation to confer with his team when he knew the enemy was just going to kill everyone anyway. "Ninety seconds, Moldark."

"What is it?" Caldwell asked Willowood in a more severe tone then he meant it to be. He would apologize for it later—if there were a later.

"I think we can stop him," she replied.

"Stop Moldark?" He wasn't sure he was hearing her right. "If you haven't noticed, he's got a ship we can't track and a forcefield we can't punch through."

"That's just it," she replied. "I believe it's Unity powered."

Caldwell blanched. "But I thought Moldark couldn't use—"

"He can't." Willowood shook her head. "But he's gotten ahold of something that does and is. That thing, that ship isn't something he made. But it's omitting the largest Nexus signature I've ever seen. And whoever built it is doing a good job at keeping that part hidden."

"So you're saying you can disrupt whatever's powering it?"

"Not just powering it: holding it together."

"Well, hell, Felicity. Let's get the shindig up and running."

She put a hand on his forearm. "It's not that simple. We're gonna need to get inside it. And we'll need extra hands."

"Inside it?" Caldwell balked. "And by extra hands, you mean, Unity users?"

She nodded.

"Well, hell, we've got you, Paladia Company, the narskill..."

Willowood didn't seem to buy it.

"You need Piper," he added.

She nodded and gave him a raised eyebrow. There was something more.

Caldwell's mind raced and then stopped on the only thing he could think of. "Hold up. You mean to tell me that you need Crazy Britches over there?" He pointed to So-Elku, which was an action that drew the Luma Master's attention. "Aw, hell no, Felicity. Tell me that's not what you're thinking right now."

"It is, William. And it's the only chance we have at shutting that ship down. Even then, I'm not sure it's enough. But he'll take out the city whether or not we comply."

"I already guessed as much." Caldwell sighed. "And how do we know they're not working together on this—So-Elku and Moldark?"

"We don't," Willowood said. "But if we don't try something, we're dead anyway."

"Time's up, Colonel Caldwell," Moldark said from the ramp. "What will it be?"

25

"Everyone take cover," Magnus yelled as the point defense turrets started picking out targets. There was only one problem with the order—he couldn't see anything robust enough to protect them from death from above. That was, more than likely, by design, he knew. No good defense engineer would install ceiling-mounted turrets only to add armored shelters below them. Still, there had to be something they could do to find cover.

And there was. It was called an Awen.

"Awen," Magnus said. "We need a Unity shield, now!"

Rix went down as blaster fire poured from the turrets over Magnus's shoulder. The gladia yelled—which meant he was alive—but Magnus saw a burning hole in Rix's side and another in his leg.

A split second later, a simmering yellow bubble snapped to life around the fire team as more energy bolts crashed against the outside. Magnus guessed Awen wouldn't be able to hold it for long, so they needed a plan. And he needed to know how second squad was doing.

"Silk, patch him up," Magnus said, pointing to Rix.

"On it."

Then to Zoll, Magnus said, "You find cover?"

"Thanks to Wish and company, yeah. But it's hot over here, LT."

"Roger." Magnus double-checked the roster. Granther Company had nineteen gladias, and Wobix's narskill still totaled twenty-five. "Bixy, you still present?"

"Yes, manservant."

"Is there another way into the command center besides the front doors?"

"You mean like a basement entrance or something?"

Magnus pumped a fist. "Hell yeah, Bixy!"

"No."

"Wait, what?"

"No other entrances. We are on the ocean floor, manservant."

Magnus pinched the bridge of his nose. "Then it looks like we're doing this the hard way."

From Alpha Team's position against the guard station, Magnus started counting the Li-Dain that still occupied the command building's lawn. "I've got fifty on the southwest side," he said to Zoll.

"Same on the southeast."

"The rest look to be taking up defensive positions on the high ground," Dutch said. "I'm counting a dozen sniper positions on those balconies."

"Then we stagger our approach and keep moving," Magnus said. He glanced back at Rix. "How's he looking, Silk?"

"I can still shoot," Rix answered for her.

"He's gonna need some serious attention when this is all done," she added. "But the nanobots are doing their work, and I've stopped most of the bleeding."

"Well, we need every gun we can get. Just don't look to run any marathons today. Copy?"

Rix nodded.

Magnus reviewed the team stats and flipped back to the company channel. "We've got to gain access to that building and smoke 'em out. We are the last option."

"La-raah," Abimbola said over the company channel.

"Mystics, keep our cover up," Magnus added. "Everyone else, let's show 'em what the Gladio Umbra do to unwelcome guests. Move out!"

"We've got to close the gap and get close enough for Rohoar to do some damage," Magnus said. The others nodded, and the Jujari gave a low growl. Then Magnus ordered covering fire on the closest cluster of Li-Dain. He didn't expect the munitions to catch the enemy off guard—not that he would refuse an unexpected kill. Instead, he just needed a window to run forward and dive behind a cluster of boulders turned decorative planters. Awen and the others followed close behind as soon as Magnus assumed the role of doling out covering fire.

Alpha Team leapfrogged one more time, all while being pelted from turret fire overhead. They took cover behind a berm bordering the lawn and forced the enemy back with a near-constant but highly disciplined fire rate. Such use of ammunition couldn't be sustained indefinitely, but it didn't need to be.

"Rohoar," Magnus said with a thumbs up. "You good?"

Rohoar replied with an awkward attempt at a thumbs up. "Rohoar is always good." Then the Jujari mwadim bounded over the berm and drove straight for three Li-Dain. The Luma weren't expecting to see a three-meter armor-encased Jujari hunt them down, at least by the way the enemies held their hands up in terror. Rohoar stepped within their protective shields and relieved the center Luma of his head. The outside two, Rohoar slashed with his claws and then pounced upon to slit their throats.

Meanwhile, Magnus ordered Abimbola, Silk, and Rix to provide covering fire as Rohoar worked his way across the lawn.

"You all right?" Magnus asked Awen as he swapped out magazines. She sat with her back against the berm, bracing herself like some unseen wind was about to sweep her away.

"I'm okay."

"Really? Cause you don't sound all that convinced."

"I'll be fine. Just get us inside because I can't hold this much longer."

"And that's why every Awen has a Magnus." He leaned over, kissed the top of her helmet, and then resumed firing on the Li-Dain.

A sniper position on the second story balcony caught Magnus's attention. The two Li-Dain there seemed intent on stopping the Jujari's rampage, which was understandable given the warpath Rohoar was on. "Yeah," Magnus said as he lined up on the two enemies. "Not gonna happen." Two torpedo bolts screamed up the building, the first breaking the windowplex half wall, the second detonating against the chest of one Luma. The explosion not only cleaved the first man in two—the Li-Dain must've forgotten to shield himself—but also blew off half of the second victim's face and shoulder. Both victims disappeared onto the balcony floor.

A streak of blue light to the right caught Magnus's attention. He looked across a small garden and through some tree-mounted banners to see a warrior in Sekmit armor dispensing one Thørzin power bow charge after another into an entrenched line of enemies. The unit tag on Magnus's bioteknia eyes read Wobix.

The Sekmit's weapon's bolts curved around cover and took out the Li-Dain one at a time. But it was the final shot that most surprised Magnus: the bolt missed the target altogether, but just before it struck the building face, the energy round redirected and hit the Li-Dain in the back of the head.

"That settles it, Bixy," Magnus said. "You're setting me up with one of those when we're done."

But Wobix seemed too focused to respond as he drew his staff on another Li-Dain who charged him. For a moment, Magnus was sure the narskill warrior had made a fatal mistake in choosing the wooden stick over the power bow. But then long stretches of the shaft began emanating blue light, and Magnus wondered if he'd underestimated the cat-man.

When the Li-Dain brought glowing hands around to strike Wobix, the Sekmit blocked the blow with his staff. But unlike any normal parry, the Luma's arm flew back the way it'd come, accompanied by a *boom* that made the leaves move. A dazzling display of sparks burst from the impact too, followed by a second *boom* and shower of light as Wobix struck the enemy in the chest. The Luma flew backward and hit the command building's base with a sickening *thud*.

"And I want a stick too," Magnus added.

Even though both squads continued to gain ground, the enemy sent what felt like an endless supply of reinforcements to defend the building and drive the gladias and narskill back.

Magnus knew ammunition was getting low, and his units were getting tired. Two Jujari, Graban and Redmarrow, had been injured during CQB, but still looked to be going strong, while Jaffrey and Dozer had been struck by energy rounds when straying too far from their respective Unity shields. Their vitals were stable, but they wouldn't be making any presses for the building.

Wobix had lost four narskill in hasty attempts to charge the ground-level doors. One Sekmit even got within a meter before his torso was cored by a Li-Dain who stepped around a decorative bush. The robed warrior drove two beams of light into the narskill's abdomen, leaving a gaping hole where vital organs should have been.

Even Awen was moving more slowly. Despite her objections to the contrary, Magnus knew her shield was moments from collapsing. Without the mystics, the turrets would pick the fire teams off, and the whole assault would be over.

"If anyone's got any bright ideas, now's the time," Magnus said. He fired on a Li-Dain who was powering up for a shot at Rohoar. But the round went low, so when the torpedo bolt exploded, it blew the ground out from under the Luma. The woman flipped backward, missing both feet, and landed some four meters away amidst a shower of grass, dirt, and bone fragments.

"I'm on my last mag. But I've still got a Nick," he said, referring to his Novian combat knife.

"Charlie Team's low too," Bliss said.

"And we're not far behind," Robillard added.

A bio status alert flashed on a member from Charlie Team. It was Telwin, the fire team's mystic.

"Does someone have eyes on—"

"Gladia down," Bliss yelled over comms. "Telwin's been hit."

Splick, Magnus said to himself. "Copy that."

But Bliss wasn't through. "Dozer's—dah! Son of a bitch." More blaster fire broke over Bliss's open comm channel. "Dozer's KIA."

"Someone help secure their position," Magnus ordered. A feeling of helplessness started to creep in on Magnus. He just wanted to be free of the Li-Dain.

"Taking heavy fire," Jaffrey said from Robillard's Delta Team. "We're gonna try moving to—"

"Negative, Jaffrey," Robillard yelled. "We can't cover you."

But the kid must not have heard Robillard. That, or someone took him out before he understood his CO. Jaffrey's comm went full-static, and a red Fatal badge appeared over the kid's name in the roster.

"Ah, gods," Robillard added. "We just lost Redmarrow too. Ya gotta be splicking me right now."

"Keep it locked down," Magnus said, suppressing the emotion raging inside his chest. At this rate, there'd be nothing left of Granther Company in a few more minutes. Even if they found a way to bleed the Li-Dain's ranks, Magnus's forces were still running dangerously low on ammunition.

The only warriors who seemed to have an endless supply of energy were the narskill and the Li-Dain. But without the Gladio Umbra's mystics, Magnus doubted if the Sekmit had it in them to both keep shields up and power their energy weapons. Worse still, however, was that there was no retreat from this position: the tunnels were lined with point defense turrets. But even if they could escape, would they want to? That meant giving So-Elku control of the mine and, in turn, the planet.

Magnus secretly hoped that Forbes was on the way to relieve them. But wasn't that the wish of every trooper pinned down outside the wire? Of course it was, because no one wanted to die, and everyone wanted to believe help was on the way. But when the turrets were activated, Magnus was assured that the hovertrain tunnels were shut down too.

He and Granther Company weren't getting rescued.

"Splick," Magnus said. He dropped down and leaned his back against the berm then looked over at Awen.

She flipped up her visor and returned his stare. No doubt sensing his frustration, she spoke inside his head. *I can end this, you know.*

What do you mean you can end this? he thought back to her.

I can go nova.

Magnus didn't answer right away. Instead, he studied her face and her pained purple eyes. Then he looked over at Rix who fought despite his injuries; at Silk, who screamed as she fired on the sniper positions overhead; at Abimbola, who tried in vain to knock out the defense turrets; and at Rohoar, who wrestled two Li-Dain to the ground despite a deep gouge in his thigh armor and another along his limp left arm.

There's got to be another way, he thought. *We're so close.*

And we can still succeed, she added.

Dying is not success.

It is if it protects the ones you love.

Then Magnus thought of Piper and remembered the dream she'd had, the one where the two of them went underwater and met a power they could not defeat. She'd given Magnus all the details after he'd survived the mission at the governor's mansion.

As if reading his thoughts—because she probably was—Awen said, *It's Piper's dream, isn't it.*

Mysticsdammit, he replied. *I don't believe* it.

A lack of belief doesn't make reality any less true, she answered and then touched his hand. *Let me do it, Adonis. They don't even have to know. It will save the Sekmit and the planet.*

No, Awen. You can't.

Awen removed her helmet and threw it aside, and then she pulled her face to Magnus's and kissed him.

"Really?" Abimbola said. "Now?"

But Magnus ignored him.

"She is going to go nova."

Magnus pulled away and looked in Awen's eyes. "Yeah, Bimby. She's going nova."

The Miblimbian clucked his tongue and fell back against the berm. "I cannot say she failed to warn me. Naked monkey butts and all."

Magnus laughed, remembering the jail cell in the Dregs. "True. I suppose it was only a matter of time."

"What's all this now?" Silk said, pausing from her assault on the building.

"You'd better get it over with," Magnus said to Awen. "Or else we're gonna be a while saying goodbye to everyone. And mystics' know I hate long goodbyes."

"I love you, Magnus," Awen said as she reached up to touch his face. "We came so close."

26

Piper couldn't believe what she was hearing. She looked at her grandmother's face, shrouded in the strange ship's red light. "You really want me to let him go?" she asked.

Her grandmother nodded. "Yes, my dear. We need his help."

"But I thought he was the bad guy."

"He is. But right now, we need him to stop a worse bad guy."

"Grandpa," Piper said.

Her grandmother winced a little. "I'm afraid your grandfather has long since died, Piper."

"No," she replied, balling her hands into fists. "He's in there still. I know it."

"Be that as it may, he would also want you to do what I've asked you. We have to stop Moldark, and this is our chance."

Piper didn't like this plan. But she at least understood Mr. Caldwell's and her grandmother's line of thinking. Plus, Piper had to admit that she felt the same thing that her grandmother did: there was something inside that mysterious ship keeping it together within the Unity of all things. If they could search the ship and find the center of it, they could stop it.

Piper nodded and then turned to So-Elku, choosing to speak to him within the Unity so as not to alert Moldark. *You're a bad man*, Piper said.

So-Elku registered Piper's words by looking down at her. *Now, Piper, we both know that—*

I didn't ask for your opnin, opionin, Mr. So-Elku. I was merely saying facts.

Opinion, So-Elku said in a corrective tone. *And it's just one fact, singular.*

I'll speak the way I want to. And with that, Piper pinched So-Elku's ear within the Unity. She'd never done that to anyone before, but she'd seen it in the old holo movies when a teacher wanted to reprimand a student. When So-Elku jerked away from the pain, she admitted that it worked rather well.

I'm going to release you from your restraints, she continued. *And when I do, you're going to help us disable Moldark's ship.*

So-Elku eyed her. *Disable his ship?*

The Unity powers it. Well, the Nexus.

Does it now.

Focus, Piper said and then stabbed his ear again.

So-Elku made a sound under his muzzle, then said, *I'm focused. I'm focused.*

Good. When I let you go, you will follow my grandmother and me into the ship where we're gonna look for its drive core. Then you're gonna help us blow it up. When we're done, you'll be back under my control. And if you do anything that I don't like, anything at all, then I won't hesitate to hurt you worse than this.

Come, come, small one, So-Elku said. *We both know that—*

Piper jabbed both ears at the same time, which made the Luma Master cry out. *It's yes or no, Mr. So-Elku. I didn't ask for your oh—opinin.*

So-Elku took a deep breath. *Very well. But can we please stop with the ear pinching?*

No. Not unless you mind your manners.

"TIME'S UP, COLONEL CALDWELL," Moldark said. "What will it be?"

Caldwell didn't like the plan. He hated the plan. But he also couldn't see any other way around this predicament. Moldark and his mystery ship were literally right on top of them, and he'd be a flea monger's wartorn kitten mat before letting the dark lord have the Luma master.

But that left the Gladio Umbra and Sekmit without any leverage, and Caldwell knew the lunatic Paragon leader would blow them all to splick without thinking twice. Likewise, the colonel guessed his forces couldn't win against the dark lord in a fair fight, or else Moldark wouldn't have been so bold. But with Willowood's plan, they didn't have to win—they just needed to keep Moldark and his minions occupied long enough for the mystics to disrupt the ship's Nextgen Unity power something or other.

"You can have him," Caldwell said at last.

"Excellent," Moldark said. "You have chosen wisely."

"We don't need your flattery, Molsnark."

"It's Mol—" The dark lord hesitated, apparently picking up on the pun a moment too late.

"Just do me a favor," Caldwell said. "Make the coward pay, would you?"

"Pay?" Moldark cocked his head.

"Yeah. You're not the only one he betrayed, you know."

The dark lord gave a small chuckle. "Yes, he has betrayed many. Don't worry, Colonel. I won't let his misdeeds go unpunished."

Satisfied, Caldwell nodded and then waved for the prisoner to be brought forward.

Piper held her grandmother's hand as they pulled So-Elku along behind them. The older woman spoke without looking down at her.

As soon as we step inside the ship's force field, you know what to do?

Yes, Nana, Piper replied.

Good. Get ready.

When the trio came even with Mr. Caldwell, Piper studied Moldark's face. The man had grown even more disfigured since she'd last seen him. She noticed new scabs and scars and new folds of skin. Even his eyes seemed darker, as if that were possible, accented by heavy bags and dry skin. He was—he was old. And that's when Piper realized the truth of what was happening. Moldark, or rather his grandfather's body, was dying.

"Child," Moldark said as she neared.

"I have nothing to say to you, Moldark," she replied with a lift of her chin. "You're a bad person, and you are killing my grandfather."

Moldark gave her what amounted to a surprised look, but it came off as some gross sneer. "You speak only of the dead."

"No, I don't. Wendell Kane's alive. I can feel him."

"He is not," Moldark spat.

"Enough of this," Mr. Caldwell interjected. Then he motioned for So-Elku to be taken forward. "He is your prisoner now, Moldark."

The dark lord raised a hand and waved several Paragon Marines out of his ship. Piper didn't know how many more were inside, but they didn't seem like they'd be too much of a problem, at least not once she opened the gap in the ship's force field.

Piper's grandmother strode forward, pulling Piper along with her, and together, the three mystics stepped through the barrier to stand at the end of the ramp.

"When we release him," Nana said. "You will only have a moment to take control of him."

"I understand," Moldark said.

"If you wait too long, he will be able to—"

"I said, I understand. Let me have it."

"Your words," Nana said, and then she gave Piper a wink.

Piper did let So-Elku go, but not before pushing out from within the Unity. It was as if she opened an umbrella and raised it underneath a waterfall. Nexus energy cascaded off the awning, opening a hole in the force field that stretched from one side of the hangar bay to the other.

Before Moldark could react, blaster fire from the gladias and Repub Maines and Unity-powered bolts from the narskill filled the air. The Paragon Marines returned fire, taking cover around the crushed Repub shuttle, while Moldark backpedaled up the ramp. The dark lord stretched out his ethereal presence in an attempt to catch Piper, her grandmother, and So-Elku on the ends of black tendrils. But Nana was too fast and beat the attack back with several energy blows.

"Traitors." Moldark seethed as he backed away from the mystics proceeding up the ramp.

Piper left her imaginary umbrella under the force field for the other mystic gladias to sustain and then made sure to stay as close to Moldark as possible so that the Paragon troopers didn't try and shoot her or her grandmother. Not that the enemy seemed intent on doing so—they were far too busy keeping Mr. Caldwell's forces at bay.

"I've got So-Elku," Nana said as she followed the dark lord up the ramp and into the ship. "You know what to do."

"I do," Piper replied. "Good luck, Nana."

"You too."

Caldwell's initial impression of the unfolding battle changed several times within a few seconds. First, there was the sight of twenty-some Paragon Marines in black Mark VII armor and carrying MAR30s, which did not sit well with Caldwell. He thought most of Moldark's assault force had been killed in the orbital conflict following the attack on Capriana Prime. Then again, there were only twenty of them, as compared to the colonel's nearly 240 units. In a fair fight, there was no contest.

But this wasn't a fair fight.

The Li-Dain were still closing in from behind, as no one had told them about Moldark's arrival or the plan to use the LAW's master to take down the Paragon mystery ship. Caldwell didn't like being assaulted on two sides, but the Li-Dain would be on them any second.

Lastly, and most dangerous of all, was that Moldark had stumbled up the ramp to seek refuge inside his ship. He was wise to run: Caldwell wouldn't want to face Willowood and Piper in a fight either. Add So-Elku into the mix, who no doubt had some severe grievances against the dark lord, and you had an inescapable three-versus-one scenario, at least as far as Caldwell was concerned.

But Moldark's retreat also meant that Willowood and Piper were entering into the enemy's lair, and that bothered Caldwell most of all. As soon as they vanished into the ship's bowels, he felt his gut tighten. He'd be damned if he was going to leave them in there all alone.

"They're here," DiAntora said, nodding back toward the hover-train's port. Terminal doors opened, and dozens of Luma warriors raced out, their force fields casting the reception hall in a yellow hue.

"Nelson," Caldwell said over comms. "I want second and third platoons redirected to engage the enemy at our rear."

"Hard copy, Colonel," Nelson replied and then reissued the order to his platoon commanders.

Caldwell watched two platoons of gladia do an about-face and take cover against the Li-Dain. Concentrated NOV2 fire poured through the reception hall, bouncing off Unity shielding and filling the far end with sparks.

"Do whatever you can to keep them busy, Nelson," Caldwell shouted. "We've gotta buy Willowood and Piper as much time as we can."

THE FIRST THING that shocked Willowood was just how fast Moldark could run. Granted, her ex-husband had always been in top physical condition, which was something he'd maintained ever since playing spaceball in the academy. But given how badly the alien presence had degraded Kane's body, Willowood was surprised to see the dark lord outrun both her and So-Elku.

The second thing that surprised Willowood was just how large the enemy ship was—a fact made more apparent as she and So-Elku raced farther down each long black-lined corridor. For some reason, she first imagined the vessel was a transport shuttle. But now that she was on board, she understood it to be far more substantial—perhaps even a Battleship-class sized ship. And yet, questions remained about how such a spacecraft could enter the atmosphere unheard and unseen. But she reminded herself that this was no ordinary ship, and the Nexus power could account for all of her lingering questions.

"Ironic, isn't it?" So-Elku said between breaths. "That you and I would be fighting alongside one another again?"

"Less talking, more running," Willowood replied.

"You got it."

Just as Willowood rounded the next turn, she felt something strike her chest. She looked up to see Moldark standing five meters down the hall. The pain seared her rib cage, reminding her of a red-hot speartip trying to penetrate her chest. She batted the probe away and then flung a yellow orb of light at the enemy.

So-Elku, likewise, seemed caught off guard by the sudden attack and stumbled backward. But he pushed Moldark's tendril aside and sent his own Unity blast downrange.

Moldark dodged both attacks with reflexes that seemed far too fast for a human's. The motion made his body appear like an arachnid's that jumped on nimble legs and then pressed off the wall using quick arm thrusts. He came back with new stabs at Willowood and So-Elku's souls, trying to latch on with his other-worldly tendrils.

Willowood not only batted away the black finger that reached for her chest but also the one that lunged at So-Elku.

"Why, Willowood," So-Elku said. "You care."

"Yup." She pointed at Moldark, who turned left at the hallway's far end. "But only about stopping him. You're a means to an end, Teerbrin. Nothing more."

"And here I thought you were warming to me again."

"Not a chance." Willowood took off after Moldark. "Come on."

It wasn't long before Piper had gone far enough into Moldark's ship that she couldn't hear the blaster battle anymore. Even her grandmother's and So-Elku's footsteps had faded away down the long corridors. She was alone, wandering the halls of a dark and dangerous ship.

But Piper wasn't really wandering. She had the Unity of all things and her training to guide her. Awen's voice was in her head still, as was her grandmother's. And while Moldark's ship felt foreign, the Unity was not. In fact, Piper felt more at home there than she did anywhere else in the galaxy, so what did it matter if her feet were on a strange ship if her spirit was within the Unity?

A renewed wave of confidence surged through Piper and warmed her tummy. She could do this—hunt the Nexus drive core down and break Moldark's ship. It was just a matter of listening to the music.

Piper closed her natural eyes for a moment and decided to stretch out with her senses within the Unity. There, echoing through the starship's halls, was the faint whisper of a melody. The tune sounded sad, like something she might hear at a funeral. As Piper bent her ear toward the source, she heard harmony join with the first notes, creating a dark lament that washed through the ship. Whoever had first sung these notes must have lost someone they loved.

When Piper reopened her natural eyes, she had a strong sense of where the music was coming from—the song that held the whole ship together. She quickened her pace, feeling as though she might lose the melody if she wasn't quick about her work. That, and Piper knew that her grandmother and Mr. Caldwell couldn't hold the enemy off forever.

With every turn she took, Piper thought she would meet some angry adult with a blaster. But the hallways were all so empty, as if the ship had been abandoned. She wondered how so few people could operate such a big machine. But what did she know about flying starships anyway?

The melody continued to ripple throughout the ship and bounce off the walls. Piper suddenly got the impression that the music didn't want to be discovered—didn't want to reveal its source. She thought it was like trying to find a child who was crying in a closet. But every time you got close to finding the sad boy or girl, they turned out to be somewhere else. No matter: Piper was stronger and smarter than the tune and knew she'd be able to find it soon.

At last, she followed the song into a cavernous hall that exceeded whatever ideas she had about the ship's size. The ceiling faded away into blackness, and the stone floor was covered in lines and rings that made subtle troughs. And to one side, toward the stern, she thought, was a flat black wall. A set of doors near the bottom made her think of an elevator, while an opening several stories up made her think of a balcony that someone might use to speak to a crowd.

A chill went down Piper's back even though her power suit was keeping her body warm.

This is it, she thought, looking around the giant room. She knelt and put her hand on the warm stone floor. All at once, the troughs in the ground glowed red. *I've found you, Mr. Sad Song.*

WITH SECOND AND third platoons holding off the Li-Dain from the rear, Caldwell was able to work with Captain Nelson at picking off the Paragon Marines with first platoon. Likewise, DiAntora rallied her Repub forces along with the narskill to flank the enemy position from both sides.

The enemy troopers had to know they were fighting a losing battle. Had the units been under his command, he'd be telling them to fall back into the ship for cover by now. But they remained where they were, entrenched around the Repub shuttle or under the mystery ship's boarding ramp. Whether these Marines lacked the presence of mind or they'd been given orders not to move was anyone's guess. Either way, Hedgebore Company had them on their heels, and it wouldn't be long before every last one of them was down.

"Keep it up, gladias," Caldwell said over the general channel. "Not much longer."

Caldwell sighted his NOV2 on a Paragon trooper tucked inside a crevice above the Repub shuttle's aft engine cone. The Marine kept poking his head out just long enough to fire a well-placed round and take out one Sekmit after another. One shot, one kill, repeat. *Well,* Caldwell thought, *two can play that game.* The colonel found the trooper's pattern and waited for the next appearance.

When the black helmet poked out, Caldwell squeezed his trigger and watched the cap pop off the man's armored shoulders.

"Scratch another one for Caldwell," the colonel said to himself, and then he realized the channel was still open. In his younger years, he would have apologized. But he was too old for that sort of splick. It was what it was.

He aimed at another trooper who was giving DiAntora's men a particularly hard time on the left flank. The trooper had taken up a position inside the nose landing gear assembly and was using the hull panels as near-perfect cover on all sides. What the Marine had failed to notice, however, was that part of the hydraulic system was dangling over his head by a thread, or—in this case—a small bundle of transmission wires. Caldwell drew a bead on the target and fired. As soon as the bunch snapped, the hydraulic system crushed the trooper and silenced the MAR30.

"Saw that," DiAntora said to Caldwell. "Thanks."

"I aim to please." Caldwell smiled at his pun and moved his cigar to the other side of his mouth. Then he surveyed the fast-dwindling Paragon unit strength and knew what his next move was going to be: going in after Willowood and Piper. He'd be the wrong end of a Hornsperion buttlebuck before he let his ladies down.

Caldwell opened a channel to his officers in command. "I'm headed inside. First platoon, stay outside but guard my six. Second and third, fall back to cover the ship. Keep those Li-Dain off our asses."

The OICs replied with confirmation badges in the chat window.

"Mind if I tag along?" DiAntora said.

"The more the merrier," Caldwell replied.

The last two Paragon Marines were preoccupied with flanking attackers, which gave Caldwell all the margin he needed to charge up the ramp and enter Moldark's ship. The first thing he noticed was how dark the hallways were; the second was how empty the ship seemed. Then he heard an explosion come from somewhere up ahead. "Willowood. Do you copy?"

WILLOWOOD AND SO-ELKU worked in tandem to keep Moldark's tendrils at bay, and it turned out to be harder than she imagined. The old mystic had been wise to employ the Luma Master despite how ludicrous she knew the idea must have sounded to Caldwell. There was just no way she could have done it on her own, and someone else needed to search for the ship's Unity powered drive core.

Together, the two master users of the Unity pushed Moldark down corridor after corridor, fending off his continuous attempts at their lives while sending energy blasts toward the agile foe. Moldark ducked and lunged, always a few centimeters from certain death but never succumbing. Meanwhile, he stabbed at Willowood and So-Elku with one relentless thrust after another.

Before long, the dark lord moved down a hallway that seemed to open up to a large room. *A gargantuan hall is more like it*, Willowood said to herself as she exited the tunnel. The space was truly cavernous with a ceiling that loomed clear out of sight. But Willowood didn't have time to admire her surroundings: Moldark was dashing along the floor like a spider. Whereas the corridors had at least kept the enemy bound to a limited area, the large hall gave Moldark a much wider berth to play in. His possessed body practically skipped along the floor as he dodged So-Elku's and Willowood's fire.

"I'm tiring of him," So-Elku said as he sent two Unity rounds toward Moldark.

"Keep the pressure on," Willowood replied.

"And if I choose not to?"

Willowood felt like she was arguing with a petulant child. "Then he kills us both."

"At least then I'd also have a little revenge, yes?"

She gritted her teeth, removed a section of the wall, and flung it at Moldark. The slab sailed through the air and crashed a meter from Moldark in a loud explosion. Willowood growled as she watched the menace flip over the debris and land clear of her failed attempt to crush him.

"So angry," So-Elku said as he continued to fire. "All that pent up rage."

"Just focus, you fool," she said.

"You never appreciated me, Willowood. Never saw what I was genuinely capable of."

"You're welcome to show off now," she said as they both dodged one of Moldark's long-distance lunges.

"Oh, so now you're interested in what I can do? When it serves you?"

"Shut up and shoot him!"

Willowood followed her own orders and lashed out against the enemy with a wave of power that cost her precious energy but would be difficult for Moldark to avoid. To her satisfaction, the blast struck Moldark and knocked him down. His body slid along the ground in a squeak of leather against the glossy black floor. But when he stopped, Moldark looked up and away from Willowood—something had caught his attention.

There, on the far side of the room, was a small person who knelt with her hand on the floor. And Moldark ran straight for her.

"Piper," Willowood screamed. "Look out!"

Piper could feel the ship, just like she could a living person. And the vessel seemed like it had a story to tell, and Piper was very interested in what it had to say. But she also sensed that the ship was dangerous; or, rather, that the people who had made it were dangerous. Dangerous and very powerful. In fact, the starship seemed to cower before them, like a dog cringing before a master who liked to beat it on the nose for doing even the slightest things wrong.

If Piper could reach inside the ship, to its heart, she thought she could set it free—loose its enslavement to the cruel master and let the whole thing go. Maybe then, it wouldn't be so sad anymore. Everything could return to its proper place, and all would be well. At least that's what Piper said to the ship's core as she plunged deeper into its presence in the Nexus.

The vessel was, after all, a very big craft with lots of layers. So many decks made of so much material. Piper imagined that it had taken many, many people, each gifted in the Unity, to put it all together. How they had even dreamed up such an impossible task was beyond her. And whoever they were, they had to be the most powerful Unity users she'd ever met? Well, besides herself and her grandmother and Awen, of course. Because they were the most powerful of all, right?

A loud explosion sounded from somewhere in the room, but Piper knew that if she looked up now, she would lose her place in the Nexus. And if she did that, then she would let Willowood down and fail her mission. No, she'd press on. Whatever was going on around her could wait. Stopping Moldark's ship was her prememamint, prenemamant—*ugh*, it was her most important objection. Object. *Objective*. Words were hard sometimes.

So Piper willed herself to stay focused. And she was rewarded soon after with a glimpse into the ship's heart—a giant red glowing orb of energy that pulsed much like a human heart, sending power to every other part of the vessel. Waves of dissonant music rippled outward, proving to Piper that this was indeed the source of the melodies she'd heard earlier. As she moved closer and closer, the undulating ball of light grew super bright, so much that it made Piper want to shield her eyes. But that was silly: nothing like that mattered in the Unity. So she willed herself to focus on the orb and watched as the heart's vibrations trembled as Piper neared.

All at once, a familiar voice called Piper away from the heart. But she couldn't leave, not now. She was so close to puncturing the orb and releasing the energy from these ancient stones. She just needed another few seconds before—

"Piper, you've got to move now," yelled the voice—Willowood's voice. Something was wrong. Very wrong. So Piper receded from the ship's heart and rushed back to her body. When she finally opened her eyes, she saw a strange creature charging at her.

No, she corrected herself. *Not a creature*. It was her grandfather, but Moldark's presence had almost succeeded in killing his spirit.

"Piper," Willowood screamed again. "Stop him!"

But Piper knew that if she stopped him, she would kill whatever remained of her grandfather. And that, she could not do.

And yet, Moldark was going to kill her. He scampered toward her like a demonic beast—saliva flinging from his pointed teeth and a panting growl coming from his throat. His eyes looked like bottomless black pits hungry to feed on her little soul. She had to stop him, had to kill him because if she didn't, he would kill her.

Just before she released a wave of power she was sure would annihilate him, Piper wondered what it would be like to live her life knowing that she'd killed her grandfather. Though, she'd already been living in a world where she'd killed her father.

Yes, but that was an accident, she assured herself. *This is on purpose.*

That's when it happened.

The thought of hurting him—not Moldark, but Wendell Kane—overwhelmed her. Some might call her stupid. Others would say she was just a kid, and so navee. *Na-nay-eve. Whatever.* She didn't care. This was her life, and she was making her own decision. Piper knew that she'd rather die than live in a galaxy where she'd willfully taken her grandfather's life, even if he was a thin shred of his former self. She would not snuff him out. So she didn't.

27

MAGNUS EXPENDED his last mag and then slumped down against the berm again. "I'm out," he said over comms.

He looked at Awen and then took her offered hand. She looked so sad sitting there, resigned to their mutually assured destruction. But it was the only way to save lives. That, and Magnus was pretty sure no one would feel a thing. One minute they'd be pinned under heavy enemy fire, the next they'd be, well, floating around in whatever afterlife awaited them. If there was an afterlife. Magnus always toyed with the idea that maybe there was just nothing. He'd be here and then suddenly he'd be nowhere at all. *So what does it matter anyway?* In the end, that seemed far too sad of an end to believe in. So he dismissed it, choosing instead to believe there was something far away from all this. *Peace*, he thought. *I hope there's peace.*

Magnus looked Awen in the eyes and said, "Do it."

She mouthed the words, "I love you."

"I love you too," he said, just loud enough to be heard over the sound of weapons' fire and someone screaming like a mad man over comms.

Not a madman, Magnus thought. *An excited man.* It was faint, layered in static, but it was there.

"Wait," Magnus said to Awen as he squeezed her hand.

"Mystics, Magnus, you almost made me—"

"I know. Just, wait." He sat bolt upright and looked around as if trying to get his NBTI to pick up an elusive transmission signal. "You hear that?"

"No," she replied. "What are you…" Just then, Awen's gaze went somewhere else. She touched the side of her helmet as if deep in thought with the crackling audio. Then her eyes widened. "I hear—I hear it! It sounds like, like—"

"Like Captain Forbes gettin' his jollies on," Zoll interjected.

"Forbes," Magnus yelled. "Forbes! Is that you?"

"Yeeeeeehaw, Lieutenant," the captain replied. "Sure as hell is. And I hope you're standing clear of the walls."

"The walls?" Magnus looked overhead. "Of the dome?"

"Yup. Cause we're coming in hot."

"Everyone stay away from the walls," Magnus hollered over the company channel. He didn't know what to expect, but if Forbes was bringing backup, that was all that mattered.

"What's he doing?" Awen asked.

"Your guess is as good as mine," Magnus said privately. Then he was back on the company channel. "Get to cover and keep your heads down!"

"Do you feel that?" Awen asked.

Magnus was about to say he didn't know when he felt a thrum in the air. At first, he thought it was coming from somewhere beneath them. But as the aberration grew stronger, he realized it was coming from the dome—or, rather, from the outside.

"Yeah," he replied. "I definitely feel that."

"Picking up some strong vibrations, LT," Zoll said.

"Copy that." Magnus brought up his topo map. Now that he had comms with Forbes again, it only made sense that sensor tracking would be reestablished. "I'm picking up multiple friendly IFF tags converging on our location from, from—" He hesitated. "From everywhere."

"I see 'em too," Zoll replied. "You think something's gone haywire with our rig?"

Magnus looked up to the shimmering green walls. "No, Zoll. I think Forbes found Taursar Company a ride."

GIANT SPIKES DROVE into the command node's walls like a hundred carnivorous raptors plunging their beaks through sheet metal. The cacophony made Magnus throw his hands over his ears, but he couldn't stop the sound from ringing his head. One after another, more beak-like spires penetrated the dome until the whole structure appeared like an inverted spiny crustacean. Then, as one, fluted panels flared back from each beak to reveal missile-like cavities filled with armored warriors. Magnus suddenly remembered Cyril's nerd-like rant about Festoonial black marspins using their snouts to harpoon a Telderine giant sea mammoth; in this case, the node was the prey.

"You miss us, Granther Company?" Forbes yelled over VNET.

Magnus cross-referenced the topo in his HUD with the dozens of quills delivering gladias and narskill into the dome. The collective mass of reinforcements began firing Novian and Sekmit power weapons on the command building, beating the Li-Dain back and taking out the turrets. Then, amongst the light show, Magnus spotted Forbes. The captain was directly overhead, using one hand to control a descender on a cable and the other hand to fire his NOV2 on the building's upper balconies.

"Hell yeah, we missed you," Magnus replied. "But you're late, you son of a bitch."

"Eh, we'll make it up to you."

Magnus helped Awen get out of the way as Forbes and several other gladias touched down, firing at Li-Dain on the lawn.

"Here," Forbes said, tossing Magnus an NOV2. "Thought you might need this."

Magnus racked a charge and then smiled at Forbes. "All right, you're starting to make up for being late. But only a little."

"I can live with that," Forbes replied.

"Where'd you get all the other narskill?" Awen asked.

Forbes pointed at a Sekmit in one of the cat-like armored suits. Unlike the black and green ones, this one was black and red. "From Freya."

"Remind me to thank her," Magnus said.

"You can as soon as you get close enough."

"Hold up." Magnus did a double-take at the narskill in black and red. "You're saying that's—that's the pride mother herself?"

"In the flesh," Forbes said. "As soon as she saw the trinium freighter go nova, she assumed that you were heading to the mines. She also knew you'd need backup and that the hovertrains would be out of order. So, she arranged for Plan B."

"Plan B?"

Forbes pointed overhead. "They've got these wicked fast mini-subs, Adonis. Rapid breach and entry nose cowlings. You've gotta try one."

"I'll be sure to take one out for a spin later."

Forbes put a hand on Magnus's shoulder. "All right. We gonna sit around and chitchat all day? Or you gonna let me get back to doing my job?"

"Lead the way, Captain."

"Oh no." Forbes gestured toward the front doors. "After you."

Magnus charged up the lawn and bounded over Li-Dain bodies. He met Rohoar at the front doors and then dashed into the lobby. A Li-Dain warrior to his left leaped from behind the security desk, brandishing two orb-like balls of light around both fists. Magnus knew enough that being hit by either one would take him out. So he squared his sights on the Luma's head and fired. Whether because the Luma was fatigued or Magnus had forgotten how powerful an NOV2 really was, the enemy's shield dropped after the fourth blaster bolt, and the fifth streaked clean through the Li-Dain's skull.

A second enemy combatant rolled out from a side stairwell further back and gained her feet, energy blasts blazing. Magnus sidestepped where he thought she'd fire and then returned the attack with three bolts to the torso and two to the head. But the shield seemed far from dissipating as the Luma adversary continued to charge.

Magnus changed tactics then and wondered if the stone floor might play a role in putting the enemy on guard. He aimed at the ground right where he imagined the Luma's invisible force field might kiss the stone. Then he squeezed off two seconds of full-auto fire. The rounds shredded the floor and sent chunks of rock flying in all directions—including into the Luma's face.

Guessing that the force field had lessened, Magnus fired on the woman. Not only had the shield diminished, but it wasn't even strong enough to stop the first round that went straight through the enemy's chest—let alone the six additional bolts that followed it.

When the woman fell away, Magnus spotted ní Freya in her menacing battle armor, standing on the other side of the ground floor. "Hey there, pride mother."

"Greetings, manservant," she replied.

"We appreciate you showing up."

"And we appreciate you leaving some for us."

"Follow you up?" Magnus asked, gesturing to the next floor. "It's your mine, after all."

She raised her helmet's chin at him. "Your company is acceptable."

"Thought I'd never hear those words."

The two leaders met in the middle of the vestibule as more gladias and narskill poured in from the lawn. Freya looked Magnus over and then took the lead, bounding up the stairs.

"Apparently, she is not afraid to get her paws dirty," Rohoar said. "Rohoar likes this greatly. She would make a fine Jujari tribe leader. If she were not a Sekmit, of course."

"Minor details," Magnus replied as he charged up the stairs behind Freya. Granted, putting a national leader on point was extremely unorthodox. Yet she seemed to know what she was doing. And who was Magnus to argue with a woman second only to Queen Nishti? The best he could do was offer his support; hell, he shouldn't even be this far forward. Though, the more time he spent with the revered leader, the more Magnus suspected that she was, in fact, none other than the queen.

Freya fired at the top of the second floor's steps. Li-Dain were buried deep in the hallways, taking cover in offices and utility rooms and returning fire. For as much momentum as Forbes and Freya had brought to the fight, Magnus realized things weren't over yet.

Just then, he heard an order in Sekmitian go over the joint comms network. Freya was speaking. A moment later, ten narskill brushed passed Magnus and spread out on the second floor. As one, they drew back on their Thørzin power bows and held the bowstrings until the standard blue bolt changed to a deep purple hue. But unlike any conventional weapon, the narskill weren't aiming at the enemy. Hell, they didn't seem to be aiming at anything besides the hallway walls.

"You seeing this?" Magnus asked the gladias nearest him.

"Copy," Silk replied.

"Yes," Awen said too. "Looks like they're modifying their energy rounds."

Before anyone else could speak, Freya ordered the warriors to loose their arrows. The Unity bowstrings snapped the air with ten percussive *cracks*. Then the energy rounds leaped from the powerful weapons and tore into the walls.

Magnus felt bewildered as the bolts of purple energy criss-crossed through the maze of offices. Every split second or so, he'd catch a glimpse of a purple light streaking across a hall, but then it was gone. Screams and shrieks went out from those hidden around the floor, and soon bodies spilled out of their hiding places, landing facedown on the hallway carpet or sprawling out beside waiting room furniture.

A few seconds passed, and everything grew eerily quiet.

Magnus cleared his throat and then said, "That's some pretty good—"

"Not done yet."

"Uh, come again?"

"Not done yet, manservant. Silence."

Magnus was only too happy to oblige given the fact that ten narskill had just taken out what he could only assume was an entire floor of heavily entrenched Li-Dain.

Then, Magnus watched as each Sekmit bowman pressed a small glowing pad along their bows. A faint trill echoed in the office halls, and the purple shafts of Unity energy began whipping around once more. More yells went up within the office as Li-Dain met their ends.

"They're calling the energy bolts back," Awen said, her voice filled with amazement.

"Your words, not mine," Magnus said.

At last, the purple arrows slid back into the Thørzin power bows, and the energy vanished.

"Hey, Bixy," Magnus said over comms. "Can you do that? You been holding out on us?"

The cat-man growled in return. "This is level above Wobix, manservant."

"That must chap your knickers then."

"We will not talk of this," Wobix said.

"Just curious. That's all." Magnus looked at Freya. "Would you like us to clear the floor?"

"Why? It is cleared."

"Yeah, but it's our practice to double-check our work."

Freya hissed over comms. "That is because your work is imperfect."

Magnus raised a finger to protest but thought better of it. "And right you are, ní Frey-Frey."

"What?"

"Nothing." He pointed to the second set of steps. "After you."

She nodded and then bounded up the glass stairwell, followed closely by her ten narskill elites—as Magnus had come to call them.

Upon arriving on the second floor, the elites did the same as before. Their blue arrows deepened to a vibrant violet and then streaked away. The bolts whipped from room to room, tearing through walls as easily as flesh. Likewise, the cries of the dying echoed down the hallways, signaling the enemy's demise. When the floor went silent, the narskill pressed their return to home pads, and the energy bolts reversed course until they slid into place back where they'd started.

"Did you want to check, manservant?" Freya asked Magnus.

"Nah. I'm good."

Freya nodded once and then proceeded to the third floor, where the command center was.

"Things might get toasty up here," he said to Granther Company. "Stay sharp."

"Eh," Bliss said. "They've got those fancy bows. I'm not too worried."

Be that as it may, Magnus knew that an enemy who'd fought this hard to take a position would fight just as hard to keep it. And that concerned him because Freya was still leading the charge.

"Your worshipfulness," Magnus said just before Freya mounted the top steps. "If I may."

"What is it now?"

"I advise that we use caution on this floor."

"What is this caution?"

Magnus swallowed. "Well, my guess is the Li-Dain aren't going to let this position go easily. And you're, well, you're—"

"Speak plainly."

"You're a national leader. I think it best if you—"

"We Sekmit do not follow your Republic ways, human. Yes, I smell the Marine Corps all over you. It is not something you can escape so easily. Where your generals and commanders rest behind the safety of armored offices far from the front, our leaders take pointies."

"Take point."

She hissed at him.

"My bad." He raised a hand in defense. "Pointies it is."

"If I am not fit to lead here, I am not fit to lead up there."

Magnus nodded. Despite the military logic that this line of thinking flew in the face of, he had to give the Sekmit credit for their bravery. "Copy that."

"Good."

"This is a real leader," Rohoar said in a hushed tone. "Very Jujari."

"You've mentioned that already, Fluffy. And if I'm not mistaken, you already have a mate."

"This is not the reason Rohoar esteems her."

"Just keep telling yourself that, big guy."

"Rohoar still objects," Rohoar said with a soft *woof*.

"Forbes," Magnus said. "I want half your team clearing the upper floors."

"Copy that. Though, I need to point out that we should really do something about your rank, Lieutenant."

"Come again?"

"You keep giving Captains orders as an LT. That's not right."

"If we make it out of this, you can put in a good word for me."

"Done."

Freya looked back at Magnus. "Are you done preening yourselves?"

Magnus winced. "Preening?"

"That's what I thought. Here we go."

WHEN MAGNUS FOLLOWED Freya over the top step, they were met with a barrage of enemy fire that would have chewed through their armor in a second. Fortunately, Magnus had asked Awen and Granther Company's remaining mystics, Wish and Finderminth, to shield the charge. Instead, Freya and Magnus found cover behind two blastcrete columns and returned fire—Magnus with his NOV2 and Freya with her power bow.

The support columns were among those that supported the wide hallway that looked into the command theatre through the panoramic windowplex wall. As Magnus suspected, the command room was filled with what he assumed were high-level Li-Dain, or true bloods, as Awen called them. This was both good and bad. Good because it meant they'd finally reached the enemy's last stand, and bad because the enemy's last stand was staffed with the best the LAW had to offer.

Magnus and Freya continued to take rounds from 180º.

"I told you this was going to be a bad idea," Magnus yelled.

"And yet your mystics cover us." Freya turned and fired on two Li-Dain, dropping them both with the same power bolt. "No bad ideas."

Magnus sighed. Working with the Sekmit was almost as bad as working with the Jujari, but the Sekmit smelled better.

The rest of Granther Company, along with Forbes' Taursar Company, swarmed up the steps and took cover behind the hallway's many options. They shot their way to columns, decorative stone walls carved in some sort of classical relief, solid wood office furniture, metal storage units, and several stone planters. They drove the enemy back until everyone was set up and ready to storm the command room.

"Home stretch," Magnus said softly for his own benefit.

"Why do you stretch now?" Freya asked.

"No, it's more of a—just, never mind. I stretch, because—I like it."

"Strange. But acceptable."

Magnus asked for confirmation icons from the gladias. When his units reported they were ready, Magnus looked to Freya. "We're good to go when you are, Frey-Frey."

"Why do you keep calling the pride mother this term?"

"Because it—" Magnus hesitated, trying to think on his feet. "It's a sign of respect for you as a mighty military leader." Hey, this was combat, and Freya had put herself in the trenches. *Which means you're fair game for white lies*, Magnus thought.

"Ah, I see. Then I accept this name of Frey-Frey. Thank you, manservant."

"My pleasure."

"My pleasure, what?"

Magnus smiled. "My pleasure, Frey-Frey."

"That's better. Now, we advance." Then Freya turned from cover, shot through the supposedly blaster-proof windowplex wall, and leaped into the command room.

"Oh, splick," Magnus yelled and then charged after her.

MAGNUS LANDED SLIGHTLY to Freya's right and slammed into a workstation. The desk, chair, and holo computer broke under his fall. It wasn't Magnus's smoothest entry, but his NOV2 was up and firing, which was all that mattered in a situation like this. Shoot, move, repeat.

He fired on a Li-Dain to his right—a woman standing on the same level just a few workstations down. Rage flared in her eyes as she deflected Magnus's blaster rounds with a quick wave of her hand and then sent a barrage of return fire toward his head. The exchange happened so fast, Magnus almost took the strike in his forehead. Instead, he drilled the woman's shield on full auto and charged her position.

Temporarily blinded by the NOV2's withering fire rate, the Luma didn't see Magnus rush her—at least she didn't do anything about it. He slipped through the weakened force field and crashed into her, slamming her head against the floor. The woman yelled as Magnus's momentum flipped him over her head. His back hit the ground, and the Li-Dain would have had the chance to right herself and attack him—she would have, had Magnus not had his NOV2's muzzle buried in her shoulder. He squeezed the trigger and the weapon gave a muffled cough as three rounds penetrated her chest cavity and flash seared her vital organs.

"You good?" Awen asked him.

"One down," he replied.

"You're lucky. That was a true blood."

"Eh, they're not so bad."

"Well that's good to hear because you have a second one coming at you."

Magnus raised his head and saw another Li-Dain running down the row toward his feet. The Luma had an elongated face with grey skin that stretched across multiple lumps along its cheekbones. "Mystics, he's ugly too."

"A Dim-Telok," Awen said. "One of the few in the Order. Watch out for his—"

A harpoon-like spear thrust from the Li-Dain's knuckles and forced Magnus to dive down one level to his left. He crashed into the workstation, scrambled to a firing position, and unloaded on the alien's personal shield. The monster balked for a second.

"What the hell was that?" he asked Awen.

"Bone spears. I said, watch out for his retractable bone spears!"

Magnus was about to reply with something witty when the Li-Dain projected another one of its bone spears. The spike burst through a computer tower and produced a fountain of sparks. The damn things were driven by some sort of biological hydraulics that propelled the half-meter long weapons forward and then sucked them back into the wrist.

Magnus rolled away from the exploding computer tower and fired on the Dim-Telok. Again, the enemy's shield blocked the blaster fire.

Then the beasty smiled and jumped down to the next row. He was enjoying this—*the damn monster's actually toying with me.*

The next spear that shot toward Magnus glowed a bright yellow. Then, when the weapon reached its full length, a streak of Unity energy continued forward, blowing a hole in the floor several meters behind Magnus.

"And the bones shoot splick too?" Magnus said to Awen.

"He's a Li-Dain, a Luma! What did you expect?"

"I thought villains were only allowed one weird superpower at a time."

"Take your complaint up with Cyril," Awen replied. "He's our resident expert there."

"Noted," Magnus said with a grunt as he dove yet again, barely avoiding a thrust to his head. He got the feeling that if one of the Unity-powered bone spears made contact with any part of his body, the resulting energy release would be like a tiny bomb going off inside him.

As if to confirm this, the Dim-Telok drove a knuckle-spike into a digital archive cabinet, narrowly missing Magnus's head. Once impaled, the storage unit quivered as lines crackled across the surface. Then the box-like unit exploded and showered the vicinity with debris.

Magnus fired, and then fired again. But no matter how hard he tried, he couldn't seem to punch a hole through this thing's shield. Magnus looked up, hoping he might employ some of his other team members, but they were all busy with adversaries of their own. The theatre was full of blaster fire, Unity shields, and the cries of warriors engaged in mortal combat.

"Looks like we're gonna do this the hard way," Magnus said to his assailant.

The Dim-Telok gave a three-thrust right-left-right combination that forced Magnus against a wall and dropped his shielding to zero. A fourth, however, went straight through his shoulder. Magnus's joint exploded with pain but did not burst from the Unity. For whatever reason, the enemy was unable to imbue this last strike with the mystical energy source.

The Dim-Telok also failed to register the fact that Magnus was inside the enemy's Unity shield and had jammed an NOV2 under its ribs.

"Sucks to lose," Magnus said, and then he squeezed the trigger.

The Dim-Telok's innards blew out its back and showered several oncoming Li-Dain with gore. The spike in Magnus's left shoulder kept him pinned to the wall even though the creature's arm went limp. Magnus couldn't remove the spear and hold his weapon at the same time, and he counted six Li-Dain charging his position. There wasn't time to get free. So he switched his NOV2's mode to AI-assisted multi-target fire effect and watched as his NBTI work with his bioteknia eyes to acquire targets.

The Li-Dain were less than five meters away, and their fists were charging with light. As soon as Magnus's targeting system went green, he squeezed the trigger and felt the weapon's gimbaled barrel chatter. High-speed flickers flashed in his eyes and sent deafening screams to his ears. He was going to need a gene therapy treatment after this one so he could hear again.

The NOV2 drained both magazines and sent the energy into the Li-Dain, all while Magnus hung from the spike in his shoulder. Unity shields exploded, and bodies went down. One Luma warrior still managed to survive the Novian weapon's tirade. The man limped toward Magnus, right fist glowing, but the enemy made the fatal mistake of assuming Magnus was defenseless. When the man was within striking range, Magnus dropped his NOV2, whipped out his Nick, and slashed the Li-Dain across the throat.

Only the knife blade was a few centimeters too short.

"You poor fool," the Li-Dain said. He pulled his arm back to thrust the Unity energy into Magnus's chest. Instead, the man flew forward into Magnus's blade and slammed into Magnus's right shoulder.

Awen stood behind the Li-Dain with a hand on her hip. "Thought you could use some help."

"I had it under control."

"Sure, you did." She strode forward and grabbed the Dim-Telok's limp arm with both hands. "On three?"

"Yeah, okay."

He'd hardly said the words when Awen yanked the spear free of his shoulder.

"Son of a bitch," Magnus yelled. "I thought you said you were gonna count."

"Three," she said, dropping the limb to the ground. "Happy?"

When Awen and Magnus rejoined the rest of the gladias and narskill below the main screen at the theatre's bottom level, Freya had cornered what appeared to be the last remaining Li-Dain. Forbes and Freya's reinforcements had made the difference, and the LAW warriors had been beaten back. The battle had been won.

"I can give you what you want," the golden-robed warrior said to Freya.

"And what do you think I want?" Freya asked, pressing her claws into the soft flesh under the man's chin. She'd removed her helmet and stood surrounded by the ten elites.

"So-Elku. Master So-Elku. I can give him to you."

"In return for what?"

Magnus knew then that Freya was playing the Li-Dain. She already had So-Elku. The cat was toying with her prey. *Mystics help him*, Magnus said to himself, and then he thought better of it. *Nah, let him have it, Frey-Frey.*

"In return for—well, you let me go," the Li-Dain replied.

"Freedom?" Freya made a show of looking around the command theatre. "After all this? You think I'm just going to let you walk away?"

"But, So-Elku. I can give you So-Elku."

Freya's claws drew blood. "I already have So-Elku."

But then the Li-Dain gave her a confused look. "No, you don't."

"Ha—I think I know my own possessions."

To Magnus, the Li-Dain seemed genuine in his assertion. And, given the Luma's interconnectivity, Magnus wondered if there was something Freya didn't know about. Maybe Caldwell and DiAntora hadn't accomplished their half of the mission.

As if confirming Magnus's suspicions, the Li-Dain said, "You *had* him, ní Freya. But now you've lost him."

Freya cocked her head but did not reply, at least not with words: her nails went a little deeper into the man's neck.

He struggled against her, and his voice became tight with pain. "Lady Willowood set him free. They've betrayed you."

Magnus didn't doubt that Willowood might have had to do something to So-Elku. But without a stable VNET connection, there was no way to know what was happening on the surface. Even so, Willowood wasn't the betraying type. This Luma was desperate, and desperate people did irrational things.

"I have reason to doubt your claims, golden baby," Freya said.

"Check it for yourself then."

"I do not want to wait, and I much prefer killing you."

"Kill me and I take the room with me," the Li-Dain blurted out.

Magnus cast a glance at Awen. *He can do that, can't he?*

Yes, she replied in the Unity. *I'm afraid so. With no Luma left around him, he has nothing to lose.*

Would a headshot prevent it?

Awen took longer to respond than Magnus liked. *I think so.*

You think so?

It's not like I have a lot of experience blowing myself up, Adonis.

Magnus sighed. He had the Li-Dain's head in his sights, as did every other defender in the theatre. There was no way Magnus or the others could miss. But if the Li-Dain had his nova setting—for lack of a better term—on some sort of deadman's switch within the Unity, then this could go all kinds of sideways.

Exactly, Awen said. *That's what I'm afraid of. Something new in the Nexus that releases his life force—I don't know. But there's also a chance he's bluffing.*

Then it was a chance they had to take.

Magnus squeezed his trigger.

But not before Freya extended her claws into the base of the Li-Dain's skull. A fraction of a second later, the Luma's head exploded, and then the whole room went bright white.

IT WAS the ringing in his ears that woke Magnus up first, and it was the pain in his head that kept him from passing out again. He blinked several times before lifting his head and looking around. Tongues of fire licked the room's wreckage—charred and broken workstations, data terminals spewing sparks, and bodies. So many bodies.

Only these bodies were moving. Not much, at first, but moving nonetheless.

"Magnus?" Awen said if she spoke from behind a blanket. "Can you hear me?" Her face suddenly appeared in his vision.

"Yeah," he replied, but he had trouble recognizing his own voice. The fact that he was talking was positive. And he didn't feel like anything was missing on his body, even though his face felt like it had a wicked sunburn. "I'm good. I think."

Awen blew out a deep breath. "I thought I lost you there."

"What—what happened?"

"The guy went nova." Awen pushed a strand of hair behind her ear. "But we got some shields up in time."

"You saved everyone?" He took her offered hand and sat up.

"Not everyone."

Magnus studied her face and then looked around. He'd been blown back a few rows. The massive holo wall was gone and replaced with a view of the dome. And there, in the center of the lower level just outside a black blast radius, was a single body in Sekmit armor.

"Freya," Magnus whispered.

Awen helped him stand, and the two of them walked through the burning wreckage to the Sekmit leader. Magnus knelt beside her and looked over her body. The battle armor was cracked. Whole sections were missing and gave Magnus a clear view of charred fur and bloody flesh. Worst of all was her helmet. Half the visor was missing, leaving her face exposed to the Li-Dain's suicide. Whatever personal Unity shield Freya had employed, it hadn't been enough. Maybe she hadn't engaged one at all—who knew.

"Manservant." Freya's voice startled Magnus. He couldn't believe she was still alive. Then she raised the remains of a forearm to touch his chest. The attempt showcased the gruesomeness of a point-blank detonation, and Magnus willed himself to stay focused on the woman's last moments of life and not dwell on her macabre appearance.

"Hey, Frey-Frey," he replied.

"The last one—he's dead?"

"Yeah," Magnus replied. "The mine's all yours again."

"Not mine." She took breaths in short wheezes. "The queen's."

"I always kinda figured you were the queen, you know."

She rocked her head back and forth. "No. Please tell her—" A spasm made Freya's body constrict.

"Tell her what?" Magnus asked. Then he felt Awen's hand on his back, reminding him to be more soft with his tone. "What would you like me to share with her?"

Freya swallowed, and the muscles in her neck bulged. "That I endeavored to do my—my best—in her absence."

"Okay, sure. I got it."

"You"—Frey tapped his chest plate with her stub. "You are a very good manservant—"

Magnus chuckled. "Thanks."

"—for her." Freya's eyes darted to Awen.

Magnus glanced at Awen, and the two of them shared a moment staring into one another's eyes. When Magnus looked back to Freya, the pride mother's life had left her. "Ní Freya?"

"She's gone," Awen said with a gentle pat on Magnus's armor. "I'm sorry."

"Me too."

28

Piper might not have been able to kill her grandfather, but Colonel Caldwell sure as hell could. As he stepped into the vast hall, he read the situation like forecasting a stormfront. Hell, maybe he knew the kid's inner conflict before she did. Caldwell might not have special Unity powers or a sixth sense for seeing into other realms, but he knew people. And right then, he understood there was no way the child was going to liquefy her own grandfather—or whatever it was she could do to him.

But someone had to.

And that someone was going to be him.

Moldark scampered toward Piper like a bloodthirsty monster hellbent on devouring prey. The seasoned colonel had seen this kind of thing play out on battlefields all over the quadrant, and it never ended well for the victims. So Caldwell raised his NOV2, drew a bead on the demon-possessed enemy, and fired.

The round punctured Moldark's rib cage just under the armpit and came out the other side—a clean shot through the vital organs.

The enemy dropped to the deck and slid the rest of the way to stop at Piper's feet. Whatever Unity splick the megalomaniac had used to absorb blaster fire before, it wasn't working now, presumably because he was so transfixed on Piper.

Where Caldwell misjudged the child was in thinking she might shriek or cry or run away. But she didn't. Instead, she stood motionless and watched Moldark's crumpled body come to a stop, nudging her boot. Piper looked down at the man-beast and then did the most curious thing. She knelt and placed a hand on his face.

But Caldwell didn't have time to watch. As Willowood raced toward Piper, So-Elku backed away. The colonel wouldn't execute the Luma Master—that was for the Repub to decide. But he couldn't let the maniac go free either.

"Not so fast," Caldwell said to himself, and then he fired on So-Elku just as the man turned and ran for a side corridor.

"Grandpa?" Piper said in the softest tone she could manage. "Grandpa, are you there?" She stroked the side of his face, willing him to be alive, somehow. At least for a second. She had things to say. "Grandpa, please."

Suddenly, his black-pitted eyes transformed, receding to something that looked more human. He had a deep brown eye and another pinkish-white eye. His counterence, counternanse—his *face* also seemed to change, softening under her touch. The scars didn't go away, but some of the anger around his eyes and mouth disappeared.

Piper knew that Mr. Caldwell's blaster bolt had hit important parts of her grandfather's body. He would be dead very soon, which made speaking to him even more important. Wherever his soul went in the next life, he had to go there knowing what she had to say.

"Grandpa?" She patted his face. "Can you hear me?"

"Yes," Admiral Kane replied. Unlike Moldark's dark and gritty voice, this man's voice was soft. "I'm here."

Piper let out a burst of emotion but quickly pulled herself back together. Still, she couldn't help let a small flood of tears well up and run from her eyes. "It's me again, Piper. Your granddaughter."

"Yes, I remember," her grandfather replied.

"I wanted to see you again, before you, you—"

"It's nice to meet you, Piper." He coughed twice, his body spasming as he did.

"Grandpa. Your daughter, Valerie. My mom."

His eyes fluttered.

Piper suddenly thought maybe he would live long enough to hear her out. "No, no, no." She patted his face harder. "Grandpa?"

"I' m—I'm still here."

"Your daughter. You know she grew up to be an amazing person. My mom. She was the best."

"Was she?" he replied.

"Yes, she was. Strong and brave and really super smart. You should be very proud of her. Just as I am. But she was the best mom I ever could have asked for." Piper paused, trying to find the right words. Her tears were making her choke. "I know you and grandma didn't always, you know, get along and stuff. But you did do something amazing. You gave me the best mommy in the galaxy."

Piper felt like her chest was about to explode. This all felt too impossible to be real. Like it was just a dream or something. But it was the pain in her heart that let her know it was not a dream, that this was, in fact, the reality she was living in real-time.

"So, thank you," Piper said. "Thank you for giving her to me. I just wanted you to know, before, before it was too late."

Her grandfather coughed again, his body spasming less this time. He was getting weak. "Thank you for telling me, Piper. It's, it's good for me to know. And I'm—"

"Wendell?" came Nana's voice from above Piper. The older woman slid in beside Piper—knees on the ground, helmet off. "Is that you?"

"Yes," Grandpa Kane said with a cough. His voice was even weaker now.

"Hold on," Willowood said. "We're going to get you to—"

"No," he said, waving her off. "No, please. It's not—"

"Don't be silly, Wendell. We're going to—"

"Too much." Grandpa Kane coughed again. "I've seen too much. Done, too much. It's my time to go."

"But—but, you just came back to us and—"

"Felicity." He took her hand. "We both know what I've done… what I've been a part of. I want to enter whatever comes next and be free of… of this."

Nana closed her eyes and nodded. "I understand." Then she pulled his hand to her lips and kissed it. "I loved you, you know."

"And I hated you for loving me," he replied with a half-smile, wincing in pain.

"But when it was good—"

"It was great. And we have Piper."

Nana looked at Piper with eyes full of tears. Her grandmother put her other hand around Piper's neck and pulled their heads together. "And we have Piper," Nana repeated.

"I'm so sorry," Grandpa Kane said. "To both of you. For so many things I've done. Things I can never undo."

"It's okay, grandpa," Piper said. "You didn't mean to do them."

"No." Her grandfather coughed, but it was more like a wheeze. "I knew. I always knew what I chose. But I regret… so much."

Piper tried to console him. She wanted to ease his suffering, to correct his statements a little. But he moved his head away from her touch.

"Live, Piper," he said as he slipped something into her palm. "Live better than me." He took her and Nana's hands and squeezed them until his arms shook. "I found out too late—" Grandpa Kane coughed a last time. "—how much I missed."

"Grandpa?" Piper said. But his eyes went flat. "No!"

"Piper," her grandmother said, pulling the child into a tight embrace. "He's gone."

"No, Nana. It's too soon."

"Death always is, my child."

"You've been shot," said a smooth voice inside So-Elku's head. "They've betrayed you. Just as they always will."

"Who—who are you?" So-Elku replied into the darkness.

"You don't recognize me?"

"Well, no. I can't even see you."

"But you sense me."

So-Elku had to admit that, yes, despite the cold, he wasn't totally alone. There was someone else in the void with him. "I feel your presence, yes."

"But you still don't recognize me outside of Kane's mortal body."

"Kane?" So-Elku froze—at least in so much as whatever state he was in could go rigid. "You're—Moldark?"

"Very good," the being replied like a master pandering to an obedient pet.

"But I just saw the Colonel—"

"Shoot Kane's worthless rotting corpse? Yes, and good riddance."

"So, you're not dead?"

Moldark laughed in the darkness. "Do you really think a mere mortal can snuff me out? Are you that unaware of my nature?"

"Well, I just thought that—"

"That my soul is bound to flesh like yours?" Moldark's laugh became more sarcastic—more malevolent. "Oh, Teerbrin, *Teerbrin*. How much we have yet to journey together."

So-Elku furrowed his brow—at least whatever brow existed in this strange state of consciousness between death and life. "Journey? What kind of journey?"

"As fate would have it, it seems that we both possess things that the other needs. For instance, I need a body, and you need what I know about the multiverse and building an unstoppable army, among other trivialities. So, before I move on to find a willing host elsewhere—a task that requires so much work and endless amounts of persuasion. It can be downright exhausting!—I've decided to make you a proposal."

"You want to partner."

"Ha! And now you see why I've approached you? I only ask the best."

So-Elku pictured Kane's face just then. He supposed saying yes to Moldark's ethereal presence meant that something similar would befall him. *Then again*, So-Elku mused, *I am dead, aren't I?* Or dying, at least. Colonel Caldwell had seen to that—shooting him in the back. *The back!* So-Elku had been a fool to think the Sekmit and their allies were going to let him walk out of here alive. They just used him to get to Moldark.

And my how the tables have turned.

Whatever unfortunate side effects may come from a partnership with the otherworldly spirit that was Moldark, So-Elku knew a few things about the potential bond. The first was one of power, obviously. People had feared Kane—or Moldark—whatever. Even So-Elku himself had; he needed to look no further than the encounter with Nants in the bathhouse. This meant that whatever fear people had of So-Elku, and there was some—he'd seen it in their eyes—partnering with Moldark would only serve to amplify that fear.

Secondly, Moldark was a being capable of extraordinary feats—perhaps even more than Moldark realized. So-Elku's knowledge of the Unity, and more, of the Nexus, meant he could take Moldark's powers and make them more. He could turn them into something truly magnificent.

Thirdly, if Moldark did have insight about the multiverse, which he no doubt did, given his nature, and knowledge about creating some sort of "unstoppable army"—hyperbole if there ever was any—then So-Elku wanted it. Even if the information was half as good as he thought it was, it would be worth finding out about.

Last, and certainly not least, there was the fact that So-Elku liked the idea of living. He assumed he would be a dead man in a matter of moments. So bad was his state now that he felt disconnected from his mortal flesh and couldn't repair it even if he wanted to. But he'd seen what Moldark was capable of, and knew that the being could siphon another person's life force to nourish his own. Therefore, it wouldn't be long before So-Elku was revitalized and whole. Combined with his own powers of reanimation within the Unity, So-Elku wondered if their partnership would create the first real immortal being—*a god worthy of worship.*

Yes, all would see his power. They would bow before him. He would be the savior that the galaxy had always needed—a deliverer both beautiful and terrible, one impossible to resist.

"Very well," So-Elku said. "I accept. Partners."

"Partners," Moldark replied, and then fused himself with So-Elku's nature.

"I'M sorry to break this up," Caldwell said. "But we still have an enemy out there."

"But we can't leave him," Piper said, looking to her grandfather.

"Uh, yeah, we can. And we're gonna." Sensing he'd been a little too insensitive, Caldwell doubled back. "Listen, the most important thing right now is for us—"

Piper grabbed Kane's wrists and attempted to drag him across the floor. The body didn't budge. Still, the child pulled with all her might as tears streamed down her cheeks. Then there was Willowood, who looked up at Caldwell with pleading eyes.

"Oh, for all the blizzards in Blunderfield," Caldwell said, pushing Piper aside—gently. "Let me." The colonel heaved Kane's body off the deck and threw the dead weight over his shoulder. "Happy?"

Piper nodded. "Mmm-hmm. Thanks, Mr. Grandpa Caldwell, sir."

Caldwell hesitated. "What now?"

"Move along," Willowood said as she patted him on the back. "Wait. So-Elku."

Caldwell nodded to a point across the hall's floor. "I had to put him down." He was about to turn away when So-Elku's body twitched. "Dammit." Caldwell pulled his NOV2 up one-handed to finish the job. The colonel may have been coldblooded when it came to war, but he wasn't going to let anyone suffer needlessly. "You might not want to watch this."

But before Caldwell could pull the trigger, So-Elku's body rose off the floor—feet planted, chest popping upright.

"By Vespers twin bitches," Caldwell said. "Run!" Then he fired his NOV2 on full auto and headed for the nearest exit.

Sensing that he was running alone, though still carrying Piper's grandfather, Caldwell turned to account for Piper. But the child was standing beside Willowood, and both of them were staring at So-Elku—a man who had just blocked the NOV2's full-auto fusillade. "Dammit, ladies. I might not be a Unity scholar, but that thing there ain't normal."

"We know," Willowood said with a strange calmness to her voice. "Which is why we must stop him. Now."

"Stop us?" So-Elku replied to Willowood.

She thought the use of the word "us" was strange, so she tilted her head at the Luma Master. "We're taking you back into custody, So-Elku. Stand down."

"Taking us into custody?"

There it was again. Something wasn't right here. "You can come peacefully if you choose. If not, Piper and I will—"

"Piper," So-Elku said, snapping his head toward the child. "So powerful for one so young."

"Stay where you are," Willowood said, raising her hand. The power she exerted in the Nexus was considerable. But So-Elku looked down at his chest and then back at Willowood as if he regarded a flea attempting to stop a boulder. The look sent a chill down the back of Willowood's neck because something in the Luma's eyes had changed.

"What's going on?" Caldwell said. "You have this under control?"

"Yes," Willowood replied, but even she recognized the uncertainty in her voice. "Piper, we're going to—"

"Tell me, Luma Mistress," So-Elku said, his voice taking on a dark tone. "Would you forfeit your life for this one?"

Despite Willowood's attempts to keep So-Elku bound, he raised his arm and pointed at Piper. The mere fact that So-Elku could move against her made Willowood uneasy. So she pushed harder, willing unseen power to surround the man. At the same time, her anxiety grew as an explanation formed in her mind.

"Felicity," Caldwell said. "Talk to me."

"Piper," Willowood said finally. "We must subdue him."

"Okay, Nana."

Suddenly, So-Elku's arm went to his side. Piper was constricting the man's movements, which went a long way in easing Willowood's fears. The child was still more powerful.

For now, said the tiny voice in the back of Willowood's head.

"You cannot stop us!" So-Elku snarled as he struggled to remove himself from Piper's restraints.

"But we already have, So-Elku," Willowood replied. "You've met your match."

"We are *not* So-Elku," the man spat. "He is no more. We are Soldark now. And you"—the man sneered at all three of them—"you will bow before us."

Caldwell cried out as his knees hit the stone floor. He still held Kane's body over his shoulder, but the colonel seemed unable to move under his own volition. "What the hell's happening—to—me?"

Willowood could feel the same force trying to press her to her knees. But she resisted it. Piper, too, seemed to be fighting something pushing her down. "Resist him, Piper. Don't let him make you—"

"You cannot resist us," the being called Soldark said before letting out a maniacal laugh that reverberated around the hall.

"Oh yes we can," Piper said.

All at once, Willowood felt the pressure on her shoulders subside. Caldwell, too, was set free and fell on his hands. Then Piper closed her eyes, and Soldark backpedaled two meters in an attempt to stay upright.

"Can you defeat him?" Willowood said to Piper, her voice earnest.

"You mean, kill him?" Piper's eyes opened wide.

Willowood hated asking her grandchild, *any* child, if they could kill someone. But Piper knew the risks, especially after all they'd been through.

But does she, Felicity? Willowood asked herself. *Does she know about the demons that haunt a person's soul for the rest of her life?*

Willowood shrugged her inner voice and focused on Piper's innocent face. "I mean kill him, yes. Can you?"

"I'm not sure," she replied. "He is strong."

"But not as strong as you." Willowood couldn't tell if she'd made a statement or asked a question.

"I'm—I'm not sure," Piper replied.

Even as Piper spoke, Soldark took a step forward. The movement was labored, but it was a step, nonetheless. Willowood felt her own power succumb to Soldark's, which gave her even more concern. Either Piper was not trying hard enough, or—

No, Willowood thought. *I won't believe it.* Her granddaughter was the most potent agent in the galaxy. That much had been known. Whether or not Piper knew it was still to be discovered. *The child is just distraught over the death of her grandfather*, Willowood thought. *Or she's simply too young and has more to grow into.*

There was another explanation, of course. And as much as Willowood tried to keep the thought away, it still asserted itself in her consciousness like a canker sore screaming for attention. *Or Moldark's presence inside of So-Elku is a force no one could foretell, and one too great to be stopped.*

Soldark growled, and then his eyes turned black—sclera and all. He took another step toward the trio and chomped at the air.

"So you got him or not?" Caldwell said, finally regaining his feet and raising his NOV2. "Cause I'm not a fan of sticking around here unless you're sure about this."

"We need to go," Piper said. "I—I can't do—"

"Say no more."

Caldwell selected his NOV2's AI-assisted multi-target fire effect. Only, instead of identifying several targets for the weapon to unload two entire magazines on, he picked one target: *Soldark—or whatever the hell his new name is.*

When Caldwell squeezed the trigger, the NOV2 quaked in his hand as it sent both twin-mags' full loads toward the enemy. A flurry of sparks and bolts of electricity exploded against the figure as he writhed in agony. A terrifying shriek rose above the already deafening sound of blaster fire, which, to Caldwell, was a damn good sign indeed.

"Come on," the colonel yelled. "Run!"

Even as Piper took the lead and Willowood brought up the rear, Caldwell used one hand to eject his spent magazine and then reached for a fresh one on his hip. He was about to drop Kane's corpse, wondering why he was still carrying the bag of bones, when Piper looked back.

"You still got my grandpa, Grandpa?" she asked.

Son of a bitch. "Yeah," Caldwell replied with a grunt. "I do, darlin'." He managed to keep Kane slung over his shoulder and slammed two new magazines into the lower receiver.

"We need to run faster," Willowood said as the trio turned right into another hall. "I'm not sure I can keep him much longer."

"Turn left up there," Caldwell said to Piper.

"Okay."

Soldark appeared around the last turn and tried firing some sort of energy wave, but Willowood stopped it about mid-tunnel.

"He's really pissed," she yelled.

"I can see that!" Just before turning into the next tunnel, Caldwell raised his NOV2 and fired a second twin-mag MTFE volley. The fire effect was so brutal that whole sections of the walls, ceiling, and floor broke apart. Caldwell's HUD dimmed against the bright flashes. And yet Solpants still stepped through the smoke and stalked after them. "This guy's getting on my nerves more than—"

"A something pestering a nest of one thing or another," Willowood yelled. "We get, we get it! Just run!"

"I was gonna say—"

"RUN!"

"PALADIA COMPANY," Willowood shouted over VNET; she was too preoccupied to communicate in the Unity. Plus, it was probably wise that the whole unit heard her. "We're coming out of the starship hot. When we do, you fire up the ramp with everything you've got."

"We understand," Sion replied. He, Incipio, and Tora had been leading Paladia Company's three cadres of mystics against the Li-Dain. Redirecting them to focus on Soldark would give the LAW fighters a brief opportunity to gain ground against the Sekmit defenses, but it had to be done. Soldark had to be stopped.

"You want us too?" Nelson asked.

"Negative," Caldwell replied. "You hold the line against the Li-Dain. This is a job for Willowood's company."

"Copy."

Even as the opening to the outside came into view, Willowood felt Soldark's presence gaining on them. She couldn't hold the being back without Piper's help, and Willowood's strength was draining fast. The most Willowood could hope for was keeping Soldark at bay until they could figure out another way to kill him.

"Get ready," Willowood yelled over comms.

"Three," Caldwell yelled. "Two. One."

Willowood's body moved faster than her feet could carry her so that she tumbled headlong down the ramp. Somewhere in her disoriented state, she heard herself order the mystics to fire. Or maybe that was the colonel—she couldn't be sure. Willowood was too spent to focus, having given everything she had to keep the mutated enemy at bay. Even as her power suit crashed against the ramp and bounced across the asphalt, Willowood wanted nothing more than to sleep. So once she saw the hangar bay lit up in lurid color, she closed her eyes, stepped free of the Unity, and released herself to the inner folds of sleep.

"Get her the hell out of here," Caldwell yelled to one of his Lieutenants, pointing to Piper. He also nodded toward Willowood. "And her."

"On it, Colonel," the Lieutenant replied as he waved two sergeants over. A third sergeant and a PFC raced up to Caldwell and relieved him of Kane's body, for which the colonel was all too grateful.

As soon as Piper and Willowood were clear, he turned to witness the awe-inspiring firepower that the mystics unleashed against the ship's opening. It seemed as though energy from a thousand stars poured into the portal and threatened to tear the ship apart. Caldwell couldn't see Sol-face anywhere, but he knew the freak was in there. *And hopefully burning in a slow and painful death*, he thought.

The barrage lasted so long that Caldwell suspected blowing the ship apart might be more than hyperbole. Even the stone structure around the ramp started to glow red. He didn't have a clue how the damn starship was constructed, but if it could glow red, it could be blown up—and he sure as hell wanted this ship blown to Meredith's lip-beard's grave.

"We've been ordered to pull you back, Colonel," the Lieutenant yelled through comms. Even then, Caldwell could barely make out the man's voice. Instead of speaking, the colonel stepped away from the ramp and followed the officer, all while keeping his eyes fixed on the torrent of fire ripping that made the ship's underbelly glow red.

Caldwell wasn't sure how much more anyone could take—the mystics, Sol-pants, the ship, or even his own head. The headache he endured was downright horrible. But just when he thought the assault couldn't go on any longer, the enemy starship lurched upward. The Repub shuttle squealed from the sudden pressure removal, and Caldwell saw lightning flash just above the docking bay's rim. More sparks cascaded down as the ascending ship exposed broken electrical conduits in the hangar. A new wave of warning klaxons and emergency lights did their best to respond to changes in the spaceport's integrity, but they were nothing compared to the still-blistering assault from Paladia Company.

When the ship was fifty meters off the deck, Caldwell called off the attack. Rain poured into the hangar bay, shorting out connections and causing any remaining circuits to fault in a shower of liquid light. One problem had been averted, but an even bigger one had just begun.

"Azelon," he said over comms.

"Here, sir," the bot replied.

"Need you to try and track the vessel departing from our coordinates."

"Affirmative," she replied.

"And if you get a shot, take it."

"Understood, sir. You're concerned that—"

"That the maniac commanding it is going to pull a stunt like he did on Capriana Prime."

"That is not ideal," Azelon replied. "We'll do our best, sir."

"That's all we can ask for."

As soon as he closed the channel, Captain Nelson hailed the colonel.

"Go for Caldwell."

"We've got the Li-Dain on the run, Colonel."

"Hell, son. That's the best news I've heard yet." Caldwell looked skyward. *Might not have much time to enjoy it*, he thought to himself. But it was good news all the same. "Keep the pressure on, Captain. Whatever diaper babies you don't put down, I want secured and held for questioning."

"Hard copy, Colonel."

"Caldwell out."

There was one more play Caldwell had in mind, but it was a long shot. Still, he'd be damned if he went to his grave without trying everything in his power to stop Meesrin Pin from meeting the same fate at the Republic's capital.

"The Colonel is asking for you," an officer said to Piper.

She was hiding behind a stack of freight containers, guarded by some of the lower-ranking gladias.

The officer offered his hand. "He needs you right away, Miss Piper."

"Okay," she replied and gave a hesitant nod.

"This way."

Piper followed the officer to Mr. Caldwell, who stood with Admiral DiAntora in the middle of the hangar bay floor.

"Are you okay, Piper?" the colonel asked her, dropping to his knees.

"I think so." She looked up as Soldark's starship receded into the dark clouds and swirling rain. Even with her visor down, she still found herself blocking the water droplets with a hand.

"What we're wondering is if—well, what I mean to say is, if it's not too much—"

"What do you need from me, Mr. Caldwell, sir?"

"We're worried that Mr. Crazy Robes up there is—I'm not sure how to say this tactfully—"

"Blow up the planet like Capriana Prime?"

Caldwell reared his head back and then looked up at DiAntora.

"Yes, Miss Piper," DiAntora replied. "That's exactly right."

Caldwell cleared his throat. "I'm worried he's—the half that's Moldark, I mean—gonna make good on his promise to annihilate us. Assuming that's what he said back there."

"It is," Piper replied. "And yes, he's going to try and destroy Meesrin Pin."

"Splick." Caldwell shared a worried look with Admiral DiAntora, at least from what Piper could gather from the holo frames in her HUD. "I was afraid of that."

"But you don't need to worry," Piper replied. "I took care of it."

Caldwell's attention snapped back to her. "You took care of what?"

"His weapons systems. I took care of them." Piper could tell by the look of surprise in the colonel's face that he liked this news.

"Do you mind if I ask you to elaborate?" he said.

"Alambromate?"

"Uh, *elaborate*."

"It means to explain yourself," DiAntora said as she placed a paw on the colonel's shoulder.

"Oh." Piper smiled. "When I was trying to stop the ship before, I started talking to the parts of the ship that looked most dangerous. I made them go away. You know, kinda like, if I couldn't break down the whole thing at once, I would strip away layers one at a time until I got to the middle. Like licking a Super Rocket Pop. It's bad for your teeth if you bite all at once. But if you suck on it long enough, you eventually get to the candy in the middle."

"And I know from lots of Super Rocket Pop experience just what you mean," Caldwell said as he let out a laugh.

"But I thought you only like cigars, Mr. Colonel, sir?"

"Are you kidding me? I had to take up cigars just so the nitro-sugar didn't rot my teeth. Nasty habit."

"But the cigars are—"

"Way more safe than a Super Rocket Pop addiction, let me tell you, kid."

"Huh." Piper put one hand on her hip. "Never thought about it like that. Maybe I should take up cigars too."

Now it was DiAntora's turn to clear her throat. "While you two are busy discussing multiple ways of contracting mouth cancer, would you mind, Colonel, if I called in fire support against the enemy ship? I'd like to inspire it *not* to return here."

"Be my guest, Admiral. The *Spire* is at your disposal too, assuming any of our sensors can lock onto the damn ship. I've already put our ship's captain on alert."

"We'll see what our combined efforts can produce, Colonel," she replied. "Thank you." Then DiAntora nodded and stepped away to begin doing whatever admirals did when ordering strikes against enemy ships in orbit.

"About back there," Piper said to Caldwell. "I'm sorry that I couldn't stop Soldark."

"There's no need to apologize," the colonel said in a reassuring tone. "What you did saved lives. And that's more than I could have asked for given the circumstances. You're a hero in my book, Piper."

Piper appreciated his kind words. She really felt like she'd let everyone down. But Soldark had been—well, he'd scared her. Seeing both Moldark and So-Elku fused into one being was terrifying. And she felt really bad about ice-cubing under the pressure. Even now, Piper wanted to go back and try it again, thinking maybe she had enough power to stop him. But that was just it: Soldark was strong. Probably stronger than her. Which made her afraid. She didn't want to be anywhere near him. And that was the real problem: deep inside, Piper knew that before all this was over, she'd have to face him again. No one else was strong enough to stop Soldark. But Piper was. She just needed to be more sure of herself.

"My turn for a question," Mr. Caldwell said.

"Okay."

"You called me Grandpa Caldwell back there."

"Uh-huh."

"What did you mean by that?"

Piper giggled. It felt good to laugh after everything they'd just been through. "You like my grandma, right?"

Mr. Caldwell chuckled. "Well, certainly."

"No. But I mean like, like-like."

"You're asking if I like-like your grandma?"

"Yeah. Like-like is more than just like. You know."

"So it is." Mr. Caldwell laughed again. "You're a relentless little bugger, aren't you."

"Yup. I can be super annoying too."

Caldwell took a deep breath and squared himself with Piper. "Yes. I like-like her a whole lot."

"Then that's why I called you grandpa."

"I still don't see how—"

"Like-likers always get married, silly."

All of a sudden, Caldwell's smiling face turned to one of complete surprise and his cheeks turned a rosy shade of pink. "Uhhh, so—"

"Hey, you two," Willowood said. She lay on a stretcher held by two Sekmit medics. "Everything okay here?"

Piper giggled at Mr. Caldwell as he tried to respond to her grandma. "We're just feelings. I mean, it's—talking. About how we is—*are* feeling."

Nana laughed. "Sounds good, William. They're taking me to the hospital. I'll check in later."

"And I'll check in on you too."

"Oooo," Piper crooned. Then she nudged him with her elbow. "Like-like."

"Would you stop it already?" Then he winked at Nana. "Kids."

Just then, a chime trilled over VNET. The incoming transmission, meant for Grandpa Caldwell, said it was from Magnus, which made Piper's heart want to explode in a shower of rainbows. "Answer," she cried. "Please, please!"

"You'll have your chance to speak to him," Willowood said from her stretcher. "But they need to talk first."

Piper slumped her shoulders. And even as she studied her

grandmother's and Mr. Caldwell's faces in the holo frames, she thought she detected sadness in their eyes.

"Go ahead, Magnus," Caldwell said, stepping away to take the call.

The voice that replied was ragged and tired but still managed to project the elusive threads of confidence and hope. "Mine secured, Colonel."

Caldwell felt a weight lift off his shoulders. In the wake of Capriana's loss, every win, no matter how small, felt like a significant win. Every defeat taught you how to savor life just a little bit more than before. "Damn fine work, son."

"Thank you, sir."

"I'm proud of you—proud of your whole team."

Magnus nodded.

"And can I just say, you look like a sack of splick, son?" Only then did Caldwell notice that Magnus wasn't wearing a helmet. Instead, his bioteknia eyes used their reversed peripheral data interpolation protocol to send the image of Magnus's blackened and bloodied face. "You okay?"

"Eh, nothing the majority of us won't get over."

"How bad?" Caldwell asked.

Magnus took a deep breath and answered as the air rushed from his lungs. It was an old Marine trick used to psyche your head out of connecting to your heart. "Haze, Redmarrow, Jaffrey, and Dozer. Telwin's probably on her way out soon too. Wobix lost several narskill in the final moments."

"Splick, son. I'm sorry."

"Yeah." Magnus took another deep breath and held it in. There was something more.

"What is it?"

Magnus ran his tongue over his teeth and shook his head twice. "It's Freya. She's KIA."

Caldwell looked back toward DiAntora and studied the Admiral kneeling beside Piper. The news would be devastating, and he hated being the one to break it to her. He looked back at Magnus's face. Now it was Caldwell's time to sigh. He didn't know how the pride mother had gotten to the mines so quickly—she must have left as soon as the convoy departed from the palace. But Caldwell couldn't blame her for wanting to help. It was her damn planet, after all.

"She saved us," Magnus added. "Forbes did too. We were pinned down, and Awen almost…" Magnus seemed to choke back a tear. "She almost had to save us in a different way."

Caldwell guessed what Magnus meant. The colonel knew about the Luma's ability to blow themselves up or some splick. Didn't take a genius to conclude that Awen would have done something like that if it meant keeping the LAW from taking over the mine. He was just glad she hadn't needed to—for all their sakes.

"Get back here as soon as you can, Adonis."

"Copy that, Colonel. One more question."

"Shoot."

"So-Elku. Did Willowood release him?"

"Why do you ask?" Caldwell said, his curiosity piqued.

"There was a Li-Dain back here that claimed Willowood had betrayed Freya and let So-Elku go."

"We all let So-Elku go," Caldwell said with a corrective tone. "It was the only way to stop Moldark."

"The hell?"

"I'll explain when you get back, son. Just get you and your unit squared away."

"Copy."

Caldwell closed the channel and then looked back at DiAntora. There were two things that he hated about his job as a military commander. The first was sending good warriors to their deaths. He'd done plenty of it, but that was the nature of war. The second, however, was telling survivors and family members that the warrior they loved and respected had fallen in the line of duty.

"Admiral DiAntora?" he said over a private comms channel. "A word."

Caldwell saw from the look in the admiral's eye that she knew something terrible had happened. So with every step that the Sekmit took toward him, Caldwell cursed his office.

No, he corrected himself. *Not my office.* He loved being a career military commander. What he hated was the enemy.

He cursed Soldark.

EPILOGUE

Caldwell gave the Gladio Umbra three days of mandatory leave while the Sekmit picked up the pieces from the LAW's assault. Freya's office, postmortem, made guest housing arrangements for all of the gladias and provided medical treatment in the palace's private hospital.

While Magnus was grateful for the time to mend, he found himself getting restless by the second day. The only thing that seemed to calm him down were surprise visits from Awen—though he wouldn't exactly say those were much in the way of calming. It seemed the more hardship they went through together, the more he wanted to be with her. And the more he wanted to be with her, the less he wanted to do with war. Holding her in his arms made him long for the peaceful life he'd always dreamed of but knew he didn't deserve. He had too much blood on his hands.

"You good?" Awen asked as she lay in the bed beside him.

He had his hands behind his head, watching the morning

sunlight reflecting off her bare shoulder. "You ever think about what's next?"

"Well," Awen said as she propped her head up beneath her arm. "Worru hasn't reported So-Elku's return, which makes me think Soldark has headed for a different system. So if we're—"

"Not that next," Magnus said. He rolled over to look at her. "I mean, us next."

"Us?"

"After all this is done."

"That's assuming quite a lot, isn't it?"

He furrowed his brow at her. "We've got Soldark on the run, beat back the Li-Dain—"

"I didn't mean the enemy," Awen said with a coy smile. "I mean, you're assuming I want to stay with you."

"Huh." Magnus returned to his back and looked at the ceiling. "I guess I do have other options."

Awen punched him in the side.

Magnus recoiled and pulled his arms down to protect his flanks and then laughed. "What?"

"Girl in every port?" she asked.

"Maybe. Maybe not."

She tried punching him again, but he grabbed her fists and then pulled her close. "So, do you?"

"A girl's got to review her options," she said.

Magnus pulled her close and kissed her.

When it was over, Awen said, "Okay. I like this option."

"Me too," Magnus replied.

Twin chimes rang on both sides of the bed. Magnus reached over and picked up the in-ear comm that he'd purposely ported his Novona biotech interface to specifically because he didn't want the alert going off inside his head while he was with Awen. She'd done the same. The two of them inserted the comms devices into their ears and accepted the incoming transmission.

"This is Colonel Caldwell," said the holo projection that appeared twenty centimeters in front of their faces. The commander sounded perturbed.

"Yeah, we can see that, Colonel," Magnus said.

"Why aren't you on holo?" the colonel asked. "I'm only getting audio."

"Uh, because I haven't done my makeup yet?"

"Well hurry it up, Adonis. And you too, Awen."

The two of them shared a look.

"Are we missing something, Colonel?" Awen asked.

"Yeah: our battalion dinner with the Sekmit royalty. You were supposed to be here five minutes ago."

"Oh, splick," Magnus yelled as he checked the time and threw the sheets off. He'd lost track of the day. *Days*, he corrected himself, and then he beat Awen to the shower.

"Nice of you to join us, Magnus, Awen," the colonel said as he handed them glasses of kyreethsha from an attendant's tray. "You both look"—Caldwell paused—"rested."

"Sorry to keep you waiting, Colonel," Magnus said.

The entire battalion of Gladio Umbra had gathered in the expansive vestibule outside the royal throne room. The group included Azelon and TO-96, who were busy speaking various languages with Wobix and Rohoar. Other attendees were Awen's parents, Ricio's wife and son, Jules, and Flow and Cheeks in their first time off the *Spire* in a long time. Magnus noted how well his two Fearsome Four teammates conducted themselves around Jujari without losing their splick. Jules had truly worked wonders with the men, and Magnus was proud of them all. Even Admiral DiAntora stood with the surviving members of her covert team, accompanied by the newly named Chancellor Seaman. Everyone had donned formal dress-wear fit for a gala—even the bots looked freshly polished and pretended to sip glasses of kyreethsha.

"Oh, it's not me you have to worry about," Cadwell replied. "If the royal clan asks, I'm hanging you both out to dry." An awkward beat passed before Caldwell winked. "Kidding."

Magnus let out a breath. "We appreciate it, Colonel. Thank you."

"You're terrible, William," Willowood said, striding up to the colonel's side. "Let them be."

Magnus thought he noticed the faintest sign of a flirtatious smile behind the colonel's eyes as the commander looked at Willowood in a formal dress.

Awen's voice spoke in Magnus's head. *You think they*—?

No way, Magnus replied. *But, I mean…*

Then Magnus and Awen looked at each other, and at the same time, said, *Nah.*

"Mr. Lieutenant Magnus, sir?" came a small voice accompanied by a tug on his pant leg.

Magnus turned to see Piper motioning him downward. "Hey, Piper. It's good to see you."

"You too. I'm sorry to hear about Freya. I heard you were with her when she died."

"I was, yes."

"She was a super soft kitty," Piper replied.

"You—you petted her?" Magnus was trying to think back to a point when the two had come that close, but he didn't remember any. That, and he highly doubted the famed leader of Aluross would allow a human child to treat her like a pet.

"Mmm-hmm," Piper said with a nod. "It was the only thing I asked for."

"Asked for?"

"For my birthday, silly."

"Ah, gotcha. Wait—you asked to pet her?"

"For my birthday."

"And she—"

"Said yes." Piper gave Magnus a proud smile. "I think she liked it."

"I'm sure she did," Magnus said with a chuckle, wishing Freya were here now for all of this. Then Cyril approached from behind Piper, and Magnus rose to meet him. "Hey, Mr. Code Slicer."

"Ha ha—hey, Mr. Adonis Major, sir," Cyril said.

"Wrong rank, but thanks for thinking so highly of me."

"Sure, sure, hey. It's good to see you in one piece, sir."

"You too, Cyril." He shook the skinny gladia's hand. "Oh, and about those Festoonial black marspins."

"Yes?"

"I think I know what you're talking about now."

"You mean how they harpooned the Telderine giant sea mammoth?"

Magnus smiled and then caught Forbes overhearing the conversation a few people away. Magnus sent the captain a nod and then looked back to Cyril. "Yeah. Pretty spectacular stuff."

"I'd say! And if you like that, there's this amazing documentary on—"

"Hold that thought," Magnus said, and then he headed for Wobix and Rohoar. The narskill warrior's arm was in a sling, and he was missing some fur here and there but otherwise looked okay. "Bixy. Good to see you. You're looking splotchy and generally pissed off."

"Manservant. It is good to see you looking hairless and like you need to defecate."

"Keep that up"—Magnus pointed to a few patches of bare skin—"and you'll be my twin before long."

"I would sooner slit my own throat."

"I'm sure you would," Magnus said with a smile. "Hey. Good fighting back there."

"The same can be said for you. And I am pleased to know that it was you who heard our leader's final confession."

Magnus raised an eyebrow. "I'm not sure I follow. All she said was—"

"It is for your ears only," Wobix said as he placed a paw on Magnus's chest.

"It's narskill tradition," Awen said as she approached on Magnus's right.

"A warrior's last statement is called a confession," Willowood added from Magnus's left. "Meant as the summation of their life's meaning."

"It is a distinct privilege and honor to be granted a narskill's confession," TO-96 added.

Magnus didn't doubt this new information as it seemed to

corroborate the gravity of Freya's dying statement, even if he didn't understand its full meaning.

"This is very different than Jujari customs," Rohoar said.

"And how is that?" TO-96 said.

"Wait for it," Awen whispered in Magnus's ear.

"As Jujari, we attempt to bite the head off the person who we last view, even if it is a friend." Rohoar stared at TO-96 for a long moment.

Finally, the bot took a step back. "Ah, I see."

"Don't worry, TO-96," Willowood said. "It is a seldom practiced jujari tradition. And we love you too much to let that happen to you."

"You do?" TO-96 said.

"Of course. Plus"—Willowood moved across the circle of friends—"I owe you a kiss."

"I beg your pardon?" Azelon said as her back suddenly straightened.

But Willowood was too fast, even for Azelon, and planted a kiss on TO-96's glossy faceplate. The bot touched the point of contact and his complexion glowed. Meanwhile, Azelon stepped in front of TO-96 and forced Willowood back. The whole scene made Magnus laugh, as it did the others who saw it.

"Why, Lady Willowood," TO-96 said. "Whatever was that for?"

"For saving Ricio's life over Meesrin Pin," she replied. "I told you I was going to give you a kiss, and I always keep my promises."

"You mustn't let her do that again, Tee-Tee," Azelon said to TO-96. "She's being overly flirtatious, and I do not approve."

Everyone laughed together despite Azelon's confused looks at the response, which only made the group chuckle more. Magnus had to admit that it felt good to laugh together, and the kyreethsha certainly wasn't hurting anyone.

"If we are making good on oaths," Rohoar said with a raised voice. "Rohoar has one to keep to Commander Robillard."

Everyone in the group looked for Delta Team's OIC and pointed him out. Robillard took a moment to enter the makeshift circle. "What's this about?"

Magnus nodded toward Rohoar.

"Rohoar remembers that before the assault on the Republic governor's mansion, Commander Robillard expressed how he liked Jujari meats."

Robillard looked around. "I did?"

Magnus dipped his head. "You kinda did, yeah."

"Rohoar was surprised to hear that he had such similar interests as the commander. So, with some help from our Sekmit hosts, Rohoar has prepared the rotted flesh of a local hammerbore, along with its congealed blood." Rohoar then produced a small vacuum-sealed packet from behind his back and offered it to Robillard.

The man took the translucent pouch and winced as the red and green fluids inside mixed together. "I—don't know what to say."

"Say nothing," Rohoar said with a raised paw. "Only let the delicate flavors soothe your inner war as they do Rohaor's." When everyone chuckled at the truly touching exchange, Rohoar glanced around. "What?"

"Ah," Magnus exclaimed. "Before I forget, I have something too. Rohoar, Wobix?"

The two warriors lowered their furry eyebrows and studied Magnus.

"I'd like everyone to know I've made good on my own promise."

"Which was what, scrumruk graulap?" Rohoar asked.

Magnus pulled two clear data cards from inside his suit coat pocket and tossed them to the warriors. "I got you both galactic common lessons, on me."

More laughter circled the group, and Magnus blew both fighters a kiss.

"Rohoar thinks the hairless leader insults us," Rohoar said to Wobix without looking away from Magnus.

"I agree." Then Wobix looked to Rohoar. "Perhaps we can study ways to insult him in his own tongue."

"Rohoar agrees." He held up his data card. "He will meet you this night."

"Don't look now," Awen whispered in Magnus's ear. "But someone just got a study buddy."

"And," Rohoar continued. "Rohoar will show you how to prepare a skralggrit fire. There will be much drinking and roasting of meat."

"I heard that," Abimbola said.

Just then, a loud horn blast issued from the doors leading into the royal throne room. Then a Sekmit attendant in elegant red and black silk drew everyone's attention. "Queen Nishti will see you now."

The Gladio Umbra's leaders and the Neo Republic officials were front and center as the entire battalion filed into the throne room's elongated hall. Narskill warriors bordered the aisle, their bows slung and staves at the ready. Behind them sat dozens of long dinner tables with ornate place settings. Somewhere in the distance, Magnus caught the fragrance of roasted meat, melted cheese, and fresh-baked bread. He felt his mouth fill with saliva and had to swallow twice. He was eager to get the formalities over with so everyone could get down to the serious business of eating.

Spoken like a true gladia, Awen said in his head.

Hey, a man's got needs, he replied.

Apparently, quite a few.

Magnus cast her a sideways look. While Awen's head remained fixed forward, the edge of her lips curled up in the slightest of smiles.

The mass of guests stopped short of the dais. Magnus expected to see Freya atop the throne, but it remained empty. Some small part in the back of his brain thought maybe that Freya had been saved or reanimated or something. Hell, they'd seen crazier splick than that. Then again, Freya never claimed to be queen. Whoever Nishti was, she'd been more of a token icon than a present leader. If anything, Freya deserved to be queen with the way she'd acted. But Magnus didn't write the rules.

The attendant from before stepped in front of the dais and waited for the room to settle. "On behalf of all the Sekmit, the royal house of Aluross welcomes you, the members of the Gladio Umbra and the Neo Republic, to this night of remembering the slain and celebrating our future. The feast is our show of appreciation for your valiant deeds and noble sacrifices, honoring both the living and the dead. We regret, in no small way, the passing of ní Freya ap Linux, who gave her life in the ultimate act of bravery against the Li-Dain hordes. May her spirit reside in this hall forever."

The Sekmit throughout the hall recited a short phrase in their native tongue and then made a motion in the air with their right paws. Magnus had no idea what the cats said, but he had to admit that it had its own unique beauty about it.

When the echo finally faded, the attendant continued. "Tonight, we are graced by the presence of the Elder Queen. May I present, Queen Nishti."

The narskill on either side of the aisle and the dais took a knee. Wobix and DiAntora also knelt, as did Caldwell and Willowood. Not one to disrespect the royal house further than he already had, Magnus followed suit and took a knee. Awen used Magnus's shoulder to steady herself as she knelt in her tight dress, and soon the entire hall echoed with the subtle rustle of fabric.

Magnus looked up to the dais, expecting the queen to appear from behind the throne. But she didn't, and the seat remained empty.

"What's going on?" Magnus whispered to Awen.

But she only shrugged in reply.

Then, out of the corner of his eye, Magnus caught movement. Admiral Lani DiAntora stood up and stepped out of line. Magnus heard several people gasp as the admiral mounted the steps and ascended the dais. When she reached the summit, she turned and addressed the entire hall.

"Please, my friends," she said. "Stand. All of you, stand."

Magnus helped Awen up and exchanged looks with her. He glanced over at Caldwell too; even the colonel seemed surprised.

"I'm sure that my presentation now comes as a bit of a shock, most of all to my Republic counterparts." She nodded to the chancellor and other notable officials. "However, it is my love for Aluross that called me into a life of subterfuge, and that is a decision I will never regret. I also recognize that my loyalty to the Neo Republic will be called into question, as it should be. Let me set the record straight here and now. It has ever been my intention to liberate my people, and my rise through the Galactic Republic over the course of my career ever served one end—the freedom of the Sekmit."

The room stirred. Magnus had to admit that this woman had quite the pair of brass bearings. The announcement was most likely news to her entire Repub envoy as much as it was to everyone else. It also explained several things about DiAntora and Freya that Magnus had been unable to parse in recent days, including DiAntora's original recommendation that the GU seek refuge on Aluross. Magnus realized that getting the gladias to assist in fully liberating the planet was the queen's goal after all.

Gives new meaning to our mantra, Magnus thought to Awen.

Dominate, she said.

Yeah. Liberate.

DiAntora, or Nishti—Magnus wasn't sure which anymore—turned to address the Repub officials. "Mr. Chancellor. As you can imagine, this was not the way I intended to reveal my true self to you. It is, however, the needed way, given the circumstances. I ask your forgiveness for any undue pain I have caused, though I do not regret my actions on behalf of my people."

Magnus might have been wrong, but he detected that there was something more to the queen's relationship with the chancellor. He glanced over at the man, but the Repub official was the picture of stoic Navy statesmanship. The chancellor nodded once at Nishti, and that was all.

"Needless to say, I tender my resignation as Admiral, effective immediately. If I am deemed an enemy of the Neo Republic, so be it. That said, I do look forward to negotiating a *fair* deal with any who wish to resume trade with Aluross."

Magnus guessed Nishiti's emphasis on the word fair was anything but a veiled attack on the former trade deal the Sekmit had with the Galactic Republic. Whether or not the chancellor was chagrined about this sudden turn of events was uncertain, though he guessed the officials didn't like being caught off guard with the news. Then again, they were the heads of a decades-long trade deal that had suppressed the Sekmit. If you're gonna helm a big ship, you'd better be prepared for the holes in the hull. If Chancellor Seaman was upset, he still didn't show it. Nor would he; this was not the time or place to make a scene. That would all come later.

"And to my newest friends, the leaders and members of the Gladio Umbra, I can only offer my sincere thanks for your aid in liberating my people. As with my Republic counterparts, I recognize I was not forthcoming with my true identity. For this, I seek your forgiveness. And yet, I also would ask you to recognize the crucial role that you played in ensuring the safety and longevity of Aluross, securing it from both Republic and LAW governance. For whatever harm I may have caused you, please know you have our undying thanks. You need only ask for whatever you wish, and it is ever yours. It is a bond we will never break. So if it breaks, it is your doing."

Nishti locked eyes with Colonel Caldwell.

The man raised his chin in acceptance of the generous offer, and then Nishti nodded in return.

"To you, Feared Aggressor of the Gladio Umbra," Nishti said as she descended the dais toward Caldwell. "I bestow a gift."

Caldwell looked to Willowood and then to Magnus in surprise. Clearly, the man hadn't been expecting anything. One Sekmit attendant rushed to the colonel's side and took his drink, while another attendant presented Nishti with a long item wrapped in red fabric.

Nishti took the package and stood in front of Caldwell. "Colonel. You served my people with distinction and thwarted both the Li-Dain and the unexpected attack from Moldark. For this, we are ever grateful." She unfolded the fabric to reveal a narskill staff. But unlike those employed by the warriors, this one was covered with ornate carvings and inlaid with gold. "For you, a narskill staff inscribed with the history of our people. Perhaps, someday soon, I will translate the part for you where the Gladio Umbra save Aluross."

"I would be honored, your highness." Caldwell accepted the gift and shook his head in admiration. "It is exquisite."

"To you, Lady Willowood," Nishti said next, turning to the elder mystic. "I present you with a band of friendship." The queen removed one of the gold bracelets from around her wrist and invited Willowood to extend her forearm. As Nishti slid it over Willowood's hand to join the other bangles, the queen said, "This is a symbol, a circle of everlasting means with no end, of the connection you and your line will have with our people."

"Thank you, Queen Nishti," Willowood said as she admired the golden gift. "I will wear it always."

"I'm sure you will." Nishti winked at Willowood. "And where is Piper?" The queen seemed to be making a show of searching for the child even though she stood right between Caldwell and Willowood.

"Down here, queen lady ma'am," Piper replied with a playful wave.

"Ah, yes." Nishit knelt before the girl and waved an attendant over. The servant carried a wooden box and lowered it beside the queen. "Piper. You demonstrated extraordinary bravery in the face of overwhelming odds."

"We faced odds?" Piper said up to Willowood. "I don't remember seeing any."

Willowood shushed the child and then pointed her back to the queen.

"It was your heroism and quick thinking that saved us all from certain death," Nishti continued. "For this, we are truly grateful." Then the queen opened the box's lid, reached inside, and removed a Sekmit stuffed animal.

Wait, Magnus said to Awen. *If it's a stuffed Sekmit made by a Sekmit, does that make it a doll?*

Awen stifled a chuckle and put her knuckles against her lips.

"Oh, she's so fluffy," Piper exclaimed and squeezed the animal doll thing tight against her face. "Oh, thank you, thank you, thank you, miss queen kitty cat." Then, before anyone could correct her or stop her, Piper threw her arms around Nishiti and squeezed her hard. Magnus even thought he saw Piper's little hand stroke the back of Nishti's head. To her credit, the queen let the encounter play out until Piper pulled away and returned to her place line.

The queen rose and approached Awen next. "Awen, for your fortitude in protecting the lives of your fellow warriors and those of my guard, I offer you this." Nishti unfastened a necklace from around her neck and then held it up to Awen. A small medallion hung from a gold chain. Magnus thought it resembled three Sekmit claws making golden slash marks in the air. "This is the symbol of the pride mothers, who, with the same claw, both hunt their prey and protect their young. You are such a warrior, Awen. And since it appears you have discarded the necklace of your former order, it seems only right that you receive a new one."

Awen raised her chin at Nishti's insistence, and the queen fastened the piece of jewelry around Awen's slender neck. "It's beautiful, your majesty. I will wear it always and think fondly of you."

When Nishti came before Magnus, she paused in some sort of consideration. "You are worthy of a gift, Magnus. But I will not be the one to bestow it."

Magnus raised an eyebrow, unsure what this meant. "Okay."

Nishti raised a paw and waved something over. No, not something. *Someone*. It was Wobix. The narskill warrior carried a package much like the one Caldwell had received, only it was wrapped in purple fabric. Nishti stepped aside and allowed Wobix to stand before Magnus while another attendant took Magnus's drink.

"You fought like a very aggressive hairless person, manservant," Wobix said. "And it was an integrity and advantage to—"

"Honor and privilege," Nishti whispered.

Wobix winced. "—honor and privilege to fight alongside you. So it is my"—he glanced at Nishti—"honor"—she nodded her assent—"to present you with these." Wobix opened the fabric and revealed both a Thørzin power bow and a narskill staff. He handed them to Magnus one at a time and then raised his chin.

Magnus felt overwhelmed by the gifts. He was only half-joking when he'd told Wobix he wanted them. But he wasn't going to refuse the weapons now. That, and Magnus finally understood why Freya's elites had outperformed Wobix back in the mine: those sharpshooters with purple powers had been Nishti's elites. Wobix may have been a high-ranking warrior but he was not the top-level. Magnus actually respected that more because, frankly, Magnus wasn't an apex warrior either. "Thank you, Bixy. They're truly amazing."

"Yes, and also very worthless to you, as you are not a Unity user."

Nishti scolded Wobix in their native tongue.

But Magnus tried to downplay the royal rebuke. "No, no, he's right. I'm afraid I won't be able to do these tools justice."

"Perhaps your mate can assist you then," Wobix said, nodding toward Awen.

Nishti then hissed at Wobix and sent him on his way.

But not before Magnus blurted out: "I'll make certain she does!"

MORE GIFTS WERE GIVEN to other notable members of the teams, including Captain Forbes, Captain Nelson, Ricio, and Sootriman. When Nishti finally dismissed everyone to enjoy the meal, Magnus handed over his Sekmit weapons to an attendant. Then he took Awen's arm and followed the cat to his and Awen's seats at the head table.

Halfway through the first course, Awen leaned over to Magnus and said, "This is nice, isn't it?"

"Food's delicious," he replied with half his mouth full.

"No. I mean, all of it. The food, the company, the music. Who knows, maybe there will even be dancing."

Magnus stopped chewing mid-bite. "Dancing?"

Awen laughed at him. "Oh, don't act all worried. I'll help you out." She twiddled her fingers as if to suggest she could use the Unity for his benefit.

"Good, cause I'm gonna need all the help you can give me."

Awen smiled at him. "You know what it is, right?"

"What?" He took another sip of kyreethsha. "What's what?"

"This. It's a little glimpse of what's coming." She rolled her hand around in the air a few times. "You know. *After* all the fighting?"

Magnus looked around. "Dinners in Aluross's royal palace?"

Awen punched him in the arm. "Normal life, NMB. Drinks, dinner, dancing with friends." Just then, Awen reached for her glass and looked into the near distance. She held the glass a few centimeters from her lips but didn't drink.

"What is it?" Magnus asked.

Awen snapped out of her daydream. "It's—" She sighed. "It seems like it will never get here."

"Normal life?"

She nodded and then set her glass down. "Like it's just a dream that will never come true. Like we don't actually deserve it, you know?"

"Hey, hey, whoa." Magnus picked up her glass and handed it back to her. "Of all the people in the galaxy, you deserve a normal life, Awen. Mystics, cause if you don't, no one does. Now, I'm not sure about your choice of *mates*, as Bixy might say, but I say we have a pretty good chance."

"Really?"

"Really. To normal life."

"Normal life," she replied.

Magnus touched Awen's glass with his, and they both took a sip. Then he leaned in and kissed her.

WHILE AZELON SAT at her place amongst the carbon-based sentient biologics, who ingested copious amounts of heated tissue from other biologics and liquid alcohols that impeded their behavioral coherence, she became aware of a message. Or, rather, an alert. It was faint, at first, surfacing like a small bubble that traveled up through the sea, originating under a rock or a crustacean or a plant. In truth, it was a miracle she noticed it at all amongst the ocean of data she processed at any given moment. But there it was, a blip from the Singularity's core, sent all the way from Ithnor Itheliana.

"Is something the matter?" TO-96 said.

Azelon regarded him but did not speak at first.

"Is it Willowood's kiss? Because I can assure you I feel nothing for her. Well, that's not entirely true. Of course, I feel something for her. It's just that, what I meant to say was—"

"Someone's coming," Azelon said.

TO-96 titled his head and then looked around the hall. "Yes, well, I can confirm that several people are coming and going."

"Not here." Azelon stood. Her chair toppled behind her.

Chatter around the table grew silent as people looked toward Azelon, but she didn't care. It didn't matter. None of this mattered.

"Azie," Magnus said six chairs away to her left. "You all right down there?"

"Someone's coming," she repeated to TO-96. "They're coming for the Singularity."

MAGNUS and AWEN will return in RISE OF THE GLADIAS, available to preorder now on Amazon.

For more updates on this series, be sure to join the Facebook Group, "J.N. Chaney's Renegade Readers."

CHARACTER REFERENCE

A. H. (Alvin Henry) Lovell: Human. Age: 51. Planet of origin: Capriana Prime. Brigadier General, 1st Republic Marine Division, I Marine Expeditionary Force, Galactic Republic Marines; includes 79th Reconnaissance Battalion. Dark complexion, commanding presence.

Abimbola: Miblimbian. Age: 41. Planet of origin: Limbia Centrella. Commander of Bravo Platoon, Granther Company. Former warlord of the Dregs, outskirts of Oosafar, Oorajee. Bright-blue eyes, black skin, tribal tattoos, scar running from neck to temple.

Adonis Olin Magnus: Human. Age: 34. Planet of origin: Capriana Prime. Gladio Umbra, Granther Company commander. Former lieutenant, Charlie Platoon, 79th Reconnaissance Battalion, "Midnight Hunters," Galactic Republic Space Marines. Baby face, beard, green eyes.

Allie Porteous: Human. Age: 44. Planet of origin: Capriana Prime. Paragon. Senior sensor's officer aboard the *Peregrine.*

Aubrey Dutch: Human. Age: 25. Planet of origin: Deltaurus Three. Commander of Alpha Platoon, Granther Company. Former corporal, weapons specialist, Galactic Republic Space Marines. Small in stature, close-cut dark hair, intelligent brown eyes. Loves her firearms.

Awen dau Lothlinium: Elonian. Age: 26. Planet of origin: Elonia. Commander of Echo Platoon, Granther Company. Form Special Emissary to the Jujari, Order of the Luma. Pointed ears, purple eyes.

Azelon: AI and robot. Age: unknown. Planet of origin: Ithnor Ithelia. Artificial intelligence of the Novia Minoosh ship *Azelon Spire.*

Cal Wagoner: Human. Age 31. Planet of origin: Capriana Prime. Lieutenant (Officer In Charge), first platoon, Taursar Company, Gladio Umbra. Leads defense of north tunnel in the assault on the *Black Labyrinth.*

Cyril: Human. Age: 24. Planet of origin: Ki Nar Four. Assigned to Bravo Platoon, Granther Company. Former Marauder. Code slicer, bomb technician. Twitchy; sounds like a Quinzellian miter squirrel if it could talk.

Daniel Forbes: Human. Age: 32. Planet of origin: Capriana. Captain of Taursar Company, Gladio Umbra. Former Captain of Alpha Company, 83rd Marine Battalion, Galactic Republic Space

Marines, on special assignment to Worru. Close-cropped black hair, but a swoop across his forehead. Brown eyes. Clean-shaven, angular face.

David Seaman: Human. Age: 31. Planet of origin: Capriana Prime. Captain in the Republic Navy, commander of the *Black Labyrinth's* two Talon squadrons, Viper and Raptor, and the head of SFC—Strategic Fighter Command. Promoted to Commodore (Flag Officer) of First Fleet aboard the *Solera Fortuna*.

Elias Morandu: Human. Age 50. Planet of origin: Undoria. Native Galactic Republic Planetary Governor of Undoria (Sinzagar Minor star system, Falcion Quadrant).

Emery Wade: Human. Age: 48. Planet of origin: Deltaurus Three. Galactic Republic Planetary Governor for Deltaurus Three.

Felicity Willowood: Human. Age: 61. Planet of origin: Kindarah. Luma Elder, Order of the Luma. Wears dozens of bangles and necklaces. Aging but radiant blue eyes and a mass of wiry gray hair. Mother of Valerie, grandmother of Piper, mentor to Awen.

Freya: Sekmit. Age: Unknown. Planet of origin: Aluross. Tribe (cf. pride) mother (ní) of Linux Pride (ní Freya ap Linix). Famed conqueress of Midorvia, and the slayer of Cor, King of the Rithruk. A black and white fur, lithe, dressed in translucent red silk.

Idris Ezo: Nimprith. Age: 30. Planet of origin: Caledonia. Assigned to Alpha Platoon, Granther Company. Former bounty hunter, trader, suspected fence and smuggler; captain of *Geronimo Nine*.

Jules: Human. Age: 31. Planet of origin: Capriana Prime. Sea skimmer racing champion, and proprietor of Jules Sea Skimmer Rentals franchise. Blonde and fit with a fiery attitude.

Kar Zoll: Human. AgeL 35. Planet of origin: Oorajee. Petty Officer, team leader for Charlie Team, Second Squad (Officer in Charge), 1st Platoon, Granther Company, Gladio Umbra. Tall, dark hair. Competent leader and tactician.

Lani DiAntora: Sekmit. Age: 29. Planet of origin: Aluross. Flag Captain of the *Soloar Fortuna*, under Commodore Seaman. Feline-like humanoid species, blonde hair. Inquisitive, analytical, and unafraid of senior officers.

Lor: Elonian. Age: 48. He serves as So-Elku's newly appointed Intelligence Minister in the LAW.

Mauricio "Ricio" Longo: Human. Age: 29. Planet of origin: Capriana Prime. Republic Navy, squadron commander of Viper Squadron, assigned to the *Black Labyrinth*.

Michael "Flow" Deeks: Human. Age: 31. Planet of origin: Vega. Assigned to the *Azelon Spire.* Former sergeant, sniper, Charlie Platoon, 79th Reconnaissance Battalion, "Midnight Hunters," Galactic Republic Space Marines. One of the "Fearsome Four."

Miguel "Cheeks" Chico: Human. Age 30. Planet of origin:

Trida Minor. Assigned to the *Azelon Spire.* Former corporal, breacher, Charlie Platoon, 79th Reconnaissance Battalion, "Midnight Hunters," Galactic Republic Space Marines. One of the "Fearsome Four."

Minx: Sekmit. Age: Unknown. Planet of origin: Aluross. Elder clan leader (mit'a), Fînta, Linix Pride (Mit'a Minx).

Moldark (formerly Wendell Kane): Human. Age: 52. Planet of origin: Capriana Prime. Dark Lord of the Paragon, a rogue black-operations special Marine unit. Former fleet admiral of the Galactic Republic's Third Fleet; captain of the *Black Labyrinth.* Bald, with heavily scared skin; black eyes.

Nants: Human. Age: 25. Planet of origin: Worru. Apprentice to So-Elku.

Penn Franks: Human. Age: 60. Planet of origin: Minroc Santari. Admiral, Chief of Naval Operations, Galactic Republic Navy, CENTCOM.

Piper Stone: Human. Age: 9. Planet of origin: Capriana Prime. Assigned to Echo Platoon, Granther Company. Daughter of Senator Darin and Valerie Stone. Wispy blond hair, freckle-faced.

"Rix" Galliogernomarix: Human. Age: Unknown. Planet of origin: Undoria. Assigned to Bravo Company, Granther Company. Wanted in three systems, sleeve tattoos, a monster on the battlefield.

Robert Malcom Blackman: Human. Age: 54. Planet of origin:

Capriana Prime. Senator in the Galactic Republic, leader of the clandestine Circle of Nine. A stocky man with thick shoulders and well-groomed gray hair.

Rohoar: Tawnhack, Jujari. Age: Unknown. Planet of origin: Oorajee. Commander of Delta Platoon, Granther Company. Former Jujari Mwadim.

Sandy LeMaster: Human. Age: 31. Lieutenant in the Gladio Umbra; Officer in Charge of Security, Hedgebore Company, 2nd Platoon.

Silk: Human. Age: 30. Planet of origin: Salmenka. Assigned to Bravo Platoon, Granther Company. Former Marauder, infantry. Slender, bald, tats covering her face and head.

Teerbrin Vanik So-Elku: Human. Age: 51. Planet of origin: Worru. Luma Master, Order of the Luma. Baldpate, thin beard, dark penetrating eyes. Wears green-and-black robes.

Trinklyn: Human. Age: 40. She serves as the newest Minister of Foreign Affairs for So-Elku in the LAW.

Sootriman: Caledonian. Age: 33. Planet of origin: Caledonia. Assigned to Alpha Platoon, Granther Company. Warlord of Ki Nar Four, "Tamer of the Four Tempests," wife of Idris Ezo. Tall, with dark almond eyes, tanned olive skin, dark-brown hair.

TO-96: Robot; navigation class, heavily modified. Manufacturer: Advanced Galactic Solutions (AGS), Capriana Prime. Suspected modifier: Idris Ezo. Assigned to Echo Platoon, Granther Company. Round head and oversized eyes, transparent blaster visor, matte dark-gray armor plating, and exposed metallic articulated joints. Forearm micro-rocket pod, forearm XM31 Type-R blaster, dual shoulder-mounted gauss cannons.

Torrence Ellis: Human. Age: 31. Planet of origin: Capriana Prime. Serves as the *Peregrine's* captain under Moldark.

Ty Yaeger: Human. Age: 30. Planet of origin: Minrock Santari. Captain, the Paragon. Moldark's personal bodyguard and lead enforcer for the assault on Capriana.

Valerie Stone (*deceased*): Human. Age: 31. Planet of origin: Worru. Assigned to Alpha Platoon, Granther Company. Widow of Senator Darin Stone, mother of Piper. Blond hair, light-blue eyes.

William Samuel Caldwell: Human. Age 60. Planet of origin: Capriana Prime. Colonel, 83rd Marine Battalion, Galactic Republic Space Marines; special assignment to Repub garrisons on Worru. Cigar eternally wedged in the corner of his mouth. Gray hair cut high and tight.

Wobix: Sekmit. Age: Unknown. Planet of origin: Aluross. Narskill warrior and emissary of her highness, Queen Nishti.

Gladio Umbra - 1st Battalion
Colonel Caldwell

Granther Company - Special Unit

Lieutenant Magnus

First Platoon

Alpha Team

- Abimbola (RFL)
- Rohoar (JRI/SMS)
- Awen (MYS)
- Silk (SNPR)
- Haze (DEMO/MED)

Bravo Team

- Zoll (RFL)
- Longchomps (JRI/SMS)
- Wish (MYS)
- Dutch (SNPR)
- Rix (DEMO/MED)

Charlie Team

- Bliss (RFL)
- Grahban (JRI/SMS)
- Telwin (MYS)
- Reimer (SNPR)
- Dozer (DEMO/MED)

Delta Team

- Robillard (RFL) - injured
- Redmarrow (JRI/SMS)
- Findermith (MYS)
- Jaffrey (SNPR)
- Czyz (JRI/SMS/DEMO/MED)

Taursar Company - Rifle (150)
Captain Forbes

- 1st Platoon (50)
- 2nd Platoon (50)
- 3rd Platoon (50)

Hedgebore Company - Rifle (150)
Lieutenant Nelson

- 1st Platoon (50)
- 2nd Platoon (50)
- 3rd Platoon (50)

Drambull Company - Support and Intel (83)
Azelon

- 1st Platoon (21): inteligence; Cyril
- 2nd Platoon (36): logistics; Berouth
- *3rd Platoon (26): fighter support; Gilder

**Attached to Fang Company*

Fang Company - Starfighter Attack Wing (33)

TO-96

- Red Squadron (14) - Commander Ricio (*Includes Ezo, Sootriman, Gill Quo, and Dye Vallon)*
- Gold Squadron (14)
- Blue Squadron (14)

Raptor Company - Naval Operations (19)
Azelon

- Command (6)
- Fire Support (13)

Includes Flow and Cheeks.

Paladia Company - Mystics (40)
Master Willowood

- 1st Cadre (14) - Sion
- 2nd Cadre (14) - Incipio
- 3rd Cadre (12) - Tora

ACKNOWLEDGMENTS

Christopher would like to thank the esteemed members of his alpha readers group for their indispensable feedback and encouragement. They include Kevin Zoll, Jon Bliss, Matthew Titus, David Seaman, Mauricio Longo, John Walker, Shane Marolf, Aaron Seaman, Elijah Cole, Joe Wessner, Matthew Dippel, Walt Robillard, and Ollie Longchamps.

Special thanks to Caleb Baker for lending so much inspiration for the Thørzin power bow with his art and descriptions. To Ronnie Smith and Jeremy Davis for their friendship, encouragement, and enthusiasm for all things writing. And to the amazing beta readers and review team readers in both Jeff's and my Facebook groups. Special thanks to Patrick McDaniel for his keen eye that won him this book's coveted Nuance Prize.

Additional thanks to Joshua Cyzy who allowed me to use his family's cottage for writing much of this book.

I would be far from what I am in publishing without the partnership of Jeff Chaney; the editing of Jennifer Sell; the expertise of

Kayla Curry, Chloe Cotter, and James Brockwell at Variant Publications, and Vicotria Gerken, Maggie Silver, and Kyle Brunick at Podium Audio; and the love and support of my wife, Jenny—the greatest champion of my prose and the one who makes and guards space for me to write.

Lastly, to my son, Judah, who is so faithful to read everything I write. Your encouragement means the world to me, Judy. And to Levi, who sat beside me and worked on his own book during the coronavirus quarantine. May your books reach more people than mine ever could.

GET A FREE BOOK

J.N. Chaney posts updates, official art, previews, and other awesome stuff on his website. You can also follow him on **Instagram**, **Facebook**, and **Twitter**.

He also created a special **Facebook group** called "JN Chaney's Renegade Readers" specifically for readers to come together and share their lives and interests, discuss the series, and speak directly to me. Please check it out and join whenever you get the chance!

For updates about new releases, as well as exclusive promotions, visit his website, jnchaney.com and sign up for the VIP mailing list. Head there now to receive a free copy of *The Other Side of Nowhere.*

https://www.jnchaney.com/ruins-of-the-galaxy-subscribe

Enjoying the series? Help others discover the Ruins of the Galaxy series by leaving a review on **Amazon.**

ABOUT THE AUTHORS

J. N. Chaney is a USA Today Bestselling author and has a Master's of Fine Arts in Creative Writing. He fancies himself quite the Super Mario Bros. fan. When he isn't writing or gaming, you can find him online at **www.jnchaney.com**.

He migrates often, but was last seen in Las Vegas, NV. Any sightings should be reported, as they are rare.

Christopher Hopper's novels include the Resonant Son series, The Sky Riders, The Berinfell Prophecies, and the White Lion Chronicles. He blogs at **christopherhopper.com** and loves flying RC planes. He resides in the 1000 Islands of northern New York with his musical wife and four ridiculously good-looking clones.

Made in the USA
San Bernardino, CA
26 June 2020

74202901R00297